HUSH

Bethany Sustaric

*For the warrior who feels alone, overwhelmed, and left for dead.
God sees you and loves you more than you could possibly imagine.
Keep holding on to Him, keep fighting, and He will rescue you.*

-Beth

PRONUNCIATION GUIDE

Angels

Andrew (An-drew)

Kafziel (Caf-zeal)

Leon (Le-on)

Finn (Fin)

Viveka (Vi-ve-k-ah)

Kano (Kah-no)

Axum (Axe-um)

Makeal (Ma-k-eel)

Dante (Dawn-tay)

Ashanti (Ah-sh-an-tea)

Demons

Occult (Oh-cult)

Beli-yaal (Be-lie-all)

Beuxis (Be-you-k-sis)

Hexiathan (Hex-ia-than)

Ticano (Te-caa-no)

Mogrin (Mah-grin)

Shabak (Sh-A-bock)

Ketaton (Ke-ta-t-on)

These people are false apostles. They are deceitful workers who disguise themselves as apostles of Christ. But I am not surprised! Even Satan disguises himself as an angel of light. So it is no wonder that his servants also disguise themselves as servants of righteousness. In the end they will get the punishment their wicked deeds deserve.

2 Corinthians 11:13-15, NLT

One

HER LUNGS TIGHTENED WITH an inhale of the crisp April air. Despite the internal plea to go back, her feet kept moving. With eyes pushed wide, she frantically scanned the shadows as she walked alone to the click of her boots, the wail of fear difficult to ignore.

She should return to the safety of The Roasted Bean where her friends remained, but a glance behind brought reality. Home was only a few blocks away.

The hardest thing about fear—one cannot simply will it away. It sneaks in, awakening a powerful hold most cannot resist.

Thoughts of tomorrow helped put her racing mind at ease. It was her first day as an intern at the second-largest law firm in Durham, North Carolina.

She worked so hard for this. It wasn't easy to remain top of her class and beat everyone for the coveted position at Cade, Wallace, & Wright, including the friends she left at the coffee shop—Kiley, Tamika, and Brad—but she managed to pull it off.

Brad was expected to win since his father is the most sought-after defense lawyer in North Carolina. In the weeks leading up to the decision, Brad seemed overbearing and almost aggressive, leaving an unsettled knot in Charlotte's stomach. The pressure of law school can do funny things to a person.

After a grueling first year at Duke, this internship confirmed she was headed in the right direction. If you asked Charlotte's parents, Jay and Fran Scott, they would say God opened the doors toward her Heavenlyappointed destiny. She, on the other hand, wasn't so sure about all of that Jesus stuff. It's easier to believe that some cosmic power, far beyond our galaxy, aligned her dreams because she'd proven herself a good person.

For seemingly no reason, her heart picked up speed. She clutched the strap of the brown leather satchel her father gave her when she left home. Maybe she should've stayed longer or waited to walk home with someone, anyone. Her roommate, Tamika, would have come, but Charlotte didn't want to ask.

You're fine. Stop being a baby. Keep walking.

The internal pep talk didn't help. In fact, it made things much worse.

This weird anxiety had to be from the coffee. She shouldn't have had that second cup. Needless to say, sleep wouldn't come easy tonight.

Two blocks to go.

With each step in her wedged ankle boots, her mind kept busy and away from the prick of fear in her stomach.

She pictured her mother's round face and her father's long, lean frame. She missed them. The farm was only forty-five minutes away, West of Chapel Hill.

Such a terrible daughter.

She should visit more. Maybe in a few days. One weekend away from studying wouldn't kill her. Plus, it would be nice to enjoy some time with her family.

Her mom's warm hugs were the best. Charlotte's petite frame would be fully embraced by her curves. And although the beard on her father's face scratched when he kissed her cheek, she wanted nothing more than to be annoyed by it again.

Charlotte often wondered if she was adopted. Clearly, the hospital made a mistake, because she was nothing like her country folk family. They loved to plow and tend the livestock while Charlotte longed for more.

In her adolescence, she dreamed of a life in the city. She couldn't wait to leave the farm and the strict rules of the church in her wake. At seventeen, days were eagerly marked off her calendar, a countdown to freedom like a prisoner awaiting parole.

The hustle of a jiving metropolis brought excitement. When she first moved to Durham, she felt free to be whoever she chose to be, and no one, not even Jesus could stop her. She quickly learned the city, now confident in how to navigate herself around. But lately, something changed. Anxiety and paranoia crept in and plagued her. Although she'd walked this sidewalk a million times before, the terror wreaking havoc wouldn't budge.

A loud crash jerked her attention. Slamming against its enclosure, her heart raced as a gasp dove past her lips. She instinctively picked up speed.

"You're fine," she snapped a whisper to herself. *It's probably Mrs. Anderson's cat feasting in the trash again. Just breathe.*

The hair on the back of her neck stood at attention. Animalistic instinct put her on high alert, like prey being hunted. She couldn't ignore it any longer. Something was wrong.

Fear siphoned the air from the atmosphere.

Panic burned in her lungs.

A rapid assessed of her surroundings showed no rational reason for this twisted, internal dread. And yet, everything within screamed louder to run.

She looked again, slower this time.

Were her eyes playing tricks on her? She blinked her narrow gaze. In the shadows stood what looked like a person.

Her throat tightened.

She dashed toward her apartment, wishing she'd worn better shoes.

Don't stop. Keep going.

Out of breath, she frantically searched her bag for the pepper spray she bought last month. It had to be in here somewhere.

Or a weapon.

Something.

Anything.

Hyperaware, she noticed every detail around her.

The ground crunched beneath her feet. Fragments of a street light littered the sidewalk, now cloaked in obscurity.

Submerged in darkness, thick arms grabbed her from behind.

A bulky cloth pinched down over her mouth and nose, silencing her feeble cry for help.

Her blonde hair flew into a frenzy. She strategically flung her head back and kicked her feet, but missed her abductor several times. Held prisoner in his grasp, he kept her feet off the ground.

A scream caught in her breathless lungs. Time slowed, stuck in a never-ending loop of failing to get loose. The arms of her attacker were too strong, too fast—she couldn't keep up.

Her limbs flailed, losing their power with each aimlessly directed swing.

Numbness tingled across her lips and down her fingertips. The lack of oxygen caught up with her body's demand. Darkness threatened to take over.

A raven-soaked fog closed in around her vision. The maroon awning over the door of her building blurred.

She almost made it home.

The world around her faded. Darker and darker. Her limbs no longer in her control.

A sharp pinch sent a burning pain down the side of her neck. Instinctively, she swung her head back and hit nothing.

Heavy eyes rolled back into her head. The sound of gnashing teeth and the faint hum of a familiar hymn echoed in her ear. Cold, black shadows entangled her body as she slipped into forced surrender.

Two

MIA HUGHES LEISURELY DUSTED the pictures hung down the hallway of her elegantly designed home. Deep smoky blues and neutral grays touched every room, but she loved the pop of green in the corners and on the shelves filled with beautiful plants of various varieties.

Gazing at their wedding photo, she contemplated how five years already passed. Hard to believe. She lingered on the photo. It held such promise of a beautiful and vibrant life.

The day they met, his stunning eyes had stopped her in her tracks. They glowed a brilliant hazel with distinct flecks of gold.

Several glances were exchanged in the hall of the young adult Christian conference they attended. As luck would have it, they were also seated in the same section. Glances turned to coffee, and coffee to an undeniable connection. They longed to spend every moment together.

She kept her walls high. Her heart, however, begged to break them down with a sledgehammer. With almost four hundred miles between Georgia, where he lived, and Tennessee, it was destined to fail from the start. Her past—and everyone in her life who reminded her every five seconds of how things turned out—made it clear. Long-distance relationships never work.

After the conference, she fought a plethora of feelings—worry she'd let him down and guilt for the hurt in his eyes when she refused to try. She wanted to move forward with Oliver but remained stuck with a past that clouded her future.

Getting the number of a boy she knew better than to fall for had been a rookie move, and yet there she found herself, falling—hard. Several times she picked up the phone to call but chickened out. What a hypocrite. It was her idea to sever all ties, but she couldn't bring herself to let him go.

After a week of agony, her phone rang. A smile danced on her lips when she saw his name. Everything changed from that moment on. Within a few months, *hi* became *I love you*, which quickly turned into *I do*. It all happened so fast, a sweeping love story for the ages.

Amusement lingered as she recalled her wedding day. An unexpected snowstorm fell across the east from South Carolina, through Tennessee, Kentucky, and up to Pennsylvania in early May. An overturned big rig on Highway 441 blocked their guests traveling toward the Smoky Mountain venue. Shortly after, the governor shut down the freeway.

At that news, Mia had fought against her internal demand for perfection as she peered out across the mountains. The view from the bridal sweet window at The Sweet Magnolia was breathtaking. An anxious pit in her stomach threatened to ruin it all, but she refused to let the moment be spoiled by a little snow. Oliver would become her husband that day, no matter what. She couldn't let him down again.

The day may have started in chaos, but it turned into the most memorable wedding. Mia walked down the aisle as snow effortlessly floated from the gray sky. An enchanting picture of beauty. Her father and current pastor, Jack Foster, married his daughter as the quaint bridal party and families looked on.

They had been so blissfully in love on the deck that overlooked the white-dusted mountains.

It had been the happiest day of her life.

Reaching her hand up to the picture, she lightly brushed over her beaming twenty-year-old face. So full of life. So full of potential.

Discolored skin poked out from under the chunky bracelet she wore. Lowering her hand, she pulled at the long sleeve that crept up her arm.

She needed to be more careful.

⚬─✕─⚬

"Freeze!" Levi shouted, followed by a heavy sigh. "They never listen." With quick reflexes, he took off after the suspect. "Dispatch, Adam one-four-nine, I'm in foot pursuit of a possible armed suspect after driving up on a ten-thirty-one. Stand by," he huffed into his radio.

"Copy one-four-nine, standing by," a voice faintly said in the background.

With the radio back on his belt, he pulled his gun from the holster. Adrenaline exploded and left his hopes for a mundane shift behind. Locked on the man, he refused to lose sight of him as the sun gave way to the night sky.

The suspect was short, frail, and no match for the long, lean stride of Officer Levi Reed. When the man disappeared around the corner, Levi quickly paused, checking if it was clear. Luckily, the dim light of the fading sun remained long enough to see the suspect down the alley.

Rounding the corner, he quickly tackled the runner. Levi held the man steady with a knee firmly on his back as the cuffs clicked with ease around his wrists.

"Dispatch show me ten-ninety-five."

"Copy that, one-four-nine," a woman's voice acknowledged. "One-two-two is two minutes from your location."

"Copy that."

"One-two-two, ten-sixty-nine?" The sound faded into the background as Levi stood up.

"Okay, man." He turned his attention back to his suspect. "Let's get up." He pulled the man to his feet. "What's your name?"

"Mickey Mouse," the squirrely man chuckled.

"One-four-nine, what's your twenty?" a raspy voice said over the radio.

"In the alley across the street from my squad," Levi quickly responded with his radio. "Well, Mr. Mouse." He looked back at the man. "I hate to inform you, but you're pretty far from Disney World." He replaced the radio and pushed the detainee up against the brick wall of the alley. With black leather gloves, he went to search him. "You got anything in your pockets or on your person that'll stab or hurt me in any way?"

"Nah, maybe just some magical dreams," he snickered.

Levi swiftly patted him down. "No one wants to see whatever nightmare that is." He stopped on something solid. "You wouldn't've lied to me about your name, did you?" He pulled out a wallet. "Mr. Larry Griswold?" He read the name from the man's driver's license.

Larry snarled in defeat. "Look, officer, ya got the wrong guy."

"Mmm, I don't know, Larry. You see, I just so happened to pull into the parking lot of the gas station you just tried to rob and watched you, gun in hand, run out the front door while the clerk was screaming, 'He just robbed me!' So, I'm gonna say it's a safe bet you're exactly the right guy." Levi continued his search and found the ultimate prize stashed in his jacket pocket. "A gun just like this one." He held up the weapon by its grip.

"That's not mine." Larry's yellow-stained teeth held tightly together. "I swear."

"Come on, man." Levi shook his head. "I mean, you didn't even try to toss the gun or stash it. That's just laziness, my friend."

"What do ya got?" Sergeant Cole hollered as she rounded the corner.

"Mr. Griswold here tried to relieve the gas station clerk of her money."

"Oh now, wasn't that nice of him." She chuckled a laugh. "How'd you get lucky enough to catch the guy?" the sergeant asked as she pulled an evidence bag from her thigh pocket.

"I pulled up as this guy's running out of the store, gun in hand." He shook his head and handed her the gun to disassemble.

"That's one heck of a way to start your shift. Must be your lucky day." She loudly smacked the gum in her mouth. A click of the release, and the magazine fell out. Another click cleared the single bullet in the chamber of the gun. "Good job, kid." She smiled, placing all the pieces of evidence into the bag.

"Thanks, sarge." He pulled Larry off the wall. "Let's go."

"Go ahead and take this guy down to the station and book him. I'll get the statements from the clerk and bystanders." She handed him the sealed evidence bag.

"Sounds good, thanks."

On the way back to the car, Levi couldn't help but chuckle to himself. People never owned up to their crimes, even when they were caught red-handed. Human nature, he guessed. The flight or fight instinct kicks in—some dig their heels in and others run, pleading with you to have mercy.

Last month, Levi celebrated his third anniversary as a cop with the same division in the Knoxville Police Department. He liked this beat. The people were fairly decent except for a few Larrys here and there, but the Larrys of the world were everywhere.

Sometimes Levi needed to remind himself the Bible said not to judge others but to love everyone. Not always an easy task, especially as more and more people choose to hate the police.

The last of the sun's light vanished as he put Larry into the backseat of the squad car and headed for the station to book him.

"Dispatch, Adam one-four-nine, show me ten-fifteen."

"Copy, Adam one-four-nine, showed ten-fifteen."

The guilty would always run, and sometimes they'd try to kill you, but the unprovoked murders of countless officers across the nation broke his heart. The last officer gunned down was on his lunch break, eating a sandwich in his patrol car. A man walked up and shot him nine times.

More often than not, Levi cried out to God for answers. Anything to help him make sense of this vengeful cancer, killing people's ability to love. Happiness dwindled everywhere, even from his best friend from so long ago.

She was a rebellious kid who loved Jesus with all her heart. It was nice to know some things hadn't changed. But the vibrant life she once lived had since faded into oblivion.

Levi left for the Marines two weeks after his eighteenth birthday. Exactly two weeks after he got up the nerve to kiss her for the first time. She socked him in the stomach for that kiss, but it was worth it.

"Now? You wait until now to notice me, Levi Gabriel Reed?" she yelled at him with the Southern twang that magnified with her anger.

"I've noticed you since the first grade when I saw you across the yard at recess, and I've noticed you every day since." He kissed her again and whispered a plea. "Wait for me."

Unsure how long he'd be gone, it was a long shot, but he had to try. A girl like her didn't come around every day. She agreed to wait and shortly after boot camp, Levi shipped out to Afghanistan for two consecutive tours.

He ate sand in the blazing heat for almost four years. In the beginning, he wrote her almost every day and called as often as he could—right up until the day he stopped. War changes a person, and Levi battled things most were ignorant to.

When his time was done, he dropped down to the reserves to finish out the twenty years needed to retire with a full military pension. When he returned home, he didn't expect her to forgive him, but he'd found that vivacious woman a ghost. One who stayed quiet by her husband's side.

Levi couldn't exactly put his finger on it, but it had to be more than jealousy twisting in his chest. He was unsure how, but her husband, Pastor Oliver Hughes, was definitely to blame.

Mia wasn't ready to take on leading the women's ministry at their church. It had been a burden Oliver dropped on her shoulders without a second thought or discussion. Her mom made it seem effortless, like it was part of her. For Mia, things felt disjointed and awkward. Possibly, those feelings had nothing to do with her ability to lead the women and everything to do with countless empty seats on Sunday mornings.

Folding laundry kept her mind from wandering into speculation as to why so many left. Sadly, she couldn't ignore reality—Oliver was off his game, and lately, the side of him she saw most scared her.

The Lord's refinement was not an easy thing to endure. As his wife, it was her duty to stick by him through thick and thin. In doing so, she ignored the chips and cracks with herself and put on a happy face, praying the whole thing wouldn't turn to dust. The pressure of the unknown was easier than the worry that the man she loved would never resurface.

Involuntarily, she took off her bracelet and rubbed her wrist. A scrunch of pain twisted on her smooth face. Strands of her strawberry blonde hair fell around her face as she looked down, a convenient concealer for the tears she fought.

"Lord, what am I supposed to do?" she softly pleaded with her Creator.

A moment later, she heard the front door open and hit the wall like it did every time Oliver came home. Those feelings shrunk back with a clasp of the bracelet around her wrist. Time to be the fully surrendered wife she knew she could be.

"Mia?" Oliver hollered out.

"In the bedroom."

His heavy-footed stride made it down the hallway and entered their room.

"Don't you look beautiful?" He walked over and kissed her perfectly made-up cheek.

"Thank you." Mia smiled.

He seemed to be in a good mood, which helped her relax a bit.

"I wasn't sure you'd be outta bed since your laziness got the best of you this morning."

His glare intensified, burning a hole right through her. A knot coiled in the pit of her stomach. She should know what he meant by that and if she were a better wife, maybe she would. Her mind raced.

When it clicked, she let out a barely audible gasp under her breath. "Your breakfast." She dramatically put her hands on her head, pushing against her stupid brain for its absentmindedness. There was only one thing left to do. "I'm so sorry, honey. Oh gosh, could you ever forgive me?" Her stomach twisted harder in anticipation of what would be in store if he didn't.

His jaw clenched, and she internally braced herself. "It's the wife's duty to take care of her husband." His words were stern and unforgiving. A forced step forward brought him close enough to tower over her. "You're one of the lucky ones. I don't ask much from you." His tone boiled with resentment. "A Proverbs thirty-one woman makes it her *joy* to get up and make breakfast for her family."

His large hand aggressively wiped down her cheek and under her jaw. His eyes seared through her. A subtle shift burst across his face. He became a different person when this happened, someone she didn't recognize.

Pain seared in her jaw as he gripped, digging his fingers into the crevasse of her bone. Darkness flashed in his eyes.

Mia's breath shook.

"I'm sor-sorry," she stuttered through her smashed face. "You *are* my joy, Ollie."

His grip loosened. "Go on."

She swallowed the tinge of rebellion still within her. "I have no excuse for my behavior. I failed you this morning which means I ultimately failed the Lord. I'll be a better steward of the things He's blessed me with, I p-promise."

"Good girl." He smirked and let her go.

Still breathless, she rubbed her hand against the soreness that lingered on her face.

That was close. Too close.

Oliver looked at Mia. Muted shame hung on his face. His defined arms forced themselves around her. Mia stood still, like a ragdoll along for the ride, no matter where it took her.

The familiarity of being controlled both scared and comforted her. This was something she tried to leave behind, but without knowing how, it was back with a vengeance.

"I'm the one who should be sorry." He sighed. "I don't know why I keep doing that to you. Mia, please forgive me."

His words were right, but they never stopped the next punishment surely to come. This had become their new routine, a brutal and relentless cycle.

"I forgive you." The words fell from her trembling lips.

He gently rested his hands on her face and deeply kissed her with no regard for the throbbing pain left in her jaw. Mia reluctantly participated, waiting for it to be done.

The only thing left to do now was to keep the peace in her home at all costs.

⸺⸺⸺⸺⸺ ❌ ⸺⸺⸺⸺⸺

Oliver crafted a beautiful apology dinner, another prong to their new routine. The first time was special, and it seemed like forgiving him was the right thing to do. But as more dinners piled up, forgiveness simply became a habitual crutch, like scratching an itch you know you shouldn't.

Mia often wondered what life would be like if the Lord hadn't redirected Oliver's path from being a chef to pastoring a church.

Would these problems exist?

If he were a chef, Mia might not be stuck living with her version of Dr. Jekyll and Mr. Hyde. The devil himself might not be living in his eyes when he got angry. She might not be left to wonder how to stop this dreadful rhythm of rage.

Growing up a pastor's kid, she knew all too well the reality of what it meant to be a leader within the church. They were on the front lines of the spiritual battle raging all around. They shielded their flock which left bigger targets on their back for Satan.

Oliver was so sure about being a pastor, he ignored the advice of her parents to take some time to pray. Mia obediently supported her husband's decision, despite her reservations.

As a child, the Lord pulled back the curtain between this world and the spiritual one. She was far too young, in her opinion. That's something so hard for a twelve-year-old to endure. Luckily, she pushed past the fear held in the exposure to darkness and clung to the truth—the Lord was always with her.

Her older brother, Luke, on the other hand, went in the opposite direction when he saw the darkness. He ran as far away from God as he could. Alcohol became the thing he worshiped above all, effectively silencing the Lord's voice altogether. The night he graduated high school, he went to a party, drank way too much, and flipped his car coming home.

Mia examined the picture of her and Luke on the end table. Her thumb ran over his bright, beautiful smile. She loved how it beamed from his freckled face. And oh, those chocolate brown eyes. He was a ladies' man, and boy had they been lined up.

Her fingers tightened around the frame. If only she had known what would happen hours after this picture was taken at his graduation. She would've begged him to not leave. Her hug would've been a little tighter, a little longer, and she'd remind him how much she loved him.

The last time she saw her brother was in the ICU at the trauma hospital in Nashville, Tennessee. Countless tubes and wires emerged from his body, working hard to keep him alive. She remembered her parents coming out of a glass conference room with Luke's doctor. Tears drenched their faces, alerting Mia to the decision made.

She was only fourteen the summer Luke died. It was the catalyst that changed everything. She had been so free before that moment. So full of life. Ready for anything that came her way. But darkness swallowed the light, almost snuffing it out completely.

In the background of the photo, she caught the sight of Levi Reed. He was talking to his dad, Keith, probably begging him not to go to the bar and just go home. A fight he lost frequently.

Mia rarely allowed herself to think about Levi. It was too sad, too painful, and far too pointless. But occasionally, her mind wandered. Where might life be if he hadn't run off to the desert and forgotten about her—if he hadn't shattered her heart into a million pieces? Would she be happy or was misery part of normal life for everyone?

After he finally kissed her, she decided to wait for him. When he was in basic training, they talked until his timer ran out every chance they could. Mia would stop everything she was doing just for a few moments with him. When he graduated, she even drove out to Paris Island in South

Carolina to cheer him on with a sense of pride in her chest. That night they celebrated by going on a proper first date.

From the moment he picked her up, there had been no awkwardness, no hesitation, only butterflies when he slipped his hand into hers, and again when their lips touched.

Mia shook off the memory. Truth was, Levi left her. Letters and calls stopped. It was clear he no longer cared for her, and yet he wasn't man enough to just tell her.

A year and a half later, she met Oliver, and he made her feel alive again. For that, regardless of how bleak things seemed now, she'd always be grateful.

After dinner, Mia cleared the dishes and cleaned up. Hot water ran over the last dish as suds ran off and down the drain. She spent her time at the sink, lost in thought as she attempted to remember when his explosions began.

Passion defined Oliver as a person. He felt things deeper than most, a quality she once found attractive. That passion became her life preserver, her saving grace.

But sadly, something changed in the last few years, and Mia was left drowning in a sea of skepticism. Had it been something she said or did? Was it because she wasn't living up to his expectations? What could she do or change to fix this mess?

"Aren't you done yet?" Irritation seethed from his lips.

Her back immediately stiffened. "Last dish," she delightfully called out with nothing less than a smile on her face.

He relaxed his stance. "We're leaving for the church when you're done."

Four years ago, she felt safe with him. Comfortable. Oliver always protected her. But now, every day she felt less like herself and more like an Oliver-knitted Proverbs 31 wife—twisted with perversion. His recent teachings were soaked with control rather than genuine love.

Maybe this was just a phase.

She prayed eventually the control he forced in every aspect of her life would fade and he would let her be the woman he fell in love with. Mia couldn't stop the dreadful thought from coming. What if that woman wasn't enough to keep him happy anymore?

Three

A HIGH-PITCHED RING ripped through the darkness, jolting her awake. The glow from her phone on the nightstand assaulted her eyes. She knew better than to leave the brightness of her screen turned all the way up before bed. An instinctive squint helped her take note of the time. Her shift didn't start for another six hours.

Although she expected the next ring, it still made her jump.

"Do you have any idea what time it is, Sheila?" she answered with a sigh.

"Jocelyn Maddox?" an unfamiliar voice asked.

Jocelyn's eyes popped open, now wide awake. "This is Detective Maddox."

"I'm sorry to wake you, detective, but I was told to contact you."

"Who is this?"

"My name is Tara. I'm a new dispatcher. Sheila asked me to call regarding a possible case." The woman's voice shook.

"But I'm not on call. Tell Sheila it's Huxley tonight."

She rolled over and went to hang up until Sheila's nasally voice cut through.

"Joce, you might want to come in early for this one. We just got a report of a possible missing person."

With the phone pressed into her cheek, she mumbled, "Has the person been missing for twenty-four hours?"

"No, but—"

"Then there's nothing I can do. Call Huxley."

"I think it's connected to your cult murders," Sheila blurted out.

Jocelyn shot up like a rocket in bed. Her heart already raced faster than her body moved. It had been two months since the last murder. She feared the case went cold, but this was a possible opportunity for justice to finally prevail.

Roughly a year ago, she caught her first solo murder case. No amount of training could have prepared her for what she saw that day. Ivy Whitlock, a student at Duke University, was dismembered and arranged on an altar as a sacrifice to God.

Several techs and rookie beat cops lost their breakfast in the bushes surrounding the rural crime scene. Visions of the victims displayed in such a grotesque manner haunted the darkness behind her closed eyes. With seven murders since, Jocelyn carried their blood on her hands.

Three hundred and eighty-seven days. Eight victims. Sixteen parents. Too many sleepless nights to count. And worst of all, no suspects.

"Why?" she pressed.

"Female college student from Duke went missing after leaving her friends at a coffee shop to walk home. There's been no trace, no ransom call, nothing. Just like the others."

"Get Huxley on it. I'll be there as soon as I can," Jocelyn snapped into the phone and hung up.

⊙—✕—⊙

Wrapped in a towel at the bathroom sink, Levi mindlessly went about his post-shift routine. The buzz of his electric toothbrush whirred, cutting the early morning stillness. Mid-cycle, an overpowering urgency to pray for Mia came to his soul.

He immediately spit out the toothpaste seeping from the corners of his mouth and rinsed, vowing to re-brush later. His hands gripped the edge of the counter as he leaned forward.

"Lord, I don't know what's happening, but I lift up Mia to you. I pray for a hedge of protection around her, Father." He paused for direction from the Holy Spirit. "'Protect her' are the words screaming in my head. I ask that you send your angels to cover her. In the name of Jesus, I pray for Your strength to dwell within her. Be with her, Father. Show her what you need her to see." He hesitated, not wanting to pray for the other person the Lord placed on his heart.

Love your enemies and show them kindness, the Lord gently spoke.

Levi sighed in surrender. "And Father, I pray for Oliver, that he…may, um, feel you and know you fully. Amen."

Opening his eyes, he looked back at his reflection. He knew the prayer for Oliver was juvenile, but he gave what he could at that moment and asked God for the strength to give more in the next.

Levi couldn't shake the feeling something heavy and dark brewed violently in the spirit world. Things were very wrong in Mia's life, but this felt bigger than that.

His love for Mia forced him to constantly evaluate whether he'd crossed the line into obsession territory. As far as Levi could tell, God gave him the heart of a protector. He may not be with Mia anymore, but he would protect her against any threat, always.

This wasn't a choice, but an obligation, and the least he could do for her. It was a fine line to walk, but he trusted God to send conviction whenever his thoughts crossed the line.

Regret lingered in his ever-present feelings. They weren't healthy or smart to harbor, but he couldn't turn them off. He was at least partially to blame for the fracture of Mia's soul and that brought a shame he would carry forever.

Fighting a war changes a man. It warps the mind and twists reality. During his first tour, he abruptly cut off all contact. He needed to protect her from the one who threatened her the most—him.

It was in the catastrophic moments of war he reconnected with the Lord. Jesus miraculously healed Levi's heart and the wounds endured as a child. It was the turning point where a bitter and broken soldier became a warrior healed and tempered by God.

He learned firsthand what it was like to spar with Satan and his army of tormentors. In the heat of spiritual battle, the enemy tried to take him out several times, but he had been restored and protected in the midst of it.

There was one particular moment Levi held close. He should've died that day, like so many others had.

The sun beat down through a rip in the cover of the Humvee, burning his neck to a crisp. Sweat mixed with dirt formed a thick layer over his weathered face. On edge, his team carefully drove down an endless dirt road—far too many men and women were killed by IEDs hidden under the sand on roads just like this one.

When his team drove over the top of it, the blast hit his chest with such force it knocked the breath from his lungs. His eyes opened as the IED exploded in slow motion around him. Levi looked to the left, his eyes locked on Jesus. A protective bubble surrounded them both and kept him safe.

To this day, he didn't understand why the Lord spared him, but for now, he was thankful and lived his life to honor those lost.

A few years later, Levi made it home—a walking miracle—only to find Mia married.

Occasionally, Levi slipped into the back of their church on Sundays just to hear what her husband would preach. At first, the sermons were good, but over the last year things shifted and the sermons held broken theology and a fleshly understanding of Godly things.

Twisted interpretation of the Word proved deadly. It brought deceitful thinking into the minds of the flock, which became a necrotic disease to the very heart of the church. A consequence of reading the Bible and twisting it to fit our own agenda, versus allowing the Holy Spirit to guide us through.

The Word of God should convict you. It should change you. But in the last sermon he sat in, Oliver used scripture to drive home his points rather than God's.

Levi caught glimpses of Mia in the front row looking proper. He made sure she never saw him and always snuck out before it was over. Seeing her left him tormented, battling his head and his heart every time.

He begged the Lord to take these feelings away, but God remained silent about the issue. Just as well. Levi didn't think it would be that easy anyway.

Strength, Lord…give me strength.

He picked back up his toothbrush and continued with his routine.

—✕—

Charlotte fought to open her eyes, but something hindered any progress. Her arms were too weak to lift. Air forced its way past the fear knotted in her chest.

"Hello?" her feeble, raspy voice called out. The dryness in her throat threw her into a coughing fit. "Is anyone there?" She heaved.

She pushed herself past the fragility that plagued her. Every muscle screamed in defiance as her arms rose and pulled a cloth from her eyes.

She blinked several times, trying to adjust, but it was no use. The world around her was soaked in pitch-darkness. Her heart hammered against her chest.

"Hello?" she cried out stronger this time, adrenaline charging through her veins.

Her other senses heightened as the sound around her magnified. A whoosh of air came from the right with a hollow sound and tumbled across her dampened face. Every cough echoed through the space, leaving her to believe she was in some sort of room. The silence was so loud it felt like the weight of it might crush her. Then the worst sound came. An awful rodent-sized scratching that wouldn't cease.

A shiver vibrated through her body, collecting in her lips. They quivered with each pant.

Was this real? Because it felt real.

"Please. Help me." The shuddered words dropped through a whispered sob.

Misery grew, welling up in her chest. She couldn't breathe. Her lungs worked overtime, quickening with each gasp.

Her fingertips tingled like a thousand tiny needles pricked at them.

Charlotte forced herself to take a deep breath in and let it out. She soon realized the familiar smell wafting through her nostrils.

Air rushed in and reminded her of…home. Another deep breath. It smelled woodsy with a copper zing to it. She knew that smell.

She moved to get up, but a loud clank of metal startled her. In a feeble attempt to keep her nerves from falling off the edge, she silently sat in the darkness.

Eventually, shaky fingers found her knee and walked down her jeans, noticing a large rip in them. A huff of disappointment pushed out…her favorite jeans.

How ridiculous to be upset about something so trivial at a time like this. She needed to see what she was up against, to analyze her chances of survival. Yes, this was much worse than a ruined pair of designer jeans.

The tips of her fingers worked their way down her calf, stopping abruptly as they ran into something at her ankle.

Using both hands now, she felt something hard and bulky.

Cold. Like metal.

She tried to pry it apart with her hands but it didn't budge. The smooth surface wrapped around her ankle. Once she made it to the oval-shaped rings strung together off the side, the full weight of the truth became clear. She was cuffed, imprisoned, and unable to escape.

A tremor of hopelessness reverberated through her.

Reality sunk in. Torment nipped at her heels. Death likely wouldn't be the worst thing she would endure.

———✕———

The ground beneath her bare feet was damp, yet Mia felt nothing. Standing in a dreary forest filled with mist, her body waited for a shiver of coldness, but it never came. She felt nothing, and yet the world around her seemed so real. She took in the unfamiliar place.

Her hand reached out. A pine tree branch ran between her fingers, an attempt to feel each thick, pointy needle as it did.

Nothing.

Deep breaths, you're dreaming, she softly told herself.

Looking up through the trees into the stormy, gray sky, she saw something off in the distance. The faintest hint of a dark outline moved toward her. With every passing second, it grew bigger. Her feet, unable to move, made her heart coil with fear.

As it fell over the top of her, she crouched down and braced for impact. Her creamy ginger hair danced in all directions, tickling her nose amidst the wind brought around her by the darkness.

Her attention frantically swiveled back and forth. A solid row of darkness swiftly closed in. The thick ring of black moved as one, brushing against the pine needles. The rustling abruptly stopped leaving a deafening silence.

Squinting her eyes, she slowly stood, trying to make it out.

It inched closer and closer. Her heart fluttered with terror.

Multiple figures surrounded her.

Various sizes and shapes came into view—some giants, big and burly, while others were small and agile.

Mia spun around, evaluating. There were too many to count.

The smell of fresh tobacco tickled her nostrils, enticing her senses. She struggled to think. Survival mode kicked into full gear as she looked for a way past their black, scaly bodies and sharp talons.

Panic took over. Her whole body trembled, unable to stand. Powerless, Mia crumpled into a ball.

She tried to scream, but no voice came from her throat.

They caved in over the top of her.

As they pushed in on her, she felt a strong hand pull her through the thick wall of darkness.

An intense light abruptly pulled her from this nightmare.

Her eyes pressed open, before her stood an angelic being. Blue wisps elegantly flowed in all directions. The brightness burned her squinted eyes. She looked over to see Oliver sound asleep, unaffected by the blinding light of her rescuer.

Mia smiled at the blazing figure. "Thank—" Her voice cut off when something in her spirit said not to let her guard down. The scripture, *For even Satan disguises himself as an angel of light,* came to her mind. Her fingers gripped the sheets. "Um."

Before she could discern things correctly, it rushed her like a linebacker, and rapidly clawed at her like a predator desperate to devour its prey. The brute force of the attack left her breathless. Hysteria spread as it snarled in her ear. She tried to keep herself calm, but that was easier said than done.

Air finally returned to her lungs despite the invisible beast pressing into her cheeks. She had been silenced by the beast, as if her lips had been glued shut. She tried to call out for Jesus but it was too muffled to understand.

What do I do? she silently prayed.

Something warm grabbed her hand and brushed it along the invisible dominator. Its reptile-like skin was smooth against her palm. The warm guide gently directed her hand toward the appendage covering her mouth.

A gentle whisper came to her heart, *Remember who you are. You're the daughter of the Highest King. Now pull.*

She pulled with every ounce of strength, but it didn't budge.

A gurgling chuckle surged, "Puny little human."

It squeezed harder, sending sharp pains through her cheeks. It felt like her skin might rip apart at any moment.

I can do all things through Christ who strengthens me, Mia mutely prayed. *Lord, give me Your strength.*

A rush of balmy heat exploded, pulsating through her veins. Her fingers dug deeper into its scales, and with a newfound strength, pulled it from her mouth.

A wail of agony came from the beast and cut through its blinding light. With another pull, she easily peeled off the demon and sat, free from its attack. The beast unsuccessfully fought against her unwavering grasp.

"In the name of Jesus, I command you back to Hell where you belong!" her voice boomed with a confidence she had long forgotten and echoed through the room. A flutter of uncertainty tumbled through her chest.

She catapulted the demon through the floor into darkness. Its shrill screams faded into the void.

A swift gulp of air forced her awake and straight up in bed. The room was quiet and nothing seemed out of place. Out of breath, she checked her body for any sign of what just happened. Oliver lay next to her, unfazed and sound asleep.

The clock read four-seventeen in the morning. She'd have to be up soon anyway. Her feet softly swung to the floor and tiptoed out into the living room.

Mia's mind raced. She thought about her actions over the last twenty-four hours. This level of attack was new, but she had failed her husband, which meant she failed God. A deserved punishment for her shortcomings as a wife and as a daughter of Christ.

She had to do better, be better. And prove to God she was worth His blessing rather than His wrath.

Four

A CRISP BREATH FILLED his lungs. The impending sun painted the sky with vivid colors of pink and orange. Levi sat in his favorite oversized chair in the backyard. The warm morning glow brought a shimmer of steam from the cup of decaf coffee next to him on the table. His focus, however, remained on the tan leather-bound Bible in his hands.

Psalm 27 was a personal favorite of his. At work, he often recited various sections in silent prayer as he drove around the desolate streets of a sleeping city, protecting it from unseen dangers. This morning, his heart focused on the last verse of that chapter, *Wait patiently for the Lord. Be brave and courageous. Yes, wait patiently for the Lord.*

After reading it several times, he knew God was telling him to relax and trust that He had everything in the palm of His very capable hands. He was to be patient and trust. Not an easy task to endure.

The sudden ring of the phone next to him demanded his attention.

"Sergeant Kizmint, what can I do for you, sir?" Why would a sergeant from the morning shift call him?

"Reed, sorry to bother you, but I needed to clarify some things from your DUI arrest last night."

"Which one?" He huffed a laugh. Thirsty Thursday at the newest sports bar in town recently made life on the night shift a lot more interesting.

"The one in the Taco Bell parking lot."

"Oh yeah, what about it?"

"Did you get him medically cleared before booking him?"

"Of course I did. He was discharged around two and booked into the drunk tank shortly after. Why do you ask?"

"He was complaining of stomach pain so he's headed back down to the hospital. I know you have to come back tonight, but I need you to come down to the ER so I can get a full statement."

Levi looked over at his coffee, seeing the need to switch to regular. "No problem, sir. I'll head that way."

<hr>

Sunlight burst through an open door in her obscure prison. It seared Charlotte's eyes, raw from the surge of emotions. Tears steadily carved a path through the certain grime on her cheeks. After a moment, she regained her bearings enough to realize that if there was light, someone she didn't want to meet was likely attached to it.

Her thin body scuffled back against the cool damp wall, pushing into it with all her might. Maybe it would open up and swallow her whole. It would certainly be better than to face whoever was on the other side of the blinding intrusion.

The door slammed shut. Another drastic shift of light left her temporarily blinded. The dull glow of a lantern floated toward her. She let out a whimper and pushed harder against the dirt wall.

"Hush now," a gentle voice said. "I'm not going to hurt you."

Charlotte didn't believe him.

"Relax, little mouse."

Charlotte's body tensed. That was the nickname her father used to call her as a child—his little mouse who was afraid of her own shadow.

"Let me take a look at ya," the voice lustfully basked.

"Don't touch me, you freak!" Charlotte screamed, aimlessly lashing out her fist. "Somebody help! Help me, please!"

"I see our little mouse has some fight in her," a rough voice came from behind the figure standing close.

Charlotte screamed obscenities, calling them every word that would make her parents' skin crawl. She had to fight. No one was coming to save her. She thought about praying, but what's the use—God didn't show up when evil took her, so why bother praying into oblivion now?

The lamp came close and forced her eyes shut. Instinctively, her hand came up to block it.

"I like the ones who fight," a voice snarled.

Black blotches filled her vision and left her, once again, reeling for sight. When her sight returned, she tried to decipher how many there were. It looked and sounded like two men. In all the prep she did for mock assault trials, rarely had a woman been involved as the dominant one.

The memory of the victims she read about and what they went through made her tremble.

Maybe a prayer or two wouldn't hurt.

"She's not ready," the softer voice said, although Charlotte couldn't see him.

"Why can't I just—"

"No! You must wait, it's imperative to His plan."

Charlotte squinted, demanding her vision to come back as the submissive one walked away. She needed to find an identifying mark like a scar or a tattoo, anything that could help pinpoint her captures.

Another light flickered to life in the corner. "This won't last long, but it'll be something." The one in charge held up an old crank-powered lantern. "I'll be back tomorrow to feed you. Get some rest."

"You're gonna need it," the grungy voice chuckled.

Her breath trembled. A few quiet sobs escaped as the door slammed shut.

———————————×———————————

The call of the alarm easily woke Oliver. He lazily rolled over and discovered the bed empty where his wife was supposed to be. A smirk grew across his lips. She must've learned her lesson yesterday. With a deep breath in and a long, oversized stretch, he detected the distinct smell of his favorite morning brew.

Dressed in boxers, he strolled down the hall, confident his house was fully in order. Mia finally let go of her rebellion and took her place by his side in full submission. Everything would be okay now.

Rounding the corner, there stood the perfect woman making him— wait—where was his breakfast?

Every ounce of joy fell from his face.

"Mia!" Oliver barked. "What are you doing?"

She jumped and turned around. "Oh gosh, honey, you scared me. I was just making my coffee. I didn't realize you were awake."

That slight southern drawl and those innocent Bambi-like eyes were adorable, but she wasn't fooling anyone with that fake and naive bologna.

It was almost six in the morning, and he *always* woke up at the same time. She could play dumb if she wanted, but Oliver was no sucker.

He looked at the clock and sternly back at her.

"Oh my gosh, I can't believe it's already six. I'll get started on your breakfast. Are eggs and toast okay? I, um, I haven't been to the store to get the—"

"Why didn't you start making it already?" He clenched his jaw. This behavior wouldn't suffice.

"I lost track of time. I've been up since four. I had the craziest—"

His large hand smacked her across the face. A twinge of regret flashed in his heart, but was quickly overthrown by an uncontrollable rage charging through him like a herd of wild thoroughbreds. It swallowed even the sincerest regret whole.

His heart thumped harder and faster. His breath mimicked each beat.

No more pathetic excuses. She needed to fall in line before it's too late.

No longer in control of his body or mind, Oliver narrowed in on the culprit—Mia.

She would learn, one way or another.

His hand forcibly clasped around her throat while the other firmly gripped the hair at her nape. The words he spit in her face were ones he never used. The noted fear in her eyes only fanned the flame of his outburst.

Something inside begged him to stop. He needed to stop. But he couldn't.

He dragged her over to the stove by her hair. With the flick of his wrist, the burner came to life. The blazing glow frolicked above the metal grate. With his hand firmly on the back of her neck, he forced her face close enough that the threat made her quake.

He should do it. He should give her a daily physical reminder of her wifely duties. It would certainly be better than the hellish fate waiting for her in eternity if she didn't get in line.

A loud roar ripped through his chest like lightning.

His trembling hands released their grip. Air caught in his throat.

Immediately, he recoiled away from her, scared of what he might do next. In a panic, he rushed off down the hall and quickly threw on the first clothes he could find. His heart raced in his throat.

He almost burned his wife's face.

Oliver did not pass "Go," he did not say a word or give an apology. Instead, he went straight out the front door as fast as possible. His tires squealed as he ripped out of their U-shaped driveway.

⚬—✕—⚬

The door to the interrogation room closed behind Jocelyn. With Charlotte Scott's file securely in her hands, she made an abrupt U-turn into the tiny room on the other side of the two-way mirror.

She analyzed the three friends who reported Charlotte missing. Tamika Lewis, the roommate, who wouldn't stop talking like a lawyer long enough to just be the girl's friend. Kiley Kent, who shoved more donuts in her mouth than Jocelyn's ever eaten in her life. And Bradley Wright, who seemed withdrawn and almost disinterested. Some friends this girl had.

"Maddox." Fellow detective and current best friend, Maya Martinez, popped in the room.

"What's up, M&M?"

"OCSD just called. They sent out an officer to the parent's house and are escorting them here now. Should be here in about twenty minutes."

Jocelyn was thankful the Orange County Sheriff's Department was willing to help them out and hoped they broke the news to her parents. It would give Jay and Fran Scott plenty of time to soak in what was happening before they got there.

She smiled at Maya, impressed at how chipper she was despite the five a.m. wake-up call to come in and help on this case.

"Thanks. And thanks for coming."

"I don't mind." A mischievous grin perched on her lips.

"Oh yeah? Why's that?"

Jocelyn turned to meet Maya's smile. She was definitely working an angle.

"Because lunch is on you," she cracked. "And you're taking me to my favorite sushi place and letting me get as much as I want."

For such a thin girl, Maya could eat her and Jocelyn's weight in sushi. This favor would cost a pretty penny, but she trusted no one more than Maya to be her number two on this.

"Indeed, lunch is on me."

"So, what'd ya think of the friends?"

"I think the girl needs better ones." Jocelyn turned back to face them. "Did the sheriff tell the parents she's missing?"

"Yes. But they didn't share any details, mainly because we didn't share any with them in the first place." Maya huffed with amusement. "Anyway, I came to tell you we started collecting video from street cams, ATMs, doorbell cameras—anything we can find in the area. I have people starting to comb through them, but it would be helpful to have a location to narrow in on."

Jocelyn looked back at Maya. The urgency twisting in her espresso-colored eyes brought a surge of anxiety.

"Maddox," a uniformed officer interrupted. "The parents are here."

"Put them in room six and I'll be right there. Please get them whatever they want to drink while they wait." The officer nodded and she turned back to Maya. "After I speak with the parents, I'll take a look at the search grid Huxley did and see if I can narrow it down at all."

⊶✕⊷

Levi sat in the emergency room. He pushed down the anxious lump in his throat as he waited for Sergeant Kizmint. The arrest was done by the book. There was no reason for Levi to be here, and yet, here he was, sitting in a hard plastic chair instead of sleeping in his soft, warm bed.

His thoughts landed on Mia. He desperately wanted to see her and have her see him. He wanted to reach out and touch her, to remind her of who she was and tell her she didn't have to live like this anymore.

But none of that mattered. He lost the right to weigh in on her life.

Luckily, that didn't mean he couldn't care about her well-being. It only got dicey when he ended up caught in the snare of bitterness. Oliver was certifiably the worst, but he was still her husband, even if Levi didn't like it.

It didn't take long for the sergeant's deep, booming voice to carry down the hallway. Levi thought back on his arrest. He never understood the appeal of getting so inebriated you have no idea how you got in your car, only to fall asleep behind the wheel in the Taco Bell drive-through. The selfishness of people who placed the value of a ninety-nine-cent taco above the life of another person baffled him.

Sergeant Kizmint pulled back the room's curtain and stepped inside. A massive man, he not only worked out but competed often in heavyweight competitions. The last time Levi saw him at the station gym, he'd been lifting eighty-pound dumbbells to warm up.

The fluorescent lights gleamed off his bald head. "Has anyone come to see him yet?"

"We just got placed." Levi gestured to the guard sent from the jail to escort the man in cuffs.

"Heard he gave you a bit of a hard time." Kizmint's stern face held like stone.

"Yeah, a bit, but nothing major."

"Did you tackle him or defend yourself against him in any way?"

"No. He tried to take a swing but missed. I grabbed his arm and spun him around before placing the cuffs on him. Once the ambulance crew checked him out and said he was stable. I drove him here myself."

"Do you remember the doctor who cleared him?"

"I put Dr. Mobley as the treating physician in my report, but you should be able to confirm it with the staff here since it was less than twelve hours ago."

With a simple nod, Kizmint walked over to the man and started to ask him some questions. Levi intently listened for any reason of concern.

When the last of the questions were asked, Kizmint motioned for Levi to step outside the room.

"Well, Reed, I think it's safe to say you're good to go home. Hangovers are a nasty beast and this guy is certainly feeling it today." Levi sighed with relief. "Go get some rest."

"Thank you, sir."

This whole thing seemed like a waste of time, and thanks to the regular coffee he switched to, sleep wouldn't come for hours. Levi decided to run a quick errand.

— ✕ —

She rigidly gripped her wallet in hands that hadn't stopped shaking since Oliver's outburst. The heaving onslaught of her heart against her chest was enough to drown out any conversation the male clerk at the grocery store tried to start. Mia couldn't break his rules, no matter how daunting they were.

A patch of black and blue skin peaked out from under the sleeve of her turtle neck, catching her eye. Quickly she tugged the fabric back down to cover her wrist, covertly looking to see if anyone noticed. She ignored the line of sweat building on her brow.

The searing pain in her throat at every breath became hard to overlook. It was certainly enough to remind her that despite his best efforts, she was still alive. She'd endured her punishment the way she had so many times before, obediently and submissive like a good wife should.

Sadly, Mia lost the ability to enjoy life around her long before today. One would even think she'd grown used to this cold, lifeless approach to the world.

God felt so far away.

Her heart ached to engage with the guy scanning her groceries. It was hard to be something she wasn't. She always took an interest in others and enjoyed making connections with various people throughout her life. If she hadn't, she never would've met Oliver.

The moment their eyes met had felt like magic in her heart.

It had been a long time since she'd felt anything close to that from him or their marriage.

The cashier's wedding ring flickered in the sunlight coming through the windows lining the front of the store. She yearned to ask him about his wife and if they had any kids, hoping he lived a happy and fulfilled life. With as many trips as she'd made to this store over the last few years, they should have been old friends by now, but instead, they were still awkward strangers. Too bad. He seemed like such a nice man.

The fan sitting next to the cash register hummed, drowning out the sound of this morning's horror now graphically turning in her mind. Her breath shook as she fought back her emotions. She couldn't break down. Not here. Not like this.

A soft touch on her shoulder caused her hands to instinctively ball into fists. The fight had been long over, but the throbbing pain of his explosive wrath lived on.

"Uh, ma'am," the pale-skinned bagger meekly spoke. "Paper or plastic?"

Mia disguised her desperation with a smile as she looked at the young girl. Courage swelled in her chest but quickly deflated like a balloon that had been let go.

"Plastic's fine." The words lifelessly fell from her mouth in almost a whisper.

They caught eyes just in time for Mia to witness pity on the girl's young face, opening the door for shame to subtly creep in and weigh heavy.

Mia didn't dare ask herself why she stayed with him, instead the wedding ring mindlessly twisting around her finger was all the reminder she needed. They were tied together, for a lifetime. Strangers saw that ring as a flawless two-carat diamond. But to Mia, it was the hinge on the shackles binding her to the man she vowed to love until her last breath.

Her body ached with each step pushing the cart of groceries to her car. She tightly closed her eyes and tried to force the burn in them away, but nothing worked. Misery remained. Her strawberry blonde hair lightly whipped in the tranquil breeze native to Tennessee in the early spring. She tried to enjoy it. Soon the summer humidity would take over with damp suffocation.

—×—

His feet picked up speed when he saw her. Maybe this was a bad idea, but he couldn't stop himself. It felt like a sign, randomly running into her like this.

"Hey, Mia," Levi hollered after her from just a few cars down. What a coincidence.

She turned around. Her eyes darted everywhere but on him. He hoped for a smile, but instead, her entire body trembled like a leaf when they briefly locked eyes. She reminded him of the battered women he helped throughout his time in Afghanistan and on the force—exposed, vulnerable, and always terrified.

"Yeah?" she timidly asked.

"It's me, Levi." Discouragement sunk in his chest. Her brokenness up close was hard to bear.

Her vibrant blue eyes finally returned to his. A hint of stifled enthusiasm rested beneath the surface of her beautiful face. Maybe she didn't hate him after all.

"Mr. Reed." Her tone flat, she started to reach out her hand and quickly changed her mind. "It's, um, a nice, well, I didn't know you were..." Her voice trailed off.

"How are you?" He tried to steer the conversation.

She shifted her weight too many times to count, unable to stand still.

"Oh, um, yup. I'm good—great even."

Beads of sweat formed on her brow. Levi zeroed in on the anxious twitch and skittish body language. She was terrified.

"I heard you're married," he pressed.

She nervously chuckled, backing up a few steps. "Yup." She held up her hand, displaying a beautiful ring. "Just over five years now."

"Congratulations. I'm happy you found someone," he lied. "Do you have any kids?"

"Oh, uh, no. Nope. No kids."

"Are you okay?" He prayed she'd be honest with him.

"Yup, fine. I'm good." She quickly stepped further back.

"You sure?" he asked, taking a small step toward her.

"Yeah. Yes." She pulled her keys from her purse. "I gotta go," she huffed.

In a flash, she got in her car and pulled away.

Levi stood, heart in his hand, dumbfounded.

Five

MIA SAT MOTIONLESS ON her couch. She'd seen the ghost who haunted her past—one who made her seethe with anger and panic despite his handsomely chiseled face and dorky smile. The nerve of that man astonished her. What made him think she would want to see those stupid dimples or be close enough to smell the same ridiculous cologne he's worn since freshman year?

She was too mad to sit. On her feet, she paced back and forth in front of the couch with arms folded across her chest. This twist of happiness in the pit of her stomach had to go. Luckily, the anger boiling over just might do the trick.

Those stupid green eyes. They held powers she couldn't quite explain.

All so ridiculous. There was no reason for an already hard day to turn on its head because of Levi stinkin' Reed. With a heavy sigh, she went about her chores. A dark shadow caught her eye as it flitted across the wall where the television hung, but she ignored it like she had so many times before.

Once the dishes were done and the house pristine, it was finally time to relax without guilt. She sat on the couch with a hot cup of tea as she tried to forget the last twenty-four hours. No matter how lightly she walked on eggshells, they inadvertently turned to dust. The uneasiness in the pit of her stomach grew with each infringement.

She prayed for old friends to return but never expected Levi to be one of them. She cringed at how things went earlier. The smarter move would have been to walk away or chew him out like she practiced countless times, but instead, she chose to be a bumbling idiot. Perfect.

The one thing she didn't count on was the overwhelming urge to reach out and hug her oldest friend. She must really have a death wish. Luckily, she fought that adulterous desire and got out of there fast. The risk was never worth the reward when it came to Levi.

A ring out of the phone startled her.

The caller ID revealed a much-needed reminder, she had someone in her corner—her mother, Laura Foster.

"Hey, Mom," Mia eagerly answered. "How are you?"

"Hey." She pictured a wide grin on her mom's face. "I'm doing great, but I wanna hear about how things are at the church. Dad said something about attendance being down?"

"Oh, um." Mia nervously chuckled, like a kid needing to explain herself. "Yeah, well, you know how it goes. People church hop because a Lord-led sermon rubs them the wrong way. Not much you can do about that but pray, right?" Her shaky response was met with a silence that drove her anxiety. "So," Mia continued, "that's just what Ollie and I have been doin', prayin'," she lied. Truth was, she couldn't remember the last time they prayed together for anything, even the church.

"I see." Laura's voice fell flat, leaving a lump in Mia's throat.

Although a married woman, Mia did what she could to please her parents. She had always been a people-pleaser, but the pressure amped up being their only living child. Mia never thought they pressured her on purpose, but the burden she carried was a heavy one. Disappointing them made her feel like a failure, just like how she felt right now.

Laura continued. "Well, your father and I have a system so let Oliver know to follow these steps, and it'll help. First, we pray *together*," she emphasized the word. Mia swallowed hard. Her mom always could spot a lie. "The Lord will direct you to those struggling. Then you *must* sit down and openly talk with them. There's no reason things can't be resolved."

The tone of her voice deflated any confidence Mia had. She never could do anything right. Her husband knew it, her parents knew it, and Mia felt the pressure to fix it.

Eggshells to dust.

"Can I ask you something, just between us?" Mia instinctively lowered her voice.

"Absolutely."

"What would you do if Dad just didn't want to do any of that? As the pastor's wife, how would you handle it?"

The silence felt unbearable. Mia prayed for no follow-up questions. She couldn't tell her the truth. It was too heavy. Too dark. Too sad.

"I wouldn't give him the option," she sternly said. "If he refused, I'd take the reins myself."

Mia didn't know what to say to that. If she went over Oliver's head…she didn't even want to think about the consequences of such actions.

Laura cleared her throat. "Is, uh, everything okay?"

"Oh, yeah. I was just askin'. It's silly, let's just forget it. It doesn't matter."

Mia softly touched the part of her face that Oliver almost burned today. What was done couldn't be undone, not by her anyway.

"How's the pool renovation coming along?" Mia tried to pivot the conversation in a better direction.

Another silence lingered. "I may not be able to see your face, sweetheart, but I know you. You can lean on me. What's going on?"

"Nothing, Ma. I'm just tired," she offered.

⸺⸻✕⸻⸺

Durham, North Carolina was like no other. It bore a resemblance to another world when the mountains draped with the vibrant colors of fall—too bad that was a long way off from now. This place, this city, fused into her DNA. It was part of her and she wouldn't have it any other way.

Jocelyn Maddox graduated top of her class from Duke University with a bachelor's in criminal justice, decorated with Summa-Cum-Laude. It didn't take long to climb the ranks, going from Durham Police rookie to homicide detective in less than two years.

Nine hours ago, the possible ninth victim of this cult, Charlotte Scott, went missing. Jocelyn's eyes slowly scanned the plethora of pictures given to her by the victim's mother, Fran Scott. Like the other parents before her, she brought Jocelyn more photos than needed—it's how they helped. Flipping over a picture it read, *Charlotte, Easter '21.*

Charlotte appeared to be a happy and well-liked college student. Her fashionable clothes told Jocelyn she must have made decent money at Harrington, the elite steakhouse she worked at. The tight platinum highlights made her brown eyes stand out. Her beauty seemed effortless, plus she worked hard pulling a 4.2 GPA.

The Scotts talked about Charlotte's decision to be a lawyer, but the tone in their voices told Jocelyn they didn't quite approve. She could relate. Jocelyn's parents were less than thrilled about her decision to become a cop. People from her old neighborhood weren't exactly accepting either. She was seen as a traitor and called vile things because of it.

The last time anyone saw Charlotte was at the coffee shop on Lex Street. Jocelyn did her best to not think about what she might be going through.

Each victim before her had been assaulted, tortured, and dismembered while still alive. It appeared to be ritualistic. Their beaten and dismembered bodies were laid out on altars made of uncut stone. In red paint the same words were written, *The righteous cleanse the earth of all evil.*

On the last two bodies, forensics found evidence of sexual assault, a clear sign their aggression was increasing. Jocelyn wondered what sparked this new routine and analyzed every path she found for a lead, but nothing shook out.

According to previous timelines, she had roughly sixty-three hours left to find this poor girl before she ended up a jigsaw puzzle in the morgue.

Jocelyn fumbled through the nine case files at her outdated desk in hopes of finding a connection. She went over the statements from friends and family. Nothing. A scribbled-out list of places they worked and frequented was cross-referenced with what they knew about Charlotte so far. Nothing. She re-checked the statements Huxley dropped off from the professors at the university, and the workers from the coffee shop. Nothing. Once again, no leads.

The team with Huxley found a pile of cigarette butts on the corner near the coffee shop. A heavy sigh left her throat as she read the report. The DNA didn't match any in the system. It came back female—more than likely an over-caffeinated student. She looked at the calendar. Finals were only a few short weeks away.

She analyzed the search grid. Why hadn't Huxley expanded it more? Charlotte's apartment wasn't far from the coffee shop. She could've been abducted anywhere along her route home. Jocelyn pulled out her phone and brought up the map. Why didn't they search out toward her apartment?

Her fingers nervously traced around her full lips. They initially thought she'd taken an Uber because of the statement given by...she shuffled through her notes...Bradley Wright.

She softly read his statement aloud. "I'm pretty sure I saw her get into the back of a car. I just assumed it was an Uber, but I'm not sure." It was a shaky answer at best.

None of it made sense. Why would her friends let her walk alone? And why Charlotte Scott? This murderous cult didn't follow the typical serial killer rules. The victims were a string of different races, backgrounds, hair color, and height. They seemed unconnected, except by location—Duke University.

First things first.

She picked up the phone and called the dispatch center.

"Hi, yes, this is Detective Maddox, I need a couple of squad cars to meet me down at The Roasted Bean on Lex Street, please. If you have anyone that was out there earlier that would be fantastic."

"You got it, detective," a monotone voice replied.

Jocelyn grabbed her stuff and rushed out the door.

⁂

"Maddox," Craig West, one of the beat cops assigned to her request, hollered out. His long legs easily carried his lengthy stride. His partner, Pete Kelley, on the other hand, struggled to keep up. "What's up, detective?" Craig politely asked, standing in front of her with a smile.

Jocelyn felt every bit of her average height press down on her as she looked up at Craig. He was far too tall. Or maybe she was just too short. She straightened her back, a sad attempt to grow seven inches.

"Yeah, what'd ya call us out here for, Joce?" Pete tried to hide his obvious gasps for air. Jocelyn was sure the mountain of hoagies he consumed regularly was to blame for the belly and double chin.

"Well, gentlemen, I had a thought." She paused. "You two were out here this morning, right?"

They both nodded their heads.

"Do you remember exactly how far out your search grid was?" She hastily flipped through her notes, trying to find it.

"Uh yeah, they told us to search out to the next block in all directions," Craig said, looking off down the street. "I walked Vine from Lex down to Copper." He pointed to the west.

"Okay, what about you?" She looked over at Pete, whose breath finally returned.

"I walked North on Lex to Ash."

Jocelyn made a quick note of what they said.

"Either of you know why Huxley didn't expand the search south towards her apartment?"

"What are you talking about?" Craig's face looked perplexed. "Her apartment's on Vine Street, west of Copper." Now it was Jocelyn's turn to have confusion twist her face. "It's on the south west corner."

Pete pulled out his notebook, "Yeah, I've got the address right here, three-two-one-one Vine Street."

"Wait, what address did you have?" Jocelyn asked, looking through her notes.

"Three-two-one-one Vine."

"It's on Vale, not Vine."

Craig pulled his notes to confirm. "Yeah, Huxley had it on Vine. We did an extra wide search around the apartments over there and he sent forensics to apartment three-D, but looks like they haven't arrived yet." He pointed to the barely discernible four-story building with a bright blue awning over the entrance.

Exactly why she hated taking cases from Huxley. His attention to detail was abysmal at best.

"I'll call the captain. We're going to need to expand our grid and get forensics to do a quick sweep in the right place. It's possible there's an abduction site anywhere between here and her *actual* apartment," Jocelyn huffed.

⟶✕⟵

The dim light gave Charlotte enough time to survey her surroundings. Dirt walls encircled her. The chain around her ankle was anchored into the wall with a large block of cement. The chain wasn't long enough for her to reach the lamp that would likely go out at any moment. Shelves hid in the shadows under the stairs that led to a heavy wooden door.

A soiled mattress lay off to the side of her. She didn't want to think about what that would be used for. Her eyes closed to drown out the faint screams of torment playing in her mind.

Charlotte recalled the flyers warning women to be careful, urging them to not walk anywhere alone due to the eight students who had been kidnapped and murdered. She could kick herself for thinking somehow it wouldn't happen to her. She should've listened.

The room filled with a similar smell to the fields back home. Every spring, her dad tilled up the land to prepare it for sowing seed.

She grew up on somewhat of a homestead before it was popular. To her family, it wasn't some fad to jump on. It was their way of life. Charlotte spent her adolescence doing her best to avoid the pigs and their slop. They were gross and filthy, which was how she felt right now.

The chain that kept her prisoner clanked against itself every time she moved. Her red-stained hands made her wonder how far the red dirt stretched beyond where she grew up. North Carolina was notorious for their red clay dirt, and a large part of the South had it as well. The sheer size of the South made it impossible to determine where she was being held.

Yelling for help seemed futile since this prison was underground. No one would hear her. A slow, steady breath filled her lungs, an attempt to keep fear from invading. She needed to collect data about her surroundings. That was the only hope she had left.

Another distinct smell brought familiarity. She inhaled again.

This was the worst game ever. *Guess that smell. It might just save your life.*

It smelled fresh, like the pressed juice place she and Tamika frequently visited. She'd kill for a tropical smoothie right now.

There was a green shot Tamika always made her do. She thought for a moment, remembering the taste. Fresh cut...

"Wheatgrass," the word quietly fell from her mouth as the lantern flashed off.

Submerged in darkness, a swell of hope circulated within her chest. Maybe she wasn't as far from civilization as she thought.

Six

"I'VE GOT SOMETHIN'," CRAIG'S voice rang out.

Jocelyn's heart surged with hope. Her feet scurried as fast as they could in heeled boots. They weren't practical for the job, but they made her feel in charge, and with a case like this one, she needed that.

"Wha'd ya find?" she asked.

"The light here is broken." He pointed up.

Jocelyn took a few steps back as her eyes scanned the full light post. Charlotte went missing around nine o'clock last night. If this light was out, that would leave this section of the sidewalk obscured enough for something to possibly happen.

She knelt by the shattered glass on the ground. With the tip of her pen, she pushed around a few of the bigger shards. "I think you've got a point," she finally offered. "Bag everything, including the rocks right here. Maybe we'll get lucky and find a print on the smooth parts."

It was a long shot, but a long shot was all she had at the moment.

She expanded out from the glass and noticed the sidewalk was relatively clean, much different than the path she'd walked to school every day. At ten years old, it was normal to dodge used needles and gangs pushing their product.

She'd grown up in a harsh area that bred a hatred for cops and all they stood for. They kept food off the table and were also the ones to blame when a drive-by took their loved ones. They either didn't patrol the streets enough or they did it too much. A lose-lose for the good cops striving for safety and change.

Sure, Jocelyn saw her share of self-righteous cops on patrol. But to her surprise, far more did their job right. They wanted to help people in rough neighborhoods. Her neighborhood.

The community she loved turned their back on her when she put the uniform on. But she knew that even if she lost everyone who mattered to her, this was what she was meant to do.

Most cops have a catalyst, a driving force for why they wear the badge. Some follow in the footsteps of their families while others have a harsher story. Jocelyn was no different.

In high school, she ran with the Grim Disciples. They made her feel special, like family, until they pressured her to be jumped in. Despite her desperation to be accepted, something held her back. Maybe it was God or the universe or some divine power, but she was thankful for the hesitation. Her best friend, Gabby, wasn't so lucky.

With no dad and a mom strung out on drugs, Gabby solicited anyone for acceptance. The Disciples sold that exact fantasy to hopeful and naive recruits, just like her. Jocelyn begged her not to do it, but once someone committed, there was no backing out.

Little did they know what it meant to be jumped into the gang as a girl. They assumed Gabby would get punched a few times and all would be okay, but they were wrong. That night, they raped her so many times, and in so many different ways, she died from internal injuries. They discovered her body in an alley by some dumpster, thrown out like trash.

Word got back to Jocelyn that Anton Jackson, the Disciples leader, also known as Hatchet after his preferred weapon of choice, found out about Gabby's hesitation to join. As a result, Gabby became a warning for future recruits about the dangers of uncertain loyalty in his crew.

They never found justice for Gabby. "Not enough evidence" was written several times throughout the file by the detective on the case. Jocelyn sat down with Detective Abigail Harper many times in the months that followed to see if more details would spark something, anything.

Detective Harper comforted Jocelyn in any way she could and eventually became the mentor who showed her a better way to help the people she loved. To this day, they met for breakfast regularly to catch up.

Jocelyn stopped when she spotted a long needle and syringe behind a black trash bag, where the building and sidewalk met. She reached her gloved hand down and gently placed it into an evidence bag. The kidnapping site was found for three of the eight previous victims, each one with a syringe just like this. If it came back positive for ketamine, she would know this was the right spot.

Before leaving, she sent a quick text to Maya about the possible kidnapping sight, vowing to let her know the moment she knew for sure.

———————⊶✕⊷———————

Back at the station, Jocelyn waited for the lab to process the evidence. She looked over the whiteboard dressed with all the victims, a running timeline for all their murders, and all the pertinent information she had on this case. She also went through the case files again. There had to be a connection somewhere. This group had a targeted reason for taking these women. *The righteous cleanse the earth of all evil.* The only religious group that made sense was Christianity, given the wording and similarities to Biblical sacrifice. Six months ago, Jocelyn did a deep dive into Old Testament sacrifice.

She wasn't big into religion but grew up with the stories of ordinary heroes from the Bible. Her grandmother went to church every Sunday without fail. She always put on her finest dress and hat to praise the Lord. Jocelyn went with her a handful of times over the years, but by junior high lost interest.

The sacrifices in Exodus and Leviticus held similarities to each crime scene. Both were held on altars made of uncut stone. Both had blood sprinkled over the altar. Both sacrifices were dismembered with specific cuts and laid out in a particular way. The only differences being, the women's bodies were not burned and a clear message was left, as if to say, they were far from done.

"Hey!" Maya sat down at the chair next to Jocelyn's desk. "What'cha lookin at?" Maya leaned over in time to see a brutally drawn picture of a religious sacrifice. "That's weird stuff you're into, Maddox." She laughed.

"I just don't see the connection here," Jocelyn huffed. "They claim responsibility for cleansing the earth of all evil, right? But these women are all good people. We've torn their lives apart and found no dirty secrets. So why cleanse the earth of them?"

"Maybe it's personal?"

"Meaning?"

"Meaning, maybe this guy felt rejected by each of these girls so he killed them."

Jocelyn looked up from the papers in her hand. "You think one guy did all of this?" She held up a crime scene photo from the last victim, Shelby Walsh. Jocelyn held the idea of it being a cult, a group of people responsible for these murders, not a single person. Maybe she was wrong.

"Okay…" Maya drug out the word. "Maybe it's two guys then. An alpha and beta team."

Jocelyn pumped her eyebrows with a shrug of her shoulders. "Maybe."

Maya grabbed a file off Jocelyn's desk and thumbed through it.

Seven months ago, Maya transferred to homicide from narcotics. She'd spent fourteen months building a case against Juan Franco, the kingpin for meth running through Durham. They had an undercover cop planted in Franco's crew for almost six months before enough evidence was collected for a warrant to tap his phone. Within weeks of the wiretap, Franco and five of his top associates were arrested, thanks to Maya and her team. It was an honor to have her help.

The two of them quickly hit it off. Both grew up in rough neighborhoods and fought their way out, ready to save the world. Maya's family was much bigger than Jocelyn's, with four siblings and eleven cousins all on the same block.

Last month, Maya invited Jocelyn to her niece's quiceañera party. She had no clue what she was in for. Family poured in from all over the area and some from out of state. More beer and tequila flowed than Jocelyn cared to remember. She nursed that hangover for three days.

"Hang on a second," Maya breathed. "I think I found something." She looked at Jocelyn. "You said something about this girl's parents being religious?"

"The Scotts?" Jocelyn asked. Maya nodded. "Oh yeah. They prayed at least twelve times while they were here. Plus, they mentioned things like 'God's plan' and 'We trust the Lord.' Why?"

"Shelby Walsh's parents were religious as well. There are notes in here that her dad's a pastor."

"You're right." Jocelyn stood and, without a word, poured through each file. "They all had some sort of religious upbringing." Jocelyn tossed each file down as she said their name. "Ivy Whitlock. Her mother is the worship leader at their church." Maya grabbed a dry-erase marker and made a note under each photo of the victims on the whiteboard. "Cherice

Johnson regularly attended church with her aunt. Jane Harlow joined a Bible study on campus two months before she was taken. Crystal Waters. Her father serves as a deacon, but she didn't maintain her faith. Kate Jenkins grew up in church but denounced her faith as a teenager. Elena Bozzelli attended church with a friend as a teenager. She was very devoted to her faith until college. Inez Gonzales grew up Catholic, converted to Christianity, then went back to Catholicism six months before she went missing. And Shelby Walsh grew up a pastor's kid."

"I think we found our connection." Maya slapped her hand on the files.

Jocelyn fell into her chair. "Maybe. I mean, I see their faith here, but why *these* girls? How does their religious history make them a target?"

They sat in silence, their full attention on the whiteboard with the added information. The link was here somewhere. She just kept missing it.

"The righteous cleanse the earth of all evil," Jocelyn mumbled the writing from the stones. "What if that's it?"

"What?" Maya seemed more confused than ever.

"What if these girls were targeted because they weren't living in the way a Christian should?"

"You'll have to explain that one to me. I'm Catholic. There's nothing a good 'ole fashion confession can't cure for me."

"That's just it though." Jocelyn walked up to the board. "They all attended, grew up in, or were around the church for a significant period. Some walked away from their faith, others still went to church."

"Okay. I'm following."

"But none of these girls actually led a Christian life. Ivy moved in with her boyfriend. Cherice, Jane, and Inez…all three had friends-with-benefits situations going on. Not to mention Cherice had two abortions four months apart. Elena also had an abortion seven months before being taken. Kate was openly gay with a live-in girlfriend and now pagan. Crystal was a bi-sexual who frequently slept around according to her friends. And Shelby loved to party and started experimenting with drugs a month before her abduction. And Charlotte never really believed in God, even as a kid, but grew up going to church."

Maya cursed under her breath. "I think you're right. There's our connection."

"They once were righteous but turned from the Lord and this"—Jocelyn pointed to one of the crime scene photos on the board—"is their punishment."

——————————•✕•——————————

Charlotte led with her fingers along the damp dirt floor, trying to find her way in the darkness. A breath caught in her throat at the thought of her family. She missed them so much—even her annoying kid brother Jacob who towered over her the last time she saw him.

They had been a tight-knit family of six. Charlotte and her siblings were homeschooled through elementary age. As the oldest, she begged to go to public school for high school. She argued it would help her get into a better college, but she was just sick of her Bible-thumping family—the same family she'd give anything to see again right now.

She could almost hear her father's soft voice spewing off Bible verses from memory. *The Lord himself goes before you and will be with you; He will never leave you nor forsake you. Do not be afraid; do not be discouraged.* That one was his favorite, but she couldn't remember where it was from. Guess that was to be expected from a girl who never cared to listen.

Her stomach growled in protest as her tongue roughly slid over the ridges on the roof of her dry mouth. It seemed like days since she ate or drank anything. She wanted to believe that verse was true. But her current reality said God did leave her. He did forsake her and left her here to die, alone.

The deadbolt loudly scraped against the stillness. In a swirl of panic, she balled herself up against the corner.

The footsteps were heavier than before. Was this a different person? How many of them were there?

"Hello there." The man's honeyed tone made her skin crawl. The lantern flicked on. The dim light pushed back the darkness she sat in. The closer he came, the more she fought the tears. "I've had a hard day. Wanna cheer me up?" The words muffled against the black mask covering his face.

"Get away from me," she shrieked, trying to escape his strong hands. "No! Help!" she cried. A tremble of fear vibrated as he grabbed her by the hair and aggressively swiped his hand down her face. "Please. Please don't hurt me."

His huge hand covered her mouth, muffling her plea under its weight. Tears streamed down her cheeks and pooled in the crevasse of his strong grip.

He moved his hand to her throat and squeezed. Her bony fingers wrapped around his and pulled with all her might, panting for air that didn't come. Desperate for oxygen, she frantically reached out, her nails scratched anything in their path. Her powerless body crumpled to the floor.

Breath returned to her lungs when a burst of pain ripped through her stomach, knocking the wind from her.

"You think you can scratch me?" he seethed.

His foot heaved at her again and again. The sound of her grunts echoed off the walls.

He dragged her by the hair to the stained mattress in the corner.

"It's time your evil presence did something good for a change," he sneered.

"Please," the thin words fell from her trembling lips.

"Hush." He reached up and covered her mouth. "The devil himself can't save you now."

All that remained were the stifled cries of a girl begging for her nightmare to end.

———⊷✕⊷———

She pushed pause on the video. Her heart raced. So, it was confirmed. Charlotte had been targeted and taken, just like the others. The biggest hindrance that stood in the way was obscurity. Charlotte walked into the darkness, where the street light was out. They watched her legs and arms flail, and that was it. No other cameras were available to access for half a block.

Jocelyn took a deep breath. "Is the warrant back on Charlotte's financials?"

"Not yet." Detective Boscereli stood next to Jocelyn. He came and got her when they found footage of Charlotte being kidnapped on a doorbell camera across the street.

"How's it coming with interviews?"

"They've found nothing out of the ordinary as of ten minutes ago."

"Okay, keep combing through the footage and see if we can find a vehicle or where they drug Charlotte off to. With the religious connection, I think it's safe to assume this is the same group unless proven otherwise."

Back at her desk, Jocelyn's hand cramped as she scribbled down a hurried list of what she needed from Captain Ward. They needed a team of forensic scientists, the best they had, to comb through all of the evidence over the last year and search for more connections. She also needed detectives and street cops dedicated to help sort evidence as it came in, speak to families, and evaluate if there were any other common threads in the victims. There had to be a place where their lives overlapped at the hunting grounds of this psychopath.

The smell of french fries wafted into the air. Maya set a grease-soaked bag on the desk as Jocelyn wrote the words *"Task Force"* in bold letters.

"I figured a little brain food might help."

Jocelyn stifled a laugh. "I don't think greasy food counts as 'brain food.'" She smiled, shoving a handful of fries in her mouth. The crispy, salty goodness was her ultimate weakness. She wasn't much for sugar, but salty or spicy perfection was where it was at. "Thanks," she forced the word past a mouth full of fries.

"Of course." Maya pulled her burger from the bag and took a huge bite. Now it was her turn to talk with a full mouth. "Where you at?"

"I just finished my list. I need the best forensic people we can get. I think there's evidence that can help narrow things down in here." She pointed to the mountain of disjointed files. "There's red clay dirt on the stones so maybe the dirt can help identify the region?"

Maya cocked an eyebrow.

Jocelyn put a hand up. "I know I'm grasping at straws here, but this girl is going to die if we don't find her soon."

Maya offered up a sympathetic smile. "We'll find her."

"You don't know that." Jocelyn sighed. "I thought I'd find Kate Jenkins too, but we both know how that turned out."

Jocelyn was convinced Kate's art history professor, Arthur Harris, was the one who took her. She tore that man's life apart and found a history of seducing his students. When she realized Ivy Whitlock and Jane Harlow also took his class, things really amped up.

When her body was discovered the next morning, she knew Arthur couldn't have done it because he spent the night in a holding cell. The DA forced her to release him. After following him for two months, there were no further ties to the victims, leaving them back at square one.

For those months, Jocelyn protested that evidence must have been missed, overlooked, or not fully checked. How does a person murder eight people and leave no usable evidence? So now, she made a mental list once more.

The stones were uncut, but there were far too many garden stores that carried them to narrow down. The red paint was generic. There were no hairs or foreign fibers found. All of the victims were assaulted. The last two were raped, a change from the previous pattern, but a condom was used so there was nothing more. They did find two unknown DNA samples on Shelby Walsh's body, but without a match in the system, it quickly fizzled out. Jocelyn frequently ran those samples to see if any additions to the system were a match, but so far, nothing.

Charlotte was a good kid. She worked and went to school, which left little time for a social life. They tracked down her ex-boyfriend, Paul, just to feel him out, but he was genuinely devastated. None of her professors recall anyone paying her special attention. Her friends said after she broke up with Paul, Charlotte was disinterested in dating anyone. No dates, no online profiles, no casual romantic partners. Nothing.

Her parents seemed upset about her life choices, but that wouldn't explain the other eight victims.

"This is frustrating," Jocelyn growled.

"The lab just called." Captain Ward called out as he approached. Jocelyn and Maya stood. "The substance in the syringe came back positive for ketamine. This is definitely our guy."

Jocelyn's heart raced. "Yes, sir. It is."

"What do you need to help you catch this guy?"

"Well, sir, I think we need a task force, and it's worth bringing in forensic specialists. I think we need to run the DNA again and do another analysis on the dirt from all the stones. Plus, I need people to help conduct more interviews. There has to be a connection we've missed." She paused. "Do we know anyone who specializes in cold cases?"

"I'll have Dan from the lab pull his best people and get started." He sighed heavily. "I do know a guy I can call who's an expert in what you need. But, I gotta warn you, he can be a handful to deal with."

"That's okay, sir. I'll do whatever I have to, to find Miss Scott."

⸺⸺⸺⸺⸺ ⚭ ⸺⸺⸺⸺⸺

His belt clinked together as it wrapped around his waist. Charlotte lay still on the ground, afraid to open her eyes. She slowly drew her knees to her chest. Life as she knew it would never be the same.

A soft mumble echoed off the dungeon walls. To keep from breaking down, she focused on the sound of him lacing up his boots. It sounded just like her dad's.

As a kid, Charlotte would wake up early and secretly watch her father get ready for work. When she'd get caught, he would make a small glass of chocolate milk for her to drink while he ate breakfast.

Her father was so proud of her and all she accomplished. Her heart sank, knowing he would find out about this whole thing. What a waste of such a promising life. Soon she would become a statistic, eventually stored away in a file no one would ever read because it was too sad.

This monster may not have robbed her of her innocence—she gave that to her high school boyfriend right before he broke her heart—but what this guy took was so much worse. She'd never feel safe again, if she even lived through this nightmare.

She tried to blink grains of dirt from her eyes. It was hard to see. She blinked harder now, rubbing her eyes. There was too much pain in her whole body to register where it hurt the most.

His boots pounded against the stairs as he hastily left her alone. Charlotte took small sharp breaths. Her body throbbed with agony and terror.

Seven

THE SUN DIPPED BELOW the horizon. Shades of orange, pink, and purple invaded the clouds perched in the sky. Such a beautiful setting for the worry gathered in the pit of her stomach.

Dinner grew cold with every tick of the clock. She made his favorite, homemade chicken pot pie.

"You've reached Pastor Oliver Hughes. I'm sorry I can't come to the phone…" Oliver's voice faded as she hung up and brought the phone swiftly to her lap.

This wasn't like him. First, he left without a word, and now this. Her mind raced with every worst-case scenario she could think of.

She grabbed the phone from her lap, and one by one, called the elders of the church.

First up was Ken Grant, the longest-standing Elder. Ken watched five pastors come and go in his time. He was a bold man of God who unapologetically spoke the words of the Lord. That got Ken on Oliver's list several months ago when he pushed back against him during their men's Bible study.

When Oliver came home stark mad that day, Mia stayed silent. Thankfully, he put his fist through the wall instead of her.

"Hello?" a rough voice answered with a southern drawl.

"Hey, Ken, it's Mia Hughes."

"Well, hello, Mia. What can I do for ya?"

"I'm calling to see if y'all have heard from Oliver today. I haven't been able to reach him. He should've been home for dinner over an hour ago."

"Oh, I'm sorry to hear that. I just got in from checkin' cows so I can't say that I have." Ken cleared the tiredness from his throat. Mia couldn't believe that at seventy he was still out working cows on his ranch. "Let me, uh, check with Melissa."

Mia waited patiently on the phone as Ken muffled the call out for his wife. They exchanged an indiscernible conversation for a few short seconds.

"Mia?"

"Yeah, I'm here."

"Melissa hasn't seen or heard from him either."

"Okay, thank you. Sorry to bother y'all."

"Oh, you're no bother. We'll be prayin' that ya find him soon."

"Thanks."

Next was Mark Porter. He and his wife, Connie, were younger than the Grants, but retirement wasn't far off. Mark worked odd hours at the hospital as a pediatric nurse so she wasn't sure he'd be home. As a stay-at-home mom and sewing genius, Connie likely would be.

"Hello?" Connie tightly answered.

"Hi, Connie. It's Mia Hughes."

"Hey, Mia. What's up?" Connie always sounded distracted, like Mia called at the worst opportune time. Figures.

"I was just callin' to see if y'all had seen or heard from Oliver?"

Connie huffed in palpable frustration. "Mia, I'm tryin' to get dinner on the table and Mark is workin' a double. I haven't had time to shower, let alone know where Oliver might be."

"Okay," Mia's voice cracked. "Sorry to bother you."

"I'm sorry, Mia. Caleb just shoved his sister. I've got to go."

The click of the phone sounded like a gavel in her ear. Mia had been found guilty of being an incompetent annoyance.

She drew in a shaky breath and dialed the Banisters. Todd and Vivian were in their early thirties with four boys ranging in age from twelve to four. They moved out from Colorado about two years ago and last year became the newest elders at Living Waters Church.

Mia hit it off with Vivian almost immediately. There was a connection and mutual understanding between them. Vivian had a temper though and was almost aggressive at times. Mia pulled herself back, but Oliver and Todd rapidly became thick as thieves, pushing her right back in.

Before long, the men became inseparable, doing everything together including the things Mia wanted to do with her husband, like hunting and fishing. She loved being out in nature. Her father taught her to fish as a young kid, and by fifteen she cleaned and processed her own deer meat. But, Oliver always said those things weren't for women to do. Her place was right here, in the kitchen and serving his every need.

Mia didn't care too much for Todd. There wasn't anything in particular she didn't like about him. It was more of a gut feeling like her spirit warned her to tread lightly.

"Hello?"

Her whole body tensed. "Hello, Todd. I was calling to see if you've heard from Oliver today?"

"Mia? Is that you?"

"Oh heavens, where are my manners? Yes, it's me." She tried to light-heartedly chuckle at her mistake.

"It's so great to hear from you, *Mia,*" he emphasized her name. "How are you?"

"I'd be better if I knew where my husband was." Mia gulped. *Where did that come from?*

"Well, I wish I could help ya, but I haven't seen or talked to him today."

"Oh, okay. Thanks anyway. Have a good night."

She hung up before he had a chance to say anything more.

⚬➤✕➤⚬

Mia anxiously picked at her perfectly manicured nails. Fourteen hours had passed since she last saw or spoke to him. Her watch told her it was eight-thirty. Oliver hasn't been gone like this in a few years. Maybe he was helping a member of the church, but he would usually call to tell her. Her phone had never been this quiet. He usually caused more stress with all of his texts and demands for her to answer when he called. If he wasn't home by midnight, she would call the police. He might get mad, but it would be worth the punishment.

Her foot wiggled at lightning speed as she thought about her unwelcome visitor last night. It had been so different from what she'd experienced before. Her first sinister encounter was something she still thought about over a decade later.

At twelve, Mia questioned the existence of God. She asked all the typical questions like—how do we know He's real? What if you devote your life to Him and it all turns out to be a wives' tale? Have you ever actually seen God? And when Mia asked these questions, Laura shared her personal experience.

Her mother revealed the sexual abuse endured as a child and how that trauma shaped the woman she became in the worst of ways. After that, she looked for acceptance and the ability to forget her jaded past with drugs and alcohol. And lastly, she shared how Jesus came in and changed everything.

Some things He healed instantly, others He walked her through the process of forgiveness and restoration. Despite her mom's vulnerability, Mia continued to doubt.

Four days later, Mia came face to face with Hell in the middle of the night.

Out of nowhere, darkness paralyzed her with pressure. Every feeble attempt to scream fell silent in her throat. Seconds felt like an eternity as fear spread wide. Flashes of light beamed across her vision like shooting stars.

All of that paled in comparison to the shrieks that came next. They ripped through the air and Mia's heart. Heat radiated on her face. Those screams haunted her, even now.

She eventually broke free and sprinted for her parent's room.

She stopped dead in her tracks when she saw them. Her wide eyes followed up their legs, tilting her head all the way back. There were two of them. Brown leather belts crossed over their trunk-like chests and around their waists, their chest plate a shimmer of gold with weapons drawn, ready for battle.

"What the…" Her voice trailed off in awe.

She reached for the doorknob. In unison, as if they'd practiced it a hundred times before, a loud scrape of metal echoed as they crossed their giant swords over the door making an X.

"You can't come in here," one of the angels boomed down.

"What do you mean I can't go in there? Do you not see what's happening? I *need* my parents!" she demanded.

"You *need* to go back in there and deal with that, *alone*."

He pointed to her door. Light flickered through the cracks.

"I can't," she cried out. "I don't know what to do."

"You *do* know. You have everything you need to fight them. Now go." The ground beneath her feet rumbled as the tip of his sword slammed into it.

At her door, she trembled. With a crook of her neck, she gave a final plea to the mighty warriors. Their enormous swords were back in the sheaths hung from their waistbands. Mia wondered what kind of horrible things they fought with them. Were there worse creatures out there than her dark tormentors?

One looked down at her with a sternness in his eyes. She scrambled inside before she endured their angelic wrath.

The room was cold, detached like all the love had been siphoned out and replaced with anguish. She tried to hide the predominant quiver of her lips.

Movement slithered across the wall. Her focus pulled to the ceiling and her stagnant fan. Three shadows, encapsulated with pain and darkness, swirled like sharks who smelt blood in the water.

Circling.

Watching.

Waiting to strike.

Mia hiccupped a breath in her chest. She hadn't been the best kid lately. In the last few months, she tried alcohol at a sleepover, a friend's cigarette, and looked at things on the internet she shouldn't. Whatever this was, and the torture it brought, she deserved it.

It didn't take long for them to strike. The words of the angel came to mind as she desperately clenched to her sheets, fighting for sips of air.

You have everything you need to fight them.

Shrieks of torment ripped through her like flesh being torn from their bodies in a never-ending cycle of persecution. She forced the undeniable pain from her mind.

A vision became clear. She sat on her mom's lap after having a bad dream. Laura explained there was no reason to fear because we had Jesus on our side. Mia immediately knew Jesus was the only one who could save her.

Like the woman with the blood issue in the Bible, Mia thought if she could just reach him, maybe this misery would end. Pushing with all her might, her head thrashed back and forth. She needed to free herself enough to speak the words.

Their grip on her face loosened with each thrash of her head. Hope rose within, pushing her to fight harder. Her top lip broke free.

The fight raged on until she could scream out, "Jesus!"

Instantly, everything stopped.

A warm love poured through and enveloped her. Out of breath, she sat up in bed. A white glow illuminated the room. She looked down and saw a Lamb lying next to her. Its pristine wool blazed with a blinding white light. Fear should have been present, but peace remained.

It slightly cocked its head to the side and spoke straight to her heart. *Do you still doubt Me?*

A loud bang on the window startled her. The shadows pounded with fear in their eyes, pleading to come back in. She looked down at the lamb and knew what to do.

"In the Name of Jesus, get out!" she shouted.

Mia huffed a laugh of amazement at how fast it worked. They were finally gone.

Their eyes met once again as the Lamb gestured to the door. That was all she needed to race toward the comfort of her parents.

That night, she surrendered her life fully to Christ and repented from the sinful things she collected. It was rare to catch her without her Bible as she read it frequently. She grew immensely, only to falter slightly when her brother died a few years later.

Attacks like this one came and went throughout her life, but what changed was her ability to fight. She went from a terrified child unsure of how to resist things unseen to this world, into a warrior with confidence in Jesus.

Lately, however, she felt stripped of her weapons. She desperately tried to please her husband and everyone around her, but nothing ever seemed good enough. She always fell short, waited too long, or did things backward in his eyes. No matter what she did, there were harsh consequences to endure.

"Forget it," she huffed, done waiting.

The line rang twice before a sweet, unexcitable voice came through. "Nine-one-one, what's your emergency?"

It didn't take long to hear a knock at the door. She prayed this had been the right call. Knots remained ever-present in her stomach as she reached for the handle. She hesitated for just a moment with a calculated and drawn-out breath. The fist on the other side of the door slammed into the wood again, startling her.

With a shaky hand, she quickly cracked the door open and was met with those infamous dimples. Worry twisted in her heart.

"Seriously?" she scoffed under her breath.

—×—

Taking in her big blue eyes and mouth gaped open in horror, he awkwardly stood across from her. He attempted to buy some time with a shift of his duty belt, to find the right words. This was unexpected. If he had known this was her house, he would've at least tried to dodge it. It probably wouldn't work, but at least a supervisor could have responded with him.

All he could do now was accept his fate.

"Good evening, ma'am." He tucked his fingers into the neckline of his vest in an attempt to look natural. "I'm here about a missing person?"

"Oh, stop it, Levi." Mia left the door open and walked back into the house. "We have too much history for you to act like you don't know me."

Maybe she was right, nevertheless, Levi refused to step inside.

"Well, M, the truth is, I don't know you anymore. You're certainly not the girl I once knew." There was a bitterness to his words. He exhaled a sharp breath. "Let's just pause for a second. Believe it or not, M, I'm here to help you, not fight."

Mia paced back and forth. She looked uneasy. Scared. Or something worse—he could feel it.

"Okay, okay, maybe you're right," Mia's voice shook and cracked. "Listen, I'm just worried."

"Why's that?" Levi pulled out a pocket notebook and pen from the side pouch of his tactical pants.

"It's my husband, Oliver." She nervously bit her nails. "We had a disagreement earlier this morning. He left without so much as a goodbye, and I haven't heard from him all day."

"Is that out of character for your husband?"

"What do you mean?" she defensively snapped.

"Just, is it normal for you two to go all day without talking or texting?"

A long silence followed his question. Her eyes fixated on the ground, like a child who had been caught in a lie. He ignored the break in his heart seeing her like this.

"M, I'm not judging you," he reassured her. "I'm just asking if it's normal or not."

Mia lifted her gaze but refused to look Levi in the eye. "No, it's not normal. He's usually constantly calling or texting."

"This fight—"

"Disagreement." Mia cut him off with a stern correction.

"Right. This disagreement, what was it about?"

"Oh, it was nothing." Mia's breath increased as she stumbled over her answer. "A silly little thing, really. Not worth mentioning."

She was lying, but he waited to call her on it.

"It is worth mentioning. You had a fi—" She sharply looked him in the eye for the first time since opening the door. "Uh, *disagreement*, and then he takes off. Knowing what it was about just might be the key to finding him."

She huffed a nervous laugh and drug out her words. "It was about breakfast, that's all."

"What about breakfast?"

Levi tried to subdue his frustration. He couldn't understand why she was beating around the bush about this. How bad could it be?

"I forgot to make it for him this morning," she snapped.

"And that made him mad?" Levi sarcastically replied with instant regret.

"Yes, Levi, it made him upset because I always get up and make him breakfast before he goes to work," she defensively snapped.

"Oh, that's nice." He tried to recover from his snarky remark. "So, what happened this morning that you forgot?"

"I had a weird, um, it was a—a dream. It kinda freaked me out and I couldn't sleep." She tucked her hair behind her ear. "So, I came out here and read my Bible." She gestured to the living room

"I see." Levi couldn't help his curiosity. "What was the dream about?"

"Is that really necessary, Officer Reed?"

"Uh no, ma'am. No. Sorry, it's not." He cleared his throat.

—✕—

The nerve of this guy weighed thin. Her life and its details were none of his business. She was frustrated and frankly a bit angry that of all the cops to show up, it had to be him.

"Don't you call me ma'am. You know that makes me feel old." Mia attempted to calm down with a deep breath. "This is ridiculous standin' in the door like this. You're letting all the bugs in." She gestured. "Come on in. We can talk at the table."

His foot hovered over the door jam. He hesitated. She closely watched him from the corner of her eyes.

"Officer Reed?" she meekly asked.

He took a noticeable breath before he came inside and closed the door behind him. Each step made him visibly uncomfortable.

Mia led him to the dining room table. "Can I get you some coffee, tea, or water?"

"Water would be great," he said, examining the decor. "Do you know of anyone else who's seen or heard from Oliver today?"

"No," she said from the adjacent kitchen. "I contacted all of the elders as well as the administrative assistant from our church, but no one has seen or heard from him." The ice dispenser brought a brief interruption. "I also called his parents in Georgia, but they haven't heard from him either."

Mia set the glass of water in front of him.

"Thank you." He smiled. "Is there anywhere your husband might go to cool off?"

"I'm not sure." She internally beat herself up for being too stupid to have answers. "I'm sorry, I…"

"M, it's fine." Levi reached out his hand and placed it on top of hers.

Mia wanted to ignore how nice his touch felt. She should have hated it, but she didn't.

The door abruptly flung open. Mia jumped up from her seat with shame heavy in her heart. Oliver walked in, wild with anger. Calling the police was another mistake that would cost her greatly.

"Ollie!" she barked in surprise. "Thank God you're okay." Her arms tightly wrapped around him. Red dust covered his jacket.

"Mr. Hughes." Levi stood up. "I'm Officer—"

"I know who you are," Oliver sternly cut him off. "What are you doing in my house?" His eyes cut right through Mia. "What did you do?"

"Your wife was concerned for your safety, Mr. Hughes."

Oliver's giant hand raised, pointing his finger in Levi's face. "I wasn't asking *you.*"

Levi calmly picked up his radio, keeping Oliver's gaze. "Dispatch, send a supervisor to my location, please."

"Copy, supervisor en route," dispatch acknowledged.

"Adam one-nine-four, are you code four?" a woman's raspy voice came through the speaker.

"Affirmative, code-four," Levi assured without taking his eyes off Oliver. "Mr. Hughes, I'm going to need to ask you to calm down. I'm just here to help."

"Yeah, help yourself to my wife." Oliver stepped toward Levi, his fists balled with fury.

"Ollie." Mia lightly put her hand on his shoulder, placing herself between the two men. She had to neutralize the situation before Oliver killed Levi. "Ollie, it's okay. You're home now. You're safe." She tried to grab his tightly clenched hand. "Baby." She gently turned his face to her. "I'm just so happy you're okay."

When their eyes locked, he softened his stance. Mia wrapped her arms around him, thankful for his gentle embrace. She noticed Levi from the corner of her eye reholster the taser she didn't even see him pull out.

She pulled back. With her eyes on Oliver, she nonchalantly spoke. "I'm sorry for wasting your time, officer." Her hand gently caressed her husband's dirty face.

"Mr. Hughes, I do have to ask you a few questions for the report. My supervisor will be here shortly, and I would understand if you'd rather speak with her regarding this matter."

"We would," Oliver snapped.

Eight

EVERY MUSCLE BURNED WITH pain. It felt as if months had passed. There was no way to keep track of day or night enclosed in this God-awful hole. Everything within her chest shuttered and ached. She never felt so alone. So broken. Discarded. Ready to give up on everything. Curling into a ball, she tightly held her knees.

Time to accept reality.

She was going to die here. No one would look for her. No one cared.

It was the perfect fate for a horrible girl. She treated her entire family like they were less than her, her whole life. The women she helped in high school as a volunteer were seen as weak and pathetic in her mind. Getting the internship fed her need for superiority amongst her friend group. Honestly, the only one she saw as competition was Brad, but lately he seemed way more interested in hanging out than being a lawyer.

The harsh truth was she would've stepped on anyone along the way to get that internship and did. In confidence, Tamika expressed how much she disliked the firm awarding the internship, and Charlotte may have slipped that information to the TA.

And then there was Kiley, who cared more about shoving food in her face than what she looked like. Knowing Cade, Wallace, & Wright cared heavily about how their people presented themselves, Charlotte may have suggested Kiley wear an unflattering outfit to her interview with them.

It was like cutting little holes in someone's socks. The act itself almost undetectable, but eventually, it tore open a gaping hole. A giant Charlotte-sized hole.

It was entirely possible that she was as wicked and evil as the man said. No wonder God hadn't shown up to save her. She wasn't worth it.

--------------------✕--------------------

Unseen, a lanky demon with razor-sharp teeth and long piercing talons hovered, his eyes dark and evil. A hazardous smoke puffed from his thin lips as he laughed.

"That's it." He leaned over, her head engulfed with disorienting smoke. "Taking your own life is the only way out."

"Taking my life is the only way out," Charlotte whispered.

--------------------✕--------------------

Death was the only feasible solution. It was brilliant really to go out on your own terms.

Don't let them take any more from you than they already have.

The thought was clear, concise. First, a weapon, then to end this nightmare for good.

She went out as far as her chains would allow, searching for anything to help end her life, but she came up empty. These guys were too smart to leave anything in close range.

Her hand reached out as far as it could go. She was so close to the table where the light sat. She could break the lantern and cut her wrists with the jagged pieces. Her torso stretched, like an accordion. Part of her worried she would end up like the Gumby toy she stretched too far out as a kid. He never was quite the same after that.

She was so close, and yet it may as well have been a million miles away. No amount of shifting or stretching got her close enough to matter.

She leaned against the wall in defeat. Her head softly knocked back on the hardened dirt a few times. Maybe that was it.

She did it harder.

A sharp breath came in through her teeth. The back of her head throbbed.

--------------------✕--------------------

She hit her head again, each time harder than the last.

The demon shoved his claws deep into her skull and slammed her head against the wall, over and over again. A villainous smile spread across his dark, twisted face.

Her limp body eventually crumbled to the floor.

"Occult will be pleased," the dark being snickered.

—⊶✕⊷—

Her inbox flooded with messages from the lab, sergeants, and the medical examiner. All hands were officially on deck. Jocelyn kept her anxiety under control the best she could with deep breaths and constant words of affirmation to herself. As more emails came through, her lungs fought for air.

She stood and made a beeline for the bathroom.

Her hands slammed against the door so hard it hit the wall. In the security of the tile walls, she hunched over the sink. What if they didn't find her? Her chest tightened. With no suspects, she didn't even know where to start their search. Her lungs burned. Lips tingled. Everyone would watch her fail, and the blood of one more would be on her hands.

Cupping the water, she splashed some on her face. The crisp, icy blast forced a gasp in. It was enough to slow her down briefly. She splashed again.

Her frigid hands held to her face as she stood upright, meeting her own deep brown gaze in the mirror.

"Great," she sighed, looking at the massacre of mascara on her face.

She grabbed a tissue from the counter, thankful Leslie put some here last week. Although she was an older detective who gave Jocelyn a hard time, they had an unspoken bond. Being a woman in a male-dominated field, Jocelyn took allies where she could get them, even if that meant making friends with Detective Crabby Pants.

A chuckle rose in her chest, breaking her free from the last of the anxiety. She jumped when a stall door opened behind her. In the mirror stood Detective Crabby Pants. Jocelyn braced herself for whatever snarky comment was behind those nicotine-wrinkled lips.

"Listen, Kid." Jocelyn hated it when she called her that. "I didn't mean to eavesdrop. I mean, technically you barged in on me." Her voice was deep from years of smoking. "I heard your serial killer took another girl."

Leslie slowly turned on the water to wash her hands.

"It can get overwhelming pretty quick—all the people looking for you to lead them—but remember, as women our superpower is being able to multitask better than men. It's how the Good Lord created us so we could be mothers and all that crap." Leslie wasn't known for her maternal instincts or proper etiquette. "But we can tap into that and show these jerks who's really in charge around here." She gave Jocelyn one firm smack on the shoulder and left her hand on the sting of her skin. "You have a chance to save this one. So buck up, detective. That girl needs a fighter, not whatever this is."

It may not have been the most eloquent speech, but it was effective. Leslie was right. Charlotte needed a fighter, and that's exactly what Jocelyn was.

"Thank you, Detective Fields, I really needed—"

"Don't get all mushy on me now, Suzie." She tossed her paper towel in the trash and headed for the door.

"It's Jocelyn," she hollered as Leslie left without another word.

—✕—

A bright light danced across the darkness behind her closed eyes. Its warmth cascaded and wrapped around her icy body like a warm blanket. It felt nice here, lighter. She kept her eyes closed, afraid to ruin this rare moment of comfort.

"Charlotte," a gentle voice called out. "It's okay, you can open your eyes. You're safe."

She hesitated, but only for a moment because of how this felt—whole, loved, protected… safe. A soft breeze tumbled over her face as she pushed the remanence of a smile across her thin lips.

When her eyes opened, an abundance of greenery filled her vision. Breathtaking wildflowers popped through the grass, and lush trees reached their way toward Heaven. A man crouched over her, His skin a rich olive as if from a distant land. She tried to scramble out of reach, but His hand touched her before she could. A velvety kindness burst through her. His radiant skin was soft, but it was the compassion and tenderness in His eyes that made her stop.

"Jesus?" The name fell from her mouth before she could think about how ridiculous that was.

"See, you do know Me." He smiled. "Do you think you can stand?"

His hand reached out and effortlessly took hers. There was something about this man. She was drawn to Him, like her heart might explode with love. There was joy in this love, a joy she hadn't felt since she was a kid.

"My child," He lovingly said, wrapping His arms around her.

She melted in His glow as His fingers pushed into her skin. In His embrace, she was seen, valued, and safe. She didn't want this to ever end.

"Who are you?" she asked, ignoring what was said earlier.

"You always did struggle with belief." He lightly chuckled, releasing her. "Do you know why?"

She shook her head no.

"It's because you've never taken the time to get to know Me and who I really am."

"Well, I, um…" Her thin lips quivered, unsure why that reality brought on such emotions. "I'm sorry." Her voice thinned with remorse.

"I know you are." He grabbed her hand. "Sometimes it seems easier to believe in some cosmic power like the universe, but I tell you, the One who created the universe is so much more than you can imagine."

"God?"

"That's right, my Father in Heaven, the Creator of everything." His deep brown eyes peered right through her. "He created you too."

"Why?"

"Because you're precious to Him, Charlotte. The world needs someone exactly like you, and We wouldn't have it any other way."

Tears spilled over. "But, I don't know that I'm worth all this trouble," she cried out. "I'm a terrible person, Jesus."

He gently placed His hand on her shoulder. "While that may be true, none of that dampens Our love for you." He led her to a bench made of white granite. "What do you remember about Me from Sunday school?"

"Um, I remember You're the Son of God."

"Yes, what else?"

"That You came to earth and died for us."

"Did you know that *you* were on My mind as I hung on the cross?"

She looked up at him astonished. "Me? Why?"

"My Father blessed Me with the ability to see every person throughout time and was reminded through it all, what and who I was doing it for." He placed his hand on her face, warmth flushed through her cheek. "And I saw you and all of your flaws and shortcomings. I knew you would struggle with your belief, trust, and faith. I knew I needed to not quit because you, and a world filled with so many like you, need a Savior."

Charlotte desperately wanted to believe him but quickly remembered the dungeon she was thrown in. Anger flourished.

"Then why did You betray and abandon me when I needed You the most?" she snapped. "I needed You, and You just let them take me!" she yelled. "You say that You love me, but letting them hurt me the way they did isn't love. It's torture in order to control me."

"I never left you. I've been with you the whole time." His tone was unwavering.

"And You just let them… You let him…" She let out a wail of agony that left her breathless.

Jesus wrapped His arms around her again and a calming peace came over her broken soul.

"Why did You let that happen?" she whispered.

"This can be difficult for people to understand, but God doesn't orchestrate or allow terrible and awful things to happen." He choked back His own tears now. "The world you live in is broken. In the garden, when Adam and Eve ate from the forbidden fruit, they brought sin into the world and your life."

"So?"

"So, that means evil, disease, heartbreak, tragedies, natural disasters, they all exist because they were invited in by that one act. It brought separation from God."

"Well, why did God even put the tree there if He knew what would happen?" she scoffed.

"Because God always has and always will give us a choice." He tapped his finger to his chin, exposing a scar on his wrist. "Do you remember when you dated Jared?"

She sat up straight and cleared her throat. Jared wasn't a topic of conversation she enjoyed.

"You know I do." She folded her arms across her chest.

"He controlled everything, didn't he?"

With a deep breath, her shoulders sank. "Yes."

"He told you who you could see, talk to, be friends with. He even told you what you could eat." Jesus shook his head. "Now do you remember Paul?"

"My ex?"

"That's the one." He smiled. "Can you see the difference in your love for each of them?"

Charlotte mulled over it for a few moments. The two of them were very different. Jared controlled so much of her life that she forgot who she was. When that relationship ended, she built walls of anger around her to keep her safe.

Paul was sweet, compassionate, loving, and all of the wonderful things that every woman should want out of a partner. He was the only man she ever deeply loved. Things started to get too real, and Charlotte broke his heart for reasons that didn't seem to measure up now.

"Yeah."

"You loved Jared out of what felt like an obligation, but with Paul, you were free to choose and that love was genuine and deep. Free will matters. You won't have a meaningful relationship with God, or anyone for that matter, if you're not free to choose your feelings."

"So because I didn't choose God, He let this happen to me?"

"Not at all. This happened because they chose evil, and unfortunately, that evil collided with you." Jesus gently placed His hand on her shoulder. "I'm so sorry for what's happened to you."

Charlotte looked up at him like a child with tears in her eyes. "Why didn't God stop it?"

"There are things that go far beyond comprehension. I wish I could tell you, but you won't understand fully until eternity comes."

"Is this not Heaven?" She looked around. "I didn't..." Her voice trailed off.

"No, and I want you to understand it wasn't you driving those thoughts and actions."

"What do you mean?"

"Let me show you."

Jesus grabbed her hand. Everything around them shimmered out of existence as new scenery came in. It was a city, but Charlotte didn't know where. She could hear a foreign language spoken by those walking by. French maybe? Jesus pointed to a young girl who skipped around the table of an outside café.

"In this world, there's demonic influence everywhere." He gestured back to the girl. "Sometimes it comes through people we know."

The woman screamed at her child, "Stop skipping and eat your breakfast, right now, Camille!" Charlotte surprisingly understood every word of the unfamiliar language. "You're driving me crazy!"

Every word screamed ripped the little girl apart. A dark figure came into view behind the pair. It was tall and robust with evil, black eyes. She saw talons dig deeper into the woman as she backhanded the little girl. Other black figures popped up all around them, snickering as they embedded themselves into her.

Stunned, tears filled the child's large brown eyes. Her shoulders and head sank. Charlotte felt every piece of the girl's heartbreak. The intensity forced her body to hunch over.

"What's happening?" She grabbed at her chest.

"I'll explain, keep watching." He directed.

With a hand on her knee, Charlotte forced her gaze up. She couldn't stop the outpouring of tears that fell. There wasn't a word strong enough to explain the depth of sorrow in her heart.

Talons clicked against the sidewalk as a small, dark figure slowly walked over to the girl.

"It's okay, little girl." Its sultry voice, captivating. "You have every right to feel hatred right now." A smile draped its wicked lips as it drew close to whisper in her ear. "Let me in, sweetheart. Open up to me." Its forked tongue flashed over its lips as it salivated. "That's it, let me in."

Unseen by anyone, the small, slimy demon wrapped around the little girl like a boa constrictor, squeezing tight.

"That's how easy generational demonic-holds take place, Charlotte."

The ache eased in her chest. She stood and looked at Jesus. He was distorted in the pool of tears that continued to spill over.

Everything shimmered again, bringing them somewhere new.

This time they were in a grocery store. Charlotte wiped the heartache from her eyes and looked around, unsure who she was supposed to notice in the hectic crowd of shoppers. But then, out of nowhere there he was—a tall bald man with a large demon attached to his back and head. Its talons were buried so deep, you couldn't see the demon's hands anymore.

Her eyes whipped back and forth and her heart raced. This man wasn't here for anything good. She could sense the wake of destruction he left in his path. The pain. The hopelessness. The evil.

Someone had to warn them.

"Watch out!" Charlotte hollered. "This man is here to hurt your kids! Grab them and hold them close!" Her hands flew to her head trying to keep the panic from taking over, but no one listened. "Please, please listen to me!"

Charlotte frantically ran from person to person. Only a few listened, pulling their children close. One family abandoned their cart in the middle of the aisle and left.

There were still dozens unsafe.

Panic burst into horror. Her lungs burned as she helplessly watched him crouch down and silently stalk toward his prey. She screamed, but no sound came. Unwilling to give up, she sprinted for the child. Everything played out in slow motion as the bald man shrunk lower, a stuffed animal held in hand.

A wicked smile dressed his lips, waving the desirable toy at the innocent boy while the mother's back was turned. Charlotte lunged for the child, but it was too late. They were gone.

Falling to her knees, a horrific scream burst out of her as torment ripped through her chest.

Nine

DETECTIVES, UNIFORMED AND K-9 officers, lab techs, Maya, and Captain Woods all huddled around the whiteboard Jocelyn and Maya put together for the investigation. She ignored the pit in her stomach, wishing she hadn't eaten that stale donut from the breakroom. It had been a moment of weakness and stress that left her without the willpower to turn down the last maple twist, her favorite. Now, on the other side of her poor choice, she worried it would end up on the floor in front of everyone.

She swallowed hard. Her heart pounded against her chest like it was trying to get out. *Buck up*, Leslie's voice barked in her head. Straightening her navy-blue blazer, she took a deep breath and jaunted into the briefing room.

"Good evening," she said like she'd done this a million times, remembering her mantra. *When in doubt, fake it until you make it.* "If you're here, it's because you've been selected for this task force. Some of you may not be aware, but I've been working a case where I believe a cult has kidnapped and brutally murdered eight women over the last year. This case is possibly connected to a string of similar murders found through the Mountain West area of Utah and Arizona. Last night, at around twenty-one hundred hours, a confirmed ninth victim went missing."

She walked up to the whiteboard and pointed to her picture. Butterflies twisted in her stomach. "Charlotte Scott's been missing for almost twenty-six hours. If this cult sticks to their previous timeline, we've got less than sixty hours to find this girl. As you see here, Maya and I have put up a timeline that spans over the last year." She hovered her finger along the timeline. "This task force allows us to have teams working on this day and night until we find her."

Nerves swirled in the pit of her stomach and left her breathless. She sat down on the edge of the desk next to her. "I know you're all tired, and I want you to know that I appreciate you being here. Pizza should arrive in about ten minutes, so while we wait, let's break off into groups. Each group, take a case. Your team lead will divide things up for you. We have enough people. I want to go through things with a fine-toothed comb. I'm also going to pair off a few of you to make some phone calls to the families of the previous victims. We can't find Charlotte if we don't come up with any leads. Remember, every second counts here, so let's work hard and fast."

The room buzzed to life as people followed her requests.

She pointed at Dan Crumb from the lab. "Dan, we have a forensic specialist coming in, but until then, have your people focus on what was found at each crime scene. Look at the rocks, the tool marks, anything that may tell us where these women were held captive or killed."

"You got it." Dan hurried out of the room.

"Captain, do we know when your guy will be here?" Jocelyn asked.

"His flight should be here within the hour. I'll go pick him up from the airport and bring him back to the station."

"Perfect."

—⋄✕⋄—

Unseen, two large angels stood on either side of Jocelyn dressed in battle gear. Their ample hands rested on the handles of sheathed swords. Narrowed eyes scanned for any threat lurking in the dark and forgotten shadows. This detective was the key who unlocked the Almighty's plan.

Efforts here had to be protected at all costs.

With a glance, they effortlessly communicated. A simultaneous nod of agreement indicated it was time to go to work. One stayed with Jocelyn, and the other headed to the lab.

—⋄✕⋄—

Nothing compared to the utter devastation twisting within. She never knew hurt could cut this deep. Everything ached. It left her hollow like her heart had been ripped from her chest.

"Make it stop!" Charlotte pleaded.

The ground beneath her shimmered back to lush and green. The intense pain retreated, but an ever-present ache pulsated in her chest—a not-so-subtle reminder it had been real.

Tears freely fell, too quick to count. She dropped to her knees and clenched the grass between her fingers. It was soft and smelled of home.

She envisioned her childhood—swinging on the swing set, carelessly running around with a giggle in her chest. She desperately wanted to be that little girl again. She wanted to be close to her parents so she could be close to God.

Independence betrayed her.

"You can be close to Me all on your own." His kind and steady voice cut through the pain.

"Why did that hurt so bad?" she breathed.

"You felt a fraction of the heartache God feels when terrible things happen to His beautifully imperfect creations."

"Did He…" She sobbed, trying to get the words out.

"Yes, His heart broke for you the night you were taken, and again the night he hurt you like that." His voice trembled.

Warmth and Peace radiated from His hand on her back. She loosened her grip on the grass and slowly sat. He gently wiped away her tears.

"I know that was intense." He knelt next to her and brushed the hair from her face. "Are you okay?"

"I think so. I guess I don't understand why You're showing me all of this."

Sadness rolled over His face. "I need you to understand what you're up against."

"What do you mean?"

"Remember the evil I showed you and how it embedded itself so easily into people?" Charlotte nodded. "A similar evil is growing where you are."

Fear clawed its way up Charlotte's body, twisting her stomach.

"Leave," Jesus demanded.

"Me?" Charlotte's eyes carried the weight of rejection.

"No, sweet child. I was speaking to Fear." He inched closer to her. "Remember the voice that told you killing yourself would be the only way to take back control?"

"You heard that?" She wiped her tears.

"It wasn't you thinking that, it was a demon that calls himself Hopelessness. He's a dreadful creature who wreaks havoc on your emotions."

He went on to explain how that demon exploits every person, but all she could think about was death and how it was certainly coming for her.

"Am I going to die?" she blurted out, cutting Him off mid-sentence.

He didn't seem put off or surprised by her outburst. Instead, His eyes held such genuine love in them.

"I can't answer that, but know My Father is in control of everything. It's not always easy to understand the Sovereignty of God, but I promise, He *is* trustworthy."

She sniffled, wiping more tears away.

"The thing is, Charlotte, it's not about if God will save you on this side of Heaven. It's about whether or not you're saved on the other side of it. On earth, trials and hardship are part of living, but Peace comes from the Lord, and knowing your eternity is secured with God."

"I mean, can anyone ever really be secure in that? You can be a good person and do all the right things and still end up in Hell. It's a coin toss at best."

"Oh, Charlotte, that's not true at all."

"That's the way I understood it."

"Just because you interpreted things in your own will doesn't make them true." He looked at her tenderly through the sting of conviction. "Scripture should be interpreted with the Holy Spirit, not on your own. Humans tend to see things through distorted and self-serving goggles." He patted her leg. "That's one of a million ways demons get in and gain access to you."

"So, *demons* took me?" she scoffed.

"No," he chuckled. "People took you, but demons control them. They believe they're doing it out of righteousness—doing God's work as they say." He sighed. "The lure of evil easily corrupts people. You almost killed yourself simply by the power of suggestion."

Charlotte went to say something but stopped herself. He was right, even if she didn't like it.

"My Father is quite fond of you, Charlotte, and that fiery spirit you have." He smiled. "He has a significant destiny written out for you. He's just waiting for you to come to Him. Do you remember how to do that?"

"Through You?"

"That's right. It's not too late to reach out and grab onto Me. I'll make you clean, and the Holy Spirit will guide your steps."

"So I'll get into Heaven with You?"

"That isn't the full picture, it's just a fraction of it. Eternity is secured if you keep your eyes on Me. You can invite Me in and then kick me out again—free will, remember?" He tapped a finger to the side of His head. "It's about relationship, growth, and walking hand in hand with Me. It's about allowing Me to heal your wounds and unravel the evil that roots itself within you so that you may share Me with others." He pointed at her. "You've always seen belief as bondage. Rules saying do this or else. But, it's really about boundaries to keep you safe."

Charlotte thought about the local elementary school she desperately wanted to attend.

"Yes, just like that." His smile spread wide. "The school didn't have fences around it or keep kids locked up with chains. They laid out the boundary lines required to stay in for their safety."

"But doesn't that mean the bad guys can get in?"

"In regards to your soul, the bad guys are always there. Their entire purpose is to tear you apart and make you miserable. They promise lavish things but deliver harm in its place. They want you to suffer. No walls will keep them out. That's why My name is so powerful."

"In Jesus name," she muttered.

"Exactly!" He clapped His hands together in celebration. "Now you're getting it." He smiled. "They have to bow to My name, they have to be obedient to it, and they tremble at even the thought of it."

"So I can order the men to let me go?"

"No, but you can tell Hopelessness to stuff a sock in it." They both laughed.

"Wow, Jesus, that was pretty…"

"Human of Me?" He finished her thought. "It's a good thing I'm fully human and fully God then." He winked. "Charlotte, I've truly enjoyed our time together, but it's coming to an end."

At the thought of leaving the sunshine, fresh air, and undeniable love behind, her lips trembled. Tears piled against her lower lid, spilling over.

"Please, don't make me go back."

"Remember," He gently said with His hand in hers. "I'm always with you, no matter what. It's up to you how much Peace and Healing you want. I love you, more than you'll ever know."

Jesus tightly wrapped His arms around her as Charlotte sobbed.

In a breath, she was held prisoner and surrounded by four dirt walls once again. Although it was damp and cold, the warmth of Jesus lingered, holding her tight. She never wanted Him to let her go again.

"Jesus, I need You in my life. Be with me. Help me live. Please."

———×———

Levi couldn't wait for his shift to end. He finished up the additional report for the Taco Bell incident and emergency room visit for the intoxicated guy he arrested. They diagnosed him with vomit-induced stomach pain— made sense. Plus, the non-stop madness of a Friday night, and to top it off responding to Mia's house, he was over it.

You wouldn't think the extra five to six pounds of his bulletproof vest would matter much, but with a shift like this, it weighed him down. Then again, maybe it wasn't the vest that weighed heavy.

So much anger boiled in his chest. He tried to ignore it, but couldn't. On his lunch break, he skipped the enchiladas to blow off steam back at the station in the best way he knew how.

His favorite band, Skillet, blared through the wireless headphones. He didn't want to waste time changing so he decided to remove what he could—vest, duty belt, and uniform shirt—and folded sparing wraps around his hands. He bounced up and down, pivoting in various directions to warm up, his arms loose at his side.

Far too many theories ran through his head about Mia, but the one loudest was abuse. Evil lurked in that house. He felt it in the doorway, oppressive and manipulative. He knew she could kick it out, but she hadn't. Why?

He switched to jumping jacks to get his heart rate up.

In their youth, she told him about every demonic encounter she endured. Honestly, he thought she exaggerated her stories until he came face to face with evil himself.

Oliver responded with a clear sign of aggression at the house. If he was hurting her… Levi tightly clenched his fists in the gloves.

She couldn't stay there, oppressed under such evil.

He led with his left fist in front of his face, and his right just to the side of it. Outrage surged through his body. His fists clapped against the bag as he ran through a series of punches. The rattle of the chain became background noise against the hard rock blaring in his ears.

An avalanche of sweat poured down his face, tumbling from his light brown hair to the floor in front of him.

He punched again.

And again.

Harder.

Pushing further.

Again.

His breath sharpened, going into a one, two sequence. His legs burned as he bobbed and weaved through imaginary punches. Oliver's face was mentally pinned on the target as he hit harder and faster.

He reached out his left hand and stopped the swing of the bag. His muscles burned as he leaned against it. He needed answers.

Lord, bring the truth into the light for all to see. Expose Oliver. Protect her. He prayed.

Ten

HER EYES WATERED UNDER the weight of exhaustion. She lifelessly lay next to her husband, her breath shallow, too afraid to move. After Sergeant Cole left, he no longer suppressed his rage, and she took the brunt of it all.

Oliver was beyond furious she caused so much trouble. He screamed wild and odd things about how it wasn't her place, and if she didn't figure it out soon, it would be too late. Her fault, really. She was such an idiot to think she could make the right choice, the best choice. He was right about one thing, if she didn't figure it out soon, Oliver would undoubtedly kill her.

Her body pulsated with pain. She didn't dare ask him why he came home so dirty. Cleaning the red clay dirt off the hardwood floors would be a nightmare. It probably should've been done before bed, but she needed a minute to recover.

Her mind tore through visions of her fate, his enormous fist connecting with her over and over again. Her stomach throbbed where he kicked her several times just like he had six months ago.

Thrilled to see the giant plus sign on the pregnancy test, she'd lost track of time. When Oliver got home, he went into a violent frenzy about dinner not being made. She begged him to listen, to stop, but he kicked her in the stomach countless times, despite her pleas.

For the next few days, Mia hid the bleeding as she silently mourned the loss of her unborn child. For months she felt empty. Ashamed. She had been naive to be happy at all. This home was no place for a child.

Lord… Tears trickled down her face. *What's happening to my life? I just don't know what to do. Please, show me the truth and end these lies. Protect me, and save my husband from himself.*

She silently slipped out of bed, a scream of agony held in her chest. Sleep wouldn't happen tonight, even though she knew her body needed it. Too much nervous energy. With the broom and dustpan in hand, she got a head start cleaning up the mess Oliver tracked in.

Red clay dirt spanned over the majority of the southeast area of the United States. He could've been anywhere. Mia couldn't help but wonder if he had been out to the property they bought last year.

It was the perfect section of land. Secluded, green, magnificent, and they owned fifty acres of it. Mia knew the moment they drove up this was exactly where they would raise their family, tend the garden and livestock, and ultimately spend forever. They managed to buy the property for practically nothing after the existing house burned to the ground from a candle left unattended. Thankfully no one was hurt.

Looking at the then charred land, she could see the whole thing, from the beautiful two-story farmhouse they would build, to the swing she wanted hung from the majestic elm tree that managed to come away unscathed by the flames. Her dream included a barn with a matching chicken coop and plenty of outside activities to fill her time.

After losing the baby, Mia didn't dream much about that anymore.

She had no clue what Oliver wanted out there. The only remaining thing was the root cellar the previous owners built. She wanted to turn it into a tornado bunker last year when one touched down in a neighboring town, destroying homes and lives. Oliver said it would be a waste of money, so the root cellar remained, stranded with no purpose.

She tried to ignore the twist in the pit of her stomach. She wanted to trust Oliver, but everything within her screamed not to. Looking down at the dustpan, she followed her gut, dumped its contents into a Ziploc bag, and hid it under the kitchen sink, out of sight.

***

The elevator door rang out, announcing someone new arrived on the floor. Jocelyn didn't pay much attention. Instead, she quietly looked at the timeline on the whiteboard for any connection. A few discoveries were made, but nothing broke the case wide open.

There was definite overlap with each victim through classes, professors, extracurriculars, and study groups, but it left too many points of contact in the end. Not to mention the hundreds of people coming in and out of each classroom, let alone buildings—delivery people, students, teachers, parents, people checking out classes, aids, cleaning crews, the list goes on. They needed to narrow it down.

She looked at her watch. Twenty-eight hours and counting.

A loud thud on the floor briefly silenced the dull rumble of conversation between groups. Jocelyn whipped her head to the side, taking in the average-looking man in front of her, chomping loudly on a bag of pretzels.

"Hey," he said louder than necessary.

"Can I help you, sir?" Jocelyn politely asked.

"Captain Woods said you were a straight shooter." A goofy smile dressed his full lips as he reached his hand out. "AJ Spalding."

Jocelyn's face coiled, unsure who on earth this guy was in jeans and a Foo Fighters t-shirt. She reluctantly placed her hand in his and mustered up a smile.

"I'm sorry, are you here for Captain Woods?"

"Oh," he chuckled, dropping his hand to his side. "I thought you knew I was coming. I'm the specialist. I do cold cases." He dug out his wallet and pulled out a white, crisp business card. "I'm a forensic anthropologist, but I also specialize in entomology and serology." He smiled, obviously proud.

"I don't know what half of those things mean." Jocelyn huffed a laugh, thankful he'd arrived. She didn't care what his specialty was as long as he was useful to the cause.

"Well, I identify bones and decipher gender, age, and possible cause of death from them. I also pretty much do any job in any lab. As an entomologist and serologist, I know bugs and blood." He leaned over and raised his eyebrows a few times.

Her mouth slightly hung open, unsure about this guy.

She smiled, amused. "Well, Mr. Spalding, it's nice to meet you. I'm Detective Jocelyn Maddox, and this is my task force."

He waved his hand and turned back to Jocelyn. "You do know what you're doing is a huge waste of time, right?"

"Excuse me?" She shifted her weight, trying to maintain the once genuine smile.

"It's just, in my experience, answers are never found in the paperwork. They're found with the evidence and with the victims." He shoved his thick black-framed glasses up on his nose. "But, if you want to keep doing it, by all means."

"Listen, Mr. Spalding—"

"AJ."

"AJ." She forced her hands into her pockets to conceal her clenched fists. "I appreciate your opinion. I'll take it under advisement." Her chest tightened, struggling to sustain professionalism.

"Suit yourself." He turned and picked up his bag. "Where's the lab?"

"Second floor." She rigidly pointed to the elevator.

With a quick wink of his eye, he smiled and left.

Jocelyn stood, unable to move as she watched him walk back to the elevator. Captain Woods said he was difficult, but that description was certainly downplayed.

"Well, he's somethin' else," Maya mumbled.

"I couldn't agree more." Jocelyn took a deep breath. "But, if he helps us, that's all that matters."

—✕—

They spent two more hours searching through the boxes and files, and not one solid lead came from it. Jocelyn sighed heavily. AJ was right, although she'd never admit that to him—ever. Nothing she despised more than admitting she was wrong.

She turned to address the group of tired and frustrated cops. "Listen up." The murmur of conversations stopped. Others nudged those who fell asleep at the tables, forcing them awake. "We knew this was going to be a long shot, but I'm afraid we may have wasted precious time." She paced back and forth, her hands resting firmly on her hips. "Does anyone have ideas on where to go from here?"

One wary hand slowly raised in the air. Jocelyn wasn't confident the rookie would be much help, but she called on him anyway.

"Caleb?"

"Um, well ma'am, in the files I saw no one searched the women's apartments or homes." He nervously cleared his throat. "W-What if our kidnappers broke in and left evidence behind?"

She paced. "We did sweep the homes."

"Uh, I meant a detailed assessment. If these are religious-based murders, ma'am, wouldn't they need to make sure they had the right girls? That would mean checking every angle of their lives, like their home, wouldn't it?" His voice wavered as he spoke.

Jocelyn stopped to look at the twenty-something-year-old, astonished. How had she missed that?

"Nice job, Rook," Maya celebrated.

Embarrassment pricked at the back of Jocelyn's throat, disappointed at her lack of attention to detail. She'd been schooled by a rookie for Pete's sake. She'd never live this one down.

Her shoulders squared to the group. "Nice catch, Caleb. I doubt all their apartments are still available, so let's focus on the last three, Inez Gonzales, Shelby Walsh, and Charlotte Scott. Maybe we'll get lucky. If you don't have their file in front of you, start knocking on doors where those three were taken."

"Detective, it's four in the morning. Shouldn't we wait a few hours?" Caleb chimed in.

"Shut up, Rookie," Leslie scoffed. "We'll get on it, Maddox."

Jocelyn flashed a quick smile and nodded to Leslie, who rolled her eyes in return.

"Who has Charlotte?" Jocelyn asked. The group leader raised his hand. "Excellent. Lab techs were already be out there, but we'll conduct a deeper search. I'll meet you at her place after I check on progress in the lab." She loudly clapped her hands together. "Let's get moving people. The clock is ticking."

Jocelyn quickly gathered her things, ignoring the sting in her eyes.

"Hey," Maya softly said.

"Can you go to Charlotte's apartment?" Jocelyn asked without looking up.

"Um, sure, but I'm here to remind you this isn't your fault."

"What? Overlooking a crucial step in the investigation of eight murders? You're right, it's not like I'm running point on the whole thing… Oh wait, I am. So yes, it's exactly my fault," Jocelyn snapped.

"None of the women were taken from their apartments. Plus, you had uniforms do a minor search so it's not like you forgot it altogether." Maya gently placed her hand on Jocelyn's back. "You did what you thought was best."

"Yeah, and I was wrong."

"You don't know that."

With a scoff Jocelyn grabbed her things and stormed off.

Down in the lab, everyone was hard at work. Each victim's altar stones, where their bodies were found mutilated, were piled in sections. A plethora of evidence filled the already cramped space.

Off to the side, at a desk, sat AJ Spalding. Jocelyn took note of his skinny jeans and spiked blond hair. So far, she found him to be egotistical, but then again, he was on point about the paperwork so maybe he had a right to be.

Tension gathered in her shoulders as she approached him. She'd failed these women and their families time and time again. Facing someone who just might call her out on it was unappealing, to say the least.

"Any progress?" she asked, trying to sound confident.

He didn't look up from his work. "Struck out with the files, I see."

"No," she snapped back harsher than intended.

"Oh really." He turned toward her, a smug look hung on his face. "What'd ya find?"

"It's what we didn't find that's interesting." She couldn't stop herself, unsure why she was even telling him any of this. "A deep search wasn't done at any of the victims' homes."

He scoffed, returning to his work. "You're grabbing straws, at best."

"We're doing everything we can to find a young girl before it's too late. Instead of becoming engrossed with our blunder, perhaps you could help us?"

"Oh, those are some fancy words there, detective." A chuckle held in his chest. "Calm down, College," he teased. "We're combing through mountains of evidence that likely wasn't processed right in the first place."

All eyes settled on AJ. Jocelyn looked around as the work ceased to continue by everyone but him.

"You might want to give more credit to the crew of techs tirelessly working to help right now. There's too much to reprocess—" She paused, straightening her blazer with a deep breath. "We need all hands on deck to save this girl."

With a sigh, he looked back up at her. "Fair enough. We've found some arthropods on the stones. Looks like there are two layers of dirt there as well, so we're trying to narrow down the origin. We found a large amount of ultisol in the bottom layer of dirt." Jocelyn's face coiled. "It's red clay, College." AJ smirked. "The top layer of dirt, where the bodies were found, have traces of Cecil clay and D.G."

"What's D.G.?"

"I was sure that being the lead detective on this case you would've known all of this, College," he chuckled.

Jocelyn pushed past the absurd nickname and the salt now burning her emotional wounds with another deep breath.

AJ continued, "D.G. is decomposed granite. It's common throughout the nation, but mixed with Cecil clay narrows things down. It's likely from where they dumped the bodies here in the good ol' N.C."

"No one calls North Carolina, N.C." she corrected. This guy must really like to abbreviate things. Beyond annoying.

"You never know. It could catch on." He flashed an arrogant smile.

"What about the red clay?" she asked, changing the subject.

"That's going to take time to narrow down. Ultisol is found in a wide geographical area. Most of the South is riddled with the stuff."

"So, how do you narrow it down?" Anxiety twisted within her.

"Is that really the question you wanna ask me?" He raised one of his bushy eyebrows.

Jocelyn hesitated, unsure why she held back the only question that needed an answer.

"How long?" she pressed.

"It's hard to say. Most areas have specific minerals within the soil that'll narrow down the grid, but without a sample to test it against…" He raised his shoulders. "I'll narrow it down as much and as quickly as possible."

Shocked at this new attitude, she looked at him impressed.

"Believe it or not, detective, I want to find her just as much as you. I'm just not so emotional about it."

"Emotional?" She scoffed. "If I was a man, I'd just be passionate or driven, but because I'm…" Her voice trailed off. "I'll have my phone on, text me with *any* and *all* updates," she huffed as she walked out of the lab.

His condescending smirk was an image forever burned in her mind. As the door loudly closed behind her, instant regret took over.

⸺⸺⸺⸺⸺✕⸺⸺⸺⸺⸺

Mia cautiously laid on the couch, resting her depleted and achy body. She did her best to not think about the burning and relentless pain. Her mind wandered to the dirt hidden under the sink. Guilt plagued her.

Oliver had been good to her over the years. She needed to love and support him, to be the wind at his back, not the bricks tied to his feet.

An agonizing groan filled the air as she pushed herself off the couch and into the kitchen. Crouched down, she reached far back into the dark cabinet, grabbing the dirt. The bag rolled across her fingers a few times as she examined each particle. It certainly looked like it came from their property—red clay and sandy soil, mixed in harmony.

She pulled the bag closer. What was that? Her eyes sharpened trying to make it out. Opening the bag, she pulled out a long blonde strand of hair. Oliver had been with another woman.

Eleven

ADVIL HELPED EASE THE pain as she started his breakfast. Mia wondered how many times Joseph wanted to quit at Potiphar's house or in jail. Reality, a harsh reminder Joseph didn't choose his fate, but Mia had.

The diamond shackle on her finger glistened in the dim light. She paused to admire its beauty.

The day Oliver slipped this on her finger and asked her to be his wife was a happy one. With a wide smile, she'd envisioned a life flawlessly beautiful like this rock. They'd done everything right. Their marriage was built on the bedrock of Christ. Life was good. Mia had no idea where or when things went wrong, but it only seemed to get worse by the day.

The ache in her stomach and ribs remained an ever-present reminder of what her marriage had become, a crippled disregarded promise of love.

⋆⋅☓⋅⋆

With outstretched arms, his mouth opened wide with a yawn. Pain throbbed in his hand. Last night blurred in his mind.

The heavenly aroma of bacon wafted into the room. That must be his breakfast. It was about time Mia learned—took her long enough.

Order was finally being restored to his home and his life. God appreciated order and asked His followers to pursue the Son of God's example. Jesus led with precision. Even He got angry when the religious leaders made a mockery of His Father's Temple. Sometimes you have to flip a table to get a person's attention.

He prayed she would one day understand how he protected her from God's undeniable wrath.

Maybe he shouldn't have taken Todd's advice. It left him feeling dirty and slimy, but today…today he felt like he finally stepped into the fullness of God's direction.

After getting ready, Oliver came down the hall with a giddy-up in his step. Todd was right. Everything was working itself out, and all he had to do was keep moving forward.

Yesterday's worries were gone, there was no sense in dwelling on them. Tomorrow's worries were premature, so he'd focus only on today, for tomorrow wasn't promised to anyone.

"Good morning," his voice pleasantly rang out.

"Good morning, my love." Mia slowly moved.

He looked at the back of her head as she plated his food, hoping for a glimpse of her gorgeous face. Mia truly was extraordinary. Strawberry blonde hair flowed down to her shoulders, a striking contrast to her fair skin. Light freckles danced across the bridge of her cute button nose. She was everything he imagined in a wife, and once she worked through this rebellion, she'd be flawless.

"If you go sit down, I'll bring you your plate and coffee," she sweetly offered.

Oliver smiled at her demeanor and sat down on the other side of the kitchen island. She was likely hurting this morning. Last night's punishment may have been a bit harsh, but surely the table Jesus flipped hurt the next day too.

She gently slid the plate of food to him and placed the coffee next to it. His eyes grew wide with horror. Fresh blood pooled in the open wound of her lip. Various shades of purple and blue dressed her face and wrapped around her neck. Her left eye, almost swollen shut. His once extraordinary wife now looked like a pathetic Quasimodo impersonator.

His lips parted, his mouth hung open, aghast at what he had done.

Shaking the despair and regret out of his mind, he reminded himself— he'd done what he had to do. His house needed to be put in order. Sometimes a stubborn horse has to be broken.

"This looks great, honey. Thank you." Oliver ignored the disfigured elephant in the room.

"You're welcome." A slight wince gathered in her throat when she kissed him on the cheek. "I'm going to go clean up."

He turned to discreetly watch her marred body stagger off.

It's for her own good, he told himself.

Levi only slept a few hours since his shifts for the week were done. He didn't want to miss the rhythm of everyday life on his four days off. After a protein power smoothie, he got dressed and headed for Home Depot.

He put off building a fire pit in his backyard for a few months and today it would serve as the perfect distraction. A little manual labor would help clear his mind.

Cold air blasted over the top of him as he walked through the automatic doors. The luxurious fragrance of fresh-cut wood permeated the air. Memories of his father flooded his mind.

Keith Reed could build anything from a simple bench to a complex kitchen island with all the bells and whistles. He worked out of their small two-car garage and dreamt of his own shop. Levi and his father bonded by making beautiful things together.

When Levi's mom abruptly died, a piece of Keith and his dream went with her. Keith soon turned to alcohol to numb the pain. Work suffered along with his once budding relationship with his son.

Levi repeatedly begged his dad to put down the whiskey and finish the work his customers paid for. Almost a year later, a thirteen-year-old boy became a man, finishing his father's projects well into the night to put food on the table. The corner of his mouth turned upward at the memory of Mia demanding to help him. Although she slowed things down, he was grateful for the company.

As a kid, Levi wasn't sure about God, but he always attended church— more for Mia than Jesus though. But while he was there, he did listen. In the height of war, he clung to those Sunday school lessons. They brought him through the darkest times of his life.

As a senior in high school, one thing became clear—if Levi ever wanted to get out from under his father, he had to leave. Enlisting seemed like the logical choice. He didn't want to abandon his father wasting away into oblivion, but there was no fixing someone unwilling to change.

A loud crash snapped his focus down the aisle he passed by. Bright red oozed from the broken seal of a gallon-sized paint can. Levi noticed a flustered couple profusely apologizing for the mishap. When the man turned around, he recognized him from Mia's church.

Without thinking, he started down the aisle.

"Do y'all need a hand?" Levi heard himself offer, unsure why.

"Oh, no, sir, we have people on their way," the frumpy store clerk offered.

"Are you two okay?" Levi asked the couple.

"I just feel awful." Misery washed over the woman's flawless face. "It was all my fault." Her almond-colored eyes darted to the man with her.

"It's okay, sweetheart," the man assured her.

"I'm glad you're both alright." Levi for some reason pushed further. "That's a bold color choice ya got there."

"Yeah." She swept the sandy blonde hair out of her face and looked up at the man.

"What can I say, I like to make a bold statement." The man flashed his perfectly white teeth.

"You look awfully familiar. Do I know you from somewhere?" Levi asked the man.

"I don't believe so." The man looked at the woman and back at Levi. "We do attend a local church. Maybe you've seen us there?"

"Maybe. I have sat in on a few churches here and there, tryin' to find the right fit, ya know?"

"Forgive my husband's negligence. I believe I've seen you at Living Waters Church, sitting in the back." She looked at him with a softness. "We're elders there. Todd and Vivian Banister." She stuck out her hand.

"Oh, I do believe I checked out that church."

A shake of their hands left him hollow. Cold. Lifeless.

He abruptly pulled away. "Well, I've gotta run. I'm glad y'all are okay."

Levi turned on his heel and walked away. Todd hollered after him, "We didn't catch your name." But Levi ignored the request and kept walking.

He left his cart with all the supplies and went to Lowe's instead. That whole encounter made his skin crawl. Manual labor seemed necessary to keep his sanity intact today.

Back home, he unloaded a mountain of supplies into the backyard. Frustration pushed in on him. The way he handled the Banisters was ridiculous. And to top it all off, Lowe's was out of the uncut rustic stones he wanted. Luckily, he found a small mom-and-pop place that carried better ones.

Before starting, he went inside and made himself a sandwich—salami with extra mustard, just how he liked it. Exhaustion sank in soon after his belly was full. A small nap wouldn't hurt.

⸻⸻⸻⸻ ⊶✕⊷ ⸻⸻⸻⸻

Oliver surprised her when he came home for lunch. Thankfully she made it through most of her chores despite the relentless vertigo. Her body screamed for rest, but she couldn't risk it.

After lunch, she went to clear their plates.

"I'll take care of these, my love." Oliver hopped up with a smile.

That was odd, but Mia was too tired and too broken to care. She welcomed the help, praying there weren't vicious consequences on the other side of it.

Her tired feet shuffled down the hall to finish hanging the laundry. She hid the groans of pain spewing through her clenched teeth the best she could. The only thing she wanted was sleep.

Nauseous and dizzy, she sat on the edge of the bed and prayed for the strength to persevere. Calculated breaths made it worse. Each one burned more intensely than the last.

Forcing herself up, she lunged for the bathroom and heaved up lunch.

She couldn't be a good wife anymore. This facade was too hard to keep up.

Stumbling down the hall, she weakly called out to Oliver, "Honey."

Oliver came around the corner. She pushed herself as far as she could, but her body couldn't keep up anymore. Dark spots closed in around her vision.

No longer in control, everything went black. A loud thud filled her ears as she hit the floor.

⸻⸻⸻⸻ ⊶✕⊷ ⸻⸻⸻⸻

His feet dragged along the barren wilderness. Dry, almost unbearable heat encompassed him. He felt weighed down, like walking in quicksand—every move a hindrance. Quickly peeling off his vest, he ignored the absence of it hitting the ground. He had to get it all off. It would drown him if he didn't.

Piece by piece, he ripped off the military uniform he once wore, down to his boxer briefs. With all of his strength, he forced his feet to move.

"Hello?" he yelled out in an echo.

A dark, shadowy figure a good distance out caught his eye. Instinctively, he reached for his weapon in case it was the Taliban, forgetting he tossed it off with his clothes.

The obscure figure blurred in the heat of the sun. Levi became acutely aware of the fierce temperature beating down on him. His skin burned with every step closer the figure took.

Lead me, help me, be with me, Lord God.

A sharp, frigid metal pressed against his body. He looked down to see a bronze plate surrounding his chest.

The palm of his hand skated across the hard, cold surface. Strength surged, pumping divine power through his veins. He deeply inhaled as adrenaline cascaded over him. A shield perched on his arm through leather straps, a flawless sword tightly gripped in his other hand. He took note of the metal studs on the bottom of his shoes that helped pull him from the quicksand.

Whatever that figure, he didn't sense it would be friendly. He needed to be ready for anything. Crouched in an attack stance with his weapon drawn, he waited for his opponent to approach.

The closer it came, the smaller it seemed. Trails of black fabric flowed in the wind. His guard lowered at the sight of her vibrant ocean eyes. Levi lowered his shield and sword as he stood upright. Tantalized by its beauty, he tossed off his desire to fight.

His eyes fixated. Unable to peel them away, a tingling sensation crawled across him. He longed to touch it, to see what was behind the draped fabric. Pulling down a runaway piece of its robe, his heart burst with love.

"Mia," the name fell from his astonished lips. "What are you doing here?"

He reached out to softly place his hand on her face, but she backed up out of reach.

"Help me, Levi." Her soft voice echoed through the vastness around them. "Please."

Tears freely fell from his eyes. She was in trouble, and he was to blame.

His shoulders sank low. "I'm sorry I left you, Mia. I love you. I always have."

A deep malevolent snicker burst from the figure. Levi looked up just in time to see it morph into something utterly horrific. With outstretched arms, it clenched its predatorial talons into fists.

"Poor pathetic, Levi," it boomed. "Loving a girl he cannot have. Tsk, tsk, tsk." It waved its talon back and forth in front of Levi's face. "What would God have to say about that, hmm? If I'm not mistaken—and we both know I'm not—isn't there a 'thou shall not covet' rule with that guy?"

Levi froze. It was back.

"Miss me?" The demon's jagged teeth flashed as laughter vibrated its ample chest.

Levi's heart raced. His lungs worked hard to keep up but they burned with angst.

"In the name of…" Muffled sounds came out in place of the word. *Jesus.*

"Hush. You didn't think you'd get rid of me that easy, did ya?"

Levi's eyes darted to see its hideous tail wrapped tightly around his mouth.

The sun faded out. Everything around them turned gray. The wind stopped, leaving a deafening silence. Fear swallowed him whole. The weeds that popped through the dry, cracked ground shriveled to dust, and birds fell from the sky without a sound.

"Levi," the demon sing-songed through a sulfuric cloud. "Levi," it called out again.

A chill tumbled down his spine. There was no love to be found here, only torment.

"Let's not fight, Levi. Join me, and I'll make Mia yours."

Its face swirled, bringing back the beautiful blue eyes he longed for. He thought he'd kept these feelings in check, but two seconds into meeting this familiar foe, and it exploited what he hadn't let go of—hope Mia would love him again one day.

Your sword, the Lord gently whispered to him.

Levi pumped his hand a few times around the solid handle but was unable to wield it.

What do I do, Lord?

A vision came to his mind of when he battled this demon before. He had to stay calm and remember not only who he was in Christ, but who Christ was in him. Anointed, protected, washed clean, and victorious. No one, not even the strongest demon in Hell, could take that away.

Without another thought, Levi sunk his teeth into the dark tail that held his face. The foul taste of rotten eggs touched his tongue as black tar oozed from his mouth. The demon shrieked in pain, snapping its tail back to cradle it like a baby. Levi's body dropped to the hard ground.

Levi pushed himself to his feet, wiping the black sludge from his mouth. He crouched with the shield and sword in hand and called the demon by name. "Occult. You have no standing here for I belong to the King!" He slashed his sword, nicking its shoulder. A shriek of pain belted out like nails on a chalkboard. "Jesus said, 'It is finished' on the cross. All of Hell was defeated when He took his last breath."

Again, the sword slashed, catching the top of its foot. Occult whimpered and took off in a flash. Levi knelt beside the percolating tar it left behind. With a hiss, it scorched the sand, turning it black.

"Levi," a gentle voice called out. "I've prepared you for this moment. I taught you well. Purify yourself, for this won't be easily won."

A fierce wind came, and the earth violently shook under his feet. A pleasing stillness followed as the Lord ignited the fire of His Spirit within Levi.

An uncomfortable pain exploded throughout his chest, radiating everywhere. The intensity of the heat pulled him from a deep sleep with a gasp for air.

The time had come for a much different kind of war, and he knew now more than ever that Mia was somehow caught in the middle of it all.

Twelve

HOURS PASSED SINCE TEAMS went out to search the victim's homes. Promises of being on her way fell short thanks to far too many phone calls and meetings. Plus, she accidentally fell asleep at her desk replaying the surveillance footage of Charlotte being taken in hopes of finding something new.

Thirty-five hours since Charlotte went missing, and Jocelyn thought a nap was in order. She texted about a hundred apologies to Maya, who was still at Charlotte's apartment, exactly where Jocelyn *should* be. Maya, being an unexcitable detective, told her not to stress. It was all under control. But the guilt wouldn't stop growing.

A third cup of coffee seemed like the best choice at the moment. Anything to help her stay awake. The Styrofoam cup burned against the palm of her hand. Stupid cheap cups. With a grunt, she grabbed another one and doubled up—much better.

She pushed open a heavy metal door that led out to the staff parking lot. The late afternoon sun assaulted her eyes and took a minute to adjust. Her head pounded in protest. It was the worst kind of hangover, exhaustion.

Jocelyn called her mentor, Abigail, and vented for the entire drive to Charlotte's to help calm her frustration. She hoped for validation, but instead, received the reminder she needed AJ and to take the high road.

"Rise above, Joce. It's not worth getting worked up over. All that'll do is hinder your ability to do your job and a girl's life depends on you—*both* of you."

"Why do you have to bring dumb things like reason and logic into these moments?" Jocelyn protested. "Can't you just agree with me that he sucks?"

"Maybe the two of you got off on the wrong foot. But even if you didn't, don't let him run your emotions all over town. Rise above."

"You're right. I'll do my best to keep it professional."

—⁂—

Her body shook vigorously. Something around her neck kept her head from moving. She pulled at the hard plastic, wanting it off so she could catch her breath. Nausea flourished. She had to sit up. She tried, but couldn't move.

As she wretched, muffled voices echoed in the background.

"Help me turn her on her side before she chokes," one man calmly ordered.

It felt like a rollercoaster as they flipped her to the side in one swift motion. Something tight held her body in place. She pulled at the restrictive belts, but someone pushed her hands away.

"Ma'am," an assertive voice called out. "You have to leave all this on."

"Why," she forced out between dry heaves.

"Your husband said you fell. All of this is a precaution." Out of the corner of her eye, she saw him let her go. There must have been someone else in this weird room with them. "The doctor at the hospital told me to give you something for the nausea." She watched him draw the medicine into a syringe. The bag of fluid he pushed it into violently swung back and forth above her.

"Where am I?" she finally asked.

"You're in the ambulance. You fell down the stairs and are pretty banged up." He came into her vision with his black spikey hair, thick freckles, and kind eyes.

"Luke?" she whispered.

"No, ma'am, my name's Robbie. I'm a paramedic with the ambulance. We're taking you to the hospital." He looked over the straps holding her. "Do you think you're okay now?"

"I'm okay," she slurred. "You can take all this off me now."

"I'm afraid we can't do that, ma'am."

He shined a light in her eyes, but it quickly went dull as darkness claimed her once again.

———×———

Levi looked over his work with a nice cold drink in his hand. The fire pit came together perfectly. The only thing left to do was cement it together. One by one, he examined the stones from the hole-in-the-wall store. The beautifully imperfect edges and colors varied from stone to stone—hues of gray, charcoal, silver, and the occasional glimmer of sapphire. What a happy accident.

Next step, build more chairs to encircle it.

His mind drifted back to the unwanted reunion with Occult. Levi knew all too well the power and lure this evil creature possessed. He saw countless men, women, and families fall prey to it, ruining generation after generation. Hatred gushed from the mouth of this demon. It covered itself in what looked like righteousness with an enchantment over those it touched, devouring them like a lion.

He couldn't fall for the same tricks as last time. It already used Mia against him to get his guard down, and once again he fell for it.

He sunk into the deep seat of the Adirondack chair he built last year and prayed.

———×———

Faint beeps and muffled voices grew louder with each breath. Her heavy eyes seemed glued shut. She tried to speak, but only mild grunts followed. Not good.

Strangers buzzed around her. Oliver would be furious if he saw her acting like this. Her heart picked up speed as she forced her eyes open. The world around her came into better focus. She took note of a man with salt and pepper hair standing next to her, delegating orders. His demeanor was strong, assertive. He reminded her of her father.

"Dr. Freeman, she's waking up," an elegantly posh voice announced.

With all eyes on her, Mia noticed her exposed body for the first time. Alarm rose as she frantically tried to cover her bare chest. Her fingers ached, grabbing tightly at what was left of her dignity.

"Someone get a blanket and cover her up, please," the voice sternly called out. "It's okay, I've got you."

A woman came into view. With slender features and short blonde hair, a friendly smile spread wide across her face.

"How are you feeling, Mrs. Hughes?"

A warm blanket melted over the top of her.

"Mia," she grunted, everything hurt. "Please, call me Mia."

"Okay, Mia. How're you feeling?"

"My stomach really hurts and whatever they strapped me to is so uncomfortable."

It brought relief from Mia's panic when the nurse softly touched her arm. It helped the countless other hands on her seem less intrusive somehow.

"It's precautionary, dear, to keep your spine from further injury. The doctor's about done examining you, and then we'll take you to get some X-rays."

"I hurt my spine?" Mia lightly gasped.

"We aren't sure yet. Like I said, this is all precautionary for now."

"Oh."

"My name's Katie. I'll be your primary nurse so if you need anything, just holler."

Before she could walk away, Mia reached out. "Is my husband here?"

"Yes, your husband is here, but we have to get you stabilized before he can come back."

"He didn't see me exposed, did he?" Mia swallowed hard with guilt.

"No, he didn't see that." Another soft touch brushed her arm.

Relief flooded her mind. Maybe she was safe, for now.

"Mia?" Katie came back into her view. "We're going to give you something to help you relax, okay?"

"Mm-hm," she agreed, too tired to argue.

A warm sensation raced up her arm and through her body. Her mind relaxed as she noticed a tingle in her lips. As if background noise, Mia heard Katie's sweet European voice.

"Dr. Freeman, there are multiple bruises at different stages all over her body. The one around her neck looks like she was bloody choked."

"Let's get PFS in here right now."

"Patient Family Services?" Katie questioned. "I was thinking more like the police."

"Call them too," he agreed.

The drugs left her in a fog, unable to counter their suspicions. She had to pull herself together. This needed to be fixed to protect him. They couldn't know the shameful truth of her life behind closed doors.

A golden light poured into Charlotte's prison, startling her. Her afflicted and sickly body quickly recoiled into a ball against the dirt wall.

Don't let them hurt me, Charlotte internally prayed with her head buried in her arms like a frightened child.

A shudder ripped through her with every thud of his foot down the stairs.

"Where are you?" a calm, raspy voice called out. The beam of the flashlight rocked side to side in search of her, unmasking her fetal position in the corner. "I brought you food and water."

He placed the flashlight on the small table face up, toward the ceiling. A quick peek over her arms revealed the dark figure in front of her. She retreated like a turtle into its shell.

"You don't look so good." A cold hand pressed against the top of her head. "A fever."

He stepped back into the shadows. This one wasn't as big as the others. The tension trapped in her chest relaxed. With one foot, he kicked a metal tray toward her. It smelled like pig slop from the farm. Thankfully, she didn't have an appetite anyway.

"This'll all be over soon." Metal popped against the dirt until a large canister hit her. "Until then, eat and drink. We wouldn't want you to miss the fun part." An ominous chuckle sent chills down Charlotte's spine.

The door slammed as an echo clipped against dirt walls.

With dirty hands, she forced herself to take a few bites. Several gags followed and she pushed the tray away and washed her mouth out with the water. All she wanted was a dirty martini with extra olives to wash down an entire bushel of antibiotics.

Jesus' words brought the sliver of hope she needed. *My Father has a plan. You can trust Him.*

A loud ring jolted Levi upright. Groggy, he looked around at the sunset-soaked living room—he must've fallen asleep on the couch. Wiping the drool from the corner of his mouth, he cleared his throat.

He answered, doing his best to seem awake. "Hello?"

"Reed, did I wake you?" Her raspy voice broke through his exhaustion.

"No. Well, yeah, but it's fine. What can I do for ya, Sergeant Cole?" He breathed with a yawn.

"I had a few questions. Remember Oliver and Mia Hughes from last night?"

His heart quickened. "Yes."

"Well, it seemed like maybe you knew them. There was, um, a lot of tension when I got there."

"I don't know Oliver, but I've known Mia since we were kids." He raked his hand back and forth through his hair. "Is she alright?"

"Well, she's in the E.R." Levi swallowed his desire to immediately lose it. "Her husband says she fell down the stairs leading to the basement." Air trapped in his lungs, unable to move. "She was pretty out of it at first, but from what the doctor said, her spine looks good on the x-rays. There's bruising to her stomach area so they'll have to monitor her overnight to make sure there's no internal bleeding. She also sustained a bruised lung." Sergeant Cole took a deep breath. "They say she's pretty lucky, but that's not why I'm calling."

"There's more?"

"They found multiple bruises at different stages all over her body." His jaw clenched with rage. "So let me ask, would you describe Mrs. Hughes as clumsy?"

"Clumsy?" He scoffed. "I mean, I haven't been a part of her life in a long time, Sarge, but she was never clumsy before. She was MVP of our high school volleyball team, for crying out loud." Levi tried to stop what came out next. "If something happened to Mia, Oliver definitely did it."

"Why do you say that?"

"The man's a snake." His voice grew louder, unable to hold back the anger within. "He—Well, he took a beautiful and vibrant person and broke her. The woman you met last night was not the Mia I knew. The girl I knew wasn't hollow or timid."

Levi kindly left out the role he played in who Mia was now. Shame curled in the pit of his stomach.

—⋇—

Undetected, evil snickered as it twisted around him like a snake. Fear was one of Occult's devilish beasts and a loyal one at that. He'd been sent to spy on Levi and report when he was ready for Occult to strike. They needed Levi distracted, devastated, distressed, and he just might be ready earlier than they thought.

Fear hissed, "The boss'll love this."

In a puff of dark sulfur, he was gone.

———————×———————

"Look, Reed, you obviously have history with this girl," Sergeant Cole politely countered. "I'm guessing, high school sweethearts?"

"Something like that."

"Can you be objective?"

"Look, I care deeply for her, yes. But I've also seen Oliver on multiple occasions, and I'm telling you, something's off."

After a brief pause, Sergeant Cole finally spoke. "I'll quietly look into it—as a favor. But before we accuse an esteemed pastor of abusing his wife, we need evidence or omission."

His mind raced as he heard the flicker of Sergeant Cole's lighter on the other end. She smoked Virginia Slims, which was odd. They were quite dainty for a woman who was the exact opposite of the word.

"He's too smart to leave evidence lying around, Sarge. I'll help you look into it from here."

"No, you're too close to this."

"We both know I'm going to look whether you want me to or not. Can we just skip to you accepting my help rather than being shocked when I go behind your back?"

Sergeant Cole exhaled with a chuckle. Levi pictured a large cloud of smoke dispersing around her head. "If anyone asks me, I had no idea you were looking into this. Deal?"

"Deal."

Thirteen

"MRS. HUGHES," A GRUFF voice called her name. "Mrs. Hughes, can you hear me?"

Mia tried to speak, but couldn't. The exhaustion was too much. Each breath brought a greater ache to her chest and torso.

"Mrs. Hughes, I have to ask you some questions." The raspy voice echoed against her dulled senses.

She had to speak. It was the only way to save Oliver. He was all she could think of. She worried he'd be furious at her for this mess. If only she were stronger.

Get up, Mia! Get up! she internally demanded, but it wasn't enough.

"Sergeant, you'll have to return later," Katie commanded. "I know you have questions, we all do, but Mrs. Hughes needs rest."

"Where's the husband?" the sergeant asked.

"He's in the grief room. I'll show you."

Their shoes squeaked against the floor as they left. She prayed this would get straightened out soon so she could go home with Oliver—alone. The thought made her heart race, unsure how much of a welcome she'd receive. After all, she got them into this mess. He had every right to be so angry with her.

The hair on her arms caught a gust of wind. It refreshed and comforted her ragged body. It came in waves and moved quickly, little bursts of tranquility, washed over her like a hot bath in winter.

Pain no longer victimized her every move. Her eyes slowly opened and took in her surroundings. The dry, cracked ground blistered with heat as the once comforting breeze turned harsh, beating down on her. The peace that once existed met its demise like prey unable to outrun the predator. Red clay swirled amidst the sand that flowed on the dunes around her.

The sweltering heat became almost unbearable. Her tongue clicked against her cottonmouth. A violent thirst swelled, leaving one thought—water. Every move sunk the dehydration deep into her bones. Her eyes squinted against the muted rays of light.

"Hello?" Her brittle voice faded against the wind.

A figure dressed in black moved toward her. Panic amplified. She was exposed. Vulnerable.

Her feet pelted against the parched ground as fast as they could.

"Mia," it bellowed, drawing out her name. "Don't run from me," it barked.

A scream for oxygen held in her lungs against the inhaled granules of sand. She tripped over her clumsy feet, falling face down in the dirt.

Her head snapped up to reveal a figure that nightmares were made of.

It was bigger than anything she had ever seen before, cloaked in what appeared to be a black robe. Talons protruded and tapped against the brittle ground, breaking the lifeless dirt into little clouds of dust. Its raven eyes bulged. A fiery ring, full of formidable wrath, blazed around the pupils. Razor sharp teeth flashed. A contaminated venom oozed from its mouth, dripping onto the ground beneath it.

"Mia." It morphed into Oliver, dressed in his Sunday best. "My sweet, beautiful wife. Come here." He reached out his hand.

Mia shrunk back, unsure. At a second look, his golden hazel eyes penetrated hers. She relaxed at the soft smile that hung on his lips.

Instinctively she reached out. "Oliver?" she questioned.

With the precision of a snake, it struck, wrapping tight around her hand.

"Ollie, that hurts," she whined.

A low chuckle built in his chest. "You're mine now."

"Ollie, please. Let me go."

Tears spilled over. A thunderous wail escaped her lips as it clenched harder on her wrist. Strands of strawberry blonde stuck to the sweat gathered on her face.

"Maybe you'll like this better?" It snickered, morphing into Levi.

"Please. Let me go. Please. I didn't..." Mia sobbed, heavy with despair.

"Hush."

Held up by her arm, she whipped forward. A black tail emerged from behind it and covered her mouth. The torment that followed brought muffled shrieks against its reptile skin. She eventually accepted her fate. This was deserved for all she had done. Levi, Oliver, her parents, Luke… She failed them all.

A flash of light ripped down from the sky between them. Mia flew from the creature's grasp. The force of impact against the ground pushed the air from her lungs. She sputtered for the relief of oxygen.

Light flashed from the other direction this time. It was the creature's turn to shriek in pain.

"Back off," a booming voice demanded from the light.

Her rescuer stood still. Mia's eyes squinted against the pure white light. No other colors hindered its brilliance. It was pristine, purified, perfect.

The demon held up its lanky hands, exposing bony fingers and slender talons. "Okay, okay, geez." He turned to walk away but stopped. "Tell your Boss, this ain't over." He looked back at Mia. "See ya soon, sweetheart." A grin curled up the edges of its thin black lips.

A trail of darkness lingered across the sky like a wayward shooting star.

Her vision blurred against the illumination standing over her. It was the last thing she saw before everything blinked out of existence.

———×———

"Amen." Levi ended another urgent prayer, this time pulled over on the side of the road headed somewhere he definitely shouldn't be.

An unshakable warning blared in his soul. Something evil hunted them. He didn't know how to fight it or why Mia was involved, but he trusted the Lord to show him.

"Give me Your fire, Lord, and Your Wisdom. I'm ready for this fight. Equip me with ears tuned into You and eyes to see the enemy."

With his truck in gear, he continued toward the hospital. He never should have left her there alone. Oliver wasn't a good man or a godly man. He deserved to rot in his evil. Levi's hands tightly gripped the wheel, a scowl hung on his face.

Easy, Levi. The Lord softly spoke to his heart. *Your battle is with demonic forces, not Oliver.*

Levi released the tightness in his chest with a slow exhale. *Why did you choose me for this, Father? To torment me?*

The Lord spoke again. *Is that still how you see Me? I'm for you, Levi, not against you. There are reasons. You won't fully understand why I orchestrated things this way, but the real question you need to answer is, do you trust Me? Even if you don't get your heart's desire fulfilled. Even if it ruins you. And even if it takes your life. Do you trust Me?*

Levi thought of Shadrach, Meshach, and Abednego as they stood before King Nebuchadnezzar in the book of Daniel. The king threatened to throw them in the fire if they didn't bow down and worship him. The three boys profoundly pledged their allegiance to Yahweh. All they said was God would rescue them from the fire, but even if he didn't, the Lord's will would be done and they trusted him fully.

That level of trust was easier said than done, but this was what the Lord asked of him. He was given a choice. A question to answer. *Do you trust Me?*

"I trust You, come what may," Levi whispered.

Parked at the hospital, his fingers cinched around the steering wheel until it hurt. He leaned forward, his forehead resting on the hard rubber. This burden wasn't his to carry. It was too heavy. Last time he faced Occult, that was his biggest mistake. He single-handedly tried to defeat him and was devoured as a result.

Occult and his army of demons had tormented Levi day and night. The exhaustion and demonic prowl left him vulnerable, and he would regret what he did for the rest of his life.

Private First-Class Donny Williams sat at the barracks table eating oatmeal for the tenth time that week. Maybe it was the oatmeal or the fact that he sat in the chair Levi liked, but something snapped. Levi attacked him with his Ka-Bar Short USMC knife. As a result, Williams received fourteen stitches on his back.

Levi didn't like to think about what would have happened if they hadn't pulled him off the poor guy. It was a miracle he wasn't dishonorably discharged for that mishap.

It had been a while since he talked to Williams, or Corporal Williams, as he was more commonly referred to now. A few times a year, Levi made a point to catch up with him over lunch, a few beers, or hunting—a never-ending apology.

"I trust you," he exhaled one last time.

Levi envisioned himself holding a bag filled with his emotions—how he felt about Mia, his regrets, his frustrations, his uncertainty, all of it—and he laid it down at the foot of God's Throne and vowed to keep doing that until it stuck.

Fear raced as fast as he could to where Occult lay low in an abandoned barn just out of town. Excitement rested in the pit of his horrific stomach. There was nothing better than plans that came together so effortlessly. He expected more of a fight. It wasn't every day you get to cut down the awful dimwits sent by the Enemy for protection.

Nothing was appealing about humans either. They whined about everything and if something wasn't going exactly their way, they became furious. They blamed the Enemy for everything bad that happened in the world, which was great. He'd rather they blame that Imbecile than sin and wickedness. It generally kept people, even those awful Christians, in a spiral of doubt. And where there was doubt, Fear did his best work.

He wreaked havoc on that silly little pastor and his stupid wife over the last year. A snicker rumbled in his chest as he landed in the middle of an old pile of hay. Occult jerked his humongous body around, the intrusion an unwelcomed surprise.

"Fear, my longest companion. What are you doing here?" Occult seemed irritated to see him.

Fear bowed low before Occult. His gangly body trembled. This might have been a mistake.

"Speak, you idiot," Occult barked.

"I came to tell you news, sir." Drool fell from his jagged teeth, hitting the floor with a sizzle. Fear stood upright, wickedness taking over. He loved it when humans felt overwhelmed or inadequate. He loved it even more when the Enemy's little puppets doubted His ability. Fear thrived in lives everywhere, even those with that dreadful Son of Man. "It's the girl."

"Which one?" Occult demanded.

"The pastor's wife."

"Ah, little Mia. What a dreadfully terrified and incompetent girl." A sinister smile spread across his lips.

"She's in the hospital."

A burst of fiery red tumbled over Occult's narrowed eyes. "This is your big news?" He towered over Fear, forcing a step back. "You defied my orders for *this*?"

"I just thought—" Fear abruptly stopped talking when Occult wrapped his giant hand around his throat.

Sulfur flung between Occult's clenched teeth. "Who do you think ordered the beating that put her there?" he roared. Fear choked against the pressure at his throat. "I've planned every single detail of this operation. Do you take me for a fool? Do you think I can't handle that arrogant Prick and His pathetic excuse for warriors?" Occult boomed, forcing the ground to shake. "I am the greatest demon that ever lived! I turn even the most devout Christians on a war path of twisted righteousness. Humans are easily manipulated and forged into what we want them to be, and I'm the best in the business. You're nothing compared to me. Nothing!"

Occult launched Fear into the air and out of sight.

Fourteen

JOCELYN FIELDED ENDLESS PHONE calls in the parking lot of Charlotte's apartment. She watched as the sun gave way to the night, another reminder their time ran short. Far too many questions were answered, orders given, and she even squeezed in an update to the Chief.

The final call was AJ. He narrowed down the region of where the bugs on the stones came from—a range of three states, North Carolina, South Carolina, and Tennessee. At least it narrowed it down to a few states rather than the eleven that made up the South. AJ asserted his confidence the dirt analysis would match the region of the creepy crawlers they found when finished.

"Hey listen," AJ interrupted the goodbye she wanted. "I realize what I said earlier was rude. I honestly don't know why I said it, but I'm sorry, and it won't happen again."

Speechless wasn't a typical word used to describe Jocelyn, but none of this was typical. An apology wasn't expected but it was certainly warranted. *Rise above.*

He nervously cleared his throat at the silence.

"Thank you," she finally offered. "I forgive you."

"Okay," he dragged out the word. "So…" Another silence lingered.

"I appreciate the update." She tried to sway this awkwardness to an end. "Let me know when the dirt comes back."

"Hmm," he scoffed.

"Is there something else, Mr. Spalding?" She heavily sighed.

"It's doctor actually," he cut in. "It's just…" Another scoff. "No apology from you here?"

"Apology? For what?" Frustration flooded back. *Rise above.*

"For the way you've treated me since I walked off that elevator."

"The way I've treated…" She chuckled, aghast. This guy was the most— "I'm not the one who's been rude, *Doctor.* Update me when you have more information."

She abruptly ended the call. Cell phones didn't give the same satisfaction as slamming a phone down. If she could, she'd slam a thousand phones right now…against a wall.

After a few—okay, more than a few—deep breaths, regret filled her mind. Another failure on her belt. She let him get under her skin and did the exact opposite of rising above. She definitely owed him an apology now, but that was a problem for another time.

With a sigh, she headed for Charlotte's apartment on the third floor.

It was easy to spot. The open door revealed several officers hard at work. Flashlights shone in every nook, cranny, and forgotten corner of this humble apartment. Boxes of evidence collected and piled high in the corner from hair samples to the glasses of wine on the coffee table. This team worked tirelessly, providing more than Jocelyn expected.

⸻✕⸻

In the apartment stood three angels with dark brown hair. Draped in leather and bronze, their battle gear held snug around their ample bodies. Swords dangled at their sides and shields secured safely to their backs. They easily moved around the room, operating with clear orders—bring crucial evidence to light.

Two of the men took instruction from Dante, the third. His dark features made the golden hue of metal against his skin shine. Leaning against the door, his hazelnut eyes intently watched his assignment. The woman seemed frazzled and unsure of herself. If only she knew the Lord himself handpicked her for this case.

He prayed one day she would see why it had to be her.

⸻✕⸻

Jocelyn examined things from a distance as she dressed her hands with gloves. It was something Abigail taught her as a teen and reminded her of frequently. When we look too closely, we can lose perspective and miss the mindset of the criminal. That mindset came in handy a time or two over the years, but with this case, Jocelyn worried it wouldn't be enough.

She'd missed something. It had been a year that took the lives of eight girls, soon to be nine.

She noted the open Bible on the side table by the couch. Holding the place with her fingers, she looked at the cover. A thick layer of dust covered it, resembling the one Jocelyn's grandma gave her.

Flipping it back open she noticed Revelation 2:5 was underlined in red with a note scribbled next to it.

She read it softly to herself. "Consider how far you have fallen! Repent and do the things you did at first. If you do not repent, I will come to you and remove your lampstand from its place."

"Weird," Maya added over her shoulder. "But check it out, the word *lampstand* is crossed out so it reads, I will come remove you…"

"Plus the note here that says: TIME'S UP in block letters." This had to be the cult. It fits them. Not to mention the Bible clearly hadn't been touched in a long time. "Does anyone have a sample of Charlotte's writing? A notebook, journal, post-it, anything?"

Maya promptly left Jocelyn's side only to return a moment later.

"I found her notes from school."

She handed the spiral notebook with color-coded tabs sticking out everywhere to Jocelyn. As it opened it revealed the elegant scribbles of a law student desperately trying to keep up with her professor. Several pages in, Charlotte found a shorthand for her notes that helped her words to be more legible. A phantom pain popped in Jocelyn's palm remembering the countless notebooks she had that mirrored this one.

Several samples were held next to the note. Jocelyn would send this to the lab to be sure, but the neatly blocked letters didn't seem to be a match for Charlotte's bubbly cursive.

"Let's bag this," Jocelyn delegated. "The lab will need to check for prints because of the delicate pages."

She quickly grabbed her phone and called the detectives in charge with Shelby Walsh and Ines Gonzales. The team at Shelby's townhouse found a Bible with the same haunting message. Ines' parents sold her apartment six weeks ago, so that team scoured through crime scene photos and found her Bible in the background that displayed the same message in red. Bingo.

In the hours spent there, no other major developments were made. The joy of the Bible discovery quickly dissipated now that the lab had two of them to analyze and countless photos.

In an attempt to feel useful, Jocelyn decided to knock on doors. Another Hail Mary, sure to prove a waste of time.

A shimmer of light flashed across the nickel finish of Charlotte's door knob, catching her eye as she went to leave. She knelt for closer inspection. Red dust? Jocelyn's heart fluttered.

"Can someone please get me a swab? I think I found something, but there isn't much here."

"What is it?" Maya called out.

"It looks like our red clay dirt."

"Seriously?" she excitedly asked.

Jocelyn remained locked on the hue of red as Maya placed the swab and a small spray bottle in her hand. She opened and sprayed the swab. As the damp cotton drug across the silver metal, it immediately turned red.

Holding it up, she whispered to herself, "Holy crap."

⌗

The angels all smiled. Soon the pieces of Finn's plan would fall into place.

Each one of the large warriors fought alongside their fearless leader for thousands of years. He was careful and calculated. He weighed everything, always ready when the battle shifted in an unexpected direction.

With the assignment complete, two of them ascended to rejoin Finn.

Dante held a faint smile on his lips. "Good job, Jocelyn."

"Another swab," she called out, collecting more samples of the red dust on the floor around her. "I've gotta get these to the lab. In fact..." She looked around as she stood. "Toss these boxes in my car, and I'll take them with me." A picture of Charlotte with her roommate caught Jocelyn's eye. "Andrews," she shouted to one of the uniformed officers. "Get Tamika Lewis from her parent's house and bring her to the station. The address should be in the CAD computers."

"You got it," he answered and immediately went.

Dante followed her to the car. On the way back to the station, she made a call.

"Dan, let AJ know I'm coming in with priority evidence."

Fifteen

SUFFOCATION BURNED AGAINST THE drawn-out protest for air. Her weary heart fluttered against her hard and unwavering sternum.

Mia wanted out of this place.

Cool air rushed into her fiery chest. Without thought, she sat straight up, grabbed her torso, and hunched over in pain. A moan ripped through the air from behind clenched teeth. Small wisps of breath attempted to calm the agony but failed.

The curtain to the room flew back, and there stood Levi with wild eyes of heartache. He was at her side in an instant, his arms around her.

"You're okay. It's okay," he gently whispered.

A tender stroke of her hair reminded her of being a kid. It was safe in his arms, safer than she'd been in a long time. The brokenness buried deep, poured out down her face, and left behind what remained of her mascara.

Walking on eggshells for so long left her dismantled and battered in more places than her body. The woman she became to survive was a stranger. Being quiet, unexposed, and small, were the ways she endured the suffering, but that wasn't who Mia was raised to be.

Could the walls she built so high and the conjured-up meekness fall to freedom? Was that even possible anymore?

Without warning, she snapped her body back. Levi jumped, caught off guard. Another loud protest pushed through her tight lips.

"Let me get someone," he offered, darting out of the room.

A few moments later the curtain opened, and Mia's stomach turned. With wide eyes she looked up, anxiety stacked tightly in the pit of her stomach. A faint sigh of relief held within at the sight of Nurse Katie and not Oliver.

"Mrs. Hughes, what's wrong?"

Everything tensed as Levi re-entered the room. Her eyes locked on his.

"Where are you hurting?" Katie asked with a hand lightly on Mia's back.

"My stomach and the right side of my ribs," she grunted.

"Okay, try to relax. I'll ask Doctor Freeman to prescribe something for the pain."

Mia firmly grabbed Katie's arm. "No. I can't pass out like that again," she pressed, still locked on Levi. His emerald green eyes calmed her. Whatever she encountered in the desert wasn't Levi. It lacked his kindness and empathy. "Please, don't put me out like that again."

"Let's see what the doctor says." Katie smiled and motioned for Levi to stand with Mia.

He didn't take his eyes off her. When his hand touched hers, she tried to pull away, but the pain kept her close. She couldn't withstand the punishment for this level of betrayal, not now, not ever.

"Levi?" She looked up at him. "Don't let them knock me out," she pleaded.

He looked tenderly into her eyes. "I won't."

Despite the pain and heartache he caused, and against her best judgment, she trusted him.

⸻ ✕ ⸻

Her frail body shivered in the cold damp dungeon. Charlotte missed the warmth of the sun on her face. Wishes flowed through her hazed mind to return to Jesus. It was cold, dark, and lifeless here. A ton of bricks weighed on her chest.

A cough rattled and burned in her lungs. She coughed again. Unable to stop the violent bark from within, something broke loose. In her hand laid a thick glob of mucus. The burn intensified. She wiped her hand on filthy jeans. The warmth of her body radiated through.

A tremble rapidly expanded throughout her sore muscles. She ached. Every move. Every breath. A treacherous nightmare. She longed for warmth with visions of fuzzy blankets and warm fires. With eyes closed a smile danced along her dry, cracked lips. She could almost feel the heat from her daydream.

Exhaustion took over, leaving her limp body lifeless on the dirt ground.

———————— ⚬⭢✕⭠⚬ ————————

Oliver firmly rubbed his palms across his jeans as he nervously sat in a chair, isolated and alone. Not good. So not good. They wouldn't let him see his wife or even tell him if she was okay. No one said anything, and it infuriated him.

"Mr. Hughes." A broad-shoulder man walked through the door wearing a suit far too nice for the gun visible on his hip. "My name's Detective Jerry Walsh with the Knoxville Police Department." He pulled up a chair, sat down, and scribbled something in a notebook.

"I'd like to see my wife now," Oliver demanded.

He had to get to her. She had to be controlled. His wife was many things, but she couldn't handle this. He did his best to wrangle her wild and rebellious spirit and protect her from God's wrath. And now he was caught in the crosshairs.

"I'm afraid I can't do that at the moment, Mr. Hughes," Jerry flatly responded without looking up from his notepad.

"Why not?" Oliver's jaw clenched. "This is madness! My wife's hurt. I need to be with her."

"I have some questions to ask you first." Jerry looked up this time and flashed an uninterested smile.

Oliver stood. "You can't keep me here."

"Sit down, Mr. Hughes, before you make matters worse for yourself."

Oliver sat with a huff of irritation. Nonchalantly, the detective went back to writing God knows what in his stupid little notebook. This wasn't right. Mia needed to be silenced.

He worried gossip of this nightmare would spread like wildfire through his congregation. Undoubtedly, that has-been, Ken Grant, would spearhead the whole thing and turn them all against him.

Oliver believed the Lord whispered to his heart, *Don't worry, they'll all praise your strength before long.*

————————✧————————

In the unseen world, Superiority, a demon in Occult's legion, swirled around Oliver's head. For months this particularly wicked beast worked on the feeble-minded pastor with whispered words and twisted suggestions.

He was the perfect mark—arrogant with a deep desire to be praised on big stages for saving the world one pathetic soul at a time. Oliver buried these desires so deep he thought no one would find them, but Occult did.

Time to exploit it for Hell's gain.

"So many lives to be left in ruin." Superiority smiled.

————————✧————————

Detective Walsh finally looked up from writing in that ridiculous notebook. If this was some sort of intimidation tactic, it wouldn't work. Oliver did the Lord's work, and no one, not even this wicked man, would stand in the way.

"We need to discuss your relationship with your wife."

"How is my personal life any of your business?" Oliver threw his hands up in the air. "My wife fell down the stairs. It was an accident."

"Does that happen a lot?" Detective Walsh blankly stared at Oliver.

"Does what happen a lot?"

"Your wife, falling or getting hurt."

Oliver scoffed. "That other lady already asked me that. Yes, my wife has moments of being clumsy, but not all the time."

"Hmm," was all the detective said before his pen went back to the paper to do what Oliver could only assume was work on his unfinished novel. After a few moments, he held up a picture of Mia's wrist. "So this, was the result of…?" His voice trailed off.

"Could be a number of different things. I don't stay at home and babysit my wife all day, detective. I have a very important job. An entire congregation counts on me to lead them."

"So you don't know how she got these bruises?"

"No," Oliver sternly declared.

"What about this one?" He held up a picture of her throat. "Do you see these lines here?" With the tip of his pen, he hovered it over the marks. "Those are finger lines."

"What do you mean, finger lines?" Oliver swallowed.

"It means you choked her, Mr. Hughes," he bluntly accused. "I'd be willing to bet you caused the bruise on her wrist, as well as her current injuries."

"I've never laid a hand on my wife," Oliver loudly protested.

"That's what they all say, Mr. Hughes. But here's the thing, I don't believe you and neither does anyone else."

"You'll never find any proof to back that up because there's nothing to find," Oliver powerfully declared. "I would never."

"We both know that's not true, Mr. Hughes. Your wife's injuries are not consistent with a fall down the stairs. She should have more damage to her arms and legs, but things are isolated to her torso. According to experts, her injuries are consistent with being kicked repeatedly in the stomach." He flipped through more pictures, turning each one to face Oliver. "This is all your handiwork, isn't it?"

Oliver masked his anxiety with anger. "No, it's not. I would never lay a hand on my wife." He stood again. "We're done talking. I want a lawyer, *now!*" he demanded.

Sixteen

LUCKILY, THE IBUPROFEN ADMINISTERED eased her pain but didn't knock her out like before. In the alertness of her mind, Mia avoided thoughts of the certain wrath awaiting her at home. Oliver was likely throwing a fit by now. He'd really lose it if he knew Levi was here and refused to leave her side.

Out of the corner of her eye, she took Levi in. A spark resembling love still lingered, a glowing ember buried under the ruins of their once budding romance. Mia knew it was wrong to feel this way and hated herself for the adulterous thoughts in her heart.

Lord, I'm so sorry. I don't know what's happening to me. She prayed, repenting from the lust clawing at her.

An unexpected answer quickly came, *For these sins in your heart and the lust you feel within, you deserve the punishment you've received.*

An unholy demonic force whispered lies in her ear the same way he had her whole life. Beli-yaal, a high-ranking demon, sat at the left hand of Lucifer himself. He did the wicked king's bidding and tore down those against the kingdom of darkness.

The Foster family's lineage posed a profound threat for many generations. They were too bright, too anointed to be left alone—they needed to be knocked off course.

Beli-yaal was assigned to Mia's great-great-great-great grandmother, Essie Foster. He designed a flawless trap of witchcraft wrapped in perceived righteousness. That naive and stupid woman fell for it. She believed it was the Lord's work. With tarot cards and a seemingly prophetic gift of dreams, she impacted the lives of those around her with evil. All the while, she lacked the basic intelligence to see her deceiver—pathetic.

A small opening was all this wicked creature needed to dig his talons deep within their bloodline. He twisted them in knots until that wretched Jack Foster came along. He snorted a puff of sulfuric smoke.

Beli-yaal's massive body filled half the room. He salivated and seethed, impressed with his wicked ways.

As a child, Mia resisted him more than now. Growing up brought so much baggage. The threat she posed was greater than anyone before her. From the moment she took her first breath, the awful angelic glow of a high anointing blinded Beli-yaal for many years. It was clear, the threat he saw in the Foster's all those years ago was her. She held the key to whatever that Half-Witt had planned. But not to worry, arrangements to neutralize her were well underway.

He tirelessly chiseled at her, making her feel small, unworthy, and utterly useless. Then, he took her brother and used her parent's fear to stifle her more. In the desert, he sent Occult after Levi to unleash torment. That moronic man believed himself unworthy of Mia, so he broke her heart.

Chip, chip, chip. A sinister smile spread wide on his thin black lips.

Now she was wonderfully hollow thanks to Oliver, unable to tell which way was up. He'd even managed to stifle her ability to hear from the Enemy, which left her wide open for his treacherous plans to unfold.

In the last year, his talons embedded further than ever before. She was locked in his deathly grip, incapable of escape, and ready to be swallowed whole.

"You haven't upheld what a wife should be according to scripture." Beli-yaal leaned in close, spewing his manufactured tales. "Oliver reacted out of frustration and disappointment for what you've become." He thought for a moment of how else to cut her down and, with a menacing grin, continued. "You're lazy and you've put on weight. You're not nearly as pretty as you used to be. Of course, he lashed out. You brought this on yourself, Mia. It's your job to fix it." Beli-yaal covered his delight with giant fingers and foot-long talons.

Tears built up in Mia's eyes. Good, he struck a nerve. A tidal wave of worthlessness rushed over and drowned her with its bony fingers of self-pity.

"Perfect," he snickered.

———•×•———

Levi's stomach churned. Every hair on the back of his neck stood at attention. Something evil was here. He took in the room behind narrow eyes and a prayer in his heart. Waiting on the Lord, he stood, frozen yet hyper-aware, like a cat in a dark alley.

Out of the corner of his eye, a bulging black cloud hovered over Mia. It twisted around her fair skin and strawberry-kissed hair. Turning his full attention on her, he lost sight of the tormentor.

He leaned forward with elbows on his knees. Everything within him screamed to not ignore this threat.

On his feet, he looked at Mia, worried about what she might think of him. It was an unwarranted thought, but one that took him a moment to get past. She needed him, and he needed to save her.

"In the name of Jesus, get out," Levi demanded.

Within seconds, the air turned to molasses. Winded, he choked for relief. The sting of electricity crawled up his arms like a thousand needle pricks. It was close. Too close.

"I said." Hunched over, he heaved breaths, unable to speak more than a few words at a time. "Get out…right now…in the name…of Jesus!"

Without another word, the darkness vanished, along with any trace of its presence. Levi put his hands on his knees to catch his breath.

"What on earth are you doin'?" Mia asked.

"Protecting you." With a final deep breath, he straightened himself out. "There's a war happening, M, whether you see it or not."

"What do you mean?"

"I'm talking about a spiritual war." He remembered how crazy he sounded and backed off. "I know this sounds crazy. Just forget it."

"No," she blurted out. "I don't know if you remember me telling you about this stuff as a kid, but I believe you. I've lived through it. In the last few days, I've endured some pretty bizarre things."

This was the most she'd spoken to him since they were a couple. Nerves bubbled up in his throat, not wanting to ruin this moment by saying something stupid.

"Is that what did…" He pointed to her lacerations and bruises.

Levi carried physical and emotional scars with him from the spiritual war he faced all those years ago. He knew it was possible, but didn't believe it to be the cause. Oliver did this, there was no doubt, but he needed to build rapport so she'd be honest with him.

"No, I fell." She anxiously chewed on her nails. It was her tell. She just lied to him.

With no time to call her on it, Mia explained her encounter the other night and how Oliver had been off lately. Her story was too guarded to be the full truth, but she was talking to him, so it was a start.

———×———

The door to the lab burst open as Jocelyn fell through, box first. All of this needed to be cataloged and tested, but the mystery red dust was a priority. Hopefully, AJ was over himself by now, so their bickering could finally stop. Her short legs scurried across the room, ignoring the click her boots made against the linoleum.

"I found something," she hollered out.

AJ's attention popped up from his work. "Don't waste my time with some wild goose chase."

She sat the box down on the counter. "Lisa, can you take all of this and start processing?"

"Wait a minute. You don't get to come in here and boss everyone around. I was called in to give my expertise on this case and while I'm here, I call the shots. They'll do what I need them to." His lips tightened.

"This is evidence from Charlotte's apartment. We found some stuff that could be important. Plus, I think I found trace evidence of that red clay dirt on her front door." She stared him down, ignoring the apology she owed him.

"Okay, start on the box of evidence." He stuck his hand out. "Swabs," he demanded.

Jocelyn snapped them back and out of reach. "Say please."

Yes, it was petty and a girl's life was on the line, but this jackwad would respect her.

He grunted in protest. "Fine, please." He pumped his hand to tell her to hurry up.

She smiled, handing over the evidence.

While he did that, they finished canvassing the areas around each victim's home and abduction sites. They didn't have much more than they did twelve hours ago, but with an order to specifically check for red dust sent to the teams, she couldn't give up hope yet.

Seventeen

AFTER SPILLING THE DETAILS of her recent encounters, she felt better. Lighter. Less weighed down by the mountain of secrets she kept locked away.

An echo of guilt lingered for sharing this with a man who wasn't her husband. And not just any man, Levi.

Her eyes met his, searching for any reaction to indicate he thought her a lunatic. Truth be told, she felt absurd. The life she once loved no longer made sense. The man she married vanished and left behind a shell of rage. Hopelessness plagued her. She probably was crazy.

The biggest takeaway from this year? She proven herself not to be a very supportive wife and partner, and Levi's presence only solidified it. Oliver was her husband and she was supposed to be the submissive wife. Her actions were a disappointment.

"I remember you telling me about your attack as kids." Levi softly smiled. "You worried I didn't believe you then, and I didn't. But I do now." He inched the rolling stool he sat on closer. "I've seen too many things and encountered too much evil to not believe you."

"Really?" she faintly asked.

He huffed a laugh. "Yes, really."

Levi cleared his throat, shifting in his seat. He was nervous, and it amused her to see he was still the same boy he'd always been. The Marines enlisted kids and turned them into fearless soldiers, but they couldn't take away the same nervous expression he'd had since they were six. He wore the same look when they stole her daddy's tractor to catch fireflies by the pond, and when they went to the graveyard to visit her great-grandad after dark.

"What's wrong?" she finally asked, unable to keep her curiosity at bay.

"I have something to ask you, but it's going to make you mad."

Mia swallowed hard. In the pit of her bruised stomach, she knew what came next. The only thing left to decide was if she would spill those secrets as well.

"Go ahead and ask." She took a deep breath, unsure what her answer would be.

"Did your husband do this to you?" He choked on the words as pain settled across his handsome face.

Tears pooled in her eyes, escaping into a freefall down her battered cheeks. The cut on her lip oozed as it quivered under the weight of information being kept. Her lips were sealed, supportive, steadfast, but now they contemplated betrayal.

"Am I talking to Officer Reed or my friend, Levi?" Her voice trembled.

"I can't be one without the other, but I'll be here for you as your friend through this if you want." He placed his hand on her knee. She instantly pulled away out of reach and watched his heartbreak as she did. "Did he do this?"

Her lungs burned to keep up with the race in her chest. She couldn't stop it. One word. One tiny little word was about to change her whole life.

"Yes." It quietly fell from her lips.

She couldn't stop the earthquake of sobs that followed. Her trembling body folded in half as each whimper grew in her chest. Unbearable pain shot through her torso, turning her sobs into yelps of agony.

A large man in black scrubs barreled into the room.

"What happened?" he demanded with a noted Irish accent.

Levi explained everything.

"What's happening to me?" Mia grunted through gritted teeth.

"We aren't sure," the nurse quickly announced. "Dr. Thompson," he hollered.

Within seconds, the room buzzed with people in scrubs. Each one, like a choreographed routine, checked the monitors and Mia. The doctor barked orders but all she heard was Levi.

"She doesn't want to be knocked out again. Please don't do this," he pleaded.

A warm sensation flooded her tortured and damaged body. The pain was still there, but the warmer it got, the less she cared. Her body reacted on instinct, reaching out a hand to brace herself against falling into oblivion. A hand, unsure whose, grabbed her. A slow blink came across dazed eyes as she bucked against the drugs.

Her eyes locked onto Levi, her safe place. "Levi," she whispered a plea.

She helplessly watched him try to fight his way through the sea of hospital staff.

"I'm right here, M," he offered as they escorted him through the curtain.

A devilish howl of enjoyment rang out as darkness engulfed her.

⸺✕⸺

Jocelyn tapped her fingers against the desk to the tune stuck in her head. She never should have listened to MC Hammer in the car. Now she'd be humming, tapping, and singing, "Can't Touch This" all day long. She might even bust out the dance moves when alone.

I need a life, she said to herself. But first, she had to make sure Charlotte had one too.

She peeked over AJ's shoulder for the twelfth time in the last ten minutes, trying to see the results they waited on. Unfortunately, she couldn't understand or predict anything he did. So instead, she paced a few more times, continuing to tap that song against her leg until it turned into a faint hum.

"Can't Touch This? Really?" AJ laughed, not looking up from his microscope.

"I can't help it. It's catchy." She clenched her fists, forcing herself to stop. "But shouldn't you focus on the samples and not music trivia?"

"Relax, College, I'm almost done."

Jocelyn rebounded into pacing. The clock on the wall pushed heavily against her back—a loud reminder, time was running out. She aimlessly wondered about Charlotte's parents. If they failed and Jocelyn assured them they did everything they could to find their daughter, would it be true?

She jumped at the unexpected ring of her phone.

"Maddox," she answered.

"Ms. Lewis is here. Where do you want her?" Andrews offered.

"One of the interrogation rooms is fine. I'll be there in a bit."

She hung up the phone as the lab door burst open, snapping her attention. The doe-eyed rookie, Caleb, stiffly held a box marked *evidence*.

"We found something at Shelby Walsh's townhouse," he huffed, out of breath.

"Did you run here, Rook?" AJ asked, chuckling to himself.

"All the way from my car, sir," Caleb responded with pride.

Jocelyn grabbed the box and handed it to Lisa. "How did you find so much stuff?" She assumed everywhere but Charlotte's would provide little to no evidence.

"Her father wasn't ready to part with the townhouse. They left everything exactly where it was and never went inside." Caleb smiled. "Needless to say, the cereal bowl in the sink was pretty rank, but there was quite a bit of potential evidence there." He pointed to the box.

On top, nuzzled between two bagged and tagged drinking glasses, were three red-tip cotton swabs.

"Great work, officer." Jocelyn held up the swabs.

"I found it not too long after you alerted everyone. I'd walked passed it so many times and then there it was, right at my feet." Excitement ignited in his eyes—rookies, always so eager, like puppy dogs looking for a treat. "Boserelli sent me as soon as I found it."

She tossed the swabs in front of AJ.

"I'll get started." He swiped them from the desk. "Dan, Lilly, come help me with these."

The two techs quickly made their way to the table and got right to work.

—✕—

A deep blue sky illuminated the space above. She listened for the wind, but this place was eerily quiet. Her hands gripped at the blades of grass beneath her. Silence wasn't her favorite thing. Too many thoughts raced in all the wrong directions. Too many voices competed for attention. Here, she felt inadequate. Worthless. Insignificant.

Metal clanked as she stood. It wrapped around her body and sloppily hung as she fought to counter its weight. Confusion prevailed. Mia attempted to adjust the bulky breastplate. Unsteady, her feet slid around in the sandals she wore, rendering her immobile.

The sword at her side pulled her hips askew. An impossibly heavy and massive shield lay at her feet. The helmet on her head plopped to the ground as she tried to pick it up.

A loud grunt escaped as she forced the helmet back on. It swallowed her head and left her blinded. She pushed it back until it fell to the ground.

Why in the world was she wearing armor that wasn't hers? Ridiculous.

"Hello?" her voice echoed against the deafening silence.

A mirror flashed into existence before her. Curiously, she peered at the glass to find a reflection of her youth staring back. Her large round eyes and soft ringlet curls were wild as they tumbled from her head. Her child frame was swallowed whole by shiny metal.

Where'd my helmet go? Mia thought as she touched her head, young Mia following suit.

A glimmer in the mirror caught her eye.

"Keep watching," the young girl whispered like the wind.

Mia leaned closer. The image blurred and showed the girl thoughtlessly twirl in a lush green meadow. A wide smile stretched across her face, and a giggle clutched in her chest.

So innocent. So free.

"Check it out," she yelled with excitement. "I've got a sword!" Her frail arms heaved the burdensome blade, forcing it through the air uncontrollably. "You don't scare me." A swing of the sword pushed her body in circles.

She sloppily kicked her feet and karate-chopped the air. The shield lay useless on the ground ten feet from where the girl played. The sword quickly became too heavy. It dropped to the ground, abandoned. Delight clothed Mia's face, watching her.

Without warning, a shift occurred in her spirit. Alarms wailed, forcing her on high alert. Danger relentlessly lurked somewhere near. Frantic, she pressed against the glass to grab for the sweet, innocent girl, but she couldn't pass through. Nothing Mia tried could protect her from sure annihilation.

"Hey," Mia yelled at the girl, banging against the mirror to get her attention. "Hey!" She tried again, but the girl ignored every attempt.

And then she saw it—a legion of unnoticed demons dove in from above. Stuck, unable to move, Mia demanded her body to respond, but fear held tight. Naive, the girl played like an unsuspecting calf being led to the slaughter.

A quick adjustment of her oversized armor freed up her movements. Mia lunged for the mirror but tripped on her bulky shoes. Her fists pounded against the glass, desperate to get the girl's attention.

"Watch out!" she screamed.

This time, the girl looked straight at Mia and spoke with urgency. "You aren't ready for what's coming. It'll swallow you whole if you don't grow up and allow the Lord your God to temper you." Mia stumbled back with a gasp and dropped to the ground. "The Lord will use you in mighty ways Mia, but He must prepare you for the battle that's coming." The girl looked up and calmly watched a legion of evil claw over the top of itself to get to her. "Surrender yourself to Yahweh. They're coming, and He's your only hope."

The warning vibrated through Mia's soul. She watched in horror as darkness plunged in on the girl. A thunderous roar ripped through the meadow and everything went black.

———————————✕———————————

Levi paced the hall just outside her room. A few sad attempts to peek through the cracks in the curtain revealed no new information. Mia was out, and he couldn't stop it from happening. She counted on him, and he failed.

He pulled out his phone and called Sergeant Cole.

She answered on the first ring. "Reed, I haven't had time to call you."

"Sarge, Mia confessed it was Oliver who hurt her." He did his best to speak calmly but was too wound up.

"When?"

"Just a few minutes ago, but she started crying and then screaming. Something's wrong, but the ER nurses won't let me in there to find out what." His hand ran through his hair.

"Reed, you listen to me," Sergeant Cole earnestly stated. "You let them do their job and stay out of their way. That's an order."

"Yes, ma'am," he huffed.

"Wait, she's still in the ER?"

"There's no beds available upstairs so she's here until one opens up. They said it could be a while."

"Oh," she offered. "Now, I have news too. I've brought in detectives to question Oliver." Levi stopped pacing. "Walsh has been in there for a while now, but Hughes isn't cracking."

"So now that Mia admitted the truth, things can move forward, right?"

"Reed," she sighed. "Listen, I want to believe you, I do. But, we both know you have a personal interest in this case."

"Sarge." He tried to retort although he knew she was right. He wouldn't take his word for it either.

"It's not personal, Reed. We need something solid, like a recording or written statement. Or this thing will turn into a he said, she said nightmare, and I don't think that's what you want for Mia."

Levi sighed. "I don't know how long she'll be out so I can record it."

"I know that's not what you want to hear, but you know I'm right. Listen, when she admits it was him, it'll move things along, but until then, we can't hold him here forever."

"Sarge, we can't just let this guy go."

"Reed, you know how this works. It's frustrating, but if Mia wakes up and doesn't give us a statement or decide to press charges, there's nothing we can do. It's a dumb law, but we still have to abide by it. For an arrest, we need more than you claiming to hear her confess. You have no other witnesses that heard it, and she can't sign an official statement of what happened."

"I know, I know." He peeked in the room again. "I'm staying with her."

"I don't know if that's a good idea."

"She trusts me," he urged while leaving out it was more than that. He didn't trust anyone else to do this job right. No one knew her or would care about her well-being like he did. "Don't take me off this, Sarge. I can get the truth out of her."

In the long pause, he pictured Sergeant Cole's thin, deep-wrinkled lips pressed together as she bit her inner cheek. Anxiety coiled until a loud sigh came through.

"Okay, fine. You can stay, but the moment you step out of line, you're done."

"I can live with that." He grinned.

⸺⸺⸺⸺⸺ ⸙ ⸺⸺⸺⸺⸺

In the far-off distance, a handful of angelic warriors perched in the trees encompassing a decrepit structure. They moved with stealth and precision to not alert the sea of demons circling the area. They were everywhere. In the short time they watched, their numbers easily doubled.

An angel named Andrew scrunched his face at the turn of his stomach. Centuries of fighting these wicked creatures and the smell of sulfur and decay still made him nauseous.

"They'll strike soon. I'm sure of it." Leon angled toward Andrew as he tucked his long, golden-brown hair behind his ear.

Andrew tightly clenched his once olive-skinned fist until it turned white. "Looks that way."

None of them were ready for what was coming. Levi matured since the last time, but this level of threat was more than most would ever encounter in a lifetime.

"Should we tell Finn?" Leon questioned.

Blood-curdling screeches echoed off the trees, a sound detested by even the fiercest warriors.

Andrew prayed for guidance.

"Andrew." he pressed, his Slavic accent guttural.

Andrew's eyes opened. "Kafziel." He telepathically summoned the young warrior.

In the fraction of a second, Kafziel was by Andrew's side. "Sir?"

"Kaf, I need you to get word to Finn right away. Now this is important. You cannot be detected by the growing army of darkness." Andrew's deep brown eyes fixed back on the growing evil. "Tell him the army is forming for the ritual. It won't be long now." His attention returned to Kafziel as he pulled him close. "Tell him Mia and Levi must be prepared." He looked over his shoulder with a stoic and somber gaze. "War is coming."

Eighteen

JOCELYN LEISURELY WEAVED THROUGH the sea of desks toward the interrogation room where Tamika Lewis waited. She could have placed her in a private room for families, but Detective Crabby Pants, Linda frequently used them to eat weird exotic food that smelled like feet.

"Hey," Maya called out.

"When'd you get back?" Jocelyn asked.

"Just now. Where are you headed?"

"Charlotte's roommate's in interrogation three."

Maya tilted her head quizzically. "Is she a suspect?"

A light snort of amusement escaped her nostrils. "Not at all. I just wanted to ask a few follow-up questions."

"Ah. Want some company?"

"Nah, I'm good, thanks." Jocelyn took a few steps away and turned back. "Are all the teams done?"

"The only team not back yet is Boscereli's," Maya offered.

"Cool. Can you tell everyone to just sit tight while I talk to Miss Lewis?"

"Sure thing."

Oliver hung up the phone. Of course, his lawyer was out of town in Nashville and wouldn't be here to get him out of this mess for at least a few hours. Just his luck.

He paced around the small room as thoughts endlessly raced. They had no evidence to support their theory. Everything they had was circumstantial at best. As long as Mia kept her mouth shut, he would be in the clear soon enough. He watched enough cop shows to know at least that much.

A knock at the door halted his nervous movements.

"Yes?" Oliver answered, annoyed at the intrusion.

The door opened a few inches. Detective Walsh's irritating, square-shaped head poked through.

"Get a hold of that lawyer you wanted?" He smiled.

"Yup, but he's coming in from out of town. Should be here in a few hours."

"Excellent." Walsh pushed the door wide open for him and another guy to walk in.

"Who's this?" Oliver demanded.

"This is my partner, Detective Diego Maltez."

Maltez swiftly raised his hand. "Yo, what's up?" he casually asked like he was talking to his buddy.

"What's up?" Oliver wrinkled his nose. "Seriously?"

Maltez shrugged his shoulders. He dressed differently than Walsh, wearing jeans and a black V-neck tee. Taking off his leather jacket, he draped it over the chair, exposing his left arm covered in black ink.

Great, just what he needed—a few unholy, unclean, and unrighteous men judging him.

"Y'all can't question me without my lawyer present," Oliver commanded.

"Yeah, we know." A smug look tugged at the corner of Walsh's lips. He unbuttoned his suit jacket as he pulled up a chair of his own.

"We're not gonna question you, man. I'm just gonna discuss the details of the case with my partner here," Maltez offered.

Oliver rolled his eyes and went back to pacing.

"So, let's see," Walsh sighed, casually leaning back into the chair. "Looks like Mrs. Hughes has bruising consistent with long-term abuse according to three different ER doctors."

"How can they tell?" Maltez innocently asked, shrugging his shoulders as child-like innocence washed over his face.

"Well, you see, Diego," Walsh continued like he was explaining it to a kindergartener. "She has several bruises in different stages of healing on her body."

"Oh, that sounds bad. What did Mr. Hughes say about it when you asked?"

"He, uh, claimed his wife is just clumsy."

"Clumsy?" Maltez laughed. "Did he find that defense in the 'How to Get Away with Abuse' handbook?" With a scoff, he shook his head.

"It's like the oldest defense in the book besides, 'She fell down the stairs.'" Walsh's voice became high-pitched, stifling a laugh. "Oh wait, he used that one too."

Laughter erupted, like a volcano of hyenas.

Oliver's fists clenched and his face turned hot.

———✕———

Like a dark cloud of torment, Occult seeped through the wall, gliding across the floor toward Oliver. The wicked creature slithered up his body in a figure-eight.

"What they're doing to you is unjust. It's because you're a Christian," Occult whispered through thin, curled lips. "They were sent from the pit of Hell to destroy you. Demand they leave the room at once."

"Enough," Oliver growled. "My lawyer will have a field day with this." He leaned forward. "So, go ahead, keep talking." A devilish smile lingered on his face.

"There's no reason to get bent outta shape, man," Maltez huffed. They both got up. "We'll see ya soon, Mr. Hughes." Maltez grabbed his jacket with a wink.

"Real soon," Walsh followed up before they walked out of the room, closing the door behind them.

A bulging vein protruded on Oliver's forehead, and his fingers clenched into fists. Deep seething breaths spewed saliva from his mouth.

"Relax, son. You did good," Occult gently whispered.

With a chuckle, the demon left.

———✕———

The metal chair scraped against the dingy linoleum. She caught her reflection in the two-way mirror. Dark circles and bags already formed under her eyes. Plus, the light in here was anything but flattering.

"I'm Detective Maddox. We spoke earlier." In an attempt to look less tired, she smiled.

"I remember you, detective." Tamika sat up straight. "Locking me in this interrogation room violates my rights. I don't know what you think I did, but I want my lawyer present, right now."

Ugh, law students, Jocelyn privately grumbled.

"Miss Lewis, I can assure you, I did not order for you to be locked in here. This is not an interrogation. It's an interview. I was hoping you could help clarify a few things for me."

Tamika visibly released her attack stance, like a dog called off by its owner. "Oh."

Jocelyn finished adjusting in her seat and arranged the files she'd carried in with her on the table. On top sat a notepad with collected thoughts scribbled on it.

"Before we get started, would you like some water or coffee?"

"I'm good, thanks." Tamika's wide eyes locked on the files, seemingly haunted by what might be inside. "Do you have any updates on Charlie?"

"No, I don't, but we're doing everything we can to find her," Jocelyn gently explained, ignoring the growing pit of uncertainty in her chest. "At your apartment, we found some wine glasses on the coffee table. What day did you use them?"

"It was the night Charlie went missing. Kiley and I came back to the apartment to hang out once the coffee shop closed. When Charlie wasn't there, I panicked and wanted to call the cops right away. We called Brad for advice, but he said we didn't know she was missing. She just wasn't where we expected her to be, which was a fair statement to make. He then explained how most cops won't even do anything until the person's been missing for at least twenty-four hours, sometimes forty-eight. It's just—" Tamika shifted in her seat.

"What?"

"It's just I couldn't shake this feeling that something was seriously wrong. So Brad came over. He and Kiley suggested we have a glass of wine and wait for a bit. I'm not usually a lightweight when it comes to drinking, but one glass did me in. Next thing I knew, I woke up and hours had passed."

"What time was that?"

"Around three."

"Was everyone still there?"

"Brad left, Kiley was passed out on the floor, and Charlie was still nowhere to be found. I knew then, I shouldn't have waited," she cried. "Charlie's gonna die because I'm an idiot!"

"That's not true," Jocelyn consoled her. "None of this is your fault, you hear?" She reached out and grabbed her hand.

Only one question remained.

"Did you or Charlotte go anywhere recently that had red clay dirt?"

"Red clay dirt?" Tamika pondered, searching the air above for answers. "No. Most of our time lately has been spent at The Roasted Bean, studying like crazy for finals."

Nineteen

KAFZIEL DELICATELY MOVED THROUGH the forest without disruption. No surprise Andrew chose him. He was the fastest warrior they had. Even his name meant, "The speedy one of God."

With a running leap, Kafziel lunged upward, his wings tucked in, and grabbed the top of a tree. Perched like a statue, he waited. No sign indicated the disturbance alerted any wicked entity from the barn. Finally, time for super speed.

A breeze plunged through the trees as Kafziel abruptly took off, weaving through with precision. At the edge of Knoxville, he kept a low profile. Some demons would see him, but they wouldn't know who he was or what he was doing there.

His feet slammed into the concrete as he dropped down into the parking lot of the hospital. Finn set up shop here. Standing upright, his golden eyes slowly scanned the area.

"Kaf," a deep voice whispered. "Over here."

He looked to the right and between two dumpsters crouched the warrior, Axum.

"Ax." He ran to his side. "Where's Finn? I have news."

"He's incognito in the hospital," Axum whispered.

"What do you mean?" He kept his voice low.

"He went in disguise as a human to get close to Mia and Levi."

"Why in disguise?"

"Beli-yaal's here."

Kafziel's eyes widened, and his heart picked up speed. He'd never faced Beli-yaal before, but he'd heard plenty of stories and seen plenty of scars inflicted by him.

"Why's he here?" he asked.

"Finn doesn't know, but he also didn't seem surprised by it either." Axum scrunched his nose. "Let's move somewhere better where we can talk and not smell whatever that is."

They scurried away from the dumpster, doing their best to stay hidden with each step. Rounding the corner, they went through the wall. No need for doors when you're an angel.

Kafziel finally stood upright. As he did, his large hand ran through his curly brown hair. Unworldly eyes of different colors from those already there fell on him.

In the back stood a warrior he fought side by side with a few hundred years ago.

Viveka was tall and lean. Her hair, a feminine mohawk with strips of leather weaved through the sandy blonde strands that fell from her head, like a waterfall of sunkissed shoots. She looked like a Viking warrior.

"Kafziel." Viveka's silky voice echoed concern. "What's wrong?"

"I have news. Where's Finn?"

Uneasiness rested in her bright blue eyes. "He should be back soon."

Fluorescent light poured in from the hallway as a door opened. Every angel went about their business, ignoring the intrusion.

"I'll wait for Finn, but is there any way to get in touch with him? This matter is urgent," Kafziel pushed.

"Finn?" The human's voice echoed in the forgotten cement room.

A breath held tight in his chest as he and Viveka looked at the tall man in black scrubs. Wide, light green eyes stared directly at them.

A hush fell over the heavenly hosts.

"You lookin' for a Finn, lad?" an unmistakable Irish accent came from his mouth with a chuckle.

"You scared us half to death," Viveka protested.

"Oh come on, V." Finn shook off the human form he used. "Where's your sense of humor?"

"You know I don't like that nickname. I don't like any nicknames. My Father gave me a beautiful name, and I expect to be called by it."

"Okay, okay, I'm sorry, lass." Viveka gave him a hard look. "Viveka," he put his hands up in surrender.

Finn was a smidge taller than Viveka. His auburn hair looked brown in the dim lighting, but Kafziel saw the distinct freckles draped across his face. That was Finn, alright.

"I have urgent news from Andrew."

"Alright, Kaf, let's walk and talk." He pointed deeper into the room.

Jocelyn looked on as AJ and his team quickly worked. He said the geographical results of the red dust would be done any moment, but that was ten minutes ago. Waiting wasn't exactly her strong suit. There had to be something she could do in the meantime.

Maya ran point with the groups upstairs who were assigned to wade through the mountain of evidence and follow up on any leads.

She didn't want to put all of her eggs in this red dust basket so she sent Leslie and Boscereli's teams out to canvas the outlying areas with the K-9 officers. These guys were smart. Calculated. They never dumped the bodies in the same place twice. It was too much ground to cover, but maybe they'd get lucky.

A glance at her watch brought a new wave of anxiety. Forty-seven hours since Charlotte went missing. If they didn't find something within the next hour, Jocelyn didn't want to think about what that poor girl would endure.

She incessantly clicked her pen.

"Joce!" AJ snapped with a loud sigh. "Please stop."

"Sorry." A meek smile flashed.

Think, Jocelyn. Think.

An alarm sounded like she'd won the jackpot at the local casino. "What's that?"

"The geographical footprint of where the red dust originated. Looks like it's from somewhere between South-East Tennessee and North-West North Carolina," AJ said.

"That's still too wide of a range." Jocelyn sighed.

"We'll keep trying to narrow it down, but that'll be difficult to do without surface samples to cross-analyze."

"Let's pray something shakes out soon."

AJ scoffed, "I didn't take you for the religious type."

"Not that it's any of your business, but I'm willing to accept any help we can get at this point. We're running out of time." She looked down at her watch again. Less than an hour before the probability of finding Charlotte dropped significantly.

AJ put his arms up in surrender and went back to work.

Jocelyn pulled out her phone. "Hey, this is Detective Maddox, badge number one-nine-two-nine-seven-two. We need to put out information to a wide area. Can we do that?"

"Yes, ma'am, we can alert the whole nation if you need," a sassy southern voice came through the phone.

"No need for that, but I do need to send out information to police stations in all the areas of Southeast Tennessee and the Northwest of North Carolina about our serial killers."

Jocelyn opened the door to the lab and looked back at AJ. When their eyes met, he gave a nod and cracked a gentle smile. She mouthed the words "thank you" and raced out the door.

Twenty

IN THE DARK, MUSTY dungeon, a warrior named Kano stepped inside through the dirt wall. Bronze armor glistened against her pale skin. Her thin, deep-set eyes studied the girl. With every defeated groan Charlotte released, the ache of sympathy echoed louder.

Charlotte hugged her knees to her chest. Kano's body mimicked the girl as weakness from the pestilence ravaged them both. Shivers ran up their spines. They trembled. Their teeth ached against the chatter. They fought the pool of fog plaguing them.

This wasn't good. They would be back soon, and they might end Charlotte's life for this.

"Lord, I just want this to be over." Despair hiccupped in Charlotte's chest. "Jesus. I want to come home to You. I can't take much more. Let me die right here or rescue me quickly. Please, Lord."

A few strands of silky black hair framed Kano's round face as they fell from the high bun atop her head. Her stance shifted, on high alert. Evil lurked somewhere close. If she were seen, the element of surprise Finn counted on would be ruined.

The metal at her side scraped as she unsheathed her weapon. Her dark, velvety eyes peered just over her shield. Patience was a gift. Kano never reacted with haste, for God was always in control.

She noted movement in her peripheral. Steadfast in her position, she tracked its migration.

In a flash, it wrapped itself around her like a tornado. Every claw mark burned on her skin. A grimace of agony permeated her soft features.

She fought back. A slash of her sword and a kick of her feet, but the creature remained unaffected. At lightning speed, the small devil swirled its way up her body.

She relentlessly grabbed at it until it was firmly in her grasp.

Peeling it off her chest, she saw its shriveled and raisin-like face. Wild eyes swiftly darted in all directions.

"Kano," the creature hissed. "You wouldn't want to hurt *me* now would you, Kano-Banano?"

"It can't be," a feeble whisper escaped her lips.

Only one person ever called her that. A deeper gaze into its buggy eyes, past the bloodthirsty look, she saw him.

"Naru?" Bewilderment collected in her chest.

Naru had been Kano's best friend. They both learned and enjoyed Earth's pastime of martial arts together. He seemed larger than life back then, with a square jaw and signature stoic look. He resembled the deeply respected and feared Samaris on earth.

But now, he remained a shriveled existence, a nuisance, a pest.

"We were best friends once, Kano." He sucked up the toxic drool that hung from his crooked mouth. "Just let me go, for old-time sake, huh?" A rabid smile spread. "I won't tell anyone about you, I promise."

His movements were constant, like a meth addict in need of his next fix.

Kano's heart broke just like it did all those years ago when she watched her best friend fall like lightning from Heaven, his allegiance now with Lucifer.

Their friendship pulled at her heartstrings. She desperately wanted to believe him but knew better.

There was no time for the creature to retort. A loud grunt came from the demon as her blade pierced its chest. In a breath, a pile of ash fell from her hand. By the tip of her blade, Naru was sent to the deepest pit of Hell, banished for the next thousand years.

She would not mourn its banishment, for she lost Naru long before today.

Kano prayed for guidance. Without a second glance, she stepped out of the room with an update for Finn.

Ashanti came to take her place with Charlotte. The girl was in good hands. Kano trusted the African warrior.

<hr>

A distinct and rhythmic sound filled the darkness around her. Warmth dispersed throughout from the drugs she begged them not to give her. The once paralyzing agony of pain had eased, now a dull, persistent ache in her side.

The vision of her as a child wasn't less terrifying per se, but it was better than the monster from the desert.

"Can I see her?" a man's voice echoed.

The euphonious beeps mirrored her pulse as it picked up speed.

Everything within jumped when an unknown intrusion tumbled across her feet. It started up her leg, slow and methodical, like a spider working its way up the wall. A hollowness twisted in the pit of her stomach.

She was paralyzed. Vulnerable. An unwilling participant in whatever torture this brought.

Wake up, Mia! she internally demanded. *Wake up!*

Cool air rushed into her lungs, choking back the lump in her throat. She clenched the bed sheet under her. The prick of slender talons scalded her skin as it moved further up her body.

When it reached her chest, Mia braced for the impact of torment.

"Jesus," she exhaled.

Quicker than it came, it slunk off the bed.

Thank you, she prayed as her eyes softly opened.

"Mia?"

Footsteps raced toward her tensed body.

Milliseconds felt like an eternity as she waited for her fate. His green eyes were the first thing she saw, like beautiful water crashing against the sandy beach. For a brief moment, she felt safe and secure.

Instinctively her hands clenched. A frantic look around the room unleashed anxiety within.

"Oliver?" she gruffly pressed.

"He can't hurt you, M. He's not allowed to see you."

This accord brought refuge to her mutilated heart. Freedom abounded here. She could breathe in the safety of Levi.

Things had to change. An oppressive life subsisting in fear was no life at all. She couldn't be Oliver's punching bag any longer.

Her future depended on the strength to stand fully upright despite her wobbly knees and shaky hands. With the promise of emancipation so close, she had to grab hold of it.

———o-x-o———

Desperate to hold her, he reached out, stopping halfway. It would be wrong on too many levels. She was married, and although her husband was a disgusting pile of human garbage, he couldn't infringe on a covenant made before God.

Plus, Mia needed a friend more than anything else right now, and he needed to focus on getting her statement.

"It'll be okay, M," he offered.

"I decided something." Her rough voice sounded like it hurt to talk.

Levi silently grabbed a cup of water and walked over to her. "Here," he offered.

With the straw held to her mouth, she slowly sipped.

"I'm ready to give my statement," she blurted out.

He cleared the celebration from his throat. "So, you want to go on record with your statement?"

"Yes." She struggled to catch her breath. "If I don't say something, he's going to just keep doing it."

"What brought this on?"

"I don't know." She swallowed hard. "The last two times I've been under, I've had these…visions, or maybe they were encounters?" She slowly exhaled. "Something's coming and if I don't change my life, I won't be ready when it gets here."

"I'm proud of you, M. You're doing the right thing."

She did her best to hide the muted sobs. "I know." Her voice strained with emotion. "But it still feels like I'm betraying him."

"You're not. He betrayed you by hurting you." Levi sat down on the stool next to her, phone in hand, ready to record her statement, but was interrupted by a loud and persistent alert. He looked down at the screen.

"What's that?" She asked.

"It's a county-wide alert."

He read through the details and learned Durham Police had a large manhunt underway for a cult that's killed eight women, and now a ninth one was missing.

"What's it about?" Mia eventually asked as he read further.

"Apparently there was red dirt from somewhere in this region found at the apartment of a woman they believe was kidnapped by a serial killer."

"A serial killer?"

"Yeah. Says here, a religious cult kidnapped eight women and dismembered them while they were still alive. They arranged what was left of their bodies on an altar, like a sacrifice to God." A shudder tumbled down his spine as Occult came to mind. "Traces of red clay dirt were found on the altar stones and in two of the victim's homes." He looked up from the screen and noted the horrified look in her eyes.

"So, they think the red clay is from here?"

"Looks like they've narrowed it down to somewhere in this region, so it could be here, could be a hundred miles from here."

Levi analyzed Mia as her eyes searched the air. Trying to figure out this case might be easier to deal with than reality. He casually texted Sergeant Cole that Mia was ready to give her statement and asked if she could come take it so his hands were fully out of it.

"So, I should probably have you give your statement to my boss. Giving it to me could pose some coercion issues." He casually maneuvered things back to her statement because, without it, Oliver would likely walk.

"Um, Levi?" she said, almost stunned.

"Yeah?" He worried she changed her mind.

"What if... Um..." She bit at her bottom lip, and with a heavy sigh continued. "I have a thought."

"What do you mean?" His eyes narrowed with a lean forward.

"After y'all left last night, I found some red clay dirt that Oliver tracked in on his shoes."

"You don't really think..." His voice trailed off.

"I don't." She chewed at her nails. "But what if I'm wrong?"

Levi looked at his phone to check. "The girl was taken two days ago on Thursday night around twenty-one hundred hours, not last night."

Her hands rubbed together with angst. "You ever just have a gut feeling?"

He sighed. "Okay, let's say this is all true. The dirt you swept up is contaminated in the trash."

She tried to sit up but was forced to ask for help. "Can you?"

"Yeah, of course." He came in behind her and helped her up, then lifted the head on the gurney.

She immediately recoiled from his touch. He waited with anticipation as he watched the internal struggle play out on her face. Levi imagined it wouldn't be easy to turn on your husband, even if the idea was far-fetched.

"It's weird, but I saved it in a Ziploc." She refused to make eye contact. "Is that dumb?"

"No, it's not dumb at all."

The scab on her lip broke open with a slight smile. "Should I tell you where to find it?" She scoffed. "Nevermind. It's probably nothing. Oliver's a good man. He's just made some mistakes lately. That doesn't make him a killer."

Levi fidgeted with his phone. He knew as well as anyone. The smallest piece of evidence could change everything in a case like this. Plus, it could put her mind at ease. Not that Oliver deserved that much.

"I don't know if there's cause for suspicion, but maybe—"

"Do you really think?" she whispered with a crack of her voice.

"I think every possible lead is worth looking into, no matter how small or unlikely it seems." He cleared his throat. "The problem is I can't go in your house without a warrant, which we probably wouldn't get since there's no evidence linking to your husband." He hated calling Oliver that.

"You have my permission."

"It doesn't work that way." He shook his head.

Seven months ago, he made that exact mistake when he responded to a possible domestic dispute. When he arrived on scene to find a severely beaten woman on the front lawn, his heart dropped.

She stated her husband hurt her, but he was nowhere to be found. The house was locked up tight, so Levi asked for her permission to search the property and she said yes. Inside, he found illegal weapons and photographic proof of abuse. Apparently, this guy liked to take pictures of his battered masterpiece.

Months later, the judge threw out every shred of evidence when the defense argued it was an illegal search without a warrant because his client never agreed. Despite the law stating permission from one party is enough, far too many cases just like this one had been thrown out in the last year. Levi wouldn't make that mistake again. Not with Mia.

"Why not?" she questioned.

"There are rules and laws we have to follow."

She painfully grimaced at the thought behind her eyes. "What if I told you I took the trash out this morning before I ended up here?"

"Like outside the house?"

"Yes." She glumly sighed. "It's in the big can outside."

"Is it behind a gate?" Excitement clamored against his chest.

There were about a million potential explanations for the red dirt on her husband's shoes, but Levi played along with a hidden agenda. If Oliver was guilty, it meant Mia would be safe. If her safety cost him everything, it would be worth it.

"No."

"Now that I can do." A smile crooked up on one side.

The corner of her mouth twitched, but she still refused to look in his direction.

A text came through on his phone.

"Sergeant Cole will be here shortly. She'll keep you safe and get your statement."

"Levi?" He turned back to face her. "Be careful," she ominously warned.

"I will. Promise." He smiled, pressing the phone up to his ear. "Sarge, we gotta talk."

Twenty~One

OCCULT SNICKERED AS HE paced around the abandoned barn. These dreadful humans and their pathetic warriors would never put his intricately woven destruction together. That stupid little wife had been successfully removed from the equation. All the puzzle pieces now aligned flawlessly into the trap set.

He was an utter genius.

"Your Darkness?" a voice hissed.

Occult turned to see the demon Beuxis slither toward him. With every slink and coil, his long, thin body crept closer. A viper-like head stretched out its scaly skin. His thin eyes burned blood red.

Beuxis controlled the fortune-tellers, crystal ball gazers, and tarot card readers. He was here to be Occult's eyes and ears since he'd proven useful over the years. Together they spun such flawlessly twisted truths for the Enemy's pathetic humans to devour like a Thanksgiving feast— just like Essie Foster had so long ago.

A sinister smile hung on Occult's thin lips.

It would be moronic to go up against those dreadful imbeciles without a few tricks up his sleeve, and tricks Beuxis was good at.

This time revenge would be theirs.

"What can I do for you, old chum?" His sharp teeth flashed behind curled lips.

"I've seen something you should know about." His forked tongue flashed in and out of his mouth, dragging each 's' out with a hiss.

The look on the serpent's face told him bad news was here to rain on his celebration.

Delight fell from his hideous face. "What makes you brave enough to approach me without permission?" Occult demanded.

No matter how great of a team they made, *he* was worthy of that snake's fear and worship.

Beuxis slithered himself upright, suspended in the air—a ridiculous trick.

"Oh get off it already!" Occult shoved his scaly body. "Shift out of that absurd get-up you've got on," he demanded.

Beuxis coiled himself down into a knot. With a puff of midnight smoke, he shook arms from his sides and stood upright on two legs. He was still lanky and viper-like with a wide, stocky nose and his neck curled into a hook. As it deflated, scales became visible with flecks of yellow decorating the black sheen.

"Better, Your Darkness?" He bowed low before him.

Beuxis always was the loyal servant, humbled in full submission to Occult's dark will. Refusing to be disarmed with flattery, Occult rolled his eyes.

"Get on with it," he growled.

"The girl, she still poses a threat."

"Which girl, you twit?"

"The pastor's wife," Beuxis thinly offered with the slightest hiss still present.

The gangly creature's long, thin talons clicked against the wood floor. His eyes dashed to a group of tools that hung on the wall. He sprinted toward them and was back in front of Occult in seconds.

His slender hand held a large pruning knife. Examination of the gadget showed a serrated edge that delightedly made his eyes dance.

"We could send Ticano to have some fun." Villainous amusement blazed over his face.

Occult stared at the little half-wit, irritated this fool thought he could do better.

Quick and calculated, Occult snatched the traitor up.

Beuxis violently fought for air in the grasp of Occult's huge hand.

He squeezed harder. "Do you find me incompetent?"

Spit flung onto the hypocrite's thin face. Beauxis suffocated on his desperation for air.

Occult clamped tighter.

"What's that? I couldn't hear you." A sinister chuckle growled in his ample chest. "It'll do you good to remember who's in charge around here," Occult cursed in his face.

With a bend of his body, he hurled that snake across the barn.

Beuxis tumbled across the weeds surrounding the forgotten structure until he abruptly slammed into a large tree trunk.

That idiot officially ruined Occult's celebration. Smoke billowed from his flared nostrils. If that shamelessly foolish girl didn't back off, he would make her regret ever being born.

———⊶✕⊷———

Just as he lost all hope in his lawyer, the door slowly opened. There stood a tall, well-dressed man. His young face raised concern in Oliver's gut. This man-child was not his lawyer.

"Mr. Hughes?" he firmly questioned.

"Who's asking?" Oliver commanded.

"My name's Adam Cohen, sir." He stepped into the room and closed the door behind him. An outstretched hand held toward Oliver, but he didn't move. "Mr. Malloy sent me to get you out of here."

Oliver smiled, now willing to give a quick shake of his hand. "I'm glad you're here. Am I free to leave?" Oliver clasped his hands together with child-like hope.

"Almost. I'm heading out to speak with Detective, uh…" He looked down at his notepad. "Walsh. I'll be right back."

He huffed in frustration as Adam left.

The kid was confident, assertive, and strong, Oliver could sense it. Something familiar in the way he carried himself appealed to Oliver. Maybe he was a Christian too. Whatever it was, Oliver somehow knew he was in good hands.

He sat in the chair as he waited, jackhammering his leg up and down, and then paced the room. This was taking too long. Something must be wrong.

The sound of muffled voices outside the door perked him upright. A rumble of laughter broke out. Oliver immediately took back everything he thought earlier. This kid was in over his head.

The door swung open wide. "Mr. Hughes." Adam smiled. Oliver rose to his feet with a prayer of hope in his chest. "You're free to go."

145

"Seriously?" The word came out weaker than intended. He did it. This kid really did it.

"Yes. These detectives won't detain you again without probable cause." Adam wickedly smiled at the two detectives who stood in the hallway. Both men glared back, and Maltez puffed up his chest. "You ready?" Adam looked back at Oliver.

He scoffed, "More than you know. Let's get out of here."

Within a few quick moments, his things were gathered. He walked down the hall with the young man and his fancy briefcase.

"I don't know how to thank you." Oliver beamed. "I thought they'd never let me leave."

Oliver left Adam to chase after him when he turned left down the hall.

"Mr. Hughes, where are you going?"

"I'm going to see my wife," he hollered out.

The footsteps behind him picked up their pace until they traipsed alongside him, quickly cutting him off.

"You can't."

Oliver abruptly stopped with a scowl. "How about you don't tell me what to do, 'k, sport?" He tried to go by him, but Adam mirrored every move. "Get out of my way." The vein on Oliver's forehead throbbed. He would see his wife, and no one would stop him. "Move!" he barked.

"You don't understand. I can't do that, sir." Adam put both hands out in front of him, and his shaky voice turned sultry. "Listen, they've placed a temporary restraining order on you that's in effect for the next seventy-two hours. If you violate the order, they will arrest you, no questions asked. And if that happens, there won't be much I can do to help you."

The tension between them dissipated. With calculated breaths, Oliver tried to calm down. He had to get to her somehow before they brainwashed her to turn on him. Mia was weak.

"I have to see her, just for five, ten minutes, max. Please," he negotiated.

"I'm sorry, Mr. Hughes. It was the only way they agreed to release you."

"This is ridiculous."

Adam finally put his hands down. "Legally they can detain you for forty-eight hours without charging you. I figured it was most important to get you out of there, even if it meant we had to play their game." Adam slowly moved forward, his voice a gentle hum. "Besides, don't you think it's probably a good idea to leave Mia alone right now? If you push too hard, it could be detrimental to everything you've built. Let the Lord handle things from here, Ollie." His lips curled with a flash of darkness in his eyes. "Go home."

The air turned soft as a calm trance tightly wrapped around Oliver. "Good idea." The words softly fell from his lips. "Thank you."

"You're welcome," he offered with a pat on his back. "Get some rest, and Malloy will call you as soon as he can."

Like putty, Oliver easily surrendered to Adam's will.

⊙—✕—⊙

A mild tremble came from the young man as Hexiathan separated himself from Adam. The kid was a gracious host for the demon to ravage. Loneliness forces humans to look for companionship in the strangest of places.

One bushy eyebrow cocked itself higher than the other. "Brilliant." Hexiathan snickered in his pretentious accent. "Time to have some fun with that one."

Adam stood dazed. "How did I get here?" he wondered aloud.

"Your job here is done, mate. Go on home now," he whispered in Adam's ear. "It's my turn."

Hexiathan hauntingly stalked after Oliver, ready to inflict the damage he'd been instructed to do. What an honor it was to twist the minds of these puffed-out humans for the great Beli-yaal himself.

⊙—✕—⊙

Every street lamp shone bright into the cloak of night. Each house was also dressed with its own set of lights, leaving only a few thinly veiled places to hide. So much for the plan to lurk unseen. Parked several houses down from Mia's, Levi idled in his truck. He nervously tapped his fingers against the steering wheel, in need of a new plan.

A quiet opening of his door made way to slink from the driver's seat. On second thought, it was probably best to act like he belonged here to not raise suspicion. He stood tall and owned his presence.

A shivered breath vibrated through him as goosebumps collected down his arms. He should've grabbed his jacket.

On high alert, his eyes continued surveillance between each delicate stride. It was late enough most people would be asleep, but those still awake would certainly remember him.

Mia's house came into view on the right. A lean shadow ran along the fence line. He spotted the glean of a bright blue trashcan next to the house.

Showtime.

His heart beat loudly against his chest as he cautiously darted into the shadow. This was an awful idea. He didn't want to think about what Oliver would do to him or Mia if he caught him there snooping through the trash, no matter how legal it was.

The house appeared dark. The bottom line was, Mia needed him, and he refused to fail her again.

He came to a halt, a statue of his former self. His mind raced with every heaved breath.

Cautiously he moved toward the house. Mia said the bag should be close to the top. He pulled a small flashlight from his pocket and opened the lid. The flashlight morphed into a spotlight as it reflected off the sides of the can and the moisture in the air.

So much for discretion.

With bare hands, he moved the garbage around. Gloves would have been a great idea, but it was too late for all that now. He found an old newspaper and used it to push aside the used coffee grounds, egg shells, and some unknown slimy stuff that smelled rotten. Under a slew of paper towels, he saw the corner of a sandwich bag. Hunched over, he reached further until his fingertips grazed its green edge.

Of course, it was just out of reach.

A flash on the fence startled Levi. A car. With a flick of a button, he turned his flashlight off. Frozen in time, his skin instantly became slick with sweat. The vehicle pulled into the driveway. His breath held firmly in his chest as he carefully lowered the lid, hyperfocused on not letting it slip from his hand.

Tactfully, he moved along the wall, into the shadows. His mind sharpened, fully aware of the danger ahead.

At the corner, he noted the backend of the same SUV Mia got into at the store.

Oliver.

Instinctively, he reached for his duty weapon, but it wasn't there. His lack of preparedness was insulting. If his old platoon could see him now, he'd be ridiculed until the end of time.

Rational thoughts apparently didn't exist when it came to Mia.

Oliver stepped out of the car, taller than Levi remembered.

Expectant, his palms faced each other with his hands open, ready for the fight of his life. Rapid sharp breaths came from steady lips. Levi hunched on the balls of his feet, ready to lunge. Adrenaline raged through him.

The car door closed, and without a second look, Oliver walked into the house.

—✕—

Hexiathan followed close behind Oliver, along with the ruthlessly violent demon, Ticano, at his side like a loyal dog. Hexiathan surveyed the area. Those blasted posers were close.

Ticano nudged Hexiathan with an inaudible grunt.

"You feel that too?" he quietly asked.

The hideous monster grunted with a nod.

"The Heavenly Host," Hexiathan snarled.

This moron wallowed over that wretched wife of his, unwilling to listen to the threat at hand. Hexiathan didn't regret much, but he failed when he called Ticano off. He should have let him beat her to death. The boundaries placed by the Enemy were pure rubbish anyway. What's life if you can't color outside of the golden lines? Besides, if she were dead, those dreadful beings wouldn't be here.

Tears welled in Oliver's eyes. Why he loved that ridiculous little girl was beyond Hexiathan. This absurdity went on long enough.

"What was that?" he sharply whispered in his ear.

A faint clatter came from outside. Oliver looked behind him at the back door.

"Those dreadful raccoons are back. This time, they die," Hexiathan urged.

Oliver balled his fists and clenched his jaw. He grabbed his bat from the closet and stalked toward the door.

—✕—

It was now or never.

Levi flipped his body halfway inside the trash can. He reached with all he had. The very tip of the bag brushed his fingers. Miraculously, he pulled it out.

With his feet back on the ground, he closely examined the bag. Red clay dirt. This was it.

Light poured into the shrouded cove against the house. With wide eyes, Levi quickly closed the lid, but his body became cemented in place as Oliver came into view through the bay window at the sink.

Levi held his breath. He took note of the wooden bat in Oliver's hand.

Unable to move, he hoped to become invisible, like a child caught with his hand in the rotten cookie jar. It wasn't the best plan, but it was the only one he had.

⌐×¬

The devilish pair hid inside Oliver. The idiots of Heaven didn't need to know they were here yet. Oliver was their pet. He did whatever they told or forced him to do, and they wouldn't give him up without a fight.

Hexiathan peered through Oliver's eyes and saw absolutely nothing. He forced Oliver on his tiptoes to see if something was crouched down under the window. Nothing.

"Come out, come out, wherever you are," Hexiathan mumbled under Oliver's breath.

⌐×¬

Oliver stepped toward the sink. He scanned the area as he filled a glass with water from the faucet. Levi's breath shook. In his hand was evidence that might link this monster to multiple murders. He should have shoved it in his pocket and dodged out of sight, but he couldn't move. Something held him suspended in time.

Oliver drank the entire glass of water and simply walked away.

A sigh of relief pushed past his clenched lips. There was only one explanation. The Lord must've protected him somehow.

Relief was short-lived when a dark figure pulled himself from Oliver's back. Its wide jagged mouth and needle-point teeth were tightly crammed together. Noxious saliva dripped from its mouth. With wide fiery red eyes, it slowly scanned the area.

———————— o•X•o ————————

Axum stood tall and mighty between Levi and the evil creature. He didn't recognize the demon, but that didn't matter. The Lord's Glory burned through his deep brown eyes locked on the devil.

It screeched out, unknown if it was in pain or calling for reinforcements. Perhaps both.

A tall, distinguished being stepped out from behind the creature. Its allure tantalized the senses. A virulent grin curled, amusement held in his sultry red eyes.

Axum shielded Levi with his body. "Go now. Quickly and quietly," he commanded the man. He looked at Maleek, another warrior. "Go with him, and make sure he makes it back to her."

A brief nod came from Maleek as Levi scurried through the darkness.

Axum turned back and boldly stared at the demon. "Hexiathan," he grunted.

"Axum, it's been a while." Hexiathan cracked his knuckles. "All alone, are we?"

The angelic warrior pulled his sword from its sheath. "The Lord is always with me."

"Oh yes, the Incompetent Fool you all insist on following around. Tsk. Aren't you tired of being his lap dog?"

"Twisted truth may dazzle others, but it won't work on me. I've knelt before the throne of God Himself. Nothing will ever make me deny Him." Axum held steadfast.

"Have it your way, Lap Dog." Hexiathan's sinister chuckle echoed out as he slowly walked away. "Let's go, Ticano." A devilish smile curled when he looked back at Axum. "See ya soon." He winked.

It was no fluke this vile creature was here. His presence would inhibit the humans from staying upright. It was imperative for those being tempered for battle to keep their eyes on the Lord, and the prayer warriors fervently on their knees. Without that, this battle could be easily lost.

Twenty-Two

TIME MOVED LIKE MOLASSES since the alert went out. In the last thirty minutes alone, Jocelyn successfully ruined her latest manicure. At least this one held strong for two days longer than the last. Waiting for someone, anyone to call with a possible lead, was pure torture.

A low hum filled the air. Her team worked tirelessly through the boxes of evidence. Other detectives worked their cases, made phone calls, and presumably found leads—salt in an open wound. There had to be something more they could do.

She pushed through the looming exhaustion to devise an alternative plan, each one undeniably worse than the last. Charlotte's coffee order wouldn't tell them who took her or why.

Drained, she rubbed her temples. Charlotte's life was literally in her hands. A heavy burden to bear.

With quick fingers, she dialed a number.

"Lab," an exhausted voice answered.

"Crumb?" Jocelyn asked.

"Speaking," Dan Crumb, head of the lab, answered with a hint of irritation. "What can I help you with?"

"It's Detective Maddox. Any new development on your end?" She rapidly tapped the end of her pen against the small stack of files before her.

"Nothing yet, detective. We'll let you know if that changes." He abruptly hung up the phone.

Offended, Jocelyn scoffed at his rudeness and slammed the receiver down. They were all tired. No excuse for being a jerk.

The files in front of her were opened for the millionth time. She probed for something, anything to stand out.

The burn of fatigue intensified in her eyes. Her choice of shoe was a terrible idea. Kicking off the heeled boots, she rubbed her aching feet. Opening the bottom drawer of her desk, she pulled out a pair of sneakers. The memory foam liners felt like heaven.

If a new lead wasn't found soon, they would officially be dead in the water. Charlotte's body would be found mutilated and her face would haunt the darkness behind Jocelyn's eyes forever.

It would undoubtedly besiege her career. This failure would hover over countless victims to come, fueling the fear of worthlessness within. After all, she couldn't bring justice to Gabby. How did she expect to bring it for these girls?

Picture after picture, crime scene after crime scene, she flipped through them all. In each file, she stopped on the altar rocks and slowly examined the jagged edges, color, and stacking pattern. She imagined how the texture of each rock would feel on the palm of her hand.

For every case, multiple pictures were taken of the altar. Each one, a perfect replica of the one before. The close-ups showed each rock at as many angles as possible—dozens of pictures.

Jocelyn intently stared, unable to tear her focus away. The more she looked, the harder the pull. The answer was here. She just couldn't see it.

Starting over, she went back through just the altar photos, slower this time. She stopped at Jane Harlow, victim number three. With a magnifying glass from her desk, she examined the pictures closer. Something was on the side of these stones.

Her head moved to catch different angles of the clumps. Maybe it was just dirt. She wrote Harlow on a bright pink Post-it and stuck it to the photo. Jocelyn tumbled through each file and found similar black clumps on each altar. It had to mean something.

The victim's names were stuck on the photos with color-coded notes. After the last file, she headed to the lab, pictures in hand. She hated to admit it, but AJ was her best-sounding board.

⸺⸻✕⸻⸺

Ashanti's armor hugged her lean, athletic curves. The bronze on her chest complemented her deep-colored skin. She knelt beside the girl, a hand gently on her back. Charlotte's fever radiated against Ashanti's palm.

"Almighty, this isn't good," she prayed to the One in charge.

Trust Me, mighty warrior. I Am in control, He whispered to her heart.

"Finn needs to know." She stood, her deep brown eyes set on the sky.

Kano is there now.

Ashanti looked back at the girl. Her dry, cracked lips stained a reddish brown from the dirt. Countless tears carved paths down the grime on her cheeks. Strands of blonde hair stuck to her sweaty, pale face. She violently shivered with infirmity.

"What do I do?"

Built for battle, Ashanti found the softer side of war foreign and unfamiliar.

Remind her she's not alone, the Lord spoke. *She must know Heaven is here with her.*

"Yes, sir."

Uncertainty twisted in her gut. Kano was better at this stuff.

Ashanti, I created you. You can do this, the Lord encouraged the hesitant warrior.

With a slow exhale, the fierce combatant softened her stance. She reflected on her time as a young warrior. The Savior was soft and gentle—a soothing balm of comfort after her first battle against the darkness. His words carried her through countless battles and shaped her into a true warrior.

Ashanti placed a hand on Charlotte's back. Her ashen face held wide eyes.

"Wh-who are—" Charlotte coughed uncontrollably. "Is this real?"

"Yes, Charlotte. This is real. My name is Ashanti, and I've been specially selected to protect you."

"Why?" Her voice was hoarse. "Aren't I a lost cause at this point?"

"No, Charlotte, you were never a lost cause. Don't you see that?"

"See what?"

Ashanti sighed. This wasn't going well.

The Lord reminded her of the words from oh, so long ago.

"I'm going to tell you something that was said to me when I questioned my role in the Kingdom." Her accent carried a heavy British sound. "I came back from my first battle and I was terrified. Demons were nothing like I expected. Despite my extensive training, nothing ever really prepares you for battle."

Charlotte struggled to stay awake. She had to talk fast.

"Jesus met me at the gate as I came home. He already knew how I felt, but He asked me anyway. I cried and spilled everything right there in front of the Savior of all the universe. I was embarrassed and feared I would be reassigned or worse, kicked out."

Ashanti nudged Charlotte to make sure she was awake.

"But instead, He said: Ashanti, remember His roar is mightier than *any* weapon of darkness, but even so, He knew the Heavens needed you. Humanity needs you, Charlotte. You're not here by accident. You were brought into existence by Divine purpose." Ashanti smiled. "Jesus has a way of reminding us who we actually are, and it's always beyond what we think. You're more than a victim of evil. You're the daughter of the King, Charlotte, and He will never leave you nor forsake you. Rest in that."

Charlotte faintly smiled with heavy eyes. "He really loves me that much?"

"Yes, He always has. There's nothing you could do that would make Him love you less. He has plans for you, Charlotte, and they're good. Trust in Him."

"But Jesus said people have free will."

"Yes, but don't count God out just yet. He parted the Red Sea when all hope seemed lost, and He can do that again for you. Don't lose faith, and don't stop praying," Ashanti urged.

"I won't," Charlotte whispered as she passed out.

Ashanti lightly brushed the hair from her dirty, damp face.

"Keep your eyes on Him," she whispered.

Upright, she regained a warrior stance, ready to protect this fragile life at all costs.

———————— ⚊✕⚊ ————————

Mia surged through a cycle of nervous habits. Her nails were basically non-existent at this point. She chewed on the knob of her inner cheek and switched back and forth between tapping her feet and fingers. Beli-yaal's plan was working. It's good to know Hexiathan could be trusted to do what was asked.

Mia scoffed. Her nervousness visibly transformed into anger. Beli-yaal pumped wickedly designed lies into her mind, and she easily accepted them as truth. Oliver had been the perfect patsy to tear her down to the stubs.

A howl of amusement gathered in his chest.

He circled her like a shark with blood in the water, a hemorrhage of disgrace.

Suddenly, a tinge of fear ripped through him. He whipped around to scan the area, a gasp hung in the back of his throat. The Heavenly Host were near. He quickly vanished into thin air.

⊲⊷✕⊶⊳

A silent trickle of heartache tumbled down her swollen cheek. Another mistake cut at her. She was an idiot for ever trusting Levi. All he did was let her down. He was supposed to be her friend, and she betrayed her husband because of that. He'd played her like a fool.

The love she harbored was wrong, and this was her plague, her retribution for what she had become. Cheaters don't get happy endings.

"Father, I'm so sorry." She sniffled, unable to say anything else.

The metal rings on the curtain loudly scraped as it opened. There stood a blurry Levi through the shame gathered in her eyes.

"I got it," he huffed, out of breath, and rushed to her side. "What's wrong?"

"I can't do this," her voice trembled. "I'm married."

"M, I'm sorry, but I don't understand." His eyes fixated on her.

She stared straight ahead at nothing. A shard of guilt ripped through her stomach.

"Please, just go."

"What did I do wrong here?" His voice strained.

This would hurt him, but it had to be done. Betrayal hung in the air like a foul stench.

You aren't ready. Prepare yourself. They're coming. The warning rang so loud, her teeth rattled.

"I'm sorry," she sobbed, not wanting to do this without him. "I feel like I'm losing my mind."

Hunched over, she released a grunt of pain.

Levi's arms quickly wrapped around her. "I'm right here. You're okay."

The warning was clear. Something was headed for her, and if she wasn't careful, it would win. The weight of it, unshakeable. It was imperative to be ready for whatever came—lives depended on it.

Twenty-Three

FINN KEENLY LISTENED TO Kano. Time was running out. He was sent to lead the troops to battle, but the outcome was fully in the Lord's hands. The hope was for Charlotte to live a long and prosperous life. Peace remained intact because the burden of life and death would never fall on Finn's shoulders.

"So, what's the plan?" Kano pressed.

"Stay the course in what I've assigned to you. It's our job to focus on the task at hand," Finn rigidly commanded. "Head back to Ashanti, and *stay* with the girl."

Kano softly nodded her head in agreement as he noted the pain in her narrow eyes. Being a warrior in God's army wasn't easy. He wanted to comfort her in some way, but he had to keep a level head, for all their sakes.

In a shimmer of light, Kano raced out of the forgotten room in the hospital. Finn gazed upon the group of warriors. He had a plan, but they wouldn't like it.

In the corner, Viveka rested her unmatched physique against the cold, damp cinderblock wall. Her eyes zeroed in on his, unwavering in her stance. Finn gave her a quick smile and wondered if she trusted him enough to follow his plan. She was always quick to question him, and for this to work, she would need to be all in.

"Kaf." Finn broke eye contact with Viveka. "I need a different face to look in on Mia. Be on the lookout for Beli-yaal. He's still here, I can feel him."

"You got it." Kafziel enthusiastically beamed. He turned to take off.

"Whoa, there." Finn grabbed his arm. This kid was always in such a hurry, which would undoubtedly be his undoing against a demon like Beli-yaal. "Slow and steady is the name of the game. Your speed will hinder more than it helps with this task. Be sure to keep your head a swivelin' at all times. Beli-yaal cannot know we're here yet. Your main objective is to remind Mia of her value. Encourage her. Give her the strength to keep going." Finn placed his hand on Kafziel's shoulder. "May the Lord keep you safe."

With a nod of his head, Kafziel closed his eyes and shifted from mighty warrior to lowly phlebotomist ready to draw Mia's blood. His full-bodied curls were now straight, making his hair long enough to tuck behind his ears. His golden eyes toned down to a dirty hazel and his bronze dusted skin grew a few shades darker. A smooth transition for a young warrior.

Finn knelt beside him. "You ready?"

"For His glory." Kafziel placed a fist over his heart.

"Indeed, for His glory."

—◦✕◦—

"I have to tell you something." His voice unsteady, Levi pulled the bag from his pocket and held it up. "I got the dirt sample." Mia looked up at him with heartache in her eyes. "But, there's more. I came face to face with evil tonight."

"What do you mean?"

Levi explained in great detail what happened. He watched an unfamiliar emotion blend with concern on her face.

"What are you wrestling with?"

"Who says I'm wrestling with anything?" she defensively responded.

Mia might hate to admit it, but he knew her better than anyone. Her tells were all there, so he pushed harder.

"Your tone for one, two, your nails are no longer there, and three, you weren't exactly shocked when I told you about the demons. Care to share with the class?"

"It's nothing."

"M, I'm here for you, but I can't help if you don't let me."

"It's just a dream I had the last time they knocked me out." Her voice fell to a whisper as she hesitantly told him about the little girl with the oversized armor. "That little girl is me, but I don't understand why Hell is coming after me like this."

"M." Levi placed his hand on hers, holding it longer this time before she pulled away. "You're special. There's always been something about you that was radiant and powerful. I didn't understand when we were kids, but I see it so clearly now. The Lord has a huge calling on your life, an anointing Satan fears. You matter. *You* are what they're after."

"I couldn't agree more." A silky voice wafted through the room. A lab tech stood with his cart full of equipment. "You don't know me, but the Lord has given me the gift to see people in such a magnificent way."

Levi should've questioned this intrusion, but a peace blanketed the room.

"You have no idea just how valuable to the Kingdom you are. Honestly, I didn't realize it either until I saw you. It's so bright." He smiled with wonderment. "The preparation you need isn't physical."

"How'd you—"

The tech held up his hand to stop the interruption as he stepped forward. "It's not important. You need to realign your posture to the Lord. By the enemy's design, you've been demolished, and it seems impossible to stand, but that's a lie you must stop believing.

"Seek the Lord your God with all your heart and watch Him deliver you from this evil. He is your Refuge and your Strength. Peace abundantly flows from Him. He loves you, Mia, more than you know, and He created you for such a time as this. Don't shy away from the fear, but lean into the Lord for strength to stand in spite of it."

The tech reached out and touched her arm. Mia didn't pull away nor did her face twist with recoil. Instead, she stared deep into his eyes, tantalized by his profound and precise words.

"Remember, God belongs to you, but you also belong to Him. You *must* discover who you are in Him. You're more powerful than you realize." With a smile, he turned to walk away.

"Wait," Levi blurted out as he stood up. "We don't even know your name."

"It's not important. She is. Focus on her. Nothing can stand against you, Mia, for Victory has already been given through the sacrifice of Christ."

Their mouths both hung open, unable to move as he left the room. After a few moments, Levi shoved his hands into his pockets and felt the bag of evidence. Pulling it out, he examined the red dust.

"As much as I'd love to unpack all of that, we need to tell someone about this," he firmly stated, holding up the bag.

Tears smoothly dragged down her cheeks. She looked off in the distance with her jaw still slightly open.

"M?" he politely asked with a hand on her shoulder.

She cleared her throat. "Yes, uh, sorry, I just..." Her voice trailed off.

"What he said was powerful, and it's absolutely true." Her gaze was met with a brief smile. "The Lord has an incredible plan for your life."

"Call whoever you need, and get that dirt to the right people," she ordered, her voice stronger than before.

—✕—

Kafziel urgently walked down the busy hall and away from Mia's room. His eyes continuously surveyed the area. The message had been delivered, and now it was time to get out of there before Beli-yaal found him.

Just as the thought crossed his mind, like a summons to Hell, Kafziel stopped dead in his tracks. The beast and his deadly force were still unseen, but he felt the heaviness of its hate.

Goosebumps formed on his skin as a rush of wickedness circulated. In human form, a fear of inadequacy prevailed within him. There were too many people around to morph out of existence. Several closed doors lined the hall, occupancy unknown.

Blood coursed through his veins. The sharp smell of disinfectant and Jell-O tickled his nose. His fists clenched at his sides.

A blue bathroom sign stood out on the corner. *Lord, make a way,* he prayed.

Quick, calculated moves kept the attention off him. A breath hiccupped in his chest, all focus locked on the goal.

Someone rushed out from behind a closed door.

"Code blue!" an older woman in heart scrubs announced.

With quick feet, Kafziel side-stepped and spun around the woman, barely missing her. A herd of sneakers barreled down the hall behind him to lend a hand to the unresponsive patient.

In the privacy of the bathroom, an invisible threat encompassed Kafziel's neck. The young warrior instantly left this realm and reclaimed his place in God's army.

A dark figure came into view and filled the tiny one-person bathroom, its talons the length of his chest. He gasped for air against its hold.

"Where's that weasel you call Captain?" the demon seethed.

Bursts of putrid, sulfuric breath came from its mouth like an antique train.

"I don't know—" Kafziel strained.

 Enough of this.

Agility was his strength, and it was time to use it. His fist swiftly thrust against the creature's ribs, pushing the devil back enough to move.

A wail of agony released as a talon tore through the skin on his right shoulder. His cool hand against the wound helped to ease the unbearable smolder.

The ailment brought forth a renewal of his strength. Darkness would not win.

Metal ripped against metal as he unsheathed his sword. It flashed with brilliant illumination, like lightning against a dark sky. The demon rapidly recoiled. Its jowls opened wide to reveal its narrow teeth with a moan.

The light dissipated, and Beli-yaal rose.

"You puny little boy. What do you think you can do?" Darkness snickered.

Kafziel ignored him. There were more important things to take care of.

Your Majesty, tell Finn what happened here. I'll bait and switch him. It's an honor to serve Your Holiness, and it will be my virtue to sacrifice my well-being for You. Praise be to the King of all kings, and may Your Strength and Wisdom be with me now. For Your Kingdom, may Your will be done on Earth as it is in Heaven.

Kafziel blocked its venomous, razor-sharp strike with his sword and delivered an uppercut with his free hand.

Darkness bore down with a strength he didn't know existed. With both hands on his sword, his knees buckled under the weight.

He quickly dipped low into a squat and burst upward, a reminder of his best trait. The creature stumbled to regain its footing.

"Finn, I'm coming in hot. Be ready!" Kafziel yelled.

He tore through the building like a shooting star, a golden map for the beast to follow.

——————o—✕—o——————

"What do you mean we've hit a dead end?" Jocelyn scoffed.

AJ pointed to the papers in Jocelyn's hands. "The dirt took us as far as it can go. The alert you put out is as narrow as I can get it."

"Did you even look at the stones? There's something there, I just know it," she pushed.

"I told you before, those were arthropods on the stones. We collected the region from them and I have people going through the stones of the earlier victims now, but that'll take time—time we don't have."

Jocelyn's drawn-out grunt of disapproval pained her throat. This couldn't be the end. There must be something that could lead them to Charlotte.

AJ walked over and softly placed his hand on her shoulder. "Just because we've hit a snag doesn't mean it's over."

She tried to fight the anger-filled tears, but a few betrayed her. She quickly wiped them from her cheek, drawing in a deep breath.

"Do you have any other ideas?" Her words were barely audible.

He sighed. "I'm sorry."

Without another word, Jocelyn turned and walked out of the lab with her head hung low. This was it. Failure, her bitter companion. A miracle her only hope.

Please, God. Please.

The high-pitched ring from her pocket made her jump. Moving faster than her tired brain could function, she fumbled the phone to the floor. She let out a curse under her breath.

"Maddox," she finally answered.

"Joce, it's Boscereli. We're finishing up with the K-nines. We haven't found anything out here. I just wanted to let you know and check in for our next assignment."

Her excitement faded into the stillness around her. "I'm open to any ideas."

"Sorry, Maddox, my team's got nothing. We can go back and retrace the steps of the abduction." His slight New England accent was a rare gem in the South.

It was as good of an idea as any at this point. "That would be great. Take a K-nine with you," she absentmindedly stated.

"Listen, this isn't your fault, Joce. It happens. We can only take things as far as the evidence leads us, and we don't get to choose what that is. This isn't some cop show where everything works out in the end. Reality doesn't always get tied up in a pretty little bow."

In the six months she got to know Boscereli, he always knew just what to say.

"Thanks, Bos."

"Of course. We'll head out and let you know if we find anything else."

She hung up and waited at the elevators for her ride to come. Disappointment ravaged and clouded her thoughts. The stench of defeat clung to her every move.

Her phone called out once again. Expressionless, she lazily answered. "Maddox."

"Detective Maddox, I've been trying to reach you."

The elevator dinged and the doors opened. Jocelyn leisurely walked in. "Well, ya got me. What can I do for you?"

"This is Annie, from dispatch." The doors slowly drifted together. "You got a possible suspect from your alert."

Jocelyn slammed her hand between the almost closed doors. "Tell me more."

Within minutes, her sensible shoes thudded against the linoleum floor as she ran back down the hallway toward the lab.

The miracle they needed came, just in the nick of time.

Her body slammed into the lab door. "We've got a lead," she huffed.

⸺⸺⸺⸺⸺⸺⸺✕⸺⸺⸺⸺⸺⸺⸺

This speedy little imbecile thought he could trick the great Beli-yaal so easily? It would take a much bigger con to beat him. He was too big, too grand, too wicked for these naive ideas.

Such child's play.

Beli-yaal snickered, a sinister grin on his thin lips. "That's it, keep going."

⸺⸺⸺⸺⸺⸺⸺✕⸺⸺⸺⸺⸺⸺⸺

Kafziel underestimated the vile thing quick on his tail. He foolishly thought this would be easy. Luckily, the young warrior still held a few tricks up his untattered sleeves.

He bobbed, the demon weaved, and pushed him onto a new flight plan. His mind raced for a way to regain control.

Over the top of the big beautiful trees, he banked left at ninety degrees. Wherever this demon drove him, he wasn't about to go.

Kafziel weaved in and out of the trees, trying to shake his assailant, but every time he looked back, darkness remained right on his heels. He dipped low into the trees, hoping to lose him.

⊙—✕—⊙

"That's it." He grinned. "Hold," Beli-yaal ordered as he flew after the little snowflake. Excitement rustled in the trees. "Get ready," he growled.

The man-child was pleasantly distracted. This would be fun.

"Now!" he roared out.

A wall of darkness filled in the forest, fully enclosing them. Fear spread wide on that little twit's face, bringing a chuckle past Beli-yaal's lips.

⊙—✕—⊙

Kafziel made a catastrophic mistake by underestimating his adversary. The lengths it would go to take out just one of the Heavenly Hosts terrified him, but there was no turning back now.

"For God's glory," he yelled as he crashed sword first into the battle.

He zipped through the barricade of demons, rapidly slashing his sword in all directions. A ball of light flickered as he thrust his weapon through the air, banishing as many as possible.

Passing through again, he caught the puffs of ash that left a bitter taste on his tongue.

He regained confidence with every new flurry of expulsion.

Something the size of a mack-truck rammed the side of Kafziel. His body flailed through the air, reaching out for anything to save him. Everything blurred.

The ground shook as the mighty warrior hit, tumbling across a clearing among the trees.

His body was battered and bruised. He pushed to remain conscious, but the pull was too great. He gave everything he had to this fight, but it wasn't enough.

—⊶×⊷—

A low manic chuckle pushed out of Beli-yaal's chest as he crept toward the limp being. If he played fair, he wouldn't be Hell's favorite.

"Time to die." He smiled, standing over Kafziel's lifeless body. Razor sharp blades flashed from the underside of his talons held high above him. "Amateur."

Twenty~Four

THIS PATHETIC MORTAL WAS a puppet on strings with Hexiathan as his master. There was honor in being a lowly player in this cryptic game, but then again, humility never was his strong suit. He was far more valuable than most. No other creature in all of Hell could twist that Knob's truth like Hexiathan, and this plan hinged on his slimy ability to corrupt.

Humans were convinced their perception of what was happening around them was, in fact, true. The "My Truth" and "Make Love, Not War" movements were brilliantly crafted by him. Many of his plans allowed a lustful spirit to hook its claws into so many unsuspecting patrons.

Hexiathan prided himself on manipulating the foundational truths in that wretched Book the Enemy created. It was easily contorted with just the right flare of fleshly desires to make it believable. These ridiculous creations were so naive—just make it look helpful and viola, accepted.

Hexiathan yearned to face the strong ones. They gave him a good challenge and pushed him to find new and creative ways to do his dirty work. The success rate was much lower with those blokes, but when it worked, there was nothing better than watching the perceived mighty fall, just like Oliver. The poor intolerable plank of a man never stood a chance.

A wicked smile reached across his face as he stood over the top of Oliver. He was such a buzzkill at first, totally sold out to that daft Son of God. That, of course, was until just the right tale was woven. All it took was one brief pause, one moment that opened the door for Hexiathan's talons to sink deep.

It was quite literally downhill from there, as they say. A low chuckle rested in his throat.

"You need to find a way to shut Mia up," he whispered as Ticano's forked tongue flashed. "If she talks, you'll be ruined, and we can't have that."

Oliver impassively sat on the couch in the dimly lit room, a vacant stare on his face. Hexiathan knew that look well. Mia needed to be stopped, and his puppet was finally ready to do what needed to be done.

"You know who to call." Hexiathan's sultry voice was smooth like butter, leading Oliver to all the places Hell needed him to go.

⸺✕⸺

"Here." AJ handed Jocelyn a hot cup of coffee in a to-go cup from the station break room. "I have a feeling it's going to be a long night, College." He smiled as they grabbed their overnight bags and made their way to Jocelyn's unmarked police vehicle.

He was being oddly sweet, despite the nickname that seemed to have stuck. Looking at him out of her peripheral, she realized she never noticed before how richly brown his eyes were. She also took note of his full lips and that stupid crooked smile. Her attention snapped forward and she blamed her lapse in judgment on the looming exhaustion.

"Want me to drive first so you can rest?" AJ offered.

Jocelyn shook her head. "I'm way to wound up to sleep."

"You do know that if we don't find Miss Scott in time, it's not your fault, right?"

She opened the trunk, and they tossed their bags and AJ's forensic kits inside.

"Wasn't it you who told me I was going on a wild goose chase and wasting my time?" She closed the trunk and looked at him.

"That I did, but what do I know? I can be a jerk sometimes."

There was that darn crooked smile. So charming she wanted to slap it off his face.

"No argument here." She huffed a laugh to break the tension.

They got in the car and when it growled to life, AJ connected his phone to the radio. He fumbled through his playlist as she pulled out of the station, heading toward I-85 south. It would take about four hours—

only because Jocelyn intended on speeding the whole way there—to get to Regional Memorial Hospital in Knoxville, Tennessee. There they would speak with a woman who turned in some red dirt she collected off her husband's shoes.

Jocelyn considered the impossible situation and the potential danger this woman was in. Jocelyn begged Captain Woods for a flight so they could maybe catch a nap on the way, but driving was much cheaper and would take the same amount of time.

The beat of the song AJ chose was a familiar one. Jocelyn broke her somber thoughts with a chuckle.

"Seriously?" She laughed.

"I've had it stuck in my head since you were humming it in the lab."

He busted a few dance moves as they both rapped every word of "Can't Touch This" by M.C. Hammer.

"So, how are you feeling about this lead?" AJ casually asked, turning down the music when the song ended.

"Honestly, I don't know. But I do know it came from a cop in that area, so I'd say chances are in our favor. A cop isn't going to just submit a possible lead without actual cause. Plus, everything gets filtered out by each department, and this is the only nibble we've had. So, at this point, I'm just hoping it's connected in some way, shape, or form."

"That's a rather cynical outlook, don't you think?"

With a scowl, her eyes sharply darted in his direction. "How else am I supposed to look at it?"

He could be the absolute worst. If she could have gone to Knoxville without him, she would, but she needed his expertise. She must have gone temporarily insane to think, even for a moment, he was attractive. It drove her crazy when he forced his opinion on her like he was superior or something.

"Whoa, now." He put his free hand up. "I didn't mean you were wrong, but it just sounds like you've lost hope."

"Well, that's probably because I have."

She gripped the steering wheel harder and looked forward, picking up speed on the seemingly forgotten interstate. She turned the music back up.

"Joce, hold on." AJ turned the radio off. "I didn't mean to make you mad." He lightly pushed on her arm, but she pulled it away. "Look, I'm sorry."

Her glare was met with genuine sincerity in his eyes. Darn, those chocolate eyes. She looked back at the road. *Rise above,* Abigail's words echoed in her mind.

"Don't lose hope, Joce. It's what keeps everyone going, and if you lose it, it will spread like wildfire throughout your team."

No part of her wanted to admit it, but he was right.

"You"—she drug out the words, pausing between each one—"may have a point."

AJ looked around. "We never ate dinner, so how about you pull into that twenty-four-hour burger joint up ahead and let me buy you a burger, fries, and a milkshake before we get too far?" He pointed at the sign on the side of the road.

She was hungry. In fact, she couldn't remember the last time she ate, so it was at the very least, the smart thing to do.

"Make it onion rings and you have yourself a deal," she countered.

"How about we splurge and do both?"

AJ smiled, leaving butterflies in the pit of her stomach.

─────────o─✕─o─────────

Beli-yaal made a move to plunge its talons into Kafziel. In an instant, the demon clawed at its eyes, blinded by the flash of the Lord's Glory the warrior team released. A legion of screeches permeated the woods around them.

Andrew knelt next to Kafziel and picked up his lifeless body.

In unison, the warriors instantly shot through the sky like a meteor shower. Andrew looked back at the chaotic cloud of destruction below.

That was close.

─────────o─✕─o─────────

The doors to Regional Memorial Hospital opened wide, letting a tall brutish man in a tailored suit and fedora hat inside. A thin, frail scar ran down the right side of his face from his high cheeks to his squared jaw. His hat tipped on his head to block his face from the cameras.

With his long lean stride, he casually tried to walk past security into the emergency room. A large man who looked like a linebacker abruptly stopped him.

"Sir, you can't go back there without checking in," his deep voice boomed out as he adjusted his duty belt.

The man kept his face guarded by the brim of his hat. "I'm just here to deliver this get well soon card to a friend." He tried to walk around the security guard, but the man was a wall of muscle. "I won't even stay. I just need to get this to her."

"Sir, like I said, I can't just let you back there. You have two options: Get in line so we can check you in as a visitor, for which we need ID, and some other info from ya. Or, you can be escorted out."

The faceless man held his rigid stance. "What about a third option?"

"What do you mean?"

"*You* deliver this to my friend, and I'll just go home."

"I can do that." The security guard pulled out a pen and small pad of paper. "What's the patient's name?"

"Mia Hughes."

—※—

The greasy drive-thru feast hit the spot as they charged down the interstate. Jocelyn swiftly became more alert and less annoyed with her driving partner.

"I guess food was the right choice." She laughed, dusting off the mess of crumbs all over her.

"I think it's safe to say we were hungry," AJ offered with a smile, wiping the mess of from his shirt also. "Listen, Joce, I know I'm not the easiest guy to work with. I'm trying to be better, but it's hard to have all this knowledge locked in my head all the time."

"Well, just because you're smart doesn't mean you get to treat people like trash." Her tone was soft, but her words weren't.

"You're right, which is why I want to do better." He cleared his throat and picked up the empty containers. "Me, being smart, isn't exactly why I act like that." His tone shifted. Jocelyn recognized it, he was about to confess something. Her spine stiffened. "It's because I was bullied pretty hard in school growing up." He refused to look at her.

"I was always the poor kid, the dirty kid, the kid who lived in his parent's car for forty-three and a half days in middle school, and again for thirty-six days my sophomore year of high school. So being a jerk is kind of my defense. It's my wall so I don't get hurt."

"I'm so sorry," Jocelyn sincerely offered. She attempted to hide her heartache by staring straight ahead. "That's awful."

"Yeah, but it's also not my life anymore. So I have to stop acting like everyone is out to hurt me and start having some faith in people."

Jocelyn simply nodded her head in agreement, doing her best to ignore her own guilt and the apology she hadn't voiced.

"I do appreciate that you're one of the first people to call me out to my face," AJ sheepishly added. She noticed a soft smile curl on his lips out of the corner of her eye. "Most people just talk poorly about me behind my back.

"I overhear a lot. It's easy to do when you're invisible most of the time. I didn't realize how much I needed someone to be straight with me to my face, and I appreciate it. We're a team, and it's about time I act like it."

He adjusted in his seat, squaring his shoulder toward her. She briefly looked in his direction a few times as he continued.

"I know you're probably not thrilled to be on this assignment with me. I want you to know that I've got your back, and we won't stop until we solve this thing. I'm not leaving without answers. We need them, and so does Charlotte's family."

"I agree, and I think I owe you an apology as well." She kept her eyes on the road, his stare burning into her. "I tend to get defensive far too easily." Maybe it was the exhaustion or because he confessed something to her, but she couldn't stop it from spilling out.

"I grew up in the rough part of town. The part of town where everyone hates cops. But when my best friend was murdered, I felt this pull. When I told my parents I was accepted into the academy, they kicked me out and disowned me. My whole neighborhood turned their backs on me and called me things like, traitor and so much worse.

"I lived with my mentor for almost a year and once I was no longer a rookie, I managed to sloppily patch things up with my parents."

"What do you mean, sloppily?"

"Well, they talk to me now, but I'm still not someone they're proud of. Any time they bring up my job, it's always coupled with how I'm not smart enough to do this, and how I've failed my family. Needless to say, I struggle with feeling inadequate, and when you challenged me right out of the gate, it felt like a punch to the gut."

"I'm sorry." He placed a hand on her shoulder.

"I'm sorry too. You were right. It was a waste of time. I took out my frustrations on you and that's not right." She exhaled. "Truth is, I need you."

"And I need you." He smiled, sticking out his hand. "What do you say, partners?"

For a brief moment, she glanced over, noting the sincerity in his eyes, thankful no other cars were on the road. She didn't know why the butterflies in the pit of her stomach betrayed her at the thought of touching his hand. Regardless of how things started, he was the only person she saw finishing this with now.

Placing her hand in his, she smiled. "Partners."

Twenty-Five

IN AN INSTANT, HER whole life was gutted and turned inside out. Her husband just might be a serial killer, and she just might be to blame.

Mia's thoughts raced as Levi read the Durham Police report on the serial killer out loud. The details were vivid—too vivid. They left bile clawing at the back of her throat.

The nameless suspect was deemed a predator.

This couldn't be true. It just couldn't be.

She should have kept her mouth shut. Maybe if she had, she could have figured out a way to help Oliver rather than throw him under the bus like this. Thankfully, Levi's sergeant was delayed so there might still be time to fix this. Or help him somehow.

Those poor girls.

Gut-wrenching visions tore through her mind, but she couldn't allow herself to linger there. Instead, she blocked out the plethora of questions haunting her thoughts to focus only on a few. Why not kill her with the others? Why not arrange pieces of her body on an altar as a sacrifice? Is this what he meant when he said her punishments were for her own good? Was beating her better than the alternative he felt compelled to do?

Something undoubtedly shifted within Oliver, she couldn't deny that. A frenzied evil grew in his eyes, especially when he lost all control. More and more lapses in memory frequented their conversations, as if he didn't remember his outbursts.

He spent the last year stomping the very life he once gave from her soul.

It felt impossible to stand flat-footed against such immeasurable odds. She couldn't take on Oliver—the man she loved and gave herself fully to—even if he was a serial killer. She wasn't strong enough.

"Mia?" Levi's sharp tone snapped her attention away from her rollercoaster thoughts. "Are you okay?" Concern held in his eyes. She never could lie when he looked right through her like that. "You haven't said a word in almost an hour."

She cleared the horror from her throat. "It's just a lot to process." She wearily smiled. "It's..." Her voice trailed off, back on thoughts of the certain retribution awaiting her.

"What?" Levi pressed. Apparently, he didn't know how to turn off the cop side of him.

"I just need a minute," she snapped harder than intended.

Her walls were officially up. Levi sought justice for the lives taken and possibly retribution. Oliver might be a killer. A predator. A wolf in shepherd's clothing. And Mia didn't know who to trust.

This couldn't be happening.

⸺⸺⸺⸺⸺✕⸺⸺⸺⸺⸺

Kano returned to the dungeon. Charlotte's weakened body curled into the fetal position. Her soft eyes scanned the broken-down child of God. Kano might not always understand the ways of the King, but she knew better than to let pride in. God saw things she couldn't and knew things she wouldn't comprehend. To think she was smarter would be blasphemous.

She thought of Naru. He allowed Lucifer to pry open a wedge of doubt and exploit it, and look where that got him. She glanced down at a few ashened smudges on her hand. All that remained here on earth of the once strong warrior and friend.

Naru had been selected as one of a few to be on an elite team of warriors. They were the team that carried out top-secret missions and the most difficult tasks of the King. They would run operations all over the world and rescue other teams as needed. They answered only to two, the Archangel Michael and God himself.

Kano was initially disappointed when she wasn't selected for the team, but quickly realized the Almighty knew better than her. In what felt like a blink of an eye, all of Heaven watched in horror as Lucifer and all those who stood with him fell. Her heart shattered as her best friend, the one who helped make her the warrior she was today, was torn from God's presence.

"Father, no!" Naru yelled out amidst the screams of the angels as he plummeted through the barriers of Heaven, never allowed to return.

A single tear trickled down Kano's stoic, pale face. She often thought of Naru, and seeing what he became reminded her of exactly what and who she never wanted to be. She fell to her face in the presence of the Most High many times. The train of His Robe filled the Throne room, a reminder of how Victorious the Great I Am was. Her understanding of every battle paled in comparison to the Holy One.

"I think her time is short," Ashanti firmly said from behind her. "What did Finn say?"

"He said to wait and trust the Lord." Her eyes remained locked on the girl.

"Do you think the Lord will save her?"

Kano stood for a moment and thought about it. None of that was for her to know or decide. Her eyes held a somber gaze as she turned and repeated the words of Shadrach, Meshach, and Abednego in the book of Daniel.

"The God we serve can deliver her from this and their grasp. But even if He does not, we will still trust in Him and not bow to darkness."

———✕———

A howl of anger rattled the trees. Beli-yaal had that speedy little punk right where he wanted him. Those Heavenly idiots would pay for this. The ground beneath him shook with each stomp of his colossal feet. He paced back and forth, swinging his talons in every direction. Those who dared to stand too close squelched in pain, and one unlucky shadow turned to ash.

A mild protest began but instantly ceased when Beli-yaal's sharp, deadly eyes stared them down. He was more than ready for a fight, and there wasn't a devil in this place that could stand against him.

In the dead silence, a faint wheeze grew closer. Beli-yaal's gaze did not waiver from his subordinates who foolishly thought they could stand against him. When a gasp echoed through the crowd, he craned his head to see. Catching a glimpse, anger melted into shock. He told her he would handle it. Why did she send her lackey?

Everyone took a knee in respect for the messenger of the Queen of Darkness.

"Nexus," Beli-yaal said lowering to one knee, bowing his head low. "May I ask what you're doing here?"

Although this demon was small and insignificant, he was her only pet, and she protected him. Beli-yaal could not cross Nexus with disrespect or callousness unless he wanted to be banished to the depths of Hell for the next millennium. A shutter rolled down his spine at the thought of it.

"She sent me to warn you." Nexus pulled out a scroll. "She'll be here by tomorrow morning to clean up this mess if you don't."

A low growl escaped. "Everything is going according to plan. She need not worry."

Nexus straightened his stance and lifted his chin in a pathetic attempt to elude his authority. "Her exact words were, 'That deviant cop is still with Mia. He's already swayed her into giving up the dirt sample, the one *you* promised she never would.'" Nexus continued with the utmost arrogance. "The way she sees it, you haven't been living up to your potential here, Beli-yaal. You really need to tighten up," he snickered with a devilish grin.

Quick, like a cheetah, Beli-yaal lunged forward, his built-in weapon at the imp's throat.

"Care to say that again?" He forced the words through gritted teeth.

"Do it. I dare you," the pet urged.

This little jerk baited him. If he turned Nexus to ash, he would face her full wrath.

The queen transformed herself into many beautiful things. It was her greatest weapon. When humans felt rejected and they reacted sinfully, no matter how subtle, it opened the door just enough. Before they know it, she has dug her talons in deep.

For a long time, she walked undetected with Mia Hughes. She was good at what she did, but Beli-yaal saw her true form and felt her wickedness. It ran so deep and so black anyone in her wake trembled in fear.

Slowly, he lowered his hand.

"That's what I thought," Nexus barked, dusting himself off. "I can buy you an extra day *if* I like your plan for the dirt situation." He looked around. "Where's Occult?"

Beli-yaal hoped Occult would carry out his orders precisely and promptly, because if not, Jezebel, the Queen of Darkness, would have both their heads.

Twenty-Six

THE FEDORA DIPPED LOW over his face as he walked into the diner. That was a bust, but the job wasn't over until Mia Hughes was stopped. His orders were: do anything necessary.

"Can I get ya somethin', hon?" a thick southern accent asked from behind the bar.

"Coffee. Black," he barked, his gravelly voice sharp and direct.

He refused to make eye contact, removed his fedora, and ran his hand through the salt and pepper hair atop his head. From the corner of his view, big round eyes stared, fixated on the jagged scar down the side of his face. Far too many questions painted her eyes right under that curtain of electric blue eyeshadow. The bustle of the diner reminded him that too many witnesses were here to pull off the ideas in his head.

A huff of air pushed from his mouth. He was too old for these games. Prying eyes watched him with wild ideas of how he got such a heinous scar—a story they surely couldn't handle. His sharp eyes knocked her back with a gulp.

"Oh gosh, I'm so sorry. I didn't mean to stare. It's just such a unique scar."

The quick bat of her eyes mimicked the clang of the coffee cup now in front of him. Without another word, she was off to take another order.

People were the worst.

That was why he did what he did for anyone willing to pay. He didn't care about the client's reason, although they always explained with far too much detail. He was happy to inflict their desires, which they likely didn't have the stomach for anyway.

With a sip of his piping hot brew, he considered how to remove the threat Mia posed to his client. Women. Always getting themselves into situations. Why was it so hard for them to just stay in their own lane? For thousands of years, women enjoyed being homemakers. Now they wanted to castrate all the men and rule the world. Silly little girls. They didn't understand the can of worms they'd opened.

A bomb could be fun, but his one rule was no kids unless they deserved it. Verifying that would be a nightmare. It wouldn't work. She would likely be discharged soon anyway. An accidental hit-and-run always did the trick with less collateral damage.

Over his shoulder, he surveyed the street through the large front windows of the diner. He took note of the vehicles lining the sidewalk. Something large with a solid frame would get the job done nicely. He wondered how far the city yard was from here. A garbage truck would be perfect.

He wasn't hired to kill the cop, but one less pig in the world wouldn't be a bad thing. His thin lips curled up in a wicked grin. He always did like a two-for-one special.

—✕—

Ticano hid deep within the man with the scar. They were old friends by now. This loyal worshiper of Satan was always ready to do Hell's bidding. At first, they coaxed him into hurting people, but once he experienced that first taste of blood, it didn't take much convincing.

It brought satisfaction to a monster like Ticano. He not only corrupted one of the Enemy's creations, but he used him to torture and kill other humans that Idiot took time to knit together. Now that was a two for one special he could get behind.

Amusement swelled at the thought of how many cried out for their silent God to save them—pathetic.

—✕—

Restless, she lit up the screen on her phone every few seconds to check the time. It would take a few hours for the detective and analyst to arrive from Durham, but the minutes moved like watching paint dry. There was officially not enough nail left on her fingers to chew, so she mindlessly picked at her cuticles.

Levi left a while ago to talk with his sergeant and square things away before she took Mia's statement, but worry tugged at her. Thoughts spiraled into panic. The only notable perk of her anxiety was the pain in her stomach had become an afterthought.

She rechecked her phone. One measly minute managed to tick by— *great.*

"Relax, M."

The smooth sound of his voice helped put her at ease. He was her rock, right up until he wasn't. She never understood why he left her all those years ago, but maybe she didn't need to. He was here now, right when she needed him the most.

"I can't," she protested. "My mind won't quit."

He sat down on the stool beside her. "I know it feels like time has stopped altogether. Don't worry. They'll be here soon." He softly smiled.

A knock behind the drawn curtain pulled their attention. Against all logic, she couldn't stop the swell of hope in her chest it was the detective.

"Delivery," a soft young voice called out.

The curtain pulled back. A younger woman held out an envelope as she walked in with a sweet smile on her plump face.

"Thank you." Mia drug out the phrase as a question.

Levi's jaw flexed. "Did you tell people you were here?"

"No, of course not. The only one who knows I'm here besides the cops is…" Her voice trailed off. Fear gripped her throat, holding the name she didn't want to say. "Oliver."

With shaky hands, she opened the envelope. It was a card. A beautifully painted watercolor landscape dressed the front. She gently pulled it out like a bomb ready to detonate.

Tick, tick, tick.

The flap opened. A handwritten note scribbled inside, *Keep your mouth shut or die.*

And just like that… *boom…* an explosion of fear right in her face.

—✕—

His heart slammed against his chest at an unimaginable speed. Nothing prepared him for this feeling of dread, regret, and fear. The thick air burned his lungs, working overtime in his chest. His feet picked up speed. Sweat collected on his palms.

Back and forth. Back and forth.

Out of breath, Oliver grabbed the phone from his pocket and dialed a number off the paper in his hand.

A gruff voice answered. "You were instructed not to call me—"

"I know, I know," he cut him off, trying to catch his breath.

"Mr. Hughes, you hired me to do a job, not to hold your hand or soothe your guilt."

"Is this the right thing?" His voice shook. "What if I'm wrong?"

"Are you calling it off?" He growled with undeniable irritation.

Oliver quivered as fear boiled from within. This was a horrible idea.

So many thoughts raced through Oliver's mind, some his, some not, all conflicting.

If the truth gets out, if the world discovers our little secret—your Divine mission—they won't understand, and it'll all be over.

Oliver believed with all of his heart that the Lord spoke to him. If Mia had just heeded the correction of the Lord and her husband. If she had listened. He tried to warn her.

His voice evened out as breath returned to his lungs. "Finish this."

Oliver hung up the phone and ignored the tremble of his hands.

—✕—

"We're sitting ducks here, sir," Levi pointed out, piqued, with his phone pressed to his ear. "This guy tried to just walk past security. If they hadn't stopped him"—Levi paused—"I don't even want to think about the amount of damage that could've been done."

"Did they catch this guy on their video feed?" Captain Hendrix asked.

"Yeah, but he's wearing a hat that blocks his face. All we know is he's a white male, possibly in his late forties to early fifties, about six-two, and the security guard said he had a distinct scar on his face." Levi sighed. "It's not much, but the scar might be a way to ID him."

He glanced over his shoulder toward Mia's room, ignoring the look on Sergeant Cole's face. She loudly protested against moving Mia, so he went over her head.

"Sir, when security told him he couldn't go back, it didn't make him flustered or nervous. He was, and I quote, 'eerily calm.'" Levi lowered his voice and placed his mouth closer to the speaker on his phone so Mia wouldn't overhear. "I believe he's a professional, sir, and that Oliver Hughes hired him to take out his wife."

"I'll send a sketch artist down there, and we'll run what information we have through the system, but I wouldn't expect much from that." Hendrix cleared his throat. "What are you asking here, Reed?" he firmly questioned.

"She needs to be moved. I was thinkin' the motel we've used before as a temporary safe house could be a good place to lay low."

Adrenaline pulsed in his veins. Mia was in danger. Levi's fingers hastily drummed at the side of his leg, unable to stay still. He had to keep her safe. Nothing, not even Hendrix, would stop him from doing that.

Levi held his breath in the brief silence and simultaneously devised a plan to get her out of there. He refused to stay put, even if it cost him his badge. Mia's safety was all that mattered.

"What does the doctor say?" Hendrix asked.

Levi looked to his left at the seasoned doctor. They were about the same height, but the doctor was at least two decades older. The fluorescent lights gleamed off his smooth head while his small eyes magnified behind round wire frames.

His coat said Dr. Chet Rambowski, but Levi swore a nurse called him Rambo earlier. He took over Mia's care about an hour ago. The doctor's beady eyes scanned the tablet in his hands.

Levi removed the phone from his ear, put it on speaker, and held it out in front of him.

"You're on speaker with the doctor, myself, and Sergeant Cole, sir."

"What's your thought on Mrs. Hughes being moved at this point, Dr..." The captain's voice trailed off. Levi realized he hadn't told him the guy's name.

"Rambowski, but everyone calls me Rambo for short." He half smiled.

"Well, Rambo." Levi felt silly calling a grown man that.

"Dr. Rambo," he corrected him, pushing his glasses up on his thin and serious face.

Levi shifted a glance at Sergeant Cole, a feeble attempt to ask her if this guy was for real with his eyes.

He cleared his throat. "Uh, sorry. Dr. Rambo, is she stable enough to be moved?"

"Everything's looking good here." He slid his finger across the tablet, going through the chart. "The CT of her chest is clean, no bleeding." He kept scrolling. "The initial quick look with the ultrasound said her liver was possibly lacerated, but the CT of her abdomen is clear. Let me verify her last blood draw numbers, and if that's good, I say she'd be stable enough to move."

Dr. Rambo looked up at Levi over the rim of his glasses. "You know this is probably the safest place for her to be, right? There's no way that guy's getting in here."

Sergeant Cole scoffed with a deep "I told you so" scowl on her face.

"He has a point, Reed," Hendrix chimed in from the phone.

"The guy knows she's here. If we remove her and tuck her away somewhere he doesn't know, isn't that safer?" Levi contested. "Not to mention, it puts everyone here in danger."

"I agree." A soft voice came from behind them. Mia stood in the doorway of her room, using the wall to hold herself up. Levi questioned how long she had been there. "I figured I should be part of the decision about my safety." She flashed a meek smile. "And I think Levi's right. Staying here puts too many others in danger."

The corner of his mouth crooked up. She agreed with him, a rare phenomenon.

"Her labs," Dr. Rambo cut in, "look good. We're beyond overloaded here, so if Mrs. Hughes is okay with it, I'm happy to discharge her."

"Are you sure, Mrs. Hughes?" Hendrix asked.

A sour twist cascaded on her face. "Please call me Mia. And yes, I'm sure."

"Okay, Reed, devise a plan to secretly move her. Once Sergeant Cole approves, give me the details, and I'll make sure you have what you need." Levi smiled, trying very hard to not shout in celebration. "And, kid?" Hendrix continued. "Last I heard, that Durham detective is about an hour out. I'll have someone take her to the safe house."

"Thank you, sir." Levi smiled.

—✕—

Andrew gently laid Kafziel's limp body down on the ground in Heaven. He palmed the young warrior's chin, moved his face back and forth, and examined his injuries. He stopped when blood seeped from under his comrades' breastplate.

"Lord, please," Andrew begged.

"Beli-yaal hit him pretty hard." Jesus quickly scanned Kafziel's body. "There's a lot of damage here."

Andrew held his breath.

Jesus laid his scarred hands on each side of Kafziel's face and mumbled words no one understood. Bending at the waist, he outstretched his arms over the top of the warrior three times.

"Kafziel," Jesus called his name. "Get up."

His golden eyes broke open as his lungs filled with air. He hopped up, ready to fight until he realized his surroundings.

Heaven was vastly different than the world. Most humans didn't realize how wretched it smelled down there. It reeked of decay and sin. Another thing humans didn't know—sin smells terrible. But the air in heaven carried a sweetness. Light and full of pure, unfiltered love.

Kafziel caught his breath with a smile. "Thank You." He knelt before the Messiah. "I thought I'd never fight again. How can I repay this kindness, my Lord?"

Jesus reached out his hand and helped Kafziel up. "Oh young warrior, you took on a slew of evil today and sacrificed everything for the Father's Glory. I think you've done more than enough." He pointed at the blood smeared on his armor. "Go get yourself cleaned up. We're far from done here."

"Yes, sir!" Kafziel exclaimed with a big, bright smile before doing what was asked.

"Andrew." Jesus turned, his face serious. "A lot has taken place in your absence. I need your team to hurry back." He leaned closer. "They're all in grave danger."

Twenty~Seven

THEY WEREN'T FAR FROM Knoxville now. A stop for coffee and the bathroom seemed untimely, but Jocelyn barely kept her eyes open. AJ fell asleep three times in the last hour, once mid-sentence as he talked about his last case. Not to mention, her bladder was so full it literally might explode.

She now understood why that woman a decade ago wore an adult diaper to travel across three states to commit murder. Jocelyn was so determined to catch these guys that if someone suggested wearing one—even as a joke—she probably would've seen it as a stroke of genius.

A loud grunt filled the car as it came to a stop, waking AJ from another brief nap.

"How long was I out?" he asked, rubbing his eyes.

"About ten minutes." She removed her seatbelt. "I need coffee and a bathroom. You comin'?"

They hopped out of the car and headed straight for the store. As Jocelyn came out of the little girl's room, AJ poured two cups of coffee.

"One cream, two sugars, right?" he asked without looking at her.

"Better make it three sugars. It's gonna be a long night." She smiled. "Want some pretzels?"

"How'd you know they're my favorite?" He huffed a laugh.

"It's like the only thing I've seen you eat since you arrived at the station. It's kind of hard not to know."

"Fair enough." He turned and handed her the magic elixir. "Seriously?" He laughed at the bag of Flamin' Hot Cheetos in her hand.

"What? I love these things. They make my tongue and throat burn. It's the best!"

"They're toxic. That's probably why your throat burns."

"But those toxins just taste so good, I can't help it."

Back on the road, Jocelyn pushed on the gas. Twenty miles to go.

———————————×———————————

Occult stepped out from the elongated shadow cast off the side of the gas station. His mind narrowed with evil delight. That was far enough for our detective and her sidekick.

He catapulted his large, grungy frame into the air, easily catching up with the assassins of fun.

"Time to play, boys." Occult grinned at the trail of darkness on his heels. "Keep them from Knoxville, at any cost!"

A slew of delightful screeches pierced the night in celebration of their impending torment. Occult's thick black eyes locked onto the car below.

"Today, we become gods!" he yelled out. "For the Prince of Darkness!"

His words echoed through the army.

The dense evil plunged toward the car, ready for victory.

Just above the target, a streak of light plowed through them like a bowling ball.

"Warriors!" Occult shouted. "Don't let them sway you." He flashed his talons against the light. "Remember our mission!"

———————————×———————————

Sounds of war filled the stillness of the interstate, alerting both good and evil nearby to join the fight. Above the unmarked police vehicle, Leon and Viveka led the Heavenly Hosts against the attack on the detective.

Dante, the angel assigned to Jocelyn, clung to the top of her car, his massive body a shield.

"Flank right," Viveka's deep voice boomed.

Metal thrashed against metal, streaks swirled amidst the darkness. Cries of pain came from both sides. Dante watched several bursts of ash spring through the eclipse of evil.

He smiled. They were winning.

As he loosened his stiff body, an invisible evil dive-bombed him, knocking him off the side of the car. With one hand, he clung to the metal frame and fought to regain control as his mighty body flailed against the wind speed.

If he let go, she would be unprotected against them—he would sacrifice everything before he let that happen.

"Leon," he shouted, but his words were lost in the battle. "Leon." He tried one last time.

No response.

There was nothing left to do but accept his fate. It's up to him to save her, alone.

"Dios, give me strength and agility," Dante softly prayed.

With a battle cry of hope, his feet springboarded off the ground and into the air. He flipped like an Olympian going for the gold until his feet hit the roof, firmly planted. He rode, steadying his body like a surfer.

Alert, he knew they would come but vowed to stand in their way.

From the right came a body blow so hard it flung him through the air. His sword scraped along the sheath as his mighty wings spread with a push forward. His senses heightened.

With cat-like reflexes, he swung his sword into resistance. Locked within its talons, he came face to face with a smaller demon.

Two wicked fighters. He was outnumbered.

— ✕ —

"Do you feel that?" Jocelyn asked.

AJ looked around. "Feel what?"

Her heart picked up speed. Something was wrong, but she didn't know what.

"I don't know," she confessed. "Something feels off." She thought for a moment. "Like someone's staring at me, or like hiding in the closet ready to kill me."

AJ chuckled. "There's no closet in a car, Joce."

"Don't be a brat. I obviously know that, but that's how it feels."

AJ gently touched her shoulder. "It's normal to get feelings like this in the middle of a big case." He lowered his hand. "Let's be real—you haven't slept, and you just drank your tenth cup of coffee. It's probably making you jittery."

"You're right," she agreed, unsure if she actually did.

"I'm happy to drive if you'd like," AJ offered.

"Thanks, but I'm fine. We're only fifteen miles out anyway. I can get us there."

Occult wiggled his way out of the heavenly ambush and gave Fear space to work his magic. This one pathetic warrior would be no match for them. He kept pace with the car and watched Fear weave around the massive being in delight as he pushed the warrior to the breaking point—a skill Fear performed well.

Torturous thoughts ripped through his mind. He could certainly stall the engine or fry the radiator to buy time, but wouldn't it be better to take them out? The ritual for that little blonde girl started soon, and if it was done right, they could leave town before a new detective was assigned. It was such an inspired plan from the greatest demon.

With the fool's attention fully on Fear, it was time—tonight they died.

From high above, Occult dipped into a nosedive. Secluded a half mile from the fight, these two humans didn't stand a chance. The corner of his lips twitched with pleasure. This would be fun.

Occult slammed down on the roof and joined the fight.

She jumped at the loud bang above her head. Jocelyn looked over at AJ. He just sat there unfazed, eating his stupid pretzels. A huff released in her throat. She'd officially lost her mind.

A moment later, another slam hit the door. Was it possible an invisible force was trying to get in the car?

No, that couldn't be it. She believed in science, not ghosts or anything of the supernatural. A logical and scientific explanation existed somewhere in this craziness.

Her grandmother would tell her to ask God, but Jocelyn shrugged off that idea. She had survived her entire life without God. No point in asking for Him now.

This wasn't going well for Dante. He did what he could, but it became increasingly harder to dodge their relentless advances. The smaller of the two was so fast, it nicked the back of Dante's knee. He winced, but his concentration remained, standing between death and Jocelyn.

Another life would not be lost on his watch. Not today.

New strength coursed through him, providing divine precision and maneuvering ability. They went right, he beat them there. They tried to overthrow him, he stopped them as if he were in two places at once.

Gracias, Dios, he prayed.

—※—

"Enough!" Occult growled.

"Qué paso desgraciado?" the wannabe taunted. "Are you finally finished?"

A devilish grin crept across his lips revealing his jagged teeth when something foul and twisted poked out from the shadows.

"No," he snickered. "But you are."

The large thick frame emerged from the forest and slammed into the back of that moron. Occult didn't know the beasts name, but he didn't care. Tonight, he was a hero.

Delightfully torturous screams cut through the air. Occult quickly stepped aside as the wannabe and the vigilant warrior flew by and sunk between the trees, into the cloak of night.

Fear popped his head up from the side of the car. "Is it time, boss?"

"It is indeed." A growl of satisfaction vibrated in his throat. "Time to teach this meddling woman a lesson."

—※—

"Do you believe in God?" AJ casually asked as if it was something they frequently talked about.

"Uh, that's an odd question."

"Yeah, I guess, but it's just the feeling you talked about." He paused for a moment. "It's something my mom—" He abruptly stopped. "Never mind, you're going to think it's weird."

"No, no. I won't, I promise." She hoped he would go on because nothing she thought of explained what she felt.

"My mom used to say how she could feel evil, and sometimes she could see them too."

"See what?" Jocelyn pressed.

"Don't think I'm weird, okay?"

She darted a look at AJ. His hands tightly wrung in his lap. "I won't."

"Demons."

Jocelyn's stomach coiled as she shifted in her seat.

"Um."

"I knew it. You think I've lost my mind."

"No, not at all. It's just…" She tried to find the words. "I don't like talking about that stuff."

"Why? Does it scare you?"

"Yeah, actually, it does."

There was a long awkward pause. Jocelyn wondered if AJ regretted his words as much as she did hers. A grown woman scared of something that probably wasn't true seemed juvenile at best.

"Look…" She broke the silence. "It's not that I'm scared per se. I just think that if we talk about them and they're real, it opens the door for them to come in."

She watched as AJ's face twisted, perplexed.

"You do know they aren't like Beetlejuice, right? Like, if I say the word 'demon' three times they aren't going to just appear. They're already here, all around us."

That didn't make Jocelyn feel better.

Like a crack of lightning, pain tore through her head as she let out an ear-piercing scream.

—✕—

He tried to ignore the blistering hurt in his arm where a talon dug itself in. Luckily the breastplate of his armor stopped the other two from doing more damage. The dark monster tossed Dante's body into the air like a bloody ball.

Flying proved impossible with a dislocated wing. His teeth grit in pain. In order to win this, he would have to put it back in place. He clumsily tried to push out of evil's grasp but didn't quite make it. The tip of the monster's talons ripped across Dante's neck. He let out a spontaneous holler.

Sword in hand, he flipped over the beast's other limb. In the air, he did his best to spin his body despite the excruciating pain.

Its large jowls unhinged like a snake. Dante thrust his shield forward and between the rows of serrated, shark-like teeth to keep them from ripping him to pieces. Darkness swung its talons again, but this time, Dante was ready.

With a slash of his sword, black sprayed out, painting the ground around them. A thud drew his attention to the now severed foot. The demon screeched, whimpered, and cried out in pain. It tried to retreat, but this beast wasn't escaping on his watch. His sword burst into flames as it plunged into the wounded devil.

Black sludge poured out of its massive frame before it melted into black ash.

Dante limped his broken body over to a tree, dragging the lifeless wing behind. He slammed himself against the large trunk at just the right angle. A loud grunt escaped his clenched jaw, but his wing felt a lot better being back in the right place.

A skid of tires on the interstate pulled his focus.

Jocelyn.

He steadied his breath. One down, two to go.

—⋇—

Jocelyn screamed. She did her best to stop the car but was no longer in control of her body.

"Come on!" she wailed, but her limbs remained paralyzed.

The tires squealed against the asphalt. AJ's hands were warm on hers as he took over the wheel to keep them on the road. Sliding across the bench seat, he slammed against her, pushing his foot toward the brake. The gears ground against each other as the car halted to a stop. The engine cut off.

Silence intruded on her agony.

Unbearable pain, like a torrid knife, cut through her brain. Blindness held her sight hostage. She cradled her head in shaky hands and pressed in as hard as she could. If she let go, it might explode into a million pieces.

"Jocelyn?" AJ yelled over her screams. "What's happening?"

Panic saturated his voice. A moment later, a wail burst out. He shrieked like someone chased him. She felt his body tremble.

"If You're real, where are You?" she howled to God.

Twenty-Eight

HER PRISON DOOR LET out a tired screech. Charlotte worked to respond, but her eyes were too heavy to open. She remained lifeless on the ground, ready to endure her inevitable fate.

A loud thump hit the floor. A heavy-footed walk circled her limp body. She wished they would put her out of her misery rather than drag it out like this.

Her father often spoke of God's ways being higher than our ways, and His thoughts higher than our thoughts. But right now, God's plan seemed like a brutal touch.

A cool hand brushed against her cheek. "Is she alive?" A soft voice came from behind her.

The hand moved to her neck, checking for signs of life.

"Barely." The gravelly voice was so close she could smell peanut butter on his breath.

"Where is he?" the softer one demanded. "If he doesn't hurry, she'll be dead before he gets here."

A sharp squeak ripped through the small room followed by a slam. Unknown feet clobbered down the steps.

"Don't look at me like that," the third voice snapped.

"She's almost dead. We needed those antibiotics yesterday." There was a heavy sigh. "To finish the ritual, she has to walk. You know this." Charlotte noted the frustration in the softer voice.

"I know. You've taught me well. It took longer than expected to get the vet alone in the clinic. But I'm here now, and I grabbed everything they had so this won't happen next time."

Charlotte winced at the thought of another victim.

Motionless in the dirt, she intently listened with the hope of relaying this information to the police—if she made it out of here alive that is. The last shred of expectation gripped tightly in her heart.

A familiarity in the third voice left her bewildered. There was something in the rhythm and arrogance of his words, but despite her effort, no face or name came to mind.

A sting on her butt cheek demanded her attention. An invasive burn bullied its way out to her hip and down her leg. She wanted to cry out, grit her teeth—anything—but with no energy to give, she suffered through it.

"She'll feel better in a few hours," the almost recognizable voice breathed, petting her hair like a dog. He leaned close. "It's almost over."

The familiar hand forcefully pulled away.

"Let's go," the soft voice snapped with a hiss.

◦—✕—◦

Shrouded in darkness, his lanky frame hugged the wall. The place looked dead, which he'd expected this late at night. With piercing eyes, he surveyed the yard beyond the chain link for a city garbage truck ready to be plucked.

The front end poked out from behind a building. Its large side mirror shimmered in the moonlight. *Bingo.*

He focused on the corners and high vantage points, scouring for cameras so he'd know where to avoid. He usually eluded such things, but the hospital was an unfortunate incident that couldn't be avoided. That wouldn't happen again.

With small quick steps, he dashed along the fence, only stopping where the shadows cast from the buildings. Crouched down, a pair of long, sleek bolt cutters emerged from under his trench coat. Starting from the bottom, he cut straight up the fence until he could slide through.

No alarms yet. *Good.*

Like a rat, racing to find the cheese, he scurried toward the truck. His heart picked up speed. A smile cracked across his hardened face. He lived for this kind of rush.

For kicks, he tried the handle. Idiots left the thing unlocked.

In the driver's seat, he scanned. If they're dumb enough to leave it unlocked, the keys were likely in here somewhere.

Ignition? No. Under the seat? No. Dashboard? No.

He laughed at the next thought because of how ridiculous it was. So cliche. So juvenile. Pulling down the visor, the silver keys popped into his lap.

A demented laugh softly vibrated in his throat, "Showtime."

×

A wild frenzy swirled as his talons pushed further into her skull. With any luck, her arteries would burst. The shrill of her screams egged him on with delight.

Death was the only option. Rumors of the queen coming made Occult want to outshine that imbecile, Beli-yaal. His intelligence surpassed that buffoon's ten-fold. She would know, once and for all, his worthiness of her attention.

He pushed with all his might, but this dreadful woman fought the intrusion. He stretched out his other hand in preparation for phase two. Double the talons equals double the pain.

The high-pitched scream as more talons immersed into her skull made him laugh.

Death would soon follow.

×

With wings tightly tucked into his body, his weapon ignited in flames.

Dante carved the sword out in front of him across the back of the bigger devil. His right foot trailed the body as he twisted mid-air until it connected with the small one's face. In full display, his white wings steadied him despite the excruciating burn it brought.

Both diablos released an extremity from their victims, the other still fully attached.

Halfway there.

Dante dove, moving quickly around their attempts. Every part of his body relentlessly lashed out with quick strikes, like a snake.

The smaller demon left only one talon submerged in the man as he stretched out his body. Dante avoided his attack, but not the trap set before him. By the time he realized what happened, the large demon's arm plowed down out of nowhere, pinning him to the roof of the stalled car.

A chilled chuckle made his skin crawl. "You thought you could take us out?" The big devil licked his thin, black lips. "Absurd."

"Dios is worthy of my sacrifice." Dante's jaw clenched. "The Holy One of Heaven, the Leader of Heaven's Armies, is the only One worthy of praise and glory. If this is it for me, then so be it."

"Oh shut up," the small one spit. "No one cares about your ridiculous display of loyalty."

The runt of the two struggled to fully reach the warrior's detained body while still attached to his victim. Dante watched from the corner of his eye as the final talon slid out from the man. A small victory as he faced defeat.

"I've had just about enough of you," the imp continued. "It's time for us to be rid of you once and for all," he sneered.

The devil cracked its knuckles, a warm-up for Dante's impending torment. Narrow talons outstretched, revealing the hidden razors underneath—its own personal executioner's sword, travel size.

Dante prayed for Jocelyn and AJ to remember the things taught to them by their families and for another rescuer to come quickly—an intrepid and resolute warrior to the very end.

"Time to die," the hefty one growled. "Do it," he ordered.

The small one raised its hand. Dante closed his eyes and focused on the Lord, surrendering his fate.

"Para gloria de Dios." The words fell from his lips.

He courageously waited for his affliction…and waited…and waited…

A faint grunt forced his eyes open. The demon and its built-in sword were nowhere to be found. Perhaps luring him into a false sense of security was their way of torture.

Another grunt. This time, the big one's weight ripped off his body. Something was happening. Dante seized the opportunity and stood, sword in hand. A flash of light streaked in front of him.

Reinforcements.

———————✕———————

Occult fought to catch his breath. Covered in dirt and leaves, he grabbed ahold of his aching talon. It was ripped from that woman's head with such force he was lucky it remained intact. Anger saturated him as he brushed off the debris. These brats needed to be taught a lesson, and Occult couldn't think of anyone better to teach it to them.

His monstrous feet heaved against the ground with each step.

A flash of light. His body whipped around at the sting of the sword plaguing him. A quick gasp escaped as he came face to face with an angel back from the dead.

"I heard Beli-yaal got the best of you, boy. You're supposed to be dead," Occult snarled.

"Guess he wasn't fast enough," the arrogant, obnoxious fool smirked.

"Well," Occult grinned. "I'm faster."

He lunged like a lion and encircled his prey.

———————✕———————

Jocelyn's pain eased, still ever present but tolerable. Her eyes rapidly blinked, an attempt to release the darkness that took her sight. She clumsily rummaged her hands around the car in search of her phone, the radio, anything to call for help.

"AJ? Are you there?"

She reached over and found his quivering body. A quick scoot brought her close enough to make out what he said.

"What was it she used to say? Help me. Help me remember. It was something important. What was it? Mom, help me. Help me remember," AJ muttered.

Jocelyn wrapped her arms around him. "Keep fighting, AJ. We can't give up now."

He rocked back and forth. She listened as he muttered the same things over and over. Jocelyn rubbed at her eyes with a closed fist. Internally she ran down the list of things learned in the academy, then moved on to the classes she took to become a detective. There was no manual for this. How do you fight a threat you can't see and don't understand?

"Jesus!" AJ shouted out, making her jump. "Jesus, help us!"

——————————— ⊲⋈⊳ ———————————

Darkness swirled around the young warrior, leaving him unable to see or fight. He was incapacitated, a sitting duck as the humans would say. Dante came in fast and hard, an attempt to knock darkness off its warpath. All three bodies tumbled across the forest floor. Dante let out several grunts as his injured wing hit the compacted dirt and downed tree branches.

When he came to a stop, he popped up on his feet and scanned for his opponent and ally. There, on the right, darkness scrambled to its feet. Speedy steps approached from behind.

"Have you spotted him?" the ally pressed.

"Fifteen feet out." Dante raised his ample arm and pointed at the beast. The warriors exchanged a silent nod. "Watch your back, there's a smaller devil around here too, and they work as a team."

The young warrior with golden eyes gave a quick nod and held up a fist. Dante tapped the side of his fist onto his ally's.

In unison, they rushed forward. The speedy warrior beat Dante to the threat, slamming his body into the demon.

A loud grunt exhaled from the belly of darkness.

Dante spun around in search of the pint-sized threat. Quicker than a heartbeat, the Glory of the Lord washed over him. Golden, pure light erupted from his skin, unveiling the darkness of night. Behind a tree, Dante spotted the small beast.

Shrieks of pain echoed off the mountains. Dante watched the demon claw its eyes as smoke billowed from them. Over his shoulder, the sizable menace clawed his face so hard, it broke the skin.

"Retreat!" the bigger one screamed out. "Retreat!"

Darkness fled, and the Glory of the Lord remained on the warriors.

Smiles dressed their faces, for they were victorious. The knowledge remained that the battle might be over, but war was still to come.

——————————— ⊲⋈⊳ ———————————

Jocelyn heaved several breaths, the world around her finally back in focus. AJ wrapped his arm around her shoulders and pulled her close into safety and security. She liked resting her head against his chest. The rhythmic pound of his heart calmed her.

AJ kissed the top of her head. A part of her worried the product in her hair would make him regret it, but she pushed that concern aside. They came through this together and nothing would ruin that.

Jocelyn's mind raced in the silence. God just might be a lot more real than she thought. Something or someone rescued them from the grasp of death. When the invisible threat released them, an instant safety and wholeness permeated the car. She couldn't continue to deny something she experienced so vividly.

Charlotte's face flashed in her mind. A soft voice like a gentle breeze spoke to her heart. *She's running out of time.*

Twenty~Nine

LEVI ASSUMED AS A professional hitman, the guy would do his homework. It wouldn't take a rocket scientist to know Levi would never leave Mia. This escape had to be real because the one hunting Mia wouldn't buy some phony hat trick. To sell it, Levi had no choice. He had to do the one thing he swore he'd never do again—leave her side. He simply couldn't be in two places at once.

One woman in the entire Knoxville Police Department could pass for Mia Hughes. Sondra Watkins had the same creamy strawberry-blonde hair, the same fair skin, and the same build. The only difference, Sondra had way more freckles than Mia. Luckily, no one would see her face.

She wasn't a cop. She hadn't trained for this. Sondra worked in the courier room, delivering case files and prep notes between personnel and departments.

Levi noticed her three years ago when she came in for an interview. He remembered it vividly. His heart dropped into his stomach until she turned around, and he saw it wasn't Mia. If she could fool Levi, she could fool anyone, which was why it had to be her.

Sergeant Cole obtained Mia's statement, which she signed while a plan was hastily formed and approved by Hendrix. An arrest warrant had been quickly approved by a judge and a team was currently enroute to Mia's house to take Oliver away in cuffs.

Adrenaline gathered in Levi's chest as everyone took their places. To pull this off, each part must be played perfectly.

"Sarge." Levi clenched his jaw. "She's—"

"I know she is," Sergeant Cole smiled, her hand on his shoulder. "I've got her. You have my word."

Sergeant Cole's word was as good as a signed contract. Although she didn't agree with this plan, he trusted she would give her life to protect the only woman Levi ever loved.

He pulled back the curtain of Mia's room. "Do you want to go over the plan one more time?"

"I got it," Mia laughed.

That smile. He's missed that smile.

"Okay. I'll see ya on the other side then." With a quick nod, he turned to leave.

"Wait," she called out. "Be careful." He turned and found tears pooled in her eyes. "If anything happened to you…" Her voice trailed off.

Anguish twisted on her bruised and contorted face. Levi returned, longing to touch her and hold her in his arms.

"There's no need for all of that. The plan will work."

"How do you know?" Her strained words were an arrow to his heart.

"I don't." He thought for a moment. "All I know is, it has to work because I wouldn't survive in a world without you." He choked back tears and quickly kissed her forehead. "See you in a bit."

A few steps from the door, her soft voice called out. "Levi." He stopped, unable to turn around and let her see his tears. "Thank you."

He gave a quick nod, flung open the curtain, and quickly walked into the hall. A sharp glance settled on Sergeant Cole. With a nod, the signal indicated she was ready.

Before returning the gesture, indicating it was time to go, Levi looked at Sondra—her meekness made him nervous. He prayed for her safety and theirs. If she got killed because of his plan, Levi didn't know how he would live with the guilt.

He turned back to his Sergeant and gave a firm nod.

Levi and Detective Maltez removed their jackets and placed them over Sondra's head. Her body shivered with fear.

"You've got this," Levi whispered in her ear.

With her head fully covered, Levi removed his tight grip on her to hold the HK in his hands. Walsh took the position in front, Maltez and Levi on each side of Sondra, and Officer Ellis on their six. Snipers posted up around the front entrance, out of sight and ready to defend.

Levi's eyes scanned the shadows and tops of taller buildings around them. If he was hired to kill Mia, he would sit a minimum of two to three hundred yards out with his 300 Winchester Magnum. A sit and wait tactic that worked well in a life Levi didn't care to think about. Thirty-seven marks dressed his record, faces he would forever see every time his eyes closed.

Their steps were small and precise as they crouched with bent knees, ready to fight at a moment's notice. Swift movements took them closer to the bulletproof transport vehicle waiting for them. The long narrow walkway from the door to the curb didn't seem so long coming in, but now it felt like a long walk on a short plank.

"Ten feet to go," Maltez firmly said.

"Seems all clear guys," Walsh offered.

Almost there. Quick breaths as Levi's finger gently laid along the barrel, just above the trigger.

Without warning, a long shadow quickly sprang from behind the van. Levi pulled Sondra back, forcing her behind him. In seconds, all four guns locked on the back end of the van.

His heart quickened, his focus in overdrive. This was it. A clench wrapped around his chest as the shadow drew closer.

"Freeze," Maltez commanded with a booming voice.

A middle-aged mom stood like a deer in headlights, eyes wide, mouth open, unsure what to do. She tightly clenched a young boy in her arms.

"P-P-Please don't h-h-hurt us. M-M-My son—"

They all lowered their weapons almost in unison.

Walsh delicately acknowledged her. Deescalating a tense situation was his forte as a father of three.

"Ma'am, we're sorry." Walsh slowly reached toward his belt. The woman tensed. "I'm a detective. You're both in danger here. Please, move quickly into the ER."

"Mia, get in the van. Hurry up," Levi urged Sondra with a forced touch.

A long swift push got her into the van where she was at least protected. Stress remained on Levi's face, his shoulder muscles tense. Phase one was over, two more to go.

⸺✕⸺

Sergeant Cole tightly gripped Mia's upper arm and led her through a maze of hallways. Mia had no clue where they were. She tried to plan escape routes like Levi wanted, but she was so turned around now it was no use. If something happened, she would be forced to blindly run.

Mia prayed for the safety of not only her, but everyone involved. She thought of Sondra, the woman Levi used as bait, unsure how she felt about an innocent woman in the crosshairs Mia deserved.

They moved with a brisk hustle in their step.

For some unknown reason, she flashed back to when she played basketball in high school. The coach made them run suicides for missed free throws. How many would it cost her for all the missed signs Oliver was a monster?

Her mind swirled in a million directions all at once. Despite all she did for him—she changed everything about herself, surrendered to him, let him lead, she made herself small to simply appease him—he hired someone to kill her. Someone who could jump out at any moment and succeed.

With each step, her heart pounded louder against her chest. Around the corner, she saw a door. Thirty steps to freedom.

Twenty-five.

Seventeen.

Twelve.

Five.

Sergeant Cole yanked her to the side and came to an abrupt stop.

"What are you doing?" Mia whispered with panic in her voice. "Aren't we goin' out that door?"

"We have to wait for the signal."

"What signal?"

"You'll know when it happens." Sergeant Cole cracked a little smile, a small gesture that made her seem so…human and relatable. "You'll be out of here in no time." She looked down at the ground and shifted her weight back and forth a few times.

"Go ahead," Mia encouraged.

"Excuse me?"

"Ask me."

Mia didn't quite know what the sergeant would ask, but she knew that look. Questions buzzed around everyone she encountered in the last few hours, questions they refused to ask.

"Do you think Reed's right and your husband hired that guy?" Heartbreak filled Sergeant Cole's brown eyes.

Mia's shoulders sank. "I honestly don't know." She did her best to look at the facts like Levi. "Well, he was the only other person who knew where I was, so I see where Levi's coming from. It's just so hard to imagine he'd go to this extreme. Then again, if I spilled the details about what happened, he'd be ruined. I imagine people have killed for less."

Truth left a sourness in the pit of her stomach.

Moments later, the radio cracked to life.

"One fish, two fish, go fish, blue fish," Levi barked.

"There's the signal." Sergeant Cole smiled, pulling Mia to her feet.

The door flew open as strangers in tactical gear surrounded her like a wall of Kevlar. Mia tripped over her own feet several times and grunted in pain. They moved faster than she, her body in full protest.

Sergeant Cole shoved her into a white pickup with blacked-out windows. Mia clumsily put on her seat belt. Her heart clamored against her sore ribs. She leaned forward, but that brought more pain. Exhaustion closed in around her.

⁌—✕—⁍

Her eyes opened to find Levi over the top of her, cradling her slick face in his ample hands. She oddly liked how his calluses felt on her cheeks.

These thoughts had to stop. This attraction was wrong. She was married.

"Um, you're here." Confusion twisted on her face. "I thought the plan was to meet in the back alley behind the abandoned gym."

Levi looked around. "That's where we are." He lovingly stroked her hair. "Are you okay?"

She abruptly pushed herself past him to sit up. Her adulterous heart did not glorify God or please Him in any way. The Bible said not to covet, and that's exactly what she was doing—lusting over what wasn't hers to have.

"I just got really tired. I'm sorry. I didn't mean to scare anyone. I figured I'd just rest for a few minutes." An internal light clicked on. "I didn't ruin the plan, did I?"

The corners of Levi's mouth gently turned up. "Of course not."

"Is Sondra okay?"

"She's fine. Maltez and Walsh are two of the best."

It was written on Levi's face and in her heart. She always made such a mess of things. This was why Oliver would get so angry. Habits rose up as she internally braced herself for what usually came next.

—※—

Levi struggled to accept the role he played in her brokenness. His past actions had sent a million cracks through her, like a fragmented windshield, intact but no longer functional. It left her vulnerable to someone who preyed upon a mangled soul.

He stopped himself from dwelling on it. There were more important things to deal with. The mission wasn't to stew in hatred. He needed to save her.

"We gotta go," he sternly said. A slight tremor rolled through her body as he helped her down from the truck. "You're okay. I've got you."

An abrupt turn had them into a vehicle hidden by a protruding dumpster. As the key turned in the ignition, the car came alive with various dings and lights.

He extended his arm into the back seat and pulled forward an oversized hoodie and two baseball caps. He handed her the black one with the words "I believe in magic" written in cursive. He put on the Dallas Cowboys hat still in his hand. If Maltez saw him wearing this, he'd never hear the end of it. The Cowboys were the worst.

A sudden glance her way brought a smile at memories long forgotten of the summer before middle school. They were obsessed with magic tricks after watching a David Copperfield Special on television. The whole summer they spent time learning card tricks, how to pull a rabbit out of a hat—thankfully Peter Cottontail, Mia's rabbit, was a good sport about it—and how to make someone disappear.

He wished a false back or trap door would help them now, but silly illusions weren't going to keep her safe this time.

—※—

His eyes followed the red dot as it trucked down the street. He knew they'd move her eventually. Whether they discharged or attempted to hide her was irrelevant. Thankfully he took precautions to ensure she couldn't hide—an ER tech planted a tracking device in the woman's shoe.

It was far too easy to pose as a cop these days, especially since it was the fastest way to get what you wanted. People trusted cops and rarely questioned why they needed the favor. Plus, the young girl was happy to make a quick buck without understanding the repercussions of her actions.

The diesel engine roared out under the weight it pulled, his foot pushed deeper on the gas to keep up. He had to get into position and he figured that pig would take a funky route to their destination.

He took a gamble, made a left, went down a few lights, and made a right. It was there he parked, like a beast crouched in the grass, waiting for its prey.

Go up one more light, then turn left. The Holy Spirit spoke to Levi's heart.

He bucked against the directions. There was an elaborate zig-zag pattern across town plotted out to the safe house. They mapped it out. There were undercover officers scattered all across this route. He couldn't deviate from it. Plus, the captain would have his backside parked behind a desk if he did.

So at the next light, he stuck to the plan and made a right.

"He didn't listen, boys," Finn yelled out over the wind speed from the moving vehicle. "Get ready."

In a flash of white, all five angels spread their wings. Every inch of the vehicle was wrapped perfectly in the Lord's protection.

"This may get dicey, but hold your position no matter what," Finn ordered. "And brace for impact!"

The man tightened his grip on the giant wheel. With headlights off, he crept up one street and into position. A smile pushed across his weathered face.

This wasn't one of Ticano's best plans. Ideally, they would plow through their car on the passenger side to ensure Mia's death, but beggars couldn't be choosers.

"The thrill of the kill," a chilling excitement rang in the man's voice.

Ticano let out a low chuckle that quickly turned into a blistering howl of intoxication. This woman, this tyrant, this *chosen one* would be dead soon and finally, Hexiathan wouldn't be able to take the credit for it. Ticano may not be refined like his wicked partner, but he grew tired of being that egotistical maniac's lap dog. The king of wicked would certainly offer up an award for something like this.

Rows of needle-like teeth flashed with a smile as he hunched over the man, egging him on.

⸺×⸺

All green lights up ahead. They were right on schedule despite the hiccup of Mia passing out. Levi questioned his choice to move her. The hospital could help with her injuries, but the internal alarms within wouldn't cease. She wasn't safe, and he couldn't stop until she was.

In a breath, a booming voice ripped through him.

PROTECT HER!

It was so loud, so invasive. Unable to stop himself, he let go of the wheel and gas to thrust his body over her, like a shield.

⸺×⸺

Lost in thought, Mia was taken by surprise when Levi heaved his entire body on hers. Every muscle screamed out in pain as she fought to catch her breath.

A bright light forced her eyes open just in time to see a tall, wide, silver grill within a foot of Levi's door. Time slowed while simultaneously moving too fast to catch.

"Lord, please," she pleaded.

The luminous glow remained, but no crash was heard. Her eyes squinted open and immediately widened. Surveying the area, she realized by some wild miracle, they were inside the engine of the garbage truck. She watched in disbelief as the pistons cranked up and down like a bicycle pedal. Time slowed to a crawl. Her face passed through the engine block as the injectors around her created small explosions, forcing the piston back down.

She thought of when her father explained how an engine worked to her as a child. He'd be so proud she remembered most of it.

Fascinated, she forgot the magnitude of what was happening. Their car was not crushed. Neither of them were hurt. They were protected. Spared. Alive.

God carved a way right through the garbage truck.

The car spun right out of the engine compartment and came to an abrupt stop when the tires slammed into the curb. Mia struggled to wrap her mind around what just happened. Her hands vigorously shook. She slowly unclenched the seat she didn't remember grabbing.

Her gaze met his, both looking for answers neither of them had. He protected her. She wrapped her shaky arms around him.

Relieved to be alive, she couldn't stop the destructive thoughts from crashing in like a tidal wave. Saving her had been a mistake. She was damaged goods. Worthless. A pathetic wife entangled with darkness.

⋯✕⋯

Levi's arms were tightly wrapped around Mia, not ready to let go. His heartbeat pulsated in his throat. He looked up in time to watch the dark green garbage truck crash into one of the large white oak trees lining the street.

Two black figures emerged from the truck, one jumped, and the other seeped out.

The assassin.

He released her and quickly grabbed his radio. "I see one, possibly two suspects fleeing the garbage truck. This might be our guy. Anyone in the area to respond?"

"Ten-four, we're on it," a voice came over the radio.

Within seconds, flashing lights filled the darkness with red and blue. A large spotlight frantically moved around the grid.

He turned to Mia. "We gotta move, now."

The tires squealed against the pavement before they took off. Levi repented of his disobedience and vowed to go the Lord's way every time from now on.

⋯✕⋯

"Nice job, lads," Finn smiled, cracking his neck as he peeled his lean body off the car. "But we ain't done yet. Keep your eyes moving, head on a swivel, ya hear?"

"Aye," they all responded.

"The war's just beginning. They want this little lass dead. It's our job to keep that from happening." Finn put his fist out. "Who's with me?"

"For the Lord's Glory," they said, overlapping each other as all four of them put their fists into the circle with Finn.

"For the Lord's Glory, indeed," Finn smiled.

Thirty

RAGGED AND RUN-DOWN, they walked into the downtown Knoxville Police Department. Jocelyn forced their bizarre encounter out of her mind the best she could. There was no time for such paranormal games.

"Can I help you?" a small, thin voice asked.

"Hi, yes." Jocelyn pulled a badge from her hip and held it up. "I'm Detective Maddox with Durham PD. I believe Capitan Hendrix is expecting us." The petite woman peered at AJ through large square frames. "This is AJ Spalding, the forensic specialist."

Without so much as a smile, the desk clerk picked up the phone and dialed, keeping an eye on them the whole time. The woman's suspicious stare crawled under Jocelyn's skin, reminding her of the looks she endured every time she went home.

She was exhausted. Remaining professional proved difficult, but not impossible. She learned the hard way how to rise above the violence of her neighborhood, the disapproval of those she loved, and the uncertainty in those she worked with. It was as if the color of her skin determined what side of the societal issues she stood on. It was a hard line to walk, but it was one she did well. Her job here was justice. Everything else paled in comparison.

She mindlessly tapped her foot in hopes to make this process go faster. Time was not on their side.

AJ eased his arm around her shoulders and pulled her into him. She fought the relaxation it brought.

"I know you're feeling the pressure of the clock. She'll be done soon and then I'll make you a cup of coffee when we get inside, okay?"

The knots building in her shoulders loosened. "Three sugars?"

He smiled. "Three sugars."

"Captain Hendrix is ready for you, detective." The mousy woman interrupted their sweet moment.

As if the light turned green, she hurriedly grabbed her things and rushed off toward the door.

"Thanks," she offered as an afterthought.

Through the heavy door, a suspiciously familiar room sat. This precinct held the same outdated desks and phones, the same exhausted and run-down looks hung on most faces, but their break room sat on the opposite side of the room. And from the looks of it, their coffee maker was much newer.

"Maddox!" Captain Hendrix said like they were old pals. "So glad y'all made it. If you come with me, I'll update you both on where we're at here. I've had a few of my best people on it."

Jocelyn tried to listen, but her attention was continuously pulled to the coffee station. AJ probably forgot his promise of another cup, but she held a current one-track mind.

Before she could speak, AJ chimed in. "Actually, sir, if you don't mind, it's been a long drive, and we could use some coffee before we get into the details."

"Oh, yes, of course." He led the way to the break room, his long stride hard to keep up with. "My wife just switched me to herbal tea to help my ticker." He tapped his finger to his chest with a wide smile, revealing a handful of crooked teeth. "But, I think tonight is one of those rare exceptions."

They arrived at the coffee machine, which was nicer than the one she owned back home. Mesmerized by the sleek shine of the stainless steel, she didn't notice the man pouring a cup.

"Just made a fresh pot." His booming voice made Jocelyn jump. "Oh, I didn't mean to scare you, ma'am," the man said with a rigid smile.

"Detective Maddox, this is one of our newest detectives, James Cott. James, this is Jocelyn Maddox from Durham PD. She's here about the serial killer."

"Oh, I heard about that. Are y'all close to catching him?" James asked.

Jocelyn stared blankly, leaving the preposterous question to hang in the air like day-old fish. Although she knew he didn't mean anything personal by his question, it still burned like salt in the wound of failure. Jocelyn wanted to scream in defense of her inadequacy.

"James." AJ interrupted the intrusive thoughts from behind her, his hand extended for a brief handshake. "I'm AJ, the forensic specialist. Nice to meet you." He turned to the captain. "Sir, why don't you and Joce head into your office and get started. I'll pour us all some coffee. How do you take it?"

She wanted to be annoyed. He just swooped in to save the damsel in distress. As a modern-day, rock-hard woman who stood clearly and concisely on her own two feet, she should hate it, but she didn't. It was rather enjoyable leaving her worries and fears buried under a thick layer of exhaustion.

Captain Hendrix carried on, in detail, about how to prepare his coffee. Jocelyn sighed.

⸻ ⚬⟩✕⟨⚬ ⸻

The run-down motel was small and definitely not a place she would choose for herself. She took in the outdated decor and stiff mattress and fought the urge to check their Yelp rating. The police department surely had more important things to spend their money on. A temporary motel room for a distraught, moronic wife whose life was falling apart was certainly low on the list, but she couldn't fight the cynical voice that wished they tried a little harder.

Guilt quickly settled. It wasn't their fault Oliver deceived her. She really was an idiot, blindly in love, not seeing what was literally right under her nose—all the late nights at the "office", the rising anger, the increased intensity of abuse, and the secrets that filled him. Oliver was no longer hers. He had fully given himself to something sinister that lurked behind his eyes. Out of love, or maybe it was foolishness, she tried to ignore it, but now it blew up right in her face.

"I know it's not much, but you'll be safe here," Levi offered. Her eyes shifted around the room, unsure she agreed. "I promise, it's safer than it looks."

She fixated on the fish proudly hung over the light pink and flower wallpaper. It was odd, to say the least. Casually she pawed at her side that had throbbed since the accident.

"Here." Levi pointed to a plush sitting chair. "How about you get off your feet for a bit?"

She hesitated, unsure which surface would be safest, the bed or the chair. Either could easily carry bed bugs or leftover fluids. Just the thought made her stomach twist.

"I'm going to wash up." She sighed.

The catalyst for this explosion was her. Soon every piece of comfort would be ripped away, leaving her with nothing. No amount of soap or scrubbing could ever wash those wounds away.

———×———

"Thanks for the update, captain, and for the coffee." Jocelyn stood, a sense of renewal within her.

The three of them shook hands.

"Can you point me to the lab?" AJ asked. He turned back to Jocelyn. "I'm going to get started on that sample. Shouldn't take long. If it's a match, we can easily attach charges for kidnapping and murder onto the warrant."

"I'll tell my detectives to hold off on arresting him for now," Hendrix offered.

"Sounds good. I'll head out to the safe house and speak with Mrs. Hughes. Call me on my cell with the results, yeah?"

"You got it." He smiled.

"I can take you to the safe house, ma'am," James Cott chimed in from the hallway.

Jocelyn noticed his well-built frame and baby face this time. He held little to no expression as he looked off in a direction that wasn't hers with anticipation of her answer.

"Marines?" Jocelyn asked.

"Army Rangers, ma'am. Three tours."

Three tours. That alone broke her heart. So young. She couldn't imagine the horrific things those deep-set eyes saw or what secrets hid behind them.

"That would be great." He knew the area much better than her, plus she could look over case files on the ride. "Thank you. Let's take my car." She handed him the keys. "I have weapons and vests in the trunk if needed." She smiled.

The car ride out was quiet. That would usually make Jocelyn nervous, but her mind was well-occupied.

The question currently on repeat—if Hughes wasn't their guy, then who could it be? Her mind flipped through the catalog of images and reports filed in her memory. She did her best to recall her thoughts on each case. She practically memorized those files before they left, but just in case, she downloaded the most recent ones to her phone.

She stopped on Shelby Walsh's file that read: unknown DNA found. Sometimes with cult-style killings, you find multiple strands of DNA, as multiple people were involved, but not here. The DNA found were from two suspects, neither in the system, both still a mystery.

Jocelyn skimmed through the rest of the report, and was shocked to find no further analysis done on each sample. This left them blind as to what to look for, such as gender, genetic markers, or diseases that could be traced back to medical records.

Her fingers quickly dialed, unwilling to wait another minute. Maybe AJ could work some magic and narrow down the suspect pool. Multiple DNA samples mean Hughes wasn't working alone.

"Hey, Joce." AJ's voice brought an unconscious smile to her full lips. "What's up?"

"Question." She shook off the juvenile flutter in her chest. "I'm looking at past cases and noticed none of the DNA samples from Walsh's body have been tested for information like gender or genetic markers. Any thought as to why?"

"That's odd." There was a brief pause, she could almost hear his wheels turning. "I'd say the most likely answer is the lab was overloaded and understaffed, so it was forgotten."

Another pause. The chair squeaked as he cleared his throat.

"Or." She gave a little nudge.

He sighed. "Or, someone in the lab is in on this whole thing and did what they could to slow things down."

Her gut flipped like a rollercoaster.

"Do you think that's possible?" She swallowed hard. "I mean, you spent time with them. What's your take?"

"Um…" He drew out the word. "Well, I don't think we can rule it out, but no one did anything suspicious when I was there."

"What's your percentage comparatively?" she urged.

"I'd say eighty, twenty in favor of it being an accident."

Her mind eased, but only for a moment. In the background, an alarm sounded.

"What's that?"

"Holy crap," AJ huffed a laugh. "The dirt sample's a match. Oliver Hughes is our guy."

Breath caught in her throat. She needed to update the arrest warrant and go with the team to help execute it, like yesterday.

"Turn around," she ordered James. "I need to go back to the precinct immediately."

"You got it," James nodded.

"AJ." She turned her attention back to her phone. "Alert Captain Hendrix and have him get started on the arrest warrant updates for Hughes." She went to hang up and then remembered a vital piece of the puzzle. "Oh, and let Hendrix know Mia Hughes is not to be let out of the officer's sight. For all we know, she's in on the whole thing." She paused again. "By the way, can you run the existing DNA samples for further information?"

"Sure. You're lucky I brought samples with me so I can analyze and cross reference. If you can get Hughes DNA, I can get you a slam dunk conviction."

⚬⚬╳⚬⚬

"I-I understand, sir." Mia tracked Levi as he paced back and forth alongside the bed. Hearing only one side of the conversation left her confused and annoyed. "I won't, but I really don't think—" He stopped to run his hand through his almond-colored hair. "Yes, sir. I won't. Okay. Mmhmm. Bye."

Mia held hope of an explanation, but one did not come. Instead, text messages flooded his phone, and she watched as he frantically responded. Not one look. Not even a glance in her direction. No flirtatious smile or longing touch.

Several anxious minutes later, he marched over and sat next to her on the bed.

"Everything okay?" she casually asked.

"I don't know yet," he sighed.

None of that was helpful—such a stubborn man.

"Whatever it is, you can tell me. I can handle it." She pushed for just a glimpse of understanding.

He looked up at her, and she ignored the butterflies it brought. Levi chewed on his inner bottom lip, a dead giveaway he kept something from her. It was a tell that told her to pull out whatever he kept hidden like the time he accidentally drove the tractor over her vegetable garden in middle school.

He tore his eyes away with a long, drawn-out sigh.

"I'm going to take a shower real quick." He patted the side of her leg and headed for the bathroom.

Her whole body tensed when she noticed his phone on the desk as he closed the door. She chewed at the skin around her nails, wrestling her consciousness. This was wrong. The punishment wouldn't be worth the information. Plus, if anyone would get caught, it would be her.

The water turned on, and she waited to hear the shower curtain slink back across the rod. Before she knew it, her feet were on the ground and she quietly trotted to his device. A swipe of her finger revealed the need for a passcode.

Of course.

She tried his birthday a few different ways, his mom's birthday, his old address. She wondered if it was his badge number, which would be unfortunate since she didn't know it. The sting of knowing there was an entire span of his life she knew nothing about hurt worse than she anticipated. A whole piece of him remained a mystery. Best friends, torn apart by hurt and time.

Decades of memories flooded through her mind. What if he used the same password he had all those years ago?

She typed in her birthday. *Click.*

Rows of texts were revealed with a brief preview for each one. He ignored most, not bothering to open them. But the one he didn't ignore was from Sergeant Cole.

The preview read, *I won't tell her, relax.*

She scrolled through and read several texts back and forth. Her heart dropped from her chest. The dirt she gave them was a match, and they now had an arrest warrant for Oliver. The hollow pit in her stomach brought tears to her eyes.

Countless thoughts ripped through her mind. Her husband brutally murdered innocent women. The thought coiled her stomach. Her husband was a monster, and she'd just turned him in.

Unwilling to let her mind go there, she continued to scroll. A gasp of disbelief held in her throat.

SERGEANT COLE:
You can't tell her any of this. Detective Maddox from Durham thinks Mrs. Hughes is in on it with her husband. They have a DNA sample and are running it to see if it's female.

And Levi, the good little soldier, agreed to keep it from her with minimal pushback.

She glared at the bathroom door. "Jerk," she scoffed under her breath.

With a quick reach for her purse and the keys, she ran out the door. She refused to stay where she was lied to. Not again. Not ever.

Her feet kept in rhythm with the rapid flutter of her heart. She was held prisoner for too long. Her marriage was a lie. Her life, a lie. And the one person she thought would be honest was also filled with lies.

The keys jingled in her grasp. In the car, she wiped the sweat from her upper lip. Evading the stupid officer in the shower was apparently more stressful than she thought.

She adjusted the seat with the abrasive reality this was a bad idea. If she left, wouldn't that make her look guilty? She let out a long-winded sigh. She didn't want to be near Levi. He betrayed her…again.

Beli-yaal slithered into the car and wrapped around Mia.

"He's betrayed you once again, dear one. You can't trust anyone but me," he snickered in her ear. "He's going to string you along just like he did all those years ago. Don't be a fool."

The engine roared to life. She aggressively put the car in drive, but stayed still. Her knuckles turned white against the pressure of them around the wheel. This idiotic girl never listened.

"You won't run. But there is nothing wrong with leaving for a bit to clear your head." An awfully brilliant idea came to mind. "There's a bar up the road. A drink'll help you relax so you can think rationally."

"I need a drink," she huffed as the tires spun against the asphalt.

Her strength returned, leaving her alert and very aware of everything. The drugs worked fast, which meant—

A squeal of the door alerted her to the threat at hand. Her soon-to-be killers returned. A hollow ache cried out in her bones as her body tensed. Charlotte coiled into the fetal position. Her heart pounded, each breath now heavier than the last.

"Ah, there's our little apostasy." The soft one walked over and used his steel-toed boot to roll her onto her back.

"I told you it would work." The familiar one celebrated.

"Let's get on with it already. The clock is ticking, Our Enemy hides somewhere close. I can feel it."

Their enemy? That question bounced around Charlotte's mind. Someone out there terrified them, but who?

She looked up in hopes of catching a glimpse, but no part of them was visible, leaving race, gender, or any defining marks or tattoos a mystery. Everything they did was well thought through.

Two of them carried a wide bucket of water and sat it down in front of her. The third one put a tightly covered smaller bucket next to it. Terror spread as they hummed a little tune in ecstasy. It reminded Charlotte of a hymn her father used to sing. The only part she remembered was the chorus. She internally sang the words and found they matched the melody seamlessly.

Trust and obey, For there's no other way. To be happy, trust and obey.

The larger one pulled out a leather-bound notebook and unwound the long tassels around it. He held it out and began with a long rhythmic hum. It reminded her of the Muslim service she and Kiley went to. Neither of them were Muslim, but they were curious as to what it was all about.

He bowed at the waist three times, his arms outstretched over the top of her. Things intensified as the two others joined, making a circle around her. The bellowing hum echoed off the walls of the hollow cave. Louder and louder until it unexpectedly stopped.

The silence was a welcome change.

Charlotte racked her memory for the details spread around campus. This had to be some sort of religious ritual because it played out like a charted and intentional pattern.

"Today," his thunderous voice made her jump. "We gather to air the grievances of the Lord God against you, Charlotte Scott."

She wondered if they would drink her blood or torture her as a sadistic game, but one thing became clear, the ritual of her death just started.

Thirty-One

THE SOLID WOOD DOOR needed her body weight to counteract the massiveness of it. Once inside, it met every expectation she had pulling in—a lonely and abandoned pool table sat isolated on one side, a jukebox on the other with half its lights working, all wrapped in a thick mysterious haze.

With only four people in the entire bar, including the bartender, all focus shifted to Mia as she awkwardly stood there. Thankfully her large sunglasses covered several bruises on her face and concealed the water gathered in her eyes from the smog.

Ignoring the unwelcomed stares, she took her place in the dark corner of the bar and double-tapped her hand on the surface.

"Whisky, neat, and make it a double."

The bartender carried a sullen look in his eyes and moved slower than she preferred. A nagging part of her wanted the whole bottle, but she settled for a glass.

She was officially a suspect in the brutal murders of eight, possibly nine women. The crazy thing was that she had never gone to Durham before, something Levi would have known if he bothered to ask.

"What's your name?" she asked as the whiskey swirled in her glass.

"Ernie." His gravelly voice was expected as a likely, two-packs-a-day man.

"Well, thank you, Ernie. Cheers." She tossed her head back and swallowed it in one gulp.

By the end of her first drink, she heard the door open. "Mia."

She refused to turn around, taking a slow exhale as the burn in her chest dissipated. She noted Ernie step to the left and slowly reach under the bar.

"I have nothing to say to you, Reed." Her jaw clenched. "Just leave me alone." The glass slammed down onto the bar.

She sat far away from the other patrons for unsociable reasons, but now he was here, bringing an anger that engulfed her.

"Mia, you need to go back to the motel." He leaned in and lowered his voice. "It might not be safe here."

"The lady asked you to leave her alone," Ernie growled.

Levi held up his badge. "Sir, I'm an officer."

"That don't mean nothin' to me." He stood up tall to reveal a wooden baseball bat in his hands.

"Oh Ernie, you're sweet. I'm okay," she sweetly offered before turning back to Levi. "Listen." She dismissed any further attempt to speak in a lady-like manner. "I'm gonna sit here and drink. I really don't care what you decide to do." Levi went to say something, but Mia cut him off. "I already know the truth so get off it already."

The whiskey worked its magic faster than ever. An empty stomach would do that.

"What truth?"

She ignored him and turned back around. "Ernie. Another, please." She pointed to her drink.

Ernie arrived in a flash, bat still in hand. Apparently tense situations put a giddy-up in his step. As the dark amber happy juice flowed into her empty glass, she glared at Levi from the corner of her eye.

"What truth?" Levi sternly asked again.

She whipped around to face him eye to eye. Rage boiled within. She hated that he was here, hated that stupid look on his face, and those piercing eyes. She hated his demand for her to answer him. But most of all, she hated that he played dumb.

"I know everything, Reed. Everything."

She grabbed her drink to shoot it back, but his firm hand grabbed her arm.

"What's that supposed to mean?"

"Well, let's see." She jerked away from him, spilling some of the needed relief from the glass. "My husband's probably being arrested as we speak, and if that's not bad enough"—she flung back what was left in the glass—

"y'all think I've got somethin' to do with it." Her Southern flourished as she double-tapped the glass on the bar. "Another."

"I think she's had enough… Ernie is it?" Levi put his hand over her glass.

Mia shoved him away. "It's not up to *you* when I'm done." Ernie nervously poured her drink as Mia stared down Levi. "You know, I get *them* thinkin' I'm somehow in on it, but I thought we knew each other better than that. I thought you loved me." The slurred words from her mouth stung. She tried to correct her mistake. "You know, like a friend or whatever."

"Mia." Levi spoke soft yet firm. "We need to get out of here."

"No, I'm stayin'."

"You're not going to find what you're looking for at the bottom of that glass."

"Sure I will. I'll find the ability to forget this entire day and you, Levi Reed." She picked up the tumbler and tossed back the whole thing. "Another." The thick glass slammed back down on the solid wood.

"Okay, yes, tonight you'll forget, but tomorrow you'll wake up, and it'll all be real again."

"Cool story, bud."

A refill of her drink was poured in front of her, this time she sipped it slower. Her lips tingled as the room spun.

"Look, I'll make a deal with you, okay? If you come with me back to the motel, I'll buy that bottle of whiskey and take it back with us for you."

"But what about the amazing ambiance here, Levi? How ya gonna get me that?" Sarcasm saturated Mia's words.

"Please."

"What do you care anyway? I'm a suspect, remember?"

"Mia, I'm sorry. Of course I don't think you could be in on it. But I didn't want to chance them deciding to replace me with someone else because I defended you. No one is as invested in your safety as I am, and I know the truth will come out." His hands felt heavy when he placed them on her shoulders. "I'm sorry, M. Please, I'm begging you, let me buy the bottle, and we'll go back where it's safe. I can't lose you, not again."

The bartender placed a half-full bottle of Jack Daniel's on the bar.

She wanted to go but struggled to let him win. No one here needed to see her cry, but she despised how he ordered her to go, so she dug her heels in and negotiated.

"That whiskey and all the cherries they got—final offer." She slammed back the rest of her glass.

Levi looked up, and the guy behind the counter gave a subtle nod. No one wanted her around, not even frizzy-haired Ernie.

Mia wrestled down sadness, swiped the bottle off the bar, and guzzled another shot. It wasn't long before the cherries were bagged up and they were on their way.

⸺✕⸺

Her cold naked body shivered on the dirt floor. This would be mortifying if she wasn't already terrified to her core. There was no room left, even for embarrassment. The rhythmic chanting made her head spin. Weird how it brought order to the chaos she felt.

The water in the wide-mouthed bucket brought goosebumps and uncontrollable shivers. The softer one bathed her like a baby. The dirt Charlotte laid in created mud patches on her purple skin.

The booming voice spoke out. "These are the words of the Son of God, whose eyes are like blazing fire and whose feet are like burnished bronze."

Charlotte could have sworn this was from the only book of the Bible she ever fully read, Revelation. Twisted scripture could be used to justify anything, even murder.

The man continued, "Jesus says, I know your sins, Charlotte, and I've sent these messengers to carry out my judgment on you and remove you from this earth. You're a disgrace to the Most High God and His Son. You will face judgment today for your transgressions. What do you have to say for yourself?"

Charlotte was on trial. Although she never defended herself naked in front of strangers before, she had to embrace it because her life depended on it.

"Can I plead my defense?" Charlotte mustered the strongest voice she could.

"You have one minute," the familiar voice snapped.

Charlotte took a drawn-out breath and subtly cleared her sore throat. She pushed past the scream of defiance in her body as she pushed herself to her feet. Her knees wobbled, unable to remember the last time she stood.

"Hello." A shaky start but she didn't know how else to greet them. "My name is Charlotte Scott and as you know I'm here today representing myself in this trial." She paused. Etiquette said she should thank the deciders of her fate, although these scumbags didn't deserve it.

Keep going. The Lord spoke.

"Tick-tock," the familiar one surged with palpable hate.

"Um." She searched for the words. "I want to thank you for being here today and, uh, for listening to me with an unbiased heart." Disgust collected behind her fake smile. "In this case against me, I would argue you don't have all the facts." She slowly limped into a pace back and forth in front of her tormentors. Her voice shook under the weight of her emotions. "I haven't always been on the side of God. In fact, I walked fully away from Him and denied His very existence." She gained confidence and the quiver in her voice faded. "Yes, I did some unforgivable things, but what you haven't presented is the current state of my heart. And for that, I guess I owe you a bit of gratitude." She paused. Flattery wouldn't work. "Since being in here, I've fully given my life to the Lord and have since been absolved of all sin. He has granted me immunity in those things you've accused me of." She drew another breath. "Due to this recent change of events, the charges against me no longer stand for judgment. So the way I see it, you have no other choice but to find me not guilty and let me go."

Charlotte attempted to hide the thin smile on her lips. For the first time in days, hope swelled within her. Jesus died to spare people from judgment and wrath, something she hoped even they would acknowledge.

The long silence made her uncomfortable. They had to agree. They had to let her go. This couldn't be the end. Charlotte closed her eyes. *Your will, Jesus. Not mine,* she thought.

Her eyes opened again. The three men stood like statues.

All Charlotte knew was she gave the argued with the truth to these religious predators. They were obviously delusional or maybe Charlotte was to think she could change their mind. The silence lasted for so long, Charlotte suddenly became hyper-aware of her nakedness. She attempted to cover herself with her arms and hands in hopes of taking back a sliver of dignity.

Her stomach coiled in on itself like a snake. Bile pricked at the back of her throat. Without warning, the large one put his hand up.

"Let us analyze and identify the Lord's will. It is His desire above all else," he boomed, his voice deep and grim.

A small victory celebration erupted in her heart. Hope resonated that their minds could change, or maybe she only delayed the inevitable, but soon she'd know whether the Lord would save her or not.

※

Levi helped Mia up the cement stairs and back to the motel room. She awkwardly sat on the bed, visibly struggling to control her body. Levi knew better than most how to deal with drunk people.

The day his mom died wasn't something Levi thought of often, but when he did, it always came with aching grief, even all these years later. He believed that eventually he would get used to the pain of her not being there. That one day the hole in his life would become normal. But the truth was, the nagging guilt of struggling to remember the details of his mother's face or the sound of her voice never left. And he carried a debilitating shame along with it.

His father picked up a bottle of whiskey after the funeral and then any bottle he could after that. Anything to keep the gnawing pain away that ripped one's heart to shreds. Keith Reed allowed the bottle to be the answer, and it scared Levi to know tonight, Mia did the same.

He dutifully opened and slammed every possible drawer and cabinet in search of a coffee maker until he found it. The ancient machine bucked and ground at the idea of doing its job. He grabbed a washcloth from the bathroom, soaked it in cold water, and was back at her side to wipe her face.

She lovingly looked into his eyes the same way she had so many times before destruction came for them. When he ghosted her, he did it to protect her, but now he saw the truth—the damage he caused proved catastrophic.

Those aqua eyes stopped him in his tracks. A smile danced on her face as she leaned in for a kiss. Levi's heart picked up speed. He wanted nothing more than to feel the softness of her lips on his, but the cost would be great. Last time he didn't consider the cost. If he had, things might have turned out differently. Her lips brushed his before he pulled her back.

"Not like this, M." Sorrow ignited and hung in his heart.

A longingness weighed on him. Maybe he hoped she would fight for him or maybe he just really wanted to kiss her. Either way, things couldn't go like this. It was wrong.

He expected her to push back or yell, but she didn't.

"That's okay, Mr. Reed." Her words slurred. "I know you love me because I love you." A look of shock filled her eyes. She gasped, "Oops!" A giggle followed. "I wasn't supposed to tell you that. It's a secret." She put her finger against her lips. "Shhh."

Levi left her side to make a cup of coffee with as much sugar as he could find. She had to sober up. The Durham detective would be here soon with questions this Mia couldn't comprehend, let alone answer. He held the cup close to her mouth to help steady the sway of her hands.

"This'll help."

Mia took several quick sips of the hot elixir. He hoped she'd be sober enough by the time that detective arrived. If not, this wouldn't look good for either of them.

"Where do you think the dirt sample is from?" Levi pressed. They needed answers.

"I don't know," she said like a child.

"Mia." Levi put the coffee on the table. "This is important. I need you to think."

"Maybe our property." Her eyes rolled in every direction but his.

"What property?"

"The one where I was supposed to raise my baby so I could feel like my life with you worked out." She rubbed her face.

"That place out by Sevierville?" Levi couldn't move. He never imagined she would do their life plan with someone else.

"Mmhmm. That fifty acres we said we'd buy someday. Well, I couldn't wait for you anymore so I put my dream, our dream, on Oliver's shoulders." Her words slurred with heavy eyelids. "I mean, he wanted it too. I didn't like…hijack his dreams or anything." She began to sob. "He loved me so much ya know. None of it ever made any sense. Why would he pick me to just ruin me?"

She laid down on the bed and curled up like a cat. A faint snore vibrated against him, but he still couldn't move. She put their dream on Oliver's shoulders.

The only thing that didn't make sense was they never purchased the property they wanted, plus, it was thirty acres, not fifty. He knew better than to trust the drunken ramblings of a person on the emotional edge.

⸻ ✕ ⸻

Adrenaline flooded. Her heart thundered against her chest like it always did before serving a warrant. Over her clothes, the vest hugged her body tight. She tugged on the straps and the side velcro, cinching it down like a bear hug of protection. It sported golden block letters and a sewn-on badge that popped against the black vest.

On the way to the Hughes' residence, Jocelyn studied pictures of Mia's injuries. There was no doubt Oliver Hughes had violent tendencies, so the possibility of a fight tugged at her nerves. The deep shades of a battered life forced her to question the wife's involvement.

Despite her best efforts to pass the leader role to Captain Hendrix, he insisted she take it. Her suspect, her case, and her job to lead the team. Jocelyn couldn't bring herself to tell him she had never led a no-knock warrant before. This might be the only time in her life a man's respect irritated her to no end. But, no sense crying about it. She had a job to do. Restlessness grew in her team.

She tugged once more on her vest, adjusted the helmet on her head, and checked the HK MP5 submachine weapon in her hands for the fourth time. It would be embarrassing to go in and realize the safety was still on.

She nervously checked the weapon again.

She put eyes on the house across the street where the sniper found a worthy perch. Alpha team was set at the front door and the beta team covered the back. Two teams surrounded on the perimeter, just to be safe. No room for error here.

"Beta team, ready?" Jocelyn asked into her hands-free radio.

"Beta team ready," a stern voice replied.

"Perimeter team, ready?"

"Perimeter one ready."

"Perimeter two ready."

"Sniper one, ready?"

"Sniper one ready, ma'am."

"Alpha team in position. Get ready, on my count. We breach in three…two…one."

In unison, two large men wielded their handheld metal rams and knocked in both doors. Like a strategic tidal wave, teams flooded into the house, weapons up with fingers ready to pull the trigger at a moment's notice—a calculated craft they knew well.

Teams broke off, two by two, and checked every room, closet, and forgotten space for any sign of the perpetrator.

"Clear." The word bounced from room to room on a repetitive cycle.

"Oliver Hughes," Jocelyn hollered. She did her best to sound tough despite her shaky hands. "This is the police. We have a warrant for your arrest so come out with your hands up."

No response.

"Check the attic, basement, any sheds outside—everywhere," she ordered.

The teams tore the place apart, but Oliver Hughes was nowhere to be found. Jocelyn tried to maintain hope and failed at that too.

"We're too late," she whispered.

Thirty~Two

LIKE A SHADOWY SNAKE, Hexiathan coiled around his prey. This deplorable bloke easily broke into submission. He hovered close to Oliver's ear, cementing their bond deeper. The Enemy would not win this one.

"What you're doing is right, Oliver. There are consequences for every action, some more severe than others."

The pitiful preacher concealed a sob under his breath. Hexiathan didn't want to watch this barmy twit cry like a schoolgirl. What a waste of space. He told Beli-yaal this guy wasn't tough enough. All of the weeping and sissy apologies along the way had him on Hexithan's last nerve.

"You know what needs to be done, Oliver, you're just afraid to do it." His sultry voice eased the tears. "You've worked so hard to keep everything I've given you intact. I've watched you tirelessly patch holes in your marriage, hold up a church with your blood, sweat, and tears, and still remain devoted to me." Hexiathan stifled a giggle at his spot-on impersonation of that Knob. "I have one last task for you, son. Soon you'll be aptly welcomed into my arms."

In the privacy of his car, parked on some forgotten stretch of road, Oliver openly conversed with evil.

"Whatever you ask of me, God, I'll do," he faintly whimpered.

"Mia will be managed, but it's time for you to come home to me."

Hexiathan waited silently to see if he pushed him too far, too fast. Oliver's face twisted with wide eyes. The internal wrestling match that occurred in his spirit was unmistakable.

Such an ankle-biter.

Hexiathan needed to salvage this. The final request was non-negotiable. It came from the highest level. Oliver Hughes must die.

Her body floated through a veil of darkness. The midnight gloom suddenly shimmered with light. Mia forced her eyes open and found herself enjoying a relaxing bath at home.

Her bright eyes scanned the room. An amber glow of a dozen candles flickered around her.

Is this a dream?

Sudsy water dripped from her arm as she pulled it from the tub. A good pinch would bring clarity. She grabbed skin and clamped as hard as she could.

"Ouch!" She heaved a breath. *Man that hurt*, she thought with a rub of her arm.

None of this made sense.

The atmosphere quickly shifted. Relaxation was abandoned and replaced with dread. A sting at her back alerted her to the danger she was in.

Something sharp pierced deep into her spine. Hot breath saturated her cheek. The mere weight of the creature rocked her back and forth, pushing waves of suds to the floor. A low gutter growl intensified in her ear.

Her lips quivered, a reminder that her greatest weapon remained free.

"In the name of Je—s, get—" She pushed, choking back the words when its forked tail whipped over her mouth.

"Nuh—uh—uh," it hissed in her ear. "Leave your nose out of things you don't understand," it snapped. Her body lifted completely from the bathtub, suspended in the thick air. "Or else."

Powerless to this dreadful darkness, she trembled like a leaf. A pulse of electricity vibrated through her body. Every nerve howled in searing pain. A muffled cry was lost against the mass of its tail. Her cheeks throbbed. Blood trickled from under the weight covering her mouth. Every last bit of strength was siphoned from her body.

One thought crossed her weary mind—*pray*. With her mouth unable, her heart would have to be enough.

Jesus, she cried. *Help me, please. I can't stop this from happening.*

Despite the sporadic pulses of excruciating pain, the Lord spoke to her heart.

Alone you are vulnerable and at the mercy of the evil one, but in Me and through Me, you're stronger than you know. Stop trying to defeat this in your strength and power and do it in Mine. Remember who you are in Me, Mia. You're so much more than you've allowed yourself to be. It's time to stop being the victim and through Me become the conqueror I created you to be.

A surge of power like never before coursed through her body. A fiery balm exploded across her chest and radiated from the top of her head to the tip of her fingers and toes. She bit into the darkness until tar filled her mouth. The demon screeched in pain and whipped its tail from her, but refused to let go of her back.

"Enough!" Mia bellowed, violently shaking the world around her.

Still suspended in the air, a bright light expanded throughout the room. The demon wailed in pain but refused to let go. Mia peered at the wall next to her and noticed the beast's shadow cast—triple the size of her.

Panic clawed its way in. *Remember who you are in Me*, the Lord whispered. Without thinking, she reached back and grabbed the sizable threat. It whooped and hollered at the intrusion.

A powerful battle cry formed deep within and tore from her chest into the air. Her fingers dug deep into the scaly skin of her tormentor and peeled the devil off her back like a Band-Aid. Each talon unhooked, one by one.

With it firmly in her grasp, she fell to her feet, now dressed in the armor of God like a seasoned warrior. The shield of Faith rested on her back while she held the tip of the Sword at the demon's throat.

"Who are you?" she demanded.

The demon flipped and flailed in her grasp. Its inky stare swirled with toxic yellow.

"Let me go, please. Don't send me back there." The hideous creature sputtered black tar and choked on fireless smoke. "Just let me go, and I'll leave you alone forever."

Mia scoffed, unfazed by the hazardous display and putrid stink of decay.

"Answer my question. Who are you?" she pressed.

The demon pathetically pleaded for its life, ignoring her demands. Unsure what to do, she turned to the only One able to help and prayed in her heart for a name.

Beli-yaal, the Lord answered. *It's a high-ranking demon sent to oppress you and make you believe you're worthless. It attached to your family line many generations ago, and it's time to sever its reign.*

A memory of her father came to mind when he taught her and Luke how to bind a demon shortly after her first encounter. Luke scoffed and sat with arms folded and eyes in a continuous rolling state, but Mia listened intently. She never wanted to feel as powerless as she did that first night again. But somewhere along the way, Mia believed this devil's lies and allowed them to change her in more ways than she likely knew.

No more games.

"Beli-yaal, in the authority given to me by the sacrifice and resurrection of Jesus Christ..."

Mia lifted her elbow and pressed the tip of her sword further into its throat as a trickle of tar escaped. She peered into the eyes of Hell and all that remained was fear.

"Please. No," it shrieked, revealing its jagged teeth.

"I bind you by the blood of the Lamb."

Mia looked to her right and there Jesus stood, aglow in Glory. Bright red ribbons with flecks of gold flowed freely from the scars on his extended wrists. Alive with the knowledge of exactly what to do, they easily wrapped around the beast, binding everything, including its forked tail and mouth. Muffled screams were all that remained.

"And in the Name of Jesus, I cast you back to Hell where you belong."

The floor opened a portal to where total darkness awaited with maniacal satisfaction. The heat of hell reached her face. A stench of sulfur, decay, and sweat danced at her nose.

With a simple flick of her wrist, the demon flung into darkness. Its shrieks of torment faded as it fell.

Mia sat straight up, grabbing her side in pain. She looked around at the floral wallpaper. When her eyes met the large fish mounted on the wall, it brought an odd sense of security.

"M, are you okay?" Levi was at her side in seconds with a plethora of questions that fell on preoccupied ears.

A soft exhale of relief and peace flooded her whole body. She felt lighter, stronger, and finally free from the oppression she endured.

The one who tormented her for almost three decades was finally gone.

--------×--------

Jocelyn dragged her tired, run-down body up the cement stairs. Defeat hung heavy on her shoulders. Hughes was in the wind. No closer to finding Charlotte than they had been hours ago, the only link left was a woman who'd accused her abusive husband of being a murderer. Sounded about right. This case had held on by a thread for almost a year.

Charlotte was going to die, and it would definitely be her fault... again.

She thought of AJ, and how he urged her to not give up hope, but that request seemed impossible. After forty-eight hours, the likelihood of solving a case dropped by fifty percent, and they were well past that.

Charlotte went missing around twenty-one hundred hours Thursday night. If the killers stuck to their previous timeline, she had mere hours left to live.

Every agonizing step tortured her feet. She looked down at the car and saw Detective Cott leaning against it in a signature magazine pose. She scoffed. If his peers caught him doing that, they'd call him Fabio or something, and it would haunt his whole career.

Jocelyn contemplated a friendly warning but deemed herself officially too tired to care.

She glanced at a text on her phone to find the room number.

"Two-fourteen," she whispered to herself as if it would help her locate it.

The room in front of the stairs read two-twenty-three. She looked around for a sign or anything as to which way to go. Apparently, it was dealer's choice, so she picked left. When she realized with a fifty-fifty shot, she'd chosen wrong—*figures*—she turned around.

"Sixteen... Fifteen..." She repeated the numbers on the doors.

Her hand reached up to knock when her phone went off. AJ.

She answered it quickly, stepping away from the door. "Hey, any news?"

"No hey AJ, how are you? I've missed your spiky hair and lovable personality."

"First of all," Jocelyn huffed, an attempt to not be amused by his charm. "Your hair is weird, and your personality makes me want to jam pencils in my ears," Jocelyn retorted, harsher than intended. "But, I guess I'll keep you around for the coffee." She hoped her chuckle would soften the cruelness.

"So I'm just your coffee boy now?" he playfully asked.

"And hot Cheetos." She smiled, but it quickly faded when she thought of Charlotte. "I do need to know if the DNA results are in or if there are any more developments. With Hughes MIA, we're losing momentum fast." She sighed.

"Well, I'm about to make your day then. The results are in. One of the DNA samples is from a woman. I'm running it against a water bottle Detective Walsh said Mia drank from."

"How on earth did he just randomly have that lying around?" Jocelyn asked.

"He thought Reed was being too biased about her and thinking with his…" AJ's voice trailed off. "I'll spare you the vulgar phrase, but I'm sure you get it."

"Why'd he think that?"

"I guess they used to date or at least that's the rumor floating around."

"Interesting." Jocelyn fell silent while her mind drove in circles like a NASCAR race.

Who on earth would knowingly allow a lovesick officer to babysit the only other possible suspect in a serial killer case? No way this Reed guy could stay objective. These people were either stupid, naive, or both.

She looked behind her at room two-fourteen. A horrid thought brewed deep in her mind.

What if they aren't here?

"Jocelyn?" AJ asked in the background of her focus.

"I gotta go."

⸻ ✕ ⸻

Hexiathan waited several minutes for Oliver to take action, but it didn't work. He needed to try something else.

"My son, I'm so proud of you and all you've accomplished in my name. You'll be remembered as a martyr for your faith. There is no greater accomplishment in my kingdom," he gently whispered.

Oliver softened. Hexiathan watched the imbecile consider the assignment with a wide smile. He couldn't wait to tell Jezebel about this. She would be delighted.

"Not every task assigned from Heaven is an easy one, but there is a great and mighty purpose at stake here if you say no. Your death will save thousands." He poked at Oliver's pride. "A hero of the faith, a man everyone will know."

A suppressed chuckle bucked his chest. It was working.

⌐•X•¬

Face to face with the burnt red door, the thought of Charlotte possibly being sacrificed at this very moment fed her anxiety. Her slender hand balled into a fist. Time for answers. Jocelyn aggressively racked against the door like a jackhammer. This woman better be ready because Jocelyn was in no mood to pull punches or spare feelings.

A drag of air swooped from behind her as the door whipped open, revealing a tall, handsome man. His free hand balled into a fist, his other hidden behind the door. Jocelyn moved slowly, uncertain of what he held unseen.

"I'm Detective Maddox from DPD. I'm here to speak with Mia Hughes." She gestured to her belt. "I have a badge, let me show you." Both their bodies tensed as she slowly pulled her navy blue blazer to the side. "Is Mrs. Hughes here?"

The man relaxed. She heard a click as his hand came into view with a Glock nineteen in it—a gun aimed and ready to take her out just moments ago.

"Sorry about that, detective. Can't be too careful." He smiled, holstering his weapon. "Mia, it's safe to come out."

Jocelyn heard the shower curtain pull back and through the bathroom door emerged a broken-down woman. She took notice of the multiple bruises to her face and neck, wondering what other injuries she carried under the baggy sweatshirt and pajama bottoms. Her damp hair revealed soft strawberry curls.

Jocelyn looked back at the man. "You must be Officer Reed." She stuck out her hand as a kind gesture, mostly keeping her eyes on Mia.

"It's a pleasure to meet you, detective," he kindly said.

"You too." She stepped toward her potential suspect. "I have a lot of questions for you," she said sternly. "But first, I'll need your cell phone."

The timid woman's eyes shifted between her and Levi, a potential signal for him to step in. Jocelyn waited, ready to push back if needed. Despite their height difference, she learned how to favorably use her stature early on in life. She was always ready for a fight.

Mrs. Hughes shifted in her stance. The phone twisted between her hands several times before she held it out in Jocelyn's direction. She turned off the cell, unsure what to make of this woman who held such fear in her eyes.

"I'm happy to tell you anything I know, detective," Mrs. Hughes softly offered.

"Have a seat." Jocelyn pointed to the avocado green armchair by the desk.

As Mrs. Hughes slowly moved to the chair, Jocelyn scanned the place. Hideous room. Flower wallpaper, a dead fish, and a coffee maker that was clearly from before this century.

She noted the slept-in bed and wondered if something else had gone on there. She narrowed her eyes on the officer as if some internal alarm would sound if she detected infidelity. Dark circles held under his uniquely bright green eyes.

He gently assisted Mrs. Hughes to the chair. Pain grimaced on her face. Jocelyn made a mental note of the injuries. The two of them obviously cared deeply for each other despite a deep-rooted brokenness Jocelyn sensed.

It was something in their body language or the way they looked at each other. He seemed to pity her, while she withheld from him. Those training seminars were worth the money spent a year ago—body language gives a person away every time.

"Officer Reed," Jocelyn finally spoke. "I'll need you to wait outside."

"What? Why?" He quickly became defensive.

"Because I said so, and last time I checked, I don't have to explain myself to you." Jocelyn put her hands on her hips, giving a nod in the direction of the door. Levi hesitated. "Believe it or not, Officer Reed, this case isn't about you and your love for Mrs. Hughes." He tried to voice a rebuttal but Jocelyn didn't allow him the chance. "So you have two choices, step outside or I call in your peers to forcibly remove you. Which is it gonna be?"

Officer Reed gave a swift nod. "I'll be right outside," he stated.

In silent support, he softly placed his hand on Mrs. Hughes's shoulder and left.

The door gently closed behind him. Jocelyn appreciated he didn't let his anger or frustration lead. Instead, he moved with respect.

Jocelyn walked over, turned the desk chair around, and placed it across from her suspect. She took a seat and pulled out a notebook and pen.

"Mrs. Hughes," Jocelyn evened out her voice. "I have a few—"

"Mia," she cut her off.

"Excuse me?"

"Please call me Mia. I'm not too thrilled being associated with my husband right now." She dropped her head as if on cue.

"I'm sorry that makes you uncomfortable, Mrs. Hughes, but like it or not, you *are* associated, and I'm not exactly here to spare your feelings." She thought of Charlotte. "I have a twenty-four-year-old woman who is out of time, so forgive me for not caring about *your* needs at this moment. I'm not your boyfriend out there," Jocelyn scoffed. "My job is to be the miracle that poor girl is praying for, understood?"

Tears trickled down Mrs. Hughes' face. "Understood."

Jocelyn swallowed hard. Maybe she went too far.

"Good." She clicked her pen and readied it to write. The beginning was the logical place to start, but there was no time for that. She needed answers, now. "Where did Oliver take Charlotte?"

"I-I, um, I don't know," Mia sobbed.

"We're running out of time, Mrs. Hughes. Where did he take them?"

"I don't know," Mia sobbed harder, grabbing her side.

"Where?" Jocelyn demanded.

"We have property," Mia blurted out. "We have property out near Kodak, fifty acres. I can tell you where it is."

"Why do you think he took her there?" Jocelyn pushed.

"The only thing on the property is a root cellar, plus there's red dirt everywhere up there."

"Is there any other reason Oliver would've gone up there?"

"It's secluded." She picked at her nails. "The back of our property runs up against the river. There's no one for miles around. The only people we've ever seen are the occasional cattle farmer checking fences. That's it, and it's not often." Jocelyn's stare intensified, pushing for more. "The cellar has no shelves, and no electricity. The only reason he put a lock on it was to keep squatters out."

Jocelyn's eyes grew wide. "Have you been up there recently?"

"No." Her shoulders sank.

"Why not?"

"Oliver doesn't allow me up there anymore."

Mia sobbed, the guilt surely eating her alive.

"Why?" Jocelyn raised her voice.

"I don't know."

"You've never been up there alone?" Jocelyn huffed. "So you're telling me you never broke his rules and went out there?"

"Never."

"I'm not sure I believe you."

"Well, it's the truth."

"Why should I believe that?" Jocelyn was met with silence. She slammed her hand against the table. "Why?"

"Because he would've killed me, okay?" Mia screamed. "If he knew I broke the rules…" Her voice trailed off.

"Why would Oliver do this?"

"I don't know," she faintly cried.

"I need answers, Mia," Jocelyn softened her approach.

"How could I not see it?" Mia sniffled. "How could I not know who my husband really was?"

Jocelyn placed her hand on Mia's. "How long has he been abusive?"

"A little over a year now. It's like something snapped within him, and he became a different person."

Jocelyn noted the abuse started around the same time Ivy Whitlock, the first victim, went missing. She wondered how many unfound victims there might be. She looked up at Mia, unwilling to let her off the hook quiet yet.

⸻ ✕ ⸻

Oliver's big hands cradled the steering wheel, driving himself in a familiar direction. He couldn't do this anymore. He was exhausted. It had all become too much. Self-pity slinked around his waist and up to his chest. He'd put Mia through enough. This would be best for her.

A soft whisper continued in his heart, telling him this was the right thing to do, but first, he had to confess the truth to the only person he'd ever loved.

The car finally came to a stop in the parking lot of The Sweet Magnolia's, a spot overlooking the mountains lit up by the full moon. The trees were breathtaking in the moonlight as they sparkled off the dew collected. The perfect place for his final selfless act.

He called, but it went straight to voicemail. As the recording thanked him for calling, Oliver gripped the loaded forty-caliber Smith & Wesson in his hand. If he had to say goodbye, voicemail was a great place to do it. No interruptions.

"Have a great day," Mia's voice said followed by a loud beep.

"Mia, it's me. I have so much I need to tell you," Oliver started his confession.

Thirty~Three

THE DOOR OF THE motel room swung open and exposed an overly concerned Levi Reed. Anger swirled in his eyes. The thin walls in this place must have given her away. Jocelyn stepped out of the room, forcing him against the railing.

"The look on your face tells me you heard everything." Jocelyn softened her voice in hopes of keeping Mrs. Hughes from listening. "I know you're mad, but she knows more than she's telling me."

"You're wrong," he zealously stated. "She's a victim here, and you're treating her like some…" His voice trailed off. "You still think she's a suspect?"

"Did she tell you about the property?"

"She mentioned something earlier, but it didn't make sense," he admitted.

"I'm guessing that's thanks to the whiskey I saw in there?"

Levi averted his gaze from her. "She mentioned something about a property we looked at before I left for my first tour. It was out in Sevierville, but we never bought anything, so I shrugged it off as drunken gibberish."

Jocelyn stood tall and straightened her jacket. "She told me it was located in Kodak."

They stood in silence. Jocelyn watched as Levi's mind chased the answers eluding him.

Charlotte couldn't wait for this bozo to catch up and neither could Jocelyn. She turned on her heel and marched back into the room, slamming the door shut behind her. Mrs. Hughes sat in that disgustingly colored chair, head in hands, sobbing.

"Mrs. Hughes," Jocelyn demanded her attention. Mia jumped—her bruised, puffy eyes soaked with pain. "You need to stop lying, right now."

"Lying about what?" she screeched.

"About your property. Where is it located?" Jocelyn pressed.

"I told you, it's in Kodak."

"And yet you mentioned Sevierville to Officer Reed. So, which one is true?" Mia closed her eyes tight and let out a deep wail of hurt. Jocelyn didn't know what to make of it all. This woman was officially on her last nerve while simultaneously gaining sympathy. "Listen…" Jocelyn muted her frustration. She knelt beside her on the gross carpet. "I know the last twelve hours have been overwhelming, to say the least." Mrs. Hughes continued to break down. "I know you're hurting, and I'm probably not helping." Jocelyn gently placed a hand on her shoulder and pulled a picture from inside her blazer. "I'm desperate here. This is Charlotte Scott." Jocelyn held up the picture Fran, Charlotte's mother, gave her of Charlotte at Easter. "She's just a kid in law school. She didn't ask for this any more than you did, but she's Oliver's next victim, and she's out of time. I can't take any chances here. I need the correct location or any other locations you can think of. Please, Mia, don't do it for me, do it for her."

Mia looked up at the photo, sorrow cascading down her cheeks. "The property is in Kodak. Sevierville is the place Levi and I planned to buy when he came back from the war." She lowered her head. "But, that never happened."

Jocelyn's face pushed together. "Then why lie to Levi?"

"I honestly don't remember telling him that." Mia looked over at the almost empty bottle of Jack Daniels on the nightstand. "I, um. I had a lot to drink earlier."

"Where did you get that?"

Mia explained in detail what happened.

"It was selfish. I wasn't even thinking about this poor girl." The sobs returned. "I feel like I have no idea who my husband is. Isn't that just the most pathetic thing you've ever heard?" She tried to wipe the tears away, but they kept falling. "I'm an idiot who believed his lies. I'm a freakin' statistic. And now Oliver is gonna…" She took in a sharp breath.

"You're human, Mia." Jocelyn patted her shoulder, still unsure of her guilt. "I hate to devalue your feelings, but I need an address."

Mia wrote down the address as Jocelyn opened the door and let Levi back in.

"We don't have time to waste here. I need to head out there, but I can't in good conscience leave you here," Jocelyn said to Mia. "Reed, I hope you can see how inappropriate this all is."

"Yes, ma'am," he muttered.

"Gather your things. You're both coming with me," she ordered.

As they gathered their belongings, Jocelyn ran down and instructed Detective Cott to stay at the motel in case the hitman showed up.

In a few quick minutes, the three of them packed into the car and headed to where Jocelyn hoped for a miracle.

⌾—✕—⌾

The dark countryside whipped by at lightning speed. Mia did her best to take it all in under the blaze of the full moon. She used to love this drive, but now that a horrid and evil deed was done there, it's all she would ever remember about it.

Guilt and shame overran her. Pictures of that poor girl flashed in her mind. In the photo, she looked so happy and carefree. Mia could only imagine how much of that was gone now, never to return. The damage Oliver did to her paled in comparison. Mindlessly, she reached up to her face and felt the swelling.

Father, keep her alive. Keep her safe. Please. She prayed.

"Mia." Jocelyn jolted her out of the sorrowful trance. "I almost forgot." She held Mia's phone out toward her with sympathy coiled on her face. "In case you want to contact your family and let them know you're okay. It's only a matter of time before the press get wind of this."

"Thanks," Mia breathed, unsure she wanted to call and face anyone.

Her reflection on the dark screen twisted her stomach in knots. It flashed from black to white as it came to life and loaded. On autopilot, she typed in her four-digit password. A picture of her and Oliver wrapped in each other's arms, happy, instantly filled the screen. Examining the flawless facade, sorrow trickled down. She wondered if the tears would ever run out.

The phone buzzed. A voicemail, from Oliver.

"Detective," Mia's voice shook.

"Yes?"

Jocelyn turned in the passenger seat, but Mia couldn't stop the violent shaking of fear that took over her hands and words.

"Ol-Ol-iver," she forced the words out. "He, um, left me a, ah, voicemail."

In the driver's seat, Levi shot a hard glance from the rearview mirror as Jocelyn turned herself fully around. "Play it," she demanded. "On speaker."

Mia did as instructed.

"Mia, it's me. I have so much I need to tell you." Oliver's voice sounded defeated and small. "First, I need to say how sorry I am. I've hurt you in ways I never thought I would. I wish I could say I understood where all this anger came from, but I don't—" Oliver sighed, seemingly hesitant.

"I'm sure the cops are listening to this too, so I have some confessions to make to you and them. Last night I was so angry seeing your ex standing in our house. I was furious you called the cops in the first place, but then to see that jackwad in *my* house, it was too much." Mia noticed Jocelyn's sharp look at Levi. "And I took it all out on you." His voice cracked. "Which put you in the hospital, and I want you to know how awful I feel and how sorry I am. Yes, to the cops listening, I beat my wife and have done so on multiple occasions." He hiccuped a breath and his voice strained. "I recently almost burned her face on the gas stove because she forgot to make me breakfast," he sobbed.

"But there's more. I've had a problem for about a year and a half now. Do you remember when we went hiking and broke my ankle? The doctor prescribed me Oxycontin, and at first, it worked great for the pain. My ankle felt better, but I didn't. I started to feel the full weight of living in the shadow of Levi Reed. You never talked about him, which is all I needed to confirm how you felt. So I continued using the pills to numb my pain until the refills ran out.

"But I didn't stop there. I needed to be numb to look you in the face and call you my wife. So, I found a supplier and continued to use it more and more. It consumed me," he sniffled. "Soon, I couldn't afford to buy the amount needed to sustain me, so I considered taking out a second on the mortgage, but I didn't want you to find out. Instead—" His voice strained again. "I embezzled money from the church."

He sobbed for a moment and regained his composure. "But since so many people left the church, I couldn't afford to keep the lights on and feed my addiction, so I had to get creative." He wailed in anguish. "And this part—I can't…I can't. It's too—" He howled.

"I love you more than I've ever loved anyone. I know you never fully loved me, and that's okay. I'm going to fix it and make it all better because you deserve more than I gave you. You deserve more than that jarhead gave you. You're better than either of us, Mia, and you will survive this because that's what you do. You survive, even when the people you love put you through the wringer.

"You are my one and only, forever and always. Goodbye." A loud crack whipped through the phone as the message cut off.

"What was that?" Mia cried out for answers.

Jocelyn reached back, placing her hand on Mia's arm. "It sounded like a gunshot. I'm so sorry."

Mia hiccupped in several breaths, her body contorted like an accordion. A primal wail ripped through her.

Oliver was dead. Her husband was dead. The man she shared her life with was dead.

⸻⸻ ⋅✕⋅ ⸻⸻

In a puff of black smoke, the car filled with darkness.

"Oh, the little trollop has feelings. Good to know." Hexiathan's face coiled with amusement. He slinked his thin body onto her lap and wrapped it around her. "Time to have some fun."

"My daughter," he whispered. "This is all your fault, dear. Your betrayal of love drove your husband to self-medicate, and now he's here with me, because of you." He snickered under his breath. "If you'd been a better wife, lover, and woman, you would've made him happy. It was your *job* to place his happiness above your own. You were to sacrifice everything, but you didn't, did you? You cheated on him in your heart. You refused to surrender everything to him. You refused to give up Levi Reed."

⸻⸻ ⋅✕⋅ ⸻⸻

She never stopped loving him, not even for a moment. Love was buried deep within, masking itself entirely as hate to survive. Mia begged God to let her fix this, but there was no changing what'd been done. Oliver was dead because of her.

Another shift in the atmosphere demanded her attention. The words spoken in her mind grew bigger, threatening to take over. *Jesus, help me,* she prayed, but the runaway carousel already started, leaving her powerless.

She hugged her stomach. The world around her spun faster as the lies grew louder. There was no one to blame but herself. Her wounds were her fault. Oliver was dead because of her. The church was broken because of her. And Charlotte was going to die because of her.

She couldn't breathe. Her lungs burned to keep up with the demand. *This can't be happening. This isn't real.* She clutched her chest. Her mouth endured a million needle pricks.

"Mia." Levi's voice muffled against the angst. "Are you okay?"

"I'll help her. Keep driving," Detective Maddox barked.

A thud hit the car and when she looked up, Jocelyn crawled through, invading the backseat.

"Breathe, Mia," she instructed. "In through your nose, out through your mouth."

The world around her seemed fake, like a dream. A scene from her last encounter burst through her mind. *Remember who you are, Mia,* the Lord whispered to her heart. *This is not Me. I'm not rooted in chaos and fear.*

She gulped in the air, desperate to regain control.

She looked up at the detective who offered breathing techniques, but only one thing would stop this tortuous ride.

The voice came back louder. "She'll think you're crazy, ya know. She'll probably put you in a mental institution if you say it out loud. Demons?" it snickered. "Pathetic, Mia. Absolutely pathetic."

Remember who you are.

"I don't care," Mia burst out. "In the Name of Jesus, get out!" she screamed. "You're not welcome here. You have no hold here." Her breath returned as she boldly spoke. "You *will* listen, and you *will* heed because greater is He who lives in Me. He is the King, and I am His daughter. *You* will leave, in the Name of Jesus, *now!*" she demanded. "Get out, and never come back."

⸻ ❈ ⸻

Eyes wide and lungs pumping, Levi pulled the car to the side of the road. Yes, a young girl needed them, but they couldn't go unprepared. If they did, it would be spiritual suicide. He knew this all too well. The last time he went up against hell unarmed, they just about took him out. But, not this time.

"Father God," he boldly prayed. "Be with us as we travel into enemy territory."

"What are you doing?" Jocelyn interrupted, dazed bewilderment pushed across her face. "We have to keep going," she protested.

Levi halted his prayer. "We have to go in armed and ready."

"I have at least half a dozen guns in the back and officers from Kodak will meet us there. What more do we need to check this place out, Officer Reed?" Jocelyn snapped.

"This isn't a physical war, detective. It's so much more than that."

Silence filled the cab of the still vehicle. Resolute in his stance, he watched the detective's mind work.

"Think, detective. Have there been any incidents you can't seem to explain during this investigation?"

"Yes," she reluctantly offered.

"I bet there has been. The Bible says we don't fight against flesh and blood but against evil forces."

"Evil forces?"

"Demons, detective. And I'd bet my life that's what you encountered." He turned to fully face her. "We can't just be armed physically, we have to be armed spiritually, or they will destroy us." A sorrowful look turned to Mia. "I know from experience. I lost everything when I tried to face them on my own."

Mia looked up from her phone. Their eyes met, and he hoped she now understood what happened to the future they planned.

Her eyes grew big, glancing back down at her phone. "That's got to be it," Mia whispered a revelation. "I can't believe I didn't think of this sooner."

"Think of what?" Levi pressed.

She slammed her hand on the seat. "I think we're going the wrong direction."

Jocelyn flipped her focus to Mia, clearly frustrated. "Are you serious right now?"

"Don't be mad, okay? I didn't want to tell you back at the motel because I didn't think Oliver knew about it, and I was embarrassed for Levi to know. But I re-read the transcript of Oliver's voicemail, and I don't know that the property in Kodak makes sense anymore. At the end of his message, he says he's going to fix it because I deserve better."

"What are you saying?" Jocelyn snapped.

"What if he partnered with these killers somehow?"

"Yeah, like he's the ring leader, and we're chasing him. Oh wait, that's what we're doing," Jocelyn erupted.

"But if he is the leader, wouldn't he have confessed that?" Levi asked.

"I mean, think about it, what would that gain him financially? If this is all about money for him, why kill people when he could take the killer's money instead?" Mia pressed.

"I'm not following," Jocelyn sighed.

"I am. You're thinking Oliver rented the killers the space they needed to do what they're doing?"

"Yes, exactly," Mia urged.

"But, you lost me on how we're not heading to the right place. Is there another option you know about?" Levi asked.

Mia bit her bottom lip, making it clear there was somewhere else.

"Well, I didn't exactly lie about having the place in Sevierville like you thought." She put her head down and tucked a piece of hair behind her ear. Curious, he fully turned toward her guilty stare. "*I* bought it six months after you deployed as a surprise for us when you returned."

Heartache ripped through him. No wonder why she hated him. She looked back down. "But you never came home to me." Her voice cracked. "I just couldn't bring myself to sell it so I hid it from Oliver, but he must've found out about it somehow. Maybe when he was looking for ways to get money, he found the deed I hid in the closet."

"So you think Oliver rented out *that* property?" Jocelyn inquired.

"Yes." She shifted. "Oliver was excited about the Kodak property. I can only imagine how betrayed he must've felt when he found out I pushed him to live out a dream I had with someone else." She sniffled. "If I was Oliver, I'd use the Sevierville property to further distance me from Levi in any way possible."

"You really should've told us this so much earlier than now, Mia." Levi snapped. Anger flourished within him. "I can't believe this."

He corrected himself in his seat and fell silent. After a few deep breaths, the anger dissipated and all that remained was a shattered heart, in too many pieces to count.

Jocelyn lectured Mia about her actions, but Levi couldn't bear to focus anywhere but on his own racing heart and mind. Mia lied. She has been hiding things all along. Maybe she was more involved than he originally thought.

"You said we needed to be armed?" Jocelyn interrupted his thoughts.

"This is all connected. I just don't know how, but it is. The same demon from Afghanistan is here now, and his name is Occult. From what I've learned in facing him, his main objective is to destroy or twist any belief in God or Jesus. He aims to tear Christians apart limb by limb until they are unrecognizable. Think extremes like Charles Manson to communes of people refusing to socialize with the outside world except to grow their numbers." Levi sighed. "We need to be ready for what we're facing and make sure our armor is on."

"Armor?" Jocelyn searched for clarity.

"The Armor of God. It's talked about in the Bible. God doesn't leave us here in a world filled with demonic entities unprotected. He left us tools, and we need to put each piece on before we move any further."

"Okay," Jocelyn breathed.

— ✕ —

This was all a little weird, but then again, so was what happened on the highway a handful of hours ago. She'd never experienced anything so cruel, so mind-bending. And when AJ cried out for Jesus, everything changed.

Jocelyn pondered the existence of God her whole life. Her grandma certainly wouldn't shut up about Him, so she was forced to keep her own thoughts and questions to herself because no one in their right mind went against Grams.

Somewhere around middle school, she considered that God might be okay, but everything changed when Gabby was brutally murdered. That was the breaking point that made her leave God behind for good. She could never give her life to someone who allowed such horrific things to happen to good people. Either He was the biggest jerk in history, or there was no God and it was all a hoax.

Something about this case shifted her mind. She prayed for the first time in years—a few Hail Mary's for good measure. Usually, she found a reason or explanation for just about everything, but nothing made sense of what she and AJ went through. The only thing she knew for sure was that when AJ yelled the name of Jesus, everything stopped. They were safe, and soothed by an unexplainable peace.

None of this erased her questions, but she thought it might be time to give God a chance to explain Himself when this was all over.

She looked down at her watch. A little after three in the morning. Charlotte had been missing for approximately sixty-seven hours. Jocelyn expected them to find her body somewhere in Durham by the morning. In the previous timeline of the killers, they had seventy-two hours from kidnap to murder, and yet hope shockingly remained. With Oliver dead, there was a chance Charlotte was alive, and Jocelyn had no choice but to run full speed toward it.

Trusting in some invisible force seemed crazy, but crazy was all she had right now.

Jesus, help me. Please.

Levi adjusted in his seat and bowed his head. Jocelyn watched Mia follow suit which forced her to do the same.

"Father, we come before You tonight to ask for help to place our armor on correctly. Ensure that our shoes of peace are laced up tight. Help us cinch down the belt of truth that represents not only the truth of who You are but the truth of who You've called us to be. We're the ones You've chosen to stop this threat, Lord. Help us put on the breastplate of righteousness, and lace it tight so it can hold us upright and walk in a way that glorifies You. Make sure we hook them together properly so we are not twisted in any way.

"Thank you, Jesus for the helmet of salvation which sets us apart by Your blood. Give us Your strength, wisdom, and precision so we may hold up the shield of Faith and wield the sword of the Spirit and not grow weary. Help us walk with boldness into enemy territory, and place a hedge of protection around us. Jesus, go before us and make a way, walk with us and guide us, and lastly watch our six so we make it out unharmed. We pray all this in Jesus mighty name, amen."

"Amen," the word tumbled from their lips in unison.

A flame of heat engulfed Jocelyn's chest. It intensely burned and served as proof that God was very real and was surely there with them now.

Levi put the car in drive, flipped around, and headed as fast as he could toward Sevierville. Jocelyn ordered the units in Kodak to check out the property there and requested for officers to meet them in the new location.

Thirty-Four

TWELVE MINUTES LATER, THEY came to the end of the quarter-mile dirt road that led to the property. The bushes at the road grew wild and blocked half of the driveway. It looked different than he remembered.

He put the car in park on the side of the road.

"I think we should walk in. That way we won't spook anyone here," he offered.

"Agreed," Jocelyn added.

Bright headlights fell dark. Moonlight illuminated the road, lighting the way down the obscure path cut between the glistening glow of the fields. Out of the car, a chill trembled through Levi, a reminder that April in Tennessee was not a guarantee of warmth.

Pulling herself out of the backseat, Mia folded her arms, rubbing her hands quickly up and down over them. The sweatshirt she wore wasn't enough to keep her warm. A quick shimmy freed the hoodie from his body, and he handed it to Mia.

She gave a quick smile. "I appreciate the gesture, but if I take that, you'll be cold. Besides, I don't think it's the cold making me shake. It's nerves."

His eyes stayed on her and admired the glow of the moon on her fair skin. In this light, he could barely see the bruises and to him, she looked like the old Mia from oh, so long ago.

He quickly put the sweatshirt back on, thankful it wouldn't smell like her now. After they broke up, her scent lingered on the letters she wrote and pictures she sent when things were good. He refused to take them down or throw them out, and the sweet smell of coconut penetrated his bunk until it dissipated for good. He couldn't go through that again.

Levi and Jocelyn put on the two vests in the trunk, holstered a few handguns, and loaded up with the same HKs Jocelyn said she used earlier at the Hughes residence. He admired her choice of weaponry, by far the best for something like this.

"Is there a vest for me?" Mia shivered.

"Sorry, I only had two. I didn't plan to take you with me," Jocelyn apologized.

"Maybe you should take mine," Levi offered, unwilling to leave her like a sitting duck literally in an open field.

"Absolutely not," Mia protested. "I'm not leaving you unprotected." She looked back at the car. "I'll stay here, far from danger, okay?"

He smiled, but after that stunt with the two properties, he wasn't sure he could trust her. If they left her here and she ran, he would never forgive her.

He checked his gun and counted the backup magazines, so he'd know how many bullets he had. Ninety in total. From his peripheral, he noticed Jocelyn do the same.

For a moment, he remembered gearing up with his team halfway around the world the day before the torment started. Levi took a moment to pray for God to protect them from walking into an evil ambush. It wasn't fun the first time, and he imagined round two would be even worse.

⊂→✕→⊃

Jocelyn held a fist in the air, signaling him to stop. "Okay, looks like we're about a hundred yards out," she whispered. "We need to tread lightly." She looked over her shoulder. "Let's split up, we can cover more ground that way."

She pulled her phone from her back pocket. "This is Detective Maddox, Durham Police, badge number one-nine-two-nine-seven-two, requesting an ETA for the backup at my location. Address is eight-seven-seven Heartly Drive in Sevierville, Tennessee. I repeat, eight-seven-seven Heartly Drive. We're in pursuit of our suspect at this address."

"Copy that, detective. I do show on my screen the closest unit to that location is forty-five minutes out," a ruff voice said into the phone.

"There's no one closer? What happened to the local units?"

"No, ma'am, I'm afraid not. Sevierville only has two units on patrol, and they were called to an armed robbery. I have units coming in from the surrounding area. The whole county has popped off with an overwhelming number of calls. I'm sorry, detective, but we'll have people there as soon as we can. Also, I have a note here that says units on scene in Kodak haven't found anything yet. The root cellar was clear. They're doing a quick sweep of the immediate area."

Jocelyn sighed. "Copy that. Tell the units inbound to hurry, and if nothing turns up, those units in Kodak can come this way. Also, start K-nine units and put H-one on standby. I don't have any handheld radios for us so if there is anything, call this number."

"Ten-four."

Jocelyn hung up. "Closest unit is forty-five minutes out," she huffed with irritation. "The Kodak property is clean, so if Hughes is connected to this, we're in the right place. They're sending the calvary, but we're on our own for now. I'm going in, with or without you."

"I'm with ya," Levi announced in a hushed tone.

With a silent nod, they pulled their weapons to their shoulder and skillfully crept in opposite directions. Jocelyn remained mindful of her breathing, the way Abigail, her mentor, taught her. In through the nose, out through the mouth.

Adrenaline barreled through her, sharpening her mind and eyes. Small steps, walking heel to toe, kept her crouched and ready for whatever she might encounter. Her finger softly laid against the trigger guard.

Slow and steady breaths. In and out.

She moved across the field, trying to find her bearings. Out of the corner of her eye, something flickered in the moonlight. Picking up speed, she stealthily made her way in that direction. A few feet out she saw it—a door covered with broken tree branches, leading underground.

Eyes up, she scanned the perimeter and clocked a shadowy figure coming her way. Her body tensed with a finger hovered over the trigger. There was nowhere to hide, so she steadied herself for what came next.

The shadow moved with haste and precision. Visions of demons taunted her. The hair on the back of her neck stood at attention. The threat made no sound. Maybe her eyes played tricks on her. And then she saw it, the same forest green sweatshirt Levi wore. She exhaled a breath.

"What'd ya find?" he huffed.

"Looks like an entrance to a cellar."

"Let's hope we catch 'em off guard, and Charlotte's alive," Levi whispered. "I've only got three magazines and two hand guns."

"Me too. We'll make it work." She glanced down at the handle on the door and noticed the lock was open.

They turned the flashlights attached to the MP5s on, and with a ready-nod, it was go-time.

Charlotte's body tensed at the whispers just outside the door. They must be done asking God about her plea. She prayed they would let her live. She gave it her all, the defense of her life, under the circumstances. All she hoped for was freedom on the other side of this.

Chills made her tremble. The air was so cold and damp, it wasn't a great combination for her naked and infected body. She curled into a ball, a failed attempt to warm herself.

Footsteps made their way closer. A breath caught in her throat, knowing her fate rested in whatever they said in the coming moments.

Lord, please.

The door flung open with high force. Charlotte squinted from the blinding light in her eyes. She tried to cover herself and raise her hands in surrender at the same time. The breeze that followed forced her teeth to chatter.

No words were spoken.

Levi flung the door open with haste. Jocelyn was first in and down the rickety stairs with Levi, close behind. Halfway down, they stopped. Flashlights rapidly darted from side to side.

"This can't be right," Jocelyn huffed with disbelief.

Empty.

"That's it," Levi snapped, allowing a few cuss words to slip out. "We need answers, and I'm going to get them."

"We need to search the cellar for evidence of Charlotte," Jocelyn objected, grabbing his arm.

He pulled from her grasp. "I'm not asking for permission, detective," Levi scolded as he took off in a sprint.

Thirty~Five

WITH EACH STEP FRUSTRATION gathered in Levi's chest. He'd believed her. After everything, he defended her, but things didn't add up. She sent them the wrong direction, twice. This wasn't the Mia he knew. Anger spread as he questioned what Oliver had turned her into. Was she lying? An innocent woman would die if they didn't straighten this out. It seemed unbelievable that Mia would be a part of this. That she would protect Oliver. Then again, he didn't know her that well anymore.

⸻⸻ ✕ ⸻⸻

Dante crouched through the cellar door, Ashanti on his heels. They watched as Levi stormed off, picking up speed with each step. This wasn't going to end well.

"Is it just you out here?" Dante pressed, not taking his eyes off the long dirt driveway even though Levi was no longer in sight.

"No, but I can go after the man if you'd like," she offered, hand on sword.

"Sí, por favor."

"No problem."

His stoic gaze remained locked on the driveway. A golden shimmer of light trailed along the dirt road, headed toward the battle about to begin at the car. He wondered why all of a sudden Levi would change like that. He saw no evidence of the enemy nipping at his heels or attached in any direction. He sighed. Hurt could bring forth such wicked things in the heart.

A muffled snicker alerted Dante. Scraping against its sheath, he pulled his sword with quick feet, simultaneously turning around. In seconds, the tip of his weapon rested at the throat of a dark being.

Dante glared into the ebony eyes, void of anything good, and without hesitation went to eliminate the threat forever.

"You'll never find her in time," it hissed, toxic saliva spitting from its gaping mouth. Its tongue slid around its lips. "These humans are stupid, Warrior. Why risk your life protecting them?" It slurped the hanging drool through its thin black lips.

Dante didn't waiver but thought it odd this devil would call him "Warrior." He knew they called them vile names and never, ever spared their feelings when doing so. They hated them all, but they hated the Almighty more. The names they called Yahweh made his stomach churn.

"Leave those rodents, valiant being, and help me in the woods."

"Where's the girl?" he growled.

"Come on, to the woods."

"Enough! No more games," Dante demanded. "Digame, now." He pushed the weapon into the demon until a small trail of black tar oozed. Its screech pierced the night.

"Well, sir. I—I'm not—" The demon dragged out his time.

Familiar with their trickery, Dante knew this creature wouldn't tell him anything useful. Without another word, the tip of his sword slid through the scales like a hot knife in butter. A sizzle saturated the beast. One by one its scales turned to ash, blowing in the gentle breeze.

His eyes peered into the moonlit forest, scanning for any more threats.

━━━━━━━━━━━━━━◦✕◦━━━━━━━━━━━━━━

"Move faster, you idiots!" Occult yelled, nipping at the heels of his puppets. "Move!"

They rustled quickly through the debris-covered ground amidst the trees, heaving in erratic breaths. The crunch beneath their feet could give away their location if they weren't careful.

"Halt," he snapped.

"Everyone stop," the softer one hissed.

"What on earth are you doing?" the bigger capture demanded.

They looked back in time to see the new guy lustfully gape at their worn-out prisoner. He deeply inhaled along her neck. Occult huffed a laugh at the growing desire. He loved it when Lust did her job right.

She dressed in the skin of men's desire, but Occult saw her real face far too many times to fall for the mask—no matter how good it looked. He bucked against all the changes made to bring the new guy into his plan, making his once pair a trio, but the kid turned out to be quite a wonderful addition to Occult's collection of puppets.

Despite the amusement, there wasn't time for these games.

"Lust." Occult gave one loud clap. "Enough."

Lust crept around the young capture. Those blonde pigtails, deeply revealing shirt, and short shorts, left little to the imagination. She certainly aimed to please. Occult choked back the tingle of desire in his throat.

"What's the matter, baby? You don't like me doing my job anymore?" Her bright blue eyes blinked black, wearing a look of innocence. She walked toward him with a well-rehearsed strut in her hips. "I'm just havin' a bit of fun. You jealous?" she teased, softly biting her bottom lip.

He would never admit jealousy to her. "We have to keep moving or that Idiot and his army of imbeciles will find us. If that happens, I'll have to start from scratch."

"Don't worry, Lover. I'll be sure to sit on *your* lap later." She smiled with a wink of motive. "We'll play by your rules." She paused with a devilish grin. "For now."

Occult snapped his head to the larger of the three. "Move, quietly and quickly."

"Knock that off." The big puppet pushed the kid off the girl. "We have to keep moving and find a new place to finish the ritual. Let's go." His voice cracked against the silence.

The kid peeled his eyes from the girl's naked body, pushing her forward with a shove.

The song of crickets blanketed the silence Mia sat in. Eleven minutes of waiting officially mirrored hours of anxious thought cycles. She wondered where the girl could be hidden. Thirty acres was a lot to cover. She attempted to keep the tears at bay and failed as several sporadically escaped.

The last several hours had been a lot to process. Oliver was dead, and she was the last one he called before killing himself. Her blurred eyes scanned the transcript on the screen of his last words. He gave her an apology she didn't know how to accept.

It was plausible that forgiveness didn't exist in her future. The guilt and shame she carried with her was a well-deserved punishment for being a terrible wife and partner.

Her stomach churned at the thought of what Charlotte Scott might have endured at the hands of Oliver. The bruises, the torment, the inescapable grasp of his dominating presence, those being the only thing she could stomach the thought of. The report of dismemberment, rape, and death. It was all too much to process.

A noise from the field alerted her. A rhythmic pounding against the dirt, brazen and repetitive. It quickened. She surveyed the darkness, a sad attempt to understand.

Quicker. Louder. *Thump-thump-thump-thump.* Whatever it was, it came straight for her.

Her chest and hands clinched. She tried to keep her breathing under control and failed.

Panic set in. Her body shook like an earthquake.

Down the long stretch of dirt, a shadowy figure approached. It rapidly got closer, bigger. Mia feared her heart would pound out of her chest. She placed a single hand over it and softly recited the pledge of allegiance.

"I pledge allegiance to the flag of the United States of America…"

The familiarity and repetition brought deep, calculated breaths through a core memory of her childhood. She remembered standing every morning before class started to recite these very words.

Behind closed eyes, she pictured Mrs. Griffin's fourth-grade classroom. The ABCs in cursive along the top of the whiteboard, a cutout picture of a girl and a boy smiling in lab coats, looking into a microscope, and Cody the Calculator broke down division in the corner.

A final deep breath carried a newfound clarity. She reached back and grabbed the only thing visible on the floorboard—a road flare. Pushing the door wide, she got out of the unmarked cruiser. Whatever was coming, she refused to go down without a fight.

She clenched the red tube in sweaty hands and sighed with relief when that forest green sweatshirt appeared.

Levi. A faint smile brushed her lips.

"Mia," he growled.

Her back stiffened. Last time he said her name like that was sophomore year when she tried to give him advice on how to deal with an alcoholic father—a subject she knew nothing about. But this seemed more intense somehow.

Her body habitually tensed, bracing itself for whatever explosion came next. He sprinted closer. Her hands shook like a leaf, a betrayal of the worst kind. Sweaty palms made it hard to hold on to the flare she clung to. A dull thud sounded as it hit the ground.

She muttered reminders that this was not Oliver, but biology didn't care. Previous threats just like this one ended poorly far too many times to convince the habitual response otherwise.

Instinctively, she stepped back and hunched over to make herself small. A whimper of pain let loose as he stopped right in front of her.

"Come clean right now," he demanded.

Her lips trembled with fear, fighting off the sting in her eyes as she peered up at him.

"I don't—"

"Come on, Mia!" He cut her off. "A girl's life is on the line here. Tell me the truth, right now."

"I am," she whimpered.

"The girl isn't here. Did you turn us around to cover for Oliver?" he snapped.

"No. Of course not."

Pain swelled in his eyes. "How can I trust you?" he breathed.

She sniffled, doing her best to compose herself. She held back information and considered covering up things about Oliver. If Mia was brutally honest with herself, she hadn't been very trustworthy.

"Tell me!" he begged.

"I don't know." The hidden secret fell from her lips.

He hastily stepped forward. Mia dropped into the fetal position as her last line of defense. She buried her head deep between her knees and put her hands over top. Oliver's go-to move was to drag her by the hair so she protected her head the best she could and braced for the wrath, knowing deep within, she deserved every last painful bit of it.

Soft whimpers escaped as she trembled with terror. The worst and most violent memories of her husband's torment stalked her thoughts.

She intently listened, anticipating every advance to block what she could. To her surprise, the impact never came. She noted the sounds of slow breaths and muffled emotions. But none of that helped regain her composure—frozen in panic.

Remembering a video from a few weeks back, she followed the steps for box breathing. Breathe in four seconds, hold for two seconds, and breathe out over six seconds. Counting through each action preoccupied her racing mind. The anxiety soon eased.

With her head still between her knees, she heard Levi's cell vibrate before he answered.

"What's up?" he softly asked. After a brief pause, he continued. "Really? Okay. I'm sorry. I'll be right there."

He sighed with a curse under his breath. Levi wasn't much for swear words, even when they were teenagers. In the Marines, he slipped up a few times and always apologized for it. He blamed the environment because everyone around cussed profusely and vowed to do better.

He did not allow circumstances to change the foundational things he stood on. It was something Mia deeply admired about him.

Another swear word slipped out, this time more pronounced.

"Mia," he softly spoke. "I'm—I'm really sorry. I was wrong to yell at you like that, wrong to accuse you of lying, and just plain wrong about everything."

She peeked up to see him question whether to touch her or not, horror and heartbreak held in his eyes when he looked at her.

"I have to go." He reached for her hand and helped her to her feet. "Jocelyn's sure that Charlotte was kept here in the cellar. We're going to search the woods. There's a revolver in the trunk. Please get it just in case." He placed her face in his hands. She could feel every callus against her tear-soaked skin. "Be careful, M."

Several tears escaped down her cheek as he softly kissed the top of her head and sprinted back down the dirt road.

⁃✕⁃

Rapid footsteps approached. Jocelyn mounted the submachine gun against her shoulder and aimed at the door. Adrenaline pulsed through her. At the squeak of the hinges, her finger rested on the trigger, ready to fire.

She immediately pointed the gun down when Levi walked through the door with raised hands.

"It's just me, detective," he huffed out of breath. "What'd ya find?"

Jocelyn huffed. "Well, I found some odd stuff, and I probably would've found it sooner had you not left me here to search alone so you could have a lover's quarrel with Mrs. Hughes."

Jocelyn would normally let the things she found ridiculous slide, but this juvenile stuff had to stop. They had more important things to focus on.

"You're right. I'm sorry," he offered.

"A mattress was shoved behind wooden shelves under the stairs, along with a bucket with ice-cold water and a small rickety table. I also found a lantern and what looks like the clothes Charlotte wore the night she was taken, shoved behind the table. And then there's this." Jocelyn walked to the furthest corner of the space and used her gloved hand to pick up a prisoner's chain secured into a block of cement she found hidden in the dirt wall.

"But that's not all. Check this out." She held up an empty vial and needle.

"Convenia?" Levi sounded it out like a toddler learning to speak.

"I googled it while you were off losing your crap on Mia." She ignored the look of shock on his face. "It's an antibiotic for animals."

"I remember seeing a BOLO come across my phone for a two-thousand-fifteen black Chevy Impala." He pulled out his phone and scrolled through to find what he needed. "Partial plate of Five-Victor-Charlie, last seen at a veterinary clinic downtown. The vet was found strangled to death." She watched his eyes scan for vital information. "Looks like the suspect wore a hat that blocked any cameras from catching his face, so they have no I.D. as of twenty minutes ago." He locked his screen. "That's gotta be our guy."

Levi's phone buzzed. Looking at the caller ID, his mouth stiffened.

"Mia. What's up?"

Jocelyn despised not being in on the conversation, so when Levi jerked his head to look out the door, she took a few steps forward in anticipation of a threat. Abigail often warned she was too eager, and it would get her killed, but Jocelyn ignored the advice.

"What's going on?" she asked before he hit the end call button.

Levi lowered his voice. "Mia grabbed a gun from the trunk for protection, and when she did, she saw what looked like flashlights in the woods."

Jocelyn tensed for far too many reasons. One, Mia had a gun. Two, they were outnumbered. And three, Charlotte may or may not be enduring a brutal death at this very moment.

She mounted her HK and climbed the rickety stairs behind Levi. Someone was out there, and this skeleton crew was Charlotte's last hope.

Thirty-Six

EVERY STEP WAS TORTURE on her bare feet. The feverish fog that once lingered lifted into a hard reality before her. They'd made their decision, one she prayed against. According to them, God had no room for mercy or grace toward a cautionary tale like Charlotte.

Her parents constantly preached about the forgiveness of Jesus, and now she was forced to fight against the lies for her life.

Dew collected on the dead leaves and branches that covered the ground, turning them into frigid razors that burned against her skin. Despite her upbringing, she never developed tough feet. Probably because she didn't like to walk around barefoot, even in the house.

The whole family poked fun at her aversion to being dirty. Just the thought of calluses on her hands had once made her want to gag. So petty. What she wouldn't give for one more moment of trivial fears and frustrations.

The moonlight flashed off the large weapons in the hands of her captures—a bright contrast to the black clothes and full-face ski masks they wore. She did her best to be analytical, but the shimmer of three machetes chased away her ability to focus. She assumed the gun the bigger one attempted to conceal under his jacket was loaded as well. It wouldn't be far-fetched to believe they all had guns, ready and willing to kill anyone who got in the way of this insane ritual.

Charlotte prayed. This time, there were no pleas for God to save her, only a reverberated prayer of peace for her family. She asked for Jesus to tell them He saved her before she met death, and for them to know they were on her heart in these final moments.

This was the end. Her fate was sealed. Soon Jesus would hold her in his embrace once again.

She longed to tell Tamika and Kiley how much their friendship meant. Tamika was the best roommate a girl could ask for. She wanted them to hold her memory close, as they conquered beautiful and amazing things in this life.

She and Brad were never really buddies. In fact, she couldn't remember how he, of all people, joined their little group, but she prayed for him anyway. She wanted him to know there was more to life than following in his father's footsteps. And she asked the Lord to help him find what he so obviously searched for.

An epiphany came. Success wasn't about money or status—the two things Charlotte perpetually chased. Brad had both at his disposal and still seemed so lost, so sad, and recently so angry. Maybe success looked more like a relationship of surrender and trust with Jesus, rather than how much money you have in your bank account.

"Ouch," she whispered, stumbling over a broken branch.

This minuscule pain was nothing compared to what awaited her when the walking stopped.

⸙—✕—⸙

Occult cracked his tail, like a whip, nipping at the heels of his puppets. A tingle of panic bubbled up. No one could ever know the fear he held with the Heavenly Hosts this close. The heat of their presence clawed at his back.

Luckily the humans those imbeciles protected were too stupid to figure it all out. The answers taunted them, right there in front of their faces the whole time, like a Where's Waldo game. The best way to remain undetected was to hide in plain sight for everyone to see.

Satisfaction danced with the anxiety he concealed.

A hundred yards further, and they'd be home free.

"Make them move faster," Occult barked at Fear.

The lanky little demon packed a skillful punch. Occult relished watching Fear contort his body, stretching out all four limbs, digging talons into each person.

Anxiety, alarm, and terror flooded each of them.

"That's it. Go little doggies," he growled with delight.

———————— ⚬—✕—⚬ ————————

They swiftly worked their way through the woods toward the lights. Jocelyn steadied her breathing against the flood of adrenaline. In the thick of the forest, the moonlight offered little help, so they were forced to use flashlights that gave away their position. Jocelyn abruptly stopped, signaling to Levi on her six with a fist in the air.

She pulled out her phone.

"Kind of a poor time to make a phone call, detective," Levi whispered with irritation.

"Dispatch," a rough voice answered.

"This is Detective Maddox. We're currently on scene at eight-seven-seven Hartley Drive and are in pursuit of two or three possible suspects in the woods, northeast of the driveway. I need you to get H-one started to help us search, and I need to know if there are any roads behind us or in any direction we need to be aware of?"

"We'll get H-one started. Let me pull up the address on my GPS." She heard the clacking of the keyboard as she waited. "I see two roads of concern. One at the backside of the property and one to the south of it."

"How far out are the other units?" she pressed.

"Seventeen minutes according to their GPS. They're coming as fast as they can, detective." He attempted to reassure her. "Both of those roads *will* intersect with incoming units. Do you know what type of vehicle they have so we can put out a BOLO?"

"We believe it's the same vehicle from a BOLO that was sent out earlier today after the vet robbery and murder. Black Chevy Impala—"

"Partial plate Five-Victor-Charlie," he finished her thought.

"Yes. It's very plausible that case is connected to mine. We aren't sure if they have other vehicles in the area at this time."

"Copy that. I'll alert all incoming units."

Jocelyn said thanks and hung up, replacing her phone in her back pocket.

"We need to split up."

"Negative," Levi protested. "Look, I know the roads make you nervous, but tactically it's best to stick together and work the area one step at a time."

"I'm sure you're right, but we'll cover more ground this way."

"Cover more ground with no convenient form of communication. We have no radios and no clue what we're walking into." Levi stood up straight. "So I'm saying no," he firmly stated.

Jocelyn didn't appreciate being told no by a subordinate officer. Sure, he had military training and likely knew about these scenarios better than she did, but this was her call to make.

Abigail Harper's voice rang in her ears. *Don't let your pride get in the way of what you know is right.*

She slowly exhaled. "Okay, you're right. We'll stick together, but we need to move quickly. We can't lose them."

The thought of tripping over Charlotte's lifeless body was too much to bear. She was alive. She had to be.

—⊶✕⊷—

"Almost there," a gravelly voice chuckled.

Tears effortlessly fell from Charlotte's eyes and pooled against the duct tape over her mouth. A prayer for rescue fell short as the last sliver of hope flickered out. Fear seeped in, taking its place.

Each step brought her closer to the end of the road. This couldn't be it. She lived against God her whole life and now that she surrendered, it was lights out?

There was so much to look forward to. She yearned to reconnect with her parents and siblings. She could love them for who they were and not resent them for who they weren't. She could be the woman God created her to be and help those wrongly convicted of crimes. Now more than ever, she understood what it meant to endure that level of horror and humiliation.

Someone pulled her hair, forcing her to a stop. A shuttered breath gave way to a plethora of tears that streamed down her face. The world spun beneath her feet. Something wasn't right. She didn't feel well.

She recoiled as her body was forced to her knees. Folded in half, she held herself tightly in a ball. Pain was coming. She braced for the torment, praying it would be quick.

The familiar one knelt beside her, aggressively grabbed hair at the back of her head, and forced her to sit up. He squished her face in his hand, squeezing as hard as he could. Her jaw screamed in agony. He reached up and ripped the tape from her mouth. The sting on her lips and skin forced a moan of defeat in her suffering.

"Any last words?" he hissed.

Thirty-Seven

"RUN!" OCCULT HOWLED TO his puppets, but it was too late.

Those awful maggots found them. Fighters filled the forest with a surge of strength—the Ruler of the idiots must be upon them.

Without a second thought, Lust burst through the trees and out of sight, leaving her fellow devils to deal with the onslaught of war. Typical.

Occult did his best to run, but the tip of a flaming sword caught the back of his leg. Shrieks of pain echoed through the once-still night. He watched as Fear's small and lanky frame slinked through the threatening wall of warriors, a valiant attempt to rescue his leader. The skilled creature made it past Occult with such speed and dexterity.

A blunt whimper sounded as he gaped at the sight of Fear flying through the air. The crack of his body against the tree trunk drew the attention of many angels. With them distracted, Occult had one chance to get out of this mess alive.

A little over three yards away, Fear's body lay unconscious. Rescuing him wasn't worth banishment. The depths of hell were relentless and awful and made even the most powerful demons, quake with fear.

With an internal pep talk and several huffed growls, Occult psyched himself up for his daring escape.

An enemy combatant quickly approached. He was bigger than the others and seemed determined to eliminate Occult. A glance back at Fear's lifeless body, and a vast knowledge of Lust and her self-preservation rules, confirmed his worst fear—no rescue would come. He was on his own.

"There's nowhere to run, Demon," Leon boomed as his golden, shoulder-length hair lightly tousled in the wind. "You're surrounded," he added with sharp eyes and a quick smile.

"You'll never catch us all," the creature snickered.

Leon stepped closer, the tip of his blade within an inch of its chest. Such wickedness wouldn't surrender the upper hand so easily. With eyes void of almost anything, it was easy to detect panic in them.

"I've got one of them," Leon spoke out to Finn through the Divine connection they now shared. "I'm about two clicks northeast from the cellar. Another devil lies unconscious, three yards east. Send reinforcements."

The sheer size of Leon left him vulnerable. Agility wasn't his forte, so he was thankful Viveka and Andrew came toward him from the south. Viveka carried the most agility out of all the warriors. She was well-known throughout the Heavens for her impeccable record in battle. Her coupled with Andrew's impressive mind? No one better to have at his aid.

"Split up," Leon shouted. "One takes the smaller demon, the other with me."

"What about the one who ran?" Viveka questioned.

"Leave it. These two are the priority," Leon commanded.

He watched from the corner of his eye as they split. Andrew barreled toward the unconscious one. Leon wished he and Viveka could banish this wretchedness, but the girl remained in danger.

He clocked Viveka's location, noticing a bigger problem at hand. The distinct screeches alerted him to a legion of demons in the distance. Leon wasn't the only one with backup on the way. A cloud of darkness enveloped Andrew and Viveka like a tidal wave.

His blade pushed into the beast's scales, wiping the grin off his face. Hesitation flourished. Banishment couldn't happen, not yet.

"Decisions, decisions," the devil's sinister voice growled. "Tsk, tsk. I can't believe you call yourself a warrior," he scoffed. "Pathetic."

"Silence!" Leon demanded, his eyes back and forth between this beast and the smaller one.

The creature chuckled. "Too late, Warrior Boy."

The demon rolled his body, slicing its flesh on Leon's sword. Quickly on its feet, the beast limped away with a quick step. Leon easily knocked him to the ground from behind. He flipped the demon over and slammed his ample foot onto its stomach.

"Where's the girl?" he demanded. Leon glanced behind. The slew of demons would be here any second. Out of time. "Tell me, and I'll spare you!"

"It's simply adorable you still believe you're in charge, Punkin," Darkness taunted.

"Tell me or you'll rot in the depths of Hell!"

"We both know you can't banish me yet. I'm too valuable. I hold the answers you need."

Leon grunted, slashing his sword through the demon's cheek. "Enough. Where's the girl?"

"You'll pay for that!" it snarled.

"Tell me or lose your hand."

"I'll never tell you, no matter how much you torture me."

Usually, these devils held more self-preservation than that. The girl was important enough to strike a deal, but Leon had to follow through on every threat.

Another slash of his sword cut through the creature's hand, turning it to ash.

⸻✕⸻

Occult howled in pain. This was officially the worst distraction technique ever. This idiot might be big with a Fabio-adjacent quality, but that didn't make him bright. Despite the searing pain, Occult continued to taunt as his capture watched over the wrong shoulder. Focused on the impending cloud of demons, Fabio forgot about one little ally who just came to.

Fear cautiously slinked his way up the mountainous fighter. All at once, he shoved all twelve talons into the base of his wings, rendering him useless.

Fabio squealed in pain, like the yelp of a small, pointless little dog. Fear's maniacal laugh echoed against the howls of war.

Occult chuckled. With clunky steps, he approached the otherwise occupied warrior and slashed his talons across his face.

"A little something to remember me by," Occult laughed.

"More are coming, sir," Fear warned.

Occult grabbed the pathetic fighter with his remaining hand. His talons dug into Fabio's chest. "Consider yourself lucky, you imp."

He dropped the worthless scum to the ground and scurried off into the night. The only way to salvage this was to find the new puppet and the girl.

⸻ ✕ ⸻

They moved in tandem through the unfamiliar woods. Jocelyn signed for Levi to halt with her fist. She gestured with two fingers to her eyes and then at the crumpled shirt on the ground.

Levi pulled gloves and a bag from the thigh pocket of his tactical pants. Jocelyn remounted her weapon, covering his six as he scooped up the evidence. He held it up to examine it. It looked old and so dirty he couldn't tell what color it was supposed to be. More than likely, it had nothing to do with Charlotte, but they couldn't count it out just yet. He stuffed it into the bag and sealed it closed.

Jocelyn stepped close and whispered, "Spread out. Look for anything that indicates this might be linked to any of the girls killed."

A silent nod queued them to separate and search the immediate area. Jocelyn's senses heightened, detecting a hint of sulfur in the air. Her mind raced for the smell's origin, but none of the evidence they found let off that stench.

She came across a mound of leaves and dirt. The freshness of the disturbance was unmistakable. An animal might have done this, but there was only one way to find out.

Her focus narrowed at something discolored between the leaves. She moved closer.

Scanning the horizon of the looming darkness around her, she gloved her hand and reached for the unknown substance. Pulling away, bright red harshly contrasted against the white latex glove. Blood. She scooped up a handful of debris and placed it in a bag she pulled from her back pocket.

Levi gestured for her to remain silent as he further investigated a rustle from the leaves. She quickly mounted the gun back to her shoulder and crouched her body, ready to put down whatever he found.

Jocelyn had rarely fired her weapon, and she'd never taken a life. Real police work wasn't like what people saw on TV. More paperwork and less gunfire, but the risk always lingered. She frequently practiced with various guns so that when the day came, she'd be ready.

Now that it was here, despite her chest pounding, she was confident in her ability to neutralize a threat. Her grip tightened, locked on the pile of leaves Levi crept toward.

"I see feet," Levi loudly whispered. "I'm going to move the leaves."

Jocelyn kept her weapon ready despite the burn in her arms. She held her breath as he unearthed a body.

Jocelyn steadily moved with intention toward the lifeless being on the ground.

"Is that Charlotte?" she whispered.

"I don't know."

Levi pushed more leaves away, revealing a malnourished face with dark circles under her eyes. As more debris moved, they easily saw protruding ribs under her pale, exposed skin.

"Is she alive?" Jocelyn asked.

⋅—×—⋅

"Start an ambulance to eight-seven-seven Hartley Drive. We found a victim. She's in pretty bad shape with a deep laceration to her right shoulder. I feel a pulse, but it's faint. Her heart rate is sky high, and her skin is burning up." Levi sternly spoke into his phone. "Let the crew know I'll meet them with the girl at the end of the driveway. There's an unmarked cruiser parked out there. Ya can't miss it," he huffed.

"Copy that. I've got a unit en route now. Can you confirm if this is Charlotte Scott?"

Levi looked back down at the victim's face.

"Is it Charlotte?" Jocelyn pressed, moving herself closer.

His heart picked up speed. "I don't know," he stated to both of them. "I can't tell."

A surge of defeat charged through him. If this wasn't Charlotte, how many more victims were out here?

Jocelyn laid the coat she wore over the girl's torso, and Levi did the same with his sweatshirt around her legs. Flashlight in hand, Jocelyn positioned herself over the top of the girl's shoulders. She delicately moved the jacket around, like at any moment the girl would spring up and eat her face off.

"You good?" Levi asked, unsure what to make of the scene in front of him.

"Fran Scott told me about a birthmark on Charlotte's back, flank area." Jocelyn continued to prod at the girl weirdly.

"Are you scared of her or somethin'?" Levi blurted out.

"I don't want to hurt her."

"Well, it's hurting me to watch whatever this is," he huffed.

"Looks like that Southern boy charm is gone," Jocelyn not so nicely pointed out. "Anything you wanna say here, officer?"

"I'm sorry. You're right, okay? I'm frustrated and took it out on you," he sighed. "Let me help you move her. Which side is it on?" he asked.

"I can't remember so let's just start with the right."

Levi reached over the frail body and carefully rolled her on her left side, doing his best to mind the gaping wound. Holding her with one hand, he used the other to gently lift her arm. Jocelyn searched with a flashlight, wiping away coagulated blood with a gloved hand.

"Nothing here," she sighed.

Levi swallowed back the emotions rising in his throat as they switched places. This was a lose-lose situation. If it was her, she was on the brink of death. If it wasn't, this girl and Charlotte would both likely die.

He sloppily tore a piece of his sweatshirt, and covered her wound with it to help stop the bleeding and keep it clean as they rolled her. If his marine captain saw his lack of preparedness, he would pay for it with push-ups or running. If only he'd brought the first aid kit from the car with them. By the time Levi finished, it would do the trick, for now anyway.

With a deep breath, he looked up at Jocelyn who seemed to hold similar emotions. "Here goes nothin'."

Pulling her up on her right side, he followed the same routine by lifting her left arm. He looked up to see a smile spread wide across Jocelyn's face.

"It's her," she breathed.

Before Levi could exhale, she was on the phone with dispatch. He rolled Charlotte onto her back as Jocelyn barked orders into her phone about incoming units setting up a parameter and roadblocks.

"They couldn't have gotten far," Jocelyn assured them. "They're here somewhere."

"I got you, Charlotte. You're safe now," Levi whispered to her unconscious body.

"Helo's six minutes out," Jocelyn told him. "How's she doing?"

"Still unresponsive. I've got to get her back to the car for the ambulance."

"Do you need help to carry her?"

"She's light. I've carried big 'ol soldiers out of war zones, detective. I got this," he said with more arrogance than intended. "Find these guys."

Jocelyn gave a nod and was off, weapon in hand.

Levi grabbed what remained of his sweatshirt and put it on Charlotte like she was a newborn baby, and used the jacket to wrap around her waist. At least this way, the poor girl could have a shred of dignity knowing he didn't parade her naked body through the sea of incoming officers.

She moaned when he picked her up and placed her over his shoulders into the fireman's carry.

"I've got you, Charlotte. You're safe."

⸺✕⸺

Mumbled voices faded into the background. The damp, dark forest once beneath her feet shifted into bright red clay dirt, just like the dirt back home. She now wore a flowing white dress that gently blew in the breeze.

Birds sang a song of praise as a sweet scent wafted through the air. Her long blonde hair effortlessly danced around her. Letting her head fall back, she basked in the warmth of the sun on her face.

Laughter pulled her attention. Her family ran toward her, smiles dressed their sweet faces.

"Mom! Dad!" Charlotte shouted with joy.

Tears streamed down her face as she ran toward them.

"Jacob, Maddie, Luca," she rejoiced, calling out to each sibling.

She begged for this to be real, but darkness orbited against the deep blue sky above. Suddenly, the distance between her and the ones she loved grew wider. She screamed for her parents, but no sound came.

The ground vigorously shook. To the right, a dirty, naked image of herself fell to her knees. Every bone stuck out, drawing heartache within. She noticed the wound on her shoulder as blood cascaded from it, collecting in a pool beneath her.

Looking down, red collected on her white dress. She grabbed her arm as blood pushed between her fingers, like water free flowing. A searing pain pushed a scream of anguish past her lips.

—⸙—

From the shadows, Occult cursed loudly as he watched that irritating soldier carry the girl back toward the road. This plan was going to Heaven in a handbasket because at least in hell, evil things never ceased to play out.

He paced back and forth, his limp increased with each lap. Battered, he leaked the precious toxins from his once glorious body. Plus, he only had one hand. The queen was coming, and he was in no shape to greet her. She'd have his head for this or worse, give him a one-way ticket to hell for a hundred torturous years to think about what a failure he was.

That couldn't happen. Hell was the absolute worst. Demons lurked on the earth, far away from its excruciating torment, for that reason.

The last stent he did was over eight hundred years ago, and it still haunted him. The screams there surpassed anything Earth could muster. Overplaying the mistakes, the pain, the separation from Love was too much to bear.

To remember so vividly the Enemy's love for his creations drove his hatred. His king, Lucifer, made one measly mistake and was cast out of Heaven for it, but humans failed over and over again and yet, they were forgiven. Just the thought of it made Occult's blood boil.

"Sir."

Occult erupted at the intrusion. "What?" he sternly demanded at Fear's wide expression.

"It's th-the queen, sir. She's, um, on her way."

"ETA?" he growled.

"Sunrise."

Occult got down nose to nose with Fear. "The girl must die before then."

"Which girl, sir?"

"You know which girl."

—⸙—

Alone in the dark, Mia fought against the fear that lurked. Countless prayers were made for the Lord to help them find the girl before it was too late. They had to find her. They just had to.

Fear flourished in her chest, turning her mind to her husband. For Mia, where fear existed, dreadful thoughts of Oliver weren't far behind. The knowledge of his death confused her as her angst increased. If Oliver was dead, then who was in the woods? Had he sold his soul to a cult, and she hadn't noticed? What if the voicemail was to make her think he was dead so he could get away with all of this? She trembled at the thought of him finding her here with Levi, hunting him and those he helped. He would deliver a permanent punishment.

There was no doubt in her mind that he had a plan to cover up her murder, just in case he had to dispose of her. The thought of it made her chest tighten.

A frantic search went underway for the gun she moved from the trunk to the glove box earlier. In her panic, the latch wouldn't open, but after a few tries and a deep breath, it popped. There lay a Colt Python 357 Magnum, 4-inch revolver.

A sheen of silver came off the cylinder and barrel, contrasting against the wooden grip. It looked exactly like the gun her father taught her to shoot with at the age of thirteen. She remembered how awkward and intimidated she felt holding it in her hands, but the recoil was practically non-existent, which made it easy to maneuver.

Despite how in control she felt holding the revolver, she couldn't stop the relentless tremors.

"Oliver is dead," she whispered out loud, unsure if it was true. "He can't hurt you anymore." She coaxed. "You're safe."

As the anxiety faded, one thought rang loud. The assassin. If Oliver was, in fact, dead, there was no one to call off the hit put in motion on her. She peered into the darkness surrounding the car with wide eyes and quick breaths.

Every hair rose to attention on the back of her neck.

A sharply drawn breath pierced the stillness. "He's here."

Thirty-Eight

THE PUPPETS FLED FOR their lives, deeper into the woods. Occult limped behind, nipping at their heels to move faster. The older two were of little use now, but the younger of the three showed mighty promise to take this operation to new and torturous heights. He had been worth all the effort to lure him in.

"Save yourself," Occult whispered in the apprentice's ear. "You're valuable, they're not. Leave them, and we'll build an empire together."

The prize puppet showed a hint of sinister enjoyment at the ideas dropped in his head. So many places this one would take them, so little time for suffering.

All three humans made it to the car. The best thing for him and the army that eclipsed the trees was to ensure their escape. Then he would trim the dead weight in this trio and exhale a lethal breath of depravity into the one left standing.

A genius plan thought through by a nefarious and malicious devil.

Occult was the best and brightest of his cowardly colleagues, especially Beli-yaal. That miserable excuse for a soldier paraded around like he was somehow above the rest, but Occult knew better. Beli-yaal was no more than flies on a pile of waste, and if the whispers of his banishment were true, the queen would finally see who the better devil was.

The engine of the car roared to life. Occult whispered instructions to his prized yearling. "Escape with them, then wait for further instructions."

The pup smiled with an undetected nod.

Occult turned to address the swarm of darkness. "Kill them all!"

Screeches echoed off the trees as the car moved forward. He would sacrifice his entire army to ensure his puppet's escape. This mission was more important than any of them.

∘—✕—∘

Unworldly eyes gazed upon the growing darkness around the car. His comrades were nowhere to be seen. This plan held too many flaws to calculate all the variables, but he wasn't left with much of a choice. They couldn't get away. They needed to pay for their wrongdoings, but above even that, they needed to be rescued from the clutches of evil.

There was always more than one objective at hand. Coordinating it all together took a level of finesse that stretched him past his comfort. God surely had more faith in Finn than he had in himself. He played it cool, but Viveka knew the truth. He saw it in her eyes.

He exhaled slowly. "Now," he ordered.

Hundreds of warriors dropped down from the tall trees and ambushed the oblivious evil. Finn remained on the outskirts, with Viveka to his right and Kafziel to the left. The kid was young in battle, but quick on his feet. He took on Beli-yaal alone, and that deserved respect. The others strategically fanned out around the battle to pick off those joining the fight. They were already outnumbered, ten to one.

Despite Leon and Andrew's injuries, they were still able to put up a good fight. Finn was thankful for the addition of Axum, Makeal, Kano, and Ashanti to hold the parameter.

"We have to stop that car," Viveka warned.

"Movement to the east," Finn called out as two large beasts stormed through the trees. "Viveka, Axum, cut them off!" he ordered.

Viveka shot out toward the beasts. Flashes of light and ash filled the woods as the battle to hold the line ragged on.

"South, keep it tight," Finn cautioned. "Kaf." A crooked smile pulled at his mouth. "I have a job for you."

∘—✕—∘

Ketaton, a hefty warrior of wickedness sent to clean up Beli-yaal's mess, cursed the malicious woman who lacerated his arm. The wound was now a forever reminder of the merciless female warrior he mistakenly underestimated. For centuries, he battled little annoyances like her, and today she would suffer the full extent of his wrath.

She flashed across him again and another wound emerged. He went to berate her, but her sword sliced his tongue in two. Another dive, but this time Ketaton was ready and her leg caught the tip of his talons. The satisfying rip of her flesh brought a smile to his hemorrhaging mouth.

He wiped the ebony blood running down his face with the back of his fist. His now forked tongue swirled around his thin lips, enjoying the taste of the battle on his face.

A scream of adrenaline came from the woman as she pushed herself to her feet. Her nostrils flared with anger as she let go of a few grunts from deep within. She was vulnerable in her anger. Ketaton smiled, knowing he wasn't out just yet.

The heinous threats he desired to spit couldn't get past his broken tongue. That dreadful little brat debilitated him.

The injury wasn't enough to banish him, but it distracted him long enough for the fighter to swoop back down with everything she had. Multiple slashes seared against his smooth black skin. If he wasn't careful, he'd lose this fight.

—◦—✕—◦—

Finn moved several yards down the road, leaving ample room between him and the blustering fight. All the pieces on the board moved so fast, it was difficult to keep up at times.

"Glory be to the Father, forever and always," Finn softly prayed, slamming his fist onto his chest.

Fixed in his stance, he clocked the car as it blasted from the cloud of combat. It picked up speed and barreled down the two-lane road, headed straight for him. Spiritual ash kicked up in its wake. Finn steadied his feet and gripped the long iron spear in his right hand.

With a deep inhale, he brought the spear atop his shoulder. A running start ensured power before he planted his left foot and heaved the long weapon into the air, projecting him forward as he did. Finn tracked the spear through the air until it sunk into the engine block.

The sedan sputtered and clunked. The driver tried to push the gas pedal, but the engine whined at the request. A loud crack released a cloud of smoke that consumed the front end of the car. Three doors sprung open. A flash of light weaved in and out of the car before racing away from the scene.

Finn smiled as the occupants bailed, choking on the smoke.

Now to help the detective find them.

—※—

That was hands down the coolest thing Kafziel ever saw. He whooped and hollered in celebration. Finn was without a doubt the best warrior of them all.

"Focus, lad," Finn's voice rippled through his mind.

In his hands were pieces of clothing from all three humans in the car. He prayed prison would be the wake-up call they needed for their hearts to soften so God could work on them.

It was hard for humans to understand and accept that those they hated were God's creations too, and He desired to save them also. Sometimes the warriors facilitated bringing them to their knees in prayer, and other times it happened because of their own choices and consequences. For the last eight hundred years, Kafziel proclaimed glory to the Lord when those caught in sin came to God and grieved those who continued to reject Him.

A while back, Kafziel wondered why God chased after those who hurt Him with such reckless abandon. He remembered the day, hundreds of years ago, clearly. The moment that thought popped into his heart, he turned around to see the Messiah. And right there, in the middle of everyone, Jesus explained the depth of love the God-head carried for each person. He reminded him that each one was selected before the earth was formed. They were uniquely knit together by God's hand, each one unlike any other throughout time. God saw through from the beginning to the end and determined the need for each specific person destined for this world. And although many would reject Him, it would never change the love He held for them.

Kafziel spent time reading through the entirety of the recorded histories in Heaven and began to understand the one point he needed to—it wasn't up to him. And it was pride, hidden in his heart, that made him think it was. The Father was in charge of everything. He held everything together in the palm of His hand, and it wasn't Kafziel's job to understand. It was his job to obey. Acceptance of this better helped him relate to those loved beyond comprehension.

In the dark forest, he finally reached Detective Maddox, who stood with one of the other officers now on scene with his K-9. They came in from the north somewhere along the road. No reports of anyone seen as he ventured through the trees. His dog, Rogue, showed no sign of a scent.

"ETA on the other units," she demanded into the radio the officer brought for her.

Kafziel watched her in awe. She was really good at her job. He hoped to be that good one day, like Finn and Viveka, so confident and brilliant.

"Okay," he told himself. "Time to work." Kafziel held the clothes up for the dog to smell. "Here you go. Smell that? These are who you're hunting. Yeah, that's good, huh?" When he was done, he commanded, "Get to work."

—✕—

"Detective!" the officer shouted as his dog dragged him along. "I think she's got something."

Bewildered, Jocelyn was uncertain how the dog caught a scent they hadn't introduced yet.

The loud pulsing sound of helicopter blades pulled her focus and over the radio, they beckoned her. "H-one on scene. Where do you want me, detective?"

She looked at the officer stumbling behind his dog. "East. The dog caught a scent to the east. Go out and see what you can in that area first."

"Copy that," the pilot responded.

—✕—

Five hundred feet off the ground gave a different perspective to the world. Nick Sullivan could spend his whole life under the rhythmic pop of these rotor blades. Being a pilot was all he ever wanted to do. As a boy, he flew handheld toys around the yard, and as a man, he flew an AH-64 Apache in the Gulf War.

Thinking about his time in the Gulf brought a longing for what once was. The equipment he utilized on a few covert ops blew this ridiculous long-range lens out of the water. He used to have an infrared camera for searches like this, but the recent budget cuts took those away. All he had left was a bright light and a glorified camera. It left a sour taste in his mouth.

In the middle of the search area, he began in a small circle and gradually moved outward, widening the grid. Sure, this wasn't as exciting as carrying out a search for enemy cells and eliminating them, but at least this was soothing work.

Nick's attention peaked in what looked like movement east of where he clocked that lady detective.

"This is H-one. I think I found your tangos, ma'am," Nick called over the radio with a thick southern drawl.

"Can you repeat?" She sounded confused and annoyed with his military slang.

"I think I found your suspects to the east of your location," Nick plainly stated. "They seem to be running pretty quick. I can't tell if there are two or three of 'em, but I do see two vehicles. Unable to tell if they're functional."

"Copy, H-One. Keep your eyes on them. Whatever you do, don't lose them."

"Copy that. Just a heads up, the vehicles appear to be parked about a hundred yards apart on the back road. Unable to identify the make and model of either at this time."

"Don't lose my suspects, H-one. Stay with them," she barked through the speaker.

Thirty~Nine

ON HIGH ALERT, UNABLE to move and afraid even to blink, her breath quickened as her head and shoulders tensed. Everything within cried out to run, but her legs refused to move. She tightly gripped the revolver in shaky hands.

Fear swallowed her whole. Blood violently pumped through her veins. Her heart worked double time, thrashing against her chest. It pulsed so loud she worried it would give away her location, like a drum of war leading Oliver straight to her. She needed to run.

A loud crack sounded from beyond the edges of light cascading off the lonely street lamp above. Terror trembled through her. *He's here.*

With closed eyes, she took a deep breath.

"One… two… three!" She whipped around to find nothing.

The weight of the gun was familiar in her hand despite the protest of her battered body holding it up. A glance down revealed unaligned feet so she slid them through the hard dirt and into better position. She pushed her arm straight out and rested her finger on the trigger. The weapon vigorously shook until she steadied it with her other hand.

Feet shoulder-width apart. Arms steady. Deep breath.

With narrowed vision, she scanned the darkness, praying for a miracle. Eventually, the threat would show itself, and Mia vowed to be ready when it—

The breath pushed from her lungs as something large tackled her from the left. The gun flew from her hands and skidded across the dirt and rocks. Mia struggled for air. The unknown assailant grabbed her hair. He yanked it back as hard as he could. A blinding pain ripped through her neck.

Her mouth opened to scream for help, but a large hand covered it, stifling her pathetic effort. He tossed her around like a rag doll, unfazed by her foiled defense attempts. A spin of her body brought her face to face with her soon-to-be murderer. There she saw it, the jagged scar on his leathered face.

Striking quickly like a cobra, his hands cinched down around her neck. Instinctively, she reached up, trying to peel them off, and failed like she had so many times before. Wheezes rumbled a petition for air in her throat. Her arms thrashed about, a perilous attempt to grab anything she could. She tried to scream, but her windpipe was crushed against his grip.

The pop of helicopter blades in the distance gave her hope someone would see her and come to her rescue.

—✕—

A large cloud of darkness consumed the delightful scene below. Ketaton limped along with a snicker. This moment was worth the battle wounds he gained to get here. Too many angels lurked in the shadows, but he wouldn't miss this fight for the world. Beli-yaal worked tirelessly to bring this to fruition, but Ketaton would see it through to the end as a hero.

He egged on Ticano and the man with a scar.

"Kill her," he slurred, gurgling with pleasure. "She must die." Black tar flew from his mouth.

—✕—

Jocelyn's feet moved fast to keep up with the K-9. They were on to something, and she wasn't going to miss out on finding her suspects. If they made it to one of the cars—Jocelyn couldn't focus on that now.

Rogue alerted them with a bark. Silence fell over a once-spirited search. Jocelyn's eyes darted between the handler and the K-9. Was this something or not? Her jaw clenched to keep herself from demanding an answer.

"Detective," her radio blasted out into the stillness, sparking a scramble to turn it down. "This is Sheriff Esmay, unit twelve, we are on scene on the road east of you. We found one of the vehicles. It's definitely not operational. Looks like they tried to escape. Keys are still in the ignition, and it's smoking."

"Is it on fire?" Jocelyn worried it was a distraction to keep them busy.

"No fire, detective. Just engine trouble."

"Copy. Secure the vehicle, just in case they try to double back for it."

She turned her radio down and rejoined Rogue and her handler. The dog sniffed in circles for what felt like forever. Jocelyn tried to keep her foot from tapping, but her fingers didn't get the message.

"Did she find something?" she blurted out.

"The bark means there's something here, but she needs to pinpoint which direction it went." the lean officer with the leash explained.

"How do we know what the dog found? What if it's a dog treat?"

"When you've worked with Rogue as long as I have, ma'am, you learn to trust her instincts. She hasn't let me down yet. She has the highest number of finds in the whole department. She's smart. Trust her, detective."

A long, drawn-out sigh of surrender escaped. Moments later, Rogue barked and took off, pulling her handler along for the chase. Jocelyn sprinted after them.

"There," she shouted, pointing her finger out in front of them.

"Such. Such," he commanded in what sounded like German. A few more feet forward and he barked out, "Halt." Both Rogue and Jocelyn listened.

Rogue mimicked a kid on Halloween filled with too much sugar. Her body shook with excitement against her impressive control. She did her best not to whine, stopping herself short with little squeaks. She was impressive. Her grandma's dog couldn't stop peeing in her slippers, let alone not attack when it wanted to.

The handler slowly unclipped the leash. Rogue let out a shiver of excitement, desperate for the command she patiently waited for.

A dark figure caught her eye. It barely moved in an attempt to hide, but no one could hide from this furry machine. Rogue was clearly ruthless and the best of the best. Whoever was out there didn't stand a chance.

"Fass!" the handler forcefully said, releasing the full magnitude of Rogue.

Blasting through the darkness she launched with speed and control.

"Ahhh!" a deep voice yelled out. "Get off me! Help! Someone help!"

With weapons drawn, Jocelyn and the handler swiftly moved toward Rogue. A smile spread seeing Rogue with a man dressed in all black and a full-face mask, caught in her jaw.

"One in custody," she huffed into the radio. "Spread out. There's at least one more out here."

⌐×⌐

Viveka's steel blue eyes surveyed the darkness. The pungent aroma of decay alerted the beast was close by. She quickly moved forward. A new level of intensity flourished when she saw the parked car at the end of the driveway, Mia nowhere in sight.

Without panic, Viveka stealthily moved, skirting along the edge of the overgrown bushes. She remained obscured by the long shadow cast off the hedges by the moon. Weapon in hand, she moved with grace, like a ballerina. Every step carried a purpose of poise and bravery—not a single worry about the danger she was in.

The last time Viveka came face to face with a monster this size, it left her with wounds—a pair of twelve-inch scars ran down her back. Today, she gained another reminder with three deep to her leg.

A quick peek around the car revealed Mia on the ground. The dark beast swirled around her. A flash of jagged teeth glimmered in the cloud of darkness.

Those needle teeth were unmistakable. Ticano was here too.

Viveka advanced. No angel had stood alone against such a threat, but even if it cost her everything, she refused to leave Mia to die. Without a second thought, she gripped the sword in her hand and lunged forward. The cloud of evil grunted as it rolled several feet away from Mia.

Ticano frantically slashed his talons at the warrior. A hateful snarl undercut the chomp of his teeth. Viveka moved faster than the ball of needles in his mouth. Fighting was part strategy, of which she didn't really have one, and part speed, which she had in plenty.

Tell her. The Lord broke through Viveka's thoughts.

"Mia, remember who you are and what you've trained for. Don't let fear cloud what you know you're capable of," Viveka sternly told her as she fought off Ticano.

⌐×⌐

The memory of self-defense classes rang against her chest like the blast of a gong. A few years ago, the church was broken into just minutes after Mia left. Oliver insisted she take the class. Over the last year, she'd been too afraid to use what she learned for anything but to block his torment.

In the last twenty-four hours, everything had changed. She started to see her worth and understood it was time to fight back.

An influx of strength filled her pleading body. Gasping for air, she went to work. One hand pushed onto his thigh and the other against the shoulder on the same side. This gave her the leverage she needed to slink her hips out on the opposite side. Once in position, she put her foot on his other hip and thrust all three points away.

The jolt forced his upper body back for a split second as she extended herself out with her foot still on his hip. As he dove back toward her, she flexed her other foot and slammed her heel into his face as hard as she could. Blood spattered from his nose. He called her the name Oliver usually did.

As oxygen returned to her brain, Mia was able to think. The quick scramble to her feet made her dizzy. The moonlight flickered off the barrel of the gun. She staggered, fighting to stay upright.

Stumbling over her steps, she fell to the ground just short of the gun. With a quick army crawl, her fingertips brushed along its cold metal before a robust force pulled her back. She wailed as the dirt and rocks cut deep. Another kick with her free foot against his arm jolted her leg free.

The gun. She had to get the gun.

It took seconds to reach her weapon. With a firm grip she turned to point it at her assailant, but he tackled her again before she could fire.

He searched for the gun gripped in her hands. Straddled on top of her, her legs locked in place with his feet. A sinister laugh came from his blood-soaked mouth.

"You're marked for death," he wildly grunted.

A few whimpers escaped as he gripped around the gun with both hands and twisted. Mia tried to thrust her hips up, but he had her cinched in his grasp. She tried to pull the trigger, but she couldn't move her fingers.

The gun slowly twisted as the barrel moved to face her.

"No!" she screamed.

⸻ ⊶✕⊷ ⸻

"Here, put him in your squad car," Jocelyn ordered another cop who came from the north, handing off her suspect.

"Sure thing, ma'am," the female officer acknowledged.

"Oh! One more thing," Jocelyn interrupted. "You'll need to do a thorough search before putting him in the backseat. I didn't find a wallet, but see if you can find anything that'll give us a name since he's not talking."

"Copy that." The young woman who stood eye to eye with the large man smiled.

"How tall are you, officer?" Jocelyn curiously asked, slightly jealous of her long legs.

"Six feet even, ma'am. And you can call me Bex."

"Okay…Bex. Let me know if you find anything."

"Will do."

Jocelyn returned her focus to the crime scene in front of her. She put one officer enroute to the cellar to start working the scene. The search continued for the second vehicle that seemed to have vanished. H-One lost sight of the other suspect.

"Detective." The K-9 handler got her attention. She turned to look at him. "Rogue and I are going to continue searching the area."

Jocelyn exhaled with relief. "Just mark anything you see so the analysts can come in and do their thing once the scene is code four."

"Sounds good."

Jocelyn looked down at Rouge, feeling a genuine connection to her. "Can I thank her?"

"Sorry, detective, but when she's at work you can't. But, if I see you when this is over and her gear is off, you're more than welcome to do that."

"Oh, okay." Jocelyn tried to not sound too disappointed, but she respected the protocol.

The K-9 and her handler went straight to work. Jocelyn pulled up the area map on her phone to see roughly where she was. Not too far from the back road, so maybe she'd continue on and see if she could find the second vehicle.

"H-one, have you found anything?" she huffed into the radio.

"Negative. The trees are pretty thick in this area, but I'll keep looking."

With the weapon secured at her shoulder, she continued on one steady step at a time. The second suspect could be anywhere.

———————✕———————

This princess was officially on Ketaton's last nerve. When they swerved, the wannabe warrior was there to meet them. Him and Ticano swirled around their prize killer, ready to finish the job of the pastor's wife.

A flash of light from the warrior's sword swooped through, splitting Ketaton away from the struggle. A growl of rage bellowed in his chest.

"Finish this," he ordered Ticano. "I've got the princess." He grinned, his teeth soiled with tar.

Talking was difficult and he didn't know if Ticano understood, but none of that mattered. Time for this angel brat to die.

With talons out and ready, she was right where he wanted her. He charged with a wicked slash of his claws, but she vanished before they connected.

Frantic, he looked around, unable to find her. "Hurry up!" he screamed at Ticano.

———————✕———————

Levi left Jocelyn's side with Charlotte over his shoulders, abandoning her to search alone. It wasn't long before the distinct sound of a nearby helicopter released a sigh of relief. Backup was starting to arrive.

He prayed the ambulance would be there soon, and kicked himself for getting turned around in these blasted woods. Charlotte didn't have time for mistakes like that. Her skin burned against his neck. It was uncomfortable, but he would tolerate it all day if it meant she lived.

"Hang in there, kid," he encouraged her lifeless body.

Levi made the most of his brisk walk and devised a plan for what to do once he reached the car. First, he needed an ETA from dispatch on the ambulance. Then he needed to let Jocelyn know they made it.

The manhunt underway beckoned him as blue and red lights flashed against the darkness above. He could hear a K-9 alert of something. Maybe they found the suspects, but he needed to be sure.

He still wondered about Oliver's involvement. It's plausible that he was more involved than he led on. Perhaps the voicemail was left as a decoy.

He gave Mia the benefit of the doubt when it came to what she knew. Her emotions and the role she played seemed so real and genuine, as if he could feel the shame, guilt, and fear pouring out of her.

It was only a matter of time before one of two things turned up true: she was innocent or she deserved an award for her performance.

Back when they were younger, she was so genuine. She wore her heart on her sleeve, which made it easy for him to know what she thought. He admired her ability to be so open. Levi never showed the world the storm that brewed beneath the surface.

He thought briefly about his father but it—

The crack of a gun echoed against the mountains and trees. Levi's eyes grew wide as his heart and lungs picked up speed. Adrenaline swallowed him like a tidal wave. He knew exactly where the shot came from.

"Mia!" he screamed.

Forty

VIVEKA'S LONG, LEAN FRAME stoically stood tall as she tracked the beasts. She couldn't recall a previous time two demons scattered so abruptly at the blast of a gun. She sprinted forward after them.

"Is she dead?" the bigger one growled at Ticano.

The question stopped Viveka in her tracks. Over her shoulder lay a pile of lifeless bodies. Viveka questioned if either of them survived the fatal shot.

Turning back, she lost sight of the devils. As much as she wanted to go after them, Mia was the priority. Those wicked creatures would see banishment soon enough.

"A large unknown demon and Ticano are heading north. I'm unable to leave Mia. Someone needs to go after them," she telepathically told Finn.

"On it," Finn briefly replied. "Axum, Dante, and Kano head north."

Levi sprinted passed Viveka with Charlotte over his shoulders. Time slowed. The warrior took in the young girl's face—pale, sunken in, and barren.

"Where did that shot come from?" an authoritative female voice shouted over the radio in the distance, followed by several unsure answers. "Does anyone have eyes on the potential shooter?" she demanded again.

Silence.

He sprinted toward the end of the driveway. The moon reflected off the inactive headlights of the unmarked cruiser. With caution for Charlotte's weak body, he made a minuscule effort to slow down.

Levi hated the feeling of dread in the pit of his stomach. What if—no. He couldn't play the what-if game, he knew better.

His deep feelings for her clouded his judgment around every corner. He took her protection upon his own shoulders, rather than giving it to the Lord, and then left her there, unprotected.

If she was shot, it would be entirely his fault.

An abrupt stop at the overgrown bushes gave him a chance to lay Charlotte down and slightly obscure her body with the shrubs. He hesitated to leave the defenseless woman the same way he left Mia. She was finally safe. If he left her and the suspect still at large found her, he could never forgive himself.

He looked around, unable to spot Mia anywhere in sight.

The bottom line was, he couldn't take Charlotte into unknown danger. Either option posed a risk, but leaving her seemed to be the safer of two terrible choices. He gave her one final push into the bushes to keep her hidden.

Bent at the knees, he unloaded his HK and scooted it into the bushes next to Charlotte and drew his service weapon, a trustee Glock 19. This handgun had been with him through some rather dicey encounters over the years on the night shift. It protected him during the carjacking suspect who tried to shoot his way out. Needless to say, it didn't end well for the suspect. Then again, when rival gangs went head-to-head at an ice cream shop between the two territories.

When he was moved to a less violent zone, it still protected him the night a bar fight turned deadly with a broken beer bottle that sliced a man's face wide open. And it would protect him now as he crept himself toward the car.

Crouched low, he ignored the burn in his legs and rounded the hood of the car, stopping at the edge. With the gun by his side, he slightly poked his head out and around the corner. There he saw a large body face down, not moving. Underneath, jutted out two legs.

He investigated for signs of life without giving away his position. No movement.

"No, no, no, no, no," he softly muttered.

Amidst the sorrow that burned in his eyes, a noise stopped him. He snapped back his emotions and intently listened. Something persistently scratched against the hard, dry ground.

He rocked himself forward again in time to see the man's body shift. He darted back out of sight. With a firm grip on his gun, he slowly stood. Slick steps forward left his presence unknown to the mysterious threat.

Levi zeroed his aim onto the obscured movement. His finger remained posted on the trigger guard, ready to execute the weapon at a moment's notice.

The man's body moved with a cumbersome ability. Levi's finger shifted to the trigger. Calculated breaths kept the adrenaline in check. Unsure who moved, he didn't want to blindly pull the trigger and kill the wrong person.

Unwilling to alert the suspect and leave time for him to grab an unseen weapon, Levi silently waited for the agonizing struggle to reveal who lived and who didn't. A lump remained in his throat, growing with each passing second.

With one hefty shift, the man's body flopped to the side, lifeless. Mia screamed for air as she frantically fought to free her legs from under the man. Levi stood in shock—she survived.

A large smile broke across his lips. He was at her side in less than a second. With one swift pull, Levi brought Mia into his arms. She shook like a leaf.

"You're okay. I've got you," he reassured.

He looked at the assailant's face. The assassin. He briefly let her go to ensure she was in fact safe. Two fingers pressed into the man's carotid. No pulse. He cuffed him anyway.

Scrambling to her side, he took her dirt-smudged face in his hands. "You're alive," he cried out as a few tears escaped down his face.

She smiled up at him with relief and pulled him in for a hug. "What happened to your sweatshirt?" she laughed, wiping tears from her face.

"I used it to cover up Charlotte."

He held her tight in his arms, not wanting to ever let her go, but Mia pulled away and looked at him with astonishment.

"You found her? She's alive?"

"Barely. The ambulance should be here soon." He looked around for anything that would explain this bizarre turn of events. "How did he find us out here?" he asked.

"I have no idea." Mia gently held her stomach. "Where's the girl?"

"By the bushes."

He helped Mia limp toward Charlotte. A careful tug on her hidden body brought her into view. Mia dropped to her knees and hunched over Charlotte.

"I'm so sorry," Mia repeated over and over between sobs.

<hr>

With no answers to the pressing question, Jocelyn's free hand clenched into a fist. Where did the shot come from? Did it take out an officer? What about Mia? What if something happened to Levi and Charlotte?

"H-One," she called out over the radio.

"H-One, go ahead," the man responded in his thick southern accent.

"Any sign of the second suspect?"

"No, ma'am."

"Did you see a muzzle flash or anything from the air?" Jocelyn huffed.

"Negative, ma'am."

Jocelyn fought the frustration boiling within. Someone had to know something.

"Be on the lookout for any officers who may be in trouble as you search."

"Ten-four."

She took a deep breath. "Everyone currently on scene, check in immediately," she ordered.

This was the last thing she wanted to waste time on, but she didn't have a choice. A shot went off somewhere, and she couldn't ignore it.

"Detective Maddox," a familiar voice cut through the static on her radio. "Detective Maddox, do you copy?"

"Officer Reed?" She confirmed who it sounded like past the poor connection. He must be on the car radio.

"Affirmative. Liste—I ha—informa—shoo—"

"Reed, you're breaking up. Repeat."

"I have infor—about the—ting."

"Repeat," Jocelyn yelled louder than intended.

"I have information about the shooter." Levi cut through enough so she finally understood. "We're code four. Shoot—down. Eleven-fort—four." His words broke up but she pieced it together, the shooter was dead and everyone was safe.

"Copy that, Reed. I'll get another ambulance started for the shooter. How's Charlotte?" She unintentionally held her breath, waiting for the answer.

"Unsure. She doesn't loo—good. Ya got—ETA o—EMS?"

Jocelyn went to answer, but dispatch chimed in. "EMS, two minutes out."

"Copy," his voice filled with radio noise.

Her concentration returned to the other possible suspects. "Attention all units on scene at Heartly Drive, cancel my last and continue the search grid. There are at least one, possibly two, suspects still at large. Widen your grids. No one leaves until this whole area has been swept thoroughly." Acknowledgments of her orders filed through the radio.

"All incoming units, come in from Heartly and start your search from the outside in," she continued. "All incoming K-nines, contact Officer Barnes with Officer Rogue on channel two for further instructions."

A text came through her phone from Levi.

LEVI:
The shooter was the guy caught on camera at the ER. We aren't sure how he tracked her here, but he did and attacked her. She said she fought him off the best she could, but he got his hands on the gun she had from the trunk. Sounds like it's a miracle she wasn't killed when the gun went off. I checked him and he's unresponsive, not breathing, and has no pulse, but have him cuffed and secured. Ambulance is loading Charlotte now. Sending Mia with them so she can get checked since she sustained some pretty deep cuts on her abdomen. I took detailed pictures of both women and am ready to rejoin the search. Where do you want me?

Jocelyn lingered on the text. She tried to fight it, but her suspicion continued to rise. Could it be possible Mia wasn't who she claimed? Nothing about this made sense. This woman got beaten by her husband regularly, but she just killed a professional hitman? Jocelyn would have some digging to do. She didn't think it was safe to leave the paramedics with Mia alone and unprotected.

JOCELYN:
Go with them to the ER.

LEVI:
They already left.

Jocelyn stood in silence, unsure what to think of Levi. Was there no question in his mind as to how Mia survived an attempted murder by a professional? His thought process with this girl was all over the map, leaving Jocelyn with whiplash and difficulty sorting her feelings. She couldn't allow that to sideline her. They needed to keep searching.

JOCELYN:
Head south/east of your location and work the grid from the outside in.

LEVI:
Copy. Just a heads up, the news vultures caught wind of the search and are gathering out here at the driveway.

JOCELYN:
Then hold tight. Backup should be here soon to help secure the area.

Her full lips pressed thin. When this was over, she vowed to speak to him in detail about his abysmal decisions.

"Dispatch," Jocelyn called over the radio.

"Dispatch, go ahead."

"Do you know where the ambulance is transporting their patients?"

"They're being flown to University of Tennessee Medical Center back in Knoxville due to the nature of their injuries."

"Copy. Send a few officers over to ensure their safety upon arrival. They are not to leave their side."

"Ten-four."

"Incoming units, what's your ETA?"

"Walsh and Maltez, two minutes out."

"I need your team to meet Officer Reed at the end of the driveway and set up barriers. We've got reporters gathered down that way."

"Copy," he responded.

With closed eyes, she took a long, deep breath as she contemplated her next move. She wanted to continue the search, but everyone looked to her for leadership. The smartest thing to do was head out to the driveway to ensure as more officers arrived, she could direct them properly. A few steps in, the radio stopped her.

"Second suspect in custody. Female, early thirties. Code four."

A sigh of relief escaped her lips. "Good job, guys." She congratulated them over the radio. "All units, keep looking. Unknown on the accuracy of a third, but we need to confirm."

Forty~One

HIS HANDS VIGOROUSLY SHOOK with each item frantically shoved into his suitcase. He hastily removed as much information and evidence as he could from the small motel room. By the Grace of God, and a bit of luck, he made it out of those dreadful woods without a trace—at least he was fairly confident he had.

In his escape, ten miles outside of the area, several cops flew by, oblivious they passed the one chosen to carry on the legacy. Charlotte had been a mistake, and luckily the other two weren't here to remind him of that. He should've let her go, but his desire for her burned too hot to stop. That longing, that pull she had on him, was not easily shaken.

He yearned to go back. The way she felt when he finally had his way with her was almost too much to let go. He wanted her with him forever, but she had turned from God and would pay violently for it. No mercy.

All went according to plan until those imbeciles showed up and ruined everything.

In his haste, he stopped long enough to turn on the news. This would help him know how discrete he needed to be, and if he had time to make things right.

He got his answer during the weather report as he packed the toiletries.

"We have breaking news. We've received word there is a massive manhunt underway. Let's go to Joni, who is there on the scene in Sevierville. Joni?" an older man with a thick white mustache announced.

A well-dressed and exquisite woman popped onto the screen. The petite features, the long blonde hair, those alluring eyes. She looked like Charlotte. Strands of her hair softly blew in the breeze the same way Charlotte's did the night they took her. He noted her incredible physique as his mouth hung open.

"David, we just learned from the police that they're conducting a search for possible suspects in what is being described as the manhunt of the century here in Sevierville, Tennessee. There are countless police on scene, from K-nines to helicopters, which I'm sure you can hear flying above me. We're told they're searching for a group of individuals they believe to be involved in a string of murders from the Durham area in North Carolina.

"I spoke with Captain Ben Woods out of Durham Police Department who told me they have placed two suspects in custody but are continuing to search for a possible third. However, they're unsure how accurate that information is.

"They are currently unable to release the names of those in custody, but are urging residents from Durham, Knoxville, and Sevierville to be careful, lock your doors, and stay inside. If anyone has any information about this group, you're asked to call your local police department, and they will relay the message to Knoxville PD. I have a feeling it's going to be a long night here, David, as they check and recheck their steps for another suspect. I'll stay on the scene and keep you updated as new information arrives."

"Thank you, Joni." The man she called David came back on the screen.

He quickly rewound the feed and paused it on the woman. They didn't have a clue if he even existed. His eyes centered on the beauty frozen in time on the screen.

He wanted her.

❖

He riffled through the dark and forgotten corners of the closet, searching for something specific. His hand walked across the upper shelf with ease until it ran into the hard object. A yank revealed a black specially designed carrying case. He delicately held it before placing it on the made-up bed. The latches popped with ease. He lifted the lid, displaying its precious contents.

One lowly syringe sat perfectly encompassed by the interior cushion. He lifted it out of the box, popped the needle protector off, and smiled. This would do just fine.

He anticipated that running would be hard, painful even, but no one in this life was worth staying connected to. His mother, a functioning and respected drunk. Dad, a narcissistic workaholic he barely knew. The small group of friends he found was nothing he cared about.

The only thing he considered was Charlotte. He hated to leave things undone.

I pray, Father, she is dealt with. If not by me, then by another.

Holding up his cell phone, he gazed at her picture one last time.

"Goodbye, Charlotte," he whispered before removing the SIM card and breaking it.

Time to move on. To look forward.

He put the syringe back and closed the case, setting it on top of his duffle bag. His teachers of terror would've said no to this plan, but this was *his* legacy to carry on now, and there was no one here to stand in his way.

—⋈—

Jocelyn made it to the end of the driveway, pleasantly surprised with how many officers had arrived and how fast they set up the barriers. Caution tape was strung up from the bushes across the street with officers every few feet along the line. She saw Levi from the corner of her vision checking the perimeter along the bushes to make sure no one snuck in for a breaking news clip.

She had encountered one overly aggressive reporter as a rookie cop. He snuck his way into a scene and ended up a hostage. She hoped no one was dumb enough to do that tonight.

"Detective," Levi hollered after her. She pressed forward. "Jocelyn, slow down a minute." She didn't stop, but he caught up to her anyway. *Darn these short legs.* "Can you just let me apologize?"

She stopped and turned to face him. The upper hand seemed to shrink as she crooked her neck to look up. "Go ahead."

"Look, I know I didn't handle things right back there, and I'm sorry. No excuses, no drawn-out explanation, just…I'm sorry." His wide eyes and twisted expression softened her stance. "I should've cleared sending

Mia with you first. And"—he sighed—"I should've held the press back rather than wanting to jump in the manhunt."

She took a moment to examine his face and consider his words. He looked like a puppy who just got scolded. Maybe he was remorseful, but only time would tell. She'd grown to like Levi, even if he was an idiot sometimes.

"Thanks for saving me the words I planned to yell at you," she smiled. "Maybe there's hope for you, after all, Reed." She patted him on the shoulder and went to walk away.

"There's one more thing I should tell you."

Jocelyn shifted her weight, unsure what else there could be. "Okay." She dragged out the word.

"Before I helped get Charlotte into the ambulance, she mumbled something. She said, 'He was so familiar'." He sighed at the confused look on her face. "It didn't make sense to me either, and I blew it off as ramblings, but I thought I should tell you in case I'm wrong."

"Thank you."

Jocelyn smiled at his effort and walked away to find Walsh and Maltez.

"You must be Detective Maddox," Diego Maltez called out. "What'cha doin' up here?" He walked toward her with such swagger.

"Just thought I'd check to see if you need anything."

He turned around in several directions, examining the progress. "Uh, nope, we good," he laughed. "I've got guys watching the east and west perimeters to ensure scene and civilian protection. You're welcome to head back out to the search. We've got things all locked up here."

Jocelyn softly nodded with a smile.

Another waste of precious time. Way to go, Joce.

They needed to find the second car and fast.

She caught sight of AJ in the crowd, staring at one of the newscasters. The reporter was beautiful with long blonde hair and full lips. It wasn't a shock he gaped at her, just a disappointment.

Standing there, she debated whether to talk to him or not. Odd he'd even be here.

"Spalding," she called out. When he didn't look at her, she yelled louder. "AJ!"

He finally tore his eyes off the reporter and found her in the sea of officers. Jocelyn hated these feelings that seemed to grow no matter what she did. She needed to get rid of them once and for all.

"Joce," he called. His face seemed to light up when he saw her, but who knew if that meant anything. "What are you doing over here?"

He moved toward the barrier and Jocelyn motioned the officers to let him in. "I should ask you the same thing."

As he walked closer, she swallowed hard, fighting the urge to run into his arms.

Pull it together. You're a strong, independent woman. Snap out of it.

"I saw you found Charlotte on the news and had to come down to congratulate you." He smiled that perfect, arrogant smile. Jocelyn raised one brow and just stared. There was more to his story. She could feel it. "Okay, fine, you got me. I did want to congratulate you, but I brought my stuff and thought I could start processing evidence."

"AJ, that's not—"

"I know, it's not protocol, but I don't know. I guess I'm feeling a bit left out. Plus, Joni Jacobs is here from WKT News. She's a pretty big deal."

Jocelyn looked over at the newscaster. "Yeah, I can see what a *big* deal she is," she sarcastically said, referring to the obvious boob job. Most hundred-pound girls weren't a natural double D. "A really *big* and *fake* deal."

"Oh hush," AJ laughed. "She's done some pretty major stories and seems to be ambitious. I wouldn't be surprised if she hosted sixty minutes or something one day."

"Keep telling yourself that," Jocelyn scoffed. "I gotta get back to work and you need to stand behind the line so you're safe. I'll let you know when you can process the scene."

She walked away without another word. Confusion seeped in. He didn't stop her. He didn't protest. He just let her walk away without a word. Which left the question, what on earth he was really doing here?

Forty-Two

THEY SEARCHED THE ENTIRE woods. The second vehicle H-One mentioned was nowhere to be found, and no additional suspect was picked up. It was still unknown if this phantom suspect even existed. The vehicle possibly belonged to someone unattached to this, but they couldn't rule it out. Jocelyn released the helicopter and left only a small remnant of K-9 officers to double-check the area.

Fresh tire tracks were found south of the broken-down sedan, so they needed to track down whoever took the vehicle before she could determine what happened. Hopefully, they would have a make and model soon.

She smiled briefly at AJ, who glanced up from processing the tracks. In spite of his obvious crush on the stunning reporter, her heart still went pitter-patter at the thought of him. Disgusting.

He was so not her type. She never went for guys who wore alternative band t-shirts and were know-it-alls. But with this guy... There was something about the way he smiled at her and the softness he had that she couldn't ignore.

Ugh. Stop it. Right now.

Shaking off her crush, she stalked back to the car at the end of the driveway. As she walked her mind went over what she knew to be true. Charlotte had been kidnapped, the red paint found in the vehicle and the ketamine syringe near Charlotte's apartment linked back to the other eight victims. Two suspects were in custody, Mia might still be part of it all, Oliver hadn't been confirmed dead yet, and Charlotte said something about knowing one of them. Too many questions and not enough answers.

She pulled out her phone and called Maya, who led the Durham teams in her absence.

"Maddox, what's up?" Maya picked up on the first ring.

"I think we need to go back over Charlotte's life. She said something to one of the officers here about one of the captures being familiar."

"How credible do you think that is?" she pressed.

"I'm honestly not sure. But we can't rule out a possible third suspect in this." She paused. "I think it's a viable statement we need to look into."

"What about the two you found?"

"I don't have names. I tried to question them on scene, but they're not talking. I'm headed back for a proper interrogation now."

"Sounds good. I'll get an officer to bring in Tamika Lewis, and I'll see if she can remember anyone who gave off stalker vibes or that Charlotte was afraid of."

"Yeah, sounds good. I also need you to put a rush on processing everything from Charlotte's apartment." Jocelyn bit her bottom lip. "Can you have them focus on the wine glasses? There's something Tamika said when I interviewed her that's been bothering me."

"What's that?"

"She said they had a drink to calm down and before she knew it, they were passed out. At first, I thought it was just college students being run down and exhausted, but what if it was more?"

"I'll press Miss Lewis for answers and get the lab on those glasses ASAP."

"Thanks, M&M."

Jocelyn went to hang up, but she stopped her. "Joce."

"Yeah?"

"You're doing a good job. Keep it up. Don't push too hard with these two in custody or they'll lawyer up, and we won't get anything out of them."

"I've got this."

They hung up the phone. Truth was, her confidence was as fake as that reporter's assets. On the one other high-stakes interview she'd conducted, Detective Martin, who trained her, had to jump in and finish it.

There was no time for second-guessing or worrying. She had to put her game face on and get it done.

———————————✕———————————

She stood with wobbly knees. Tall redwoods reached high into the sky for the sun. Birds sang a flawless song of praise as a single white butterfly flitted in front of her. Looking down, her feet were on a visible path that led through the forest of tall, robust trees.

Her white dress, crisp and clean. There was no sign of the blood that poured from her arm anywhere. A few steps down the road, a dirt driveway led to a charming storybook cottage. She stopped to admire the rounded corners of the roof and the beautiful vines that grew up the side by the front door. Beams of light brought elegantly golden rays of warmth through the trees.

"Charlotte!" someone called out. "Charlotte, hey! Come on over."

The girl looked like a cartoon with a snatched waist and hourglass figure. Her blonde hair was secured in low pigtails, her shirt far too low for comfort. Charlotte never understood the appeal of putting your chest on display like that. She scanned the girl to explain the sense of familiarity.

"Come on." Another girl popped out from behind the blonde.

This one was less shapely with dark hair, almost black. Her skin was pale with tired, blackened eyes. The sweet smell of coffee lingered in the air with a frigid chill.

"Oh, Charlie, don't be silly! Come with us," the blonde sweetly said, grabbing her hand and pulling her onto the property.

The only people who called her Charlie were her dad's mother, who passed away a few years back, and her roommate, Tamika. She stumbled toward them despite everything within her that screamed not to. The blonde had such a grip on her hand she couldn't wiggle out of it.

Lord, help me. What should I do?

They dragged her to the garden where a woman pleasantly tended the abundant foliage. Charlotte looked around. Despite the lush green fullness of each plant, nothing grew but leaves—no flowers, fruit, or vegetables, no sign of any production whatsoever.

What is this place?

Dread rested in the pit of her stomach.

"Charlotte, dear," the woman softly greeted. "It's so nice for you to visit."

"D-do I know you?" Charlotte finally asked.

"Oh, of course you do, dear. I'm Big Mama, remember?" Charlotte tried to jog her memory. Nothing came except an uneasy twist in her chest. "Girls, why don't you take Charlie to the beach? Maybe that'll help her to remember she belongs here, with us."

Charlotte swallowed hard.

"Oh, that's okay," she kindly declined. The blonde's hand tightened around her wrist when she tried to pull away.

"Stop fighting, Charlie. If Big Mama says to go to the beach, that's what we do. She's the boss."

"But I don't—"

"You must," the dark-haired girl snapped, shoving her from behind.

"No. Wait. Please," Charlotte protested as the two girls forced her to walk.

Lord, help me. She prayed. *This has to be a dream. Wake up, Char. Wake up.*

Through the forest, the trees quickly became sparse. The tan dirt now swirled with red. An exhaustive heat blew through and replaced the chilly breeze.

Standing at the edge of the trees, all she could see for miles was desert terrain. No water or growth in sight. Anxiety beat against her chest. Her mouth went dry. She couldn't swallow, let alone speak. It was so hot, so desolate. Love easily drained from her, leaving her hollow and alone.

The gray sky swirled with palpable hate. No part of her wanted to go here.

Jesus! Her heart internally cried out. *Help me!*

One good tug freed her wrist, and she ran back into the forest.

"Charlie! Come back!" they called after her.

But Charlotte ran as fast as her legs would carry her. Deeper and deeper into the forest she weaved through the trees. The cool air burned in her lungs.

Face to face with a beast, she abruptly stopped. It snarled as drool dripped from its barred teeth. The creature looked like a wolf, its charcoal fur mangy and wild. A low gutter growl let out in its chest. The heat of its pant made her stomach twist.

Her breath stuttered. With a hand out in front, she pleaded with it to calm down.

"Shh, it's okay. Look at me, I'm backing up. Shh. It's okay. It's okay."

Charlotte wasn't sure if she was talking more to the beast or herself, but either way, it calmed her overwhelming anxiety. The girls would catch up soon if she didn't figure out what to do.

The wolf reached out and nipped at her with aggression. The snarling increased followed by a few more nips. Of course, a plan would only work if it didn't kill her first.

Behind the beast, something caught her eye. A tall dark-skinned being shifted through the trees with purity and grace.

"Charlotte," a familiar voice whispered her name. Where did she know it from? "Charlotte, remember who you are now."

"Charlie," the blonde sing-songed, calling out for her. "Come out, come out, wherever you are."

Charlotte heard a gasp from behind her. Unwilling to take her eyes off the beast, she put her hand out, palm toward the one behind her.

"Stop," she demanded.

"Charlie," the blonde whispered. "It's not safe. Let us help you." Charlotte shook off their help. "Please, Charlie. If you're with us, he won't hurt you."

Charlotte narrowed in on the pure being behind the threat. She looked to be a warrior of some sort. Her long black hair in braids gathered at the top of her head in a ponytail. Gold feathers dressed the braids down past her shoulders. Charlotte noticed the bronze band around her forehead. Her broad nose was pierced, and her full lips urged her to remember.

Unsure what the presumed helper talked about, Charlotte ran through her options. Run and surely die. Go with the girls behind her and likely die. Trust the stranger with the familiar voice and…probably die. The odds weren't exactly in her favor.

"Call on Him!" the angel shouted.

Paralyzed in fear, Charlotte was afraid to move or speak, worried it would set the beast after her. Its massive jowls would surely rip her to shreds. Jesus couldn't save her here on the outskirts of love, could He? A slow, steady breath filled her lungs. She paused for just a moment as nerves and uncertainty twisted in her stomach.

"Jesus, help me," Charlotte belted out.

Shrieks filled the thick air as the beast contorted against an invisible pain. It violently shook its head and fled with haste. She turned around to see the girls howl in pain, covering their ears. They both sprinted away from Charlotte. In an instant, peace returned to the woods and her heart.

"Who are you?" Charlotte asked.

The warrior smiled and, with a nod, went to leave.

"Wait. Please." Charlotte cried out, stopping the angel in her tracks. She admired the bands on each arm and the length of her sword as the ample hero turned back to face her. "I know you, don't I?"

The angel nodded.

"Thank you for saving me…again." Charlotte tucked a piece of her wild hair behind her ear as the being smiled. "Can I at least know your name?"

The warrior paused. Charlotte wondered if she was thinking of her own words or waiting on God's.

"Charlotte," the warrior finally spoke. "My name is Ashanti, but you must know, I'm not the one who saved you. Jesus did." Her slight accent and tone were beautiful.

"But you have been with me, yes?"

"Yes."

"Thank you for that."

"Dear Charlotte, all Glory and Honor go to God in Heaven for sending me to look after you. I don't deserve, nor want any praise. Give it all to Him, for He is the ruler of everything."

Charlotte smiled as the edges of the world around her blackened. Trees faded out of existence, one by one. Panic crept in, but the sweet smile of the angel sent by God soothed her.

"Do not be afraid, for God is with you, always," the angel softly said.

Seconds later, everything went black, and all Charlotte could hear were the rhythmic beeps of what sounded like a heart monitor.

"Charlotte, please wake up," a soft voice sniffled next to her. "I'm so sorry."

—✕—

Levi drove Jocelyn along the desolate road back toward Knoxville. Too many thoughts tore through her mind to hold a conversation. Thankfully, the uncomfortable silence didn't seem to bother Levi. He likely had a lot on his mind too.

The more Jocelyn went back through the facts, the more details she remembered. Charlotte should have been dead hours before they found her, so what delayed their timeline? The eight previous victims all were killed within seventy-two hours, but Charlotte wasn't.

Evidence of antibiotics at the scene stumped her. The water buckets made sense though. They had to cleanse each victim for the sacrifice. At least, she assumed they followed how it was done in the Old Testament. Jocelyn flipped through the reports she had on her phone. There were no traces of antibiotics in the toxicology reports for the other victims.

Charlotte did feel warm when they found her. Maybe she got sick. Perhaps too sick for the ritual?

The last word she received from the officers at the hospital, Charlotte remained unconscious. The doctors had done all they could at this point. Now it would take time for her body to rehydrate and fight to live. Charlotte wasn't out of the woods just yet, but on her way to a hopeful recovery.

As for Mia, her wounds were cleaned out and treated. They gave her pain meds for the previous injuries and to calm her down. The officer said she hadn't stopped crying since they arrived. The detailed report was a nice change from what Jocelyn was used to.

She needed a strategy for the two suspects. They could be siblings or married, which would make this harder. A team this good would have a plan in their back pockets to protect themselves. She needed a way around whatever fictitious story they told, so she could find the truth. She needed answers.

Her phone dinged with a text.

MAYA MARTINEZ:
Tamika Lewis just arrived, and the lab is processing the glasses and hairs found at the apartment. Next, they'll process the fibers. I'll let you know what I find out.

JOCELYN:
Copy that. We're about ten minutes out from the station. I'll let you know what I get out of these two.

"Do you think there's a third person involved in all this?" Levi cut through the silence.

"What do you think?" Jocelyn turned the question on him, unsure how she felt about the whole thing.

Levi took a moment, obviously mulling it over.

"There's just something that doesn't add up. Like, where's the car?"

"What car?"

"The black Impala that was seen at the clinic where the vet was killed."

"You still think that's connected?"

"I do. We found that syringe of animal antibiotics in the cellar, which could be from a vet's office."

Jocelyn thought about it for a moment. He had a point, but there could be a million reasons for how they got ahold of it.

"I see your point, but what if it was something they had already? Or if one of them is a vet? Or maybe one person owns multiple vehicles. Or they borrowed a car." She sighed. "That's the problem. There are too many variables."

"I'm just saying, a BOLO went out on that vehicle hours ago. If it's connected, which for the record I think it is, where's the car? Why haven't we found it yet?" He tapped his fingers on the wheel. "I know BOLOs don't always get us quick information, but for a murder, I know cops are out there hunting for that car between calls."

No one found the car or even a suspicion of a car fitting that description yet. It was indeed odd.

"Okay, when we get back to the station, I want you to pull the file from the vet murder. Talk to the detectives working the case and see if there are any prints or forensics that we can link to our case. Maybe we'll get lucky and suspect three will be in the system." She ignored the smile on Levi's face. "Anything you find, give it to AJ, A-SAP."

"So, you do believe there's another suspect." Levi smiled in victory.

"Yes, I do. But I also believe we're running out of time."

Forty-Three

MAYA SAT ACROSS FROM Tamika Lewis. She analyzed the young girl as she bit at her nails and fought against the tears building in her eyes.

"I brought you water," Maya offered with a smile. She slid the cold bottle across the table.

"Thank you." Tamika softly sniffled.

Maya opened the file before her and thumbed through a few pages. There was something in the way this kid picked at her cuticles and evaded eye contact. Tamika seemed nervous or maybe just sad.

To be honest, empathy wasn't exactly Maya's strong suit. Working undercover left little room for trust. To her, everyone looked and sounded suspicious until proven otherwise. Plus, she grew up the oldest of far too many siblings and cousins. In her family, that came with a special kind of pressure to be the parent when no one was around while maintaining a good example. Needless to say, it wore down her compassion at a young age.

"We brought you in because some new information has come to light, and I'm hoping you'll be able to help us narrow it down," Maya started.

"That seems rather vague," Tamika said with a tone of authority, her watery eyes now locked on Maya.

Joce is right. Law students are the worst. Maya internally rolled her eyes.

"We believe whoever took Charlotte might be someone she knows."

"I thought you made two arrests already," she pressed, collecting her emotions.

"We did. Unfortunately, neither of them are talking." Maya pulled up photos Jocelyn took of each suspect on her phone. "Do either of these people look familiar?"

Tamika looked intently at the photos. "I don't think so."

"Take a good look. Charlotte mumbled something about one of them being familiar. Could one of them be in your classes or work at The Roasted Bean?"

A twisted look grew on Tamika's face. "No, I'm sorry."

Maya let out a deep breath. "We believe there may be a third person involved. I need you to be sure."

"I'm sure. I don't know either of them."

Tamika leaned back with a deflated posture. Her eyes collected more tears, and she pursed her full lips together to steady their quiver.

Maya gave her a moment to collect herself and thumbed through the file once more.

"Is there anyone you can think of who might have given Charlotte extra attention?"

Tamika took a moment to think it over. "Everyone paid her extra attention, detective. She's a knockout."

A tinge of jealousy briefly displayed on her face. Tamika was a beautiful girl, so the underlying covetousness she tried to hide struck Maya as odd. Could envy have played a role in Charlotte's disappearance?

"I really need you to think," Maya pushed as frustration built. "Was there anyone who might have pushed too hard for time with her or anyone who gave Charlotte or you the creeps?"

Her eyes grew wide. "There might be someone," she whispered in disbelief.

⸰⸱✕⸱⸰

Her smooth blonde hair tousled in the light breeze. The chilled air burned with every breath. Steam clouded out of his mouth and nose as he lay in wait for the right time.

Her stride proved difficult to keep up with. Those long lean legs took bigger steps than the prey hunted before her. The hunt gave such a thrill.

As a chameleon, he had fit right in on the WKT set. It was easy to get in by picking the lock of a long-forgotten door. Not a single person questioned him being there, but they did all thank him for the late-night sugar rush from the donuts he brought. After that, it was easy to find out her little routines, like how she parked her car down the same secluded alley behind the building and that she had no one waiting for her at home except a cat named Chip.

Ah, routines—helping predators isolate the prey since the beginning of time. That was something Cain understood. If Abel had been smarter, he would have survived.

He pulled back to give more space between them. The last thing he wanted was to scare her off. No time for mistakes on this one. He had to get out of town but couldn't go without her.

He matched his steps with hers in hopes of masking his presence there. A thrill jolted within him as he watched an uneasiness come over her. Staying in the shadows, he kept himself from view. A smile flashed every time she turned back to check if anything would indicate the reason for her obvious fear. He loved this part—such a rush.

Joni Jacobs was so beautiful it hurt. Maybe he'd keep this one for his own pleasure for a while before disposing of her. Thanks to the vet playing hard to get, he missed a few mandatory classes at Durham himself, but *she* would make up for it.

The freedom of having no one to tell him no or discount his ideas exhilarated him. That dreadful woman no longer snapped at him or berated him in any way. And that man was simply dead weight anyway.

Joni picked up speed as she turned down the alleyway. When she began to riffle through her purse, looking for her keys, he sprinted for her with the needle unsheathed in one hand and a rag of chloroform in the other.

Grabbing her from behind, he slammed the rag over her mouth and nose. It would be done soon. He only needed to hold on until she stopped fighting, like steering a kayak alone in a class five rapid.

Her arms flailed, grabbing for her assailant. A smile spread wide at the surge of power and dominance as each swing became less and less. He steadied the needle in his hand, easing his grip to help drug her fully.

With one last burst of energy, she swung her head back, slamming it into his face. Blood splattered from his nose, collecting in her hair as it ran down over his lips. She swung her body again, knocking the needle and rag from his grasp.

He wrestled her to the ground, overthrowing her fight with his strength. All those days in the gym paid off. The rag was nowhere in sight, so instead he wrapped his hands around her slender neck, squeezing harder and harder. Face to face with her attacker, she desperately grabbed at his hands, trying to pry them off her, slapping and pulling but unable to prevail.

The power that surged through him made it hard to pull back, but alas, the goal was to get her unconscious and finish the task. When her eyes rolled back into her head, she stopped moving. He briefly let her go and searched for the needle. Rolling her to the side, he eventually found it under her comatose body.

Thankfully, the medicine was still in there. He'd lost a little, but there was still more than enough to get the job done. The needle easily pierced her supple skin.

"Hush now, little one. It'll all be over soon," he whispered in her ear, a villainous smile on his face.

Thankfully, he'd thought ahead and parked the black Impala in the alley so no one would notice what was happening—he was on the run after all, even if no one knew for sure he existed.

After heaving her limp body into the trunk, he took one more moment to gaze at his prize. She belonged to him, and he never was good at sharing.

—◦—✕—◦—

"Finn," Andrew called out, running full speed toward him. "He took another one. Reporter, Joni Jacobs."

"Where?"

"In the alley behind the WKT news station," Andrew huffed. "By the time I found him, it was too late."

Finn drifted off past Andrew, seeking guidance from the Lord about how to move forward.

"It gets worse," Andrew continued, unfazed by Finn's silence. "I saw Ketaton, Occult, Fear, Ticano, and even Hexiathan attached to him."

Finn's attention narrowed on Andrew. "All of them?"

"All of them."

Finn couldn't recall ever seeing one human with so many strong demons attached to them before. This wouldn't be an easy battle to win. He needed to prepare the others, but more importantly, Jocelyn needed to find the DNA evidence and fast.

"Leon," Finn called out on their telepathic radio.

"Go for Leon."

"Where are we at with the lab and Tamika?"

"They're running the tests now, but it takes time to process. And the girl told Maya about a TA in their law class who is obsessed with Charlotte. She just sent uniforms to speak with him."

"Copy. Good work."

Finn wasn't sure how this would all play out. He prayed for the Lord to illuminate the right path for the detectives. They needed to see the full picture of truth before it was too late for Joni and countless others sure to follow her death.

⸺⬦⸺

Charlotte opened her eyes and found herself in her childhood bedroom, looking up at the ceiling from her bed. She slowly sat, taking it all in— the posters of Lady Gaga, 21 Pilots, and Drake strung all over her walls, the oversized stereo in the corner, her desk with all kinds of books stacked on top, and the Bible her parents got her for Christmas when she was fourteen tossed in the corner with no regard.

This room had been her safe space growing up, the one area where she was free to be who she wanted. Her parents never knew half of the things that took place in this room, but of all the bad, one thing remained good— she opened her Bible and read it a handful of times.

Much of it didn't interest her and she was unable to get past a lot of the brimstone and fire punishments, but now she hoped to survive so she could read those stories again with new eyes.

Out of the bed, she picked up the Bible, dusted it off, and gazed at it. Although she never intended on reading it, she packed it up in the last box for college before heading to Durham. She and Tamika displayed it on the side table by the couch when they moved in together last year. Charlotte wasn't fully sure why she wanted to do that other than it reminded her of home, even if all it did was sit there and collect dust.

Creeping out the door, she peered down the hall, unsure what she'd find. In what looked like her childhood home, she desperately wanted this to be real, but knew it was impossible.

"Mom?" she called out, her voice echoing off the walls. "Dad?"

"Charlotte, is that you?" an eerie voice called out.

She knew that tone and the way it said her name. Inching her way down the closed-off staircase, she saw a bluish glow illuminating downstairs. Off the last step, she gazed into the living room.

"Is someone there?" Her thin voice cracked. "Hello?"

"Charlotte, dear, there you are." A woman stepped into view, her slight European accent sweet, like Mary Poppins. "What's the matter, dear? You look absolutely dreadful."

The woman from the cottage who told those girls to take her to the beach. Charlotte didn't understand, because where they took her had no water, sunscreen, or sandcastles anywhere. Her pulse thrashed in her throat.

"There's no need to be afraid, love. I'm not here to hurt you. On the contrary, actually, I'm here to talk." She sat down on the sofa, patting the seat next to her. "You took off so quickly before, I didn't get a chance to explain what happened."

Charlotte reluctantly took a seat in one of the chairs rather than next to the woman.

"Um, Big Mama—"

"Oh Charlie, don't be silly. You can call me Bel."

"Bel?"

"Yes, it's short for Jezebel." She sweetly smiled. "My parents had quite a knack for odd names." She softly chuckled.

The name Jezebel sounded familiar, but she couldn't place how.

"There's no need to be afraid, my dear. Like I said, I just wanted to talk."

The woman muttered on while Charlotte acted like she was listening, but her mind raced to find the name Jezebel. She was pretty sure it was in the Bible somewhere. She glanced down at the book still held in her hands, wishing she could quickly thumb through it.

"Don't you think?" The woman's voice cut through.

Charlotte looked up with a blank expression. She had no clue what she was asking about. The internal debate of whether to nod and agree or fess up to her rudeness lasted too long, and Jezebel made her mind up for her.

"It's quite rude to be staring at a *book* rather than listening, don't you think?" She asked the question with such disdain.

"I-um." Charlotte looked back down at the black leather with her name engraved on the front in gold. She didn't want to let it go, but she felt like she had no choice. "Here," she sighed, handing the Bible to the woman.

Jezebel jumped back with a dramatic gasp, fear swirling in her dark eyes. "Don't hand that to me!" she shrieked. "Toss it over there." She pointed in the direction out of the living room.

Don't let it go, a voice spoke to Charlotte's heart.

"I'll just put it here, under my leg." She pulled the book back and sat on it.

That seemed to calm the woman a bit, although she was obviously unhappy about the defiance. She composed herself and continued talking while Charlotte pretended to listen. Everything within her screamed to find the answers her mind demanded.

As if a faucet had been turned on, the story of Elijah filled her thoughts. She always liked that one. The underdog going up against an entire nation alone. That guy was a legend and was one of the few who Charlotte admired. It took a lot of bravery to stand up to King What's His Face and his wife.

Didn't she send out people to hunt him down and kill him? What were their names?

And then it hit her, Ahab and Jezebel.

Suddenly everything became clear. The spirit of Jezebel represented rebellion and impurity. It craved the obliteration of all men. She was manipulative and cunning and stood in such superiority.

Charlotte tried to play it cool, but it was hard to not react.

Jezebel abruptly stopped talking.

"You're smarter than I thought." Her voice cut with hate. "I knew I shouldn't have said my full name, but you and me, we used to be so close. You belong to me, you know that, don't you? You sold your soul long ago, and I'm not leaving here without you." She lunged at her, grabbing Charlotte's wrist.

Charlotte went to call out for Jesus, but the words muffled against a thick black tail that came from behind the woman. Jezebel slinked toward her. The non-threatening mask ripped apart, revealing her real face. She looked like a jaguar with black eyes and gaping jowls. Dragon-like talons dug into Charlotte's wrist.

She tried to run, to move, but the demon gripped her tight.

"You're mine, and I never lose those who belong to me," she growled, shoving more talons in Charlotte's side.

Muted screams held gruff in Charlotte's throat. The talons went in on her left flank, sending a pulse of electricity through her. The violent sting was unbearable. Charlotte wanted it to stop.

Jesus, help me.

With a grit of her teeth and a hard grimace on her face, she forced her focus back onto the Lord. Her chaotic mind calmed and remembered the Bible underneath her.

It was difficult to move. The electric shocks left her incapacitated. She forced her hand to move despite the irrational pain, but Jezebel intensified the electrocution. Charlotte fought past the unbearable torment and worked her hand to the Holy book.

Wrapping her fingers around the soft cover, she used all her might to pull it from under her and shoved it into Jezebel's chest.

The beast let out a shrilling howl of pain as the book seared her thick skin. Black tar oozed from the wound as the beast roared and wailed. It flung itself back, knocking the Bible from Charlotte's hand, and released her from its charged grasp. The tail remained over her mouth, leaving her unable to speak.

Charlotte tried to reach the Bible but couldn't.

A memory from a year ago came to mind. She asked her mom why she listened to worship music so often, and her mom gave several reasons, one being that worship was a weapon. Her mind raced to think of any worship song eventually landing on, *This Little Light of Mine.*

Charlotte hummed the melody and sang the words within her heart. Behind closed eyes, she pictured Jesus—his loving presence and softly spoken words. She pictured kneeling before him and singing the words.

This little light of mine, I'm gonna let it shine.

Tears soon surged down her face, knowing she had put His light out so long ago. Her emotions were not rooted in shame or grief, but in a thankfulness that Jesus would come for her to reignite her heart. Charlotte ignored the whimper of the beast and fully worshiped the Lord with the words of a Sunday school rhyme she learned long ago.

The beast released her mouth, and Charlotte sang out as a beautiful declaration over her life.

"This little light of mine, I'm gonna let it shine. Let it shine, let it shine, let it shine." Charlotte smiled. "Thank you, Lord. I'll never let my light go out again, as long as I live."

Her eyes opened. The beast was gone, and Charlotte once again sat in darkness, serenaded by the rhythmic song on the machines around her.

Forty~Four

HIS FEET CLUMSILY DRUG across the dry, cracked ground. Heat radiated off the parched terrain, swallowing him whole. His dry mouth made it hard to swallow, causing him to choke on the sand surrounding him. The wind carried each grain of dust with such force that they pelted against his skin like a thousand tiny needles.

Levi scanned the horizon. Mountains reached up toward the heavens in the east, each one a desolate wasteland. Frail, decaying trees and disintegrating boulders dressed the incline. The ground swirled with colors of fiery red and tan.

This place looked similar to his last encounter, a few days ago, with Occult.

His tightly wrapped fingers held a bronze inlay handgrip of a gladius sword. His thumb casually rested against the wood guard at the base of the blade. It was lighter than expected, and it countered the massive shield in his other. He loosened his grip on the sword, shaking out his hand to relax the hold. There was a reason he was here and in full armor.

Like tiny pickaxes, the spikes on the bottom of his shoes forced their way through the parched ground. The attack was imminent. He could feel it in his bones.

Moving in a small circle, Levi continually assessed for his adversary, unsure how Occult hid himself from view.

Lord, give me discernment with eyes to see and ears to hear.

From the corner of his eye, a dark shadow swallowed him whole.

Chaos violently swirled around him like a tornado. Levi aimlessly swung the sword as panic gripped in the pit of his stomach. He wasn't sure what he expected, but it wasn't this.

Lord, how do I move forward?

His eyes popped open with total control, a master over the panic darkness tried to instill.

"Give it up, boy," Occult lashed out. "You're no match for me."

The beast wasn't wrong. After all, on his own, he couldn't stand against the darkness plaguing him. But with Jesus, he held an eternal ace up his sleeve in the form of the Savior.

Lord, help me to resist entangling myself with Hell. Keep my focus on You and not on the fight, for it all belongs to You.

Occult's face appeared in front of Levi, glaring. The putrid stink of rotting flesh on its breath made it difficult to control his gag reflex.

"Do you really think your pathetic little prayers will help you here?" Occult scoffed.

The demon's breath surpassed Levi's ability to keep the contents of his stomach from coming out. He hurled over and retched several times.

Lord, keep me safe. Levi gagged again. *I am not the boy I once was. I cannot win this on my own. Victory is mine, help me to walk boldly in it.*

Occult sized up Levi. "You think you're so tough." The devil chuckled. "I brought a few friends to help me."

Out of nowhere, Levi took several blows to his body from various directions. The hits came so hard, so fast, he couldn't recover before enduring another.

"Enough!" Levi shouted. *Lord, what do I do?* Darkness backed away from him. "In the name of, shemph." His words came out jumbled. "In the name of, chesed."

Maniacal cackles echoed through the air. From the back, something slammed into him, knocking him forward into Occult. His helmet and shield flew in opposite directions, two dull thuds against the dirt.

Occult gripped Levi's neck up under his chin, his ample arm flexed as he squeezed down on Levi's throat. Lack of oxygen bred panic as Levi grabbed and pulled at the beast. The demon's hand squeezed harder.

He cannot kill you, for you belong to Me. The Lord whispered to his heart. *Be still and see for yourself.*

Levi closed his eyes and took in a breath. It was like breathing through a blanket, restricted but effective. Occult let out a growl, placing both hands now around Levi's neck. Double the pressure, but the same amount of oxygen came in.

A chuckle built in Levi's chest. "Thank you!" he cried out to God. "I walk in victory for I belong to the One who defeated death." In palpable frustration, Occult squeezed with all his might. "Thank You for Your faithfulness even in our battles."

"Why won't you die, you menace?" Occult's distress tore through the open desert. "Die!"

"No," Levi boldly said. "You have no authority here. You have no right to put your hands on me. You cannot stand against the One who lives in me." A surge of power pulsed through his veins, bringing a deeper understanding of authority. "The Holy One of Heaven lives in me, therefore where my feet touch is Holy ground and on Holy ground, you have no standing. So back…off."

Levi shoved off the darkness. The beasts flew like dark tumbleweeds in the wind. Dusting himself off, Levi adjusted the sword in his hand. With relaxed wrists, he knelt with a prayer on his lips.

"Recuse me, Your faithful servant, Lord."

⊶×⊷

Jocelyn riffled through the suspect's belongings. Bex found their IDs in her thorough search. They were a husband and wife team, Todd and Vivian Banister. Sergeant Cole dug into both of them and found they regularly attended Oliver and Mia's church. But things got interesting when she uncovered that Todd was recently voted into an eldership position by a majority vote of the existing elders.

Sergeant Cole then called the existing elders, but only one was willing to talk, Ken Grant. He spoke in detail about the vote. He explained that he was very opposed to Todd Banister being an elder because the Lord had given him discernment of the evil attached to him and his wife. But with a majority vote, three to one, Todd was in whether Ken liked it or not. The church needed more elders since two previous elders and their families left along with several others.

Ken went on to explain weird things happened with Oliver before Todd was ever considered. Oliver became secretive and significant amounts of money vanished from the accounts. But once Todd was brought on as an elder, Oliver voted to make him treasurer, relieving Ken and his questions about the finances from his duties.

Again, he openly and publicly opposed Todd as treasurer, but the majority vote took the yes again. Ken tried to convince Mark Porter, the other elder, that this was a bad idea, but Oliver secured his vote long before the question was even asked.

She looked back over the statements again and again but found nothing to say about why this seemingly normal and nice couple would kidnap, torture, and dismember young women. These two had children and lived what appeared to be normal lives. Nothing explained why they would do this.

She flipped through what seemed like happy photos of a typical family. Jocelyn didn't know what to expect in the evidence collected from their home, but light and smiling faces, arms around each other, and the sweetest golden retriever you've ever seen weren't the typical picture of two brutal and heinous murderers.

Scanning Ken Grant's statement, she stopped at the part when he claimed Oliver became secretive and was off. She moved around the files laid out across the desk, looking for the transcript of Oliver's voicemail to Mia, but it wasn't there. Levi must have it.

She looked down at the empty coffee mug next to her. Time for a refill anyway.

Rounding the corner into the breakroom, she found Levi sprawled out on the small kitchen table. Drool seeped from smashed lips against the hardwood.

"Reed," Jocelyn loudly quipped. "Reed, wake up." He didn't move. She stepped closer and came face to face with him. "Reed," she sharply spoke, leaning over to shake his shoulder. Pushing harder this time, she got close to his ear. "Reed."

With a gasp of air, he violently woke up, whipping his hand like a sword in battle.

"Sir Lance Alot, you good?" she asked, amused.

Levi heaved several breaths as perspiration beaded on his forehead. "That was crazy," he breathed.

Her smile faded as he mumbled an indiscernible prayer. By the end, he caught his breath and wiped the moisture built up on his brow.

"Seriously, are you okay?" Jocelyn asked.

"Yeah." He drew in a final deep breath. "Yeah, I'm fine." He looked at Jocelyn. "What's up?"

Skepticism held on her face, curious as to what had him so worked up, but she didn't have time to indulge her curiosity.

"I found some things about our guests in holding, and I need to see the transcript for the voicemail Mr. Hughes left his wife." At the word "wife," Jocelyn noted a hint of pain in his eyes. "Do you have it?" she pressed when he didn't move.

"Oh, yeah." His hands crudely searched through the mess of papers that took up the diameter of the table. "Here they are." He held up the file. "Why are you going back over the transcript?" he asked, confused.

"Ken Grant said there were behavioral changes in Oliver before Todd Banister became an elder and that Oliver was the one who suggested Banister in the first place. So, I just needed to see if Oliver gave dates at all?"

"No, he didn't," Levi said matter-of-factly. Jocelyn narrowed her eyes, trying to figure this guy out. "I just read it after you gave it to me before I…"

"Fell asleep?" She finished his thought.

Levi cleared his throat. "Yes."

"Do you have the church financials in here too?"

"Yeah, should be at the back of the file."

Jocelyn flipped it open and scanned the bank transactions. Money started missing a little over eighteen months ago and then leveled out four months later. She looked closer at Ken's statement and just as she thought, fourteen months ago, Todd Banister took over the church's finances as the treasurer.

"Let me ask you a question." Jocelyn closed up the files and held them to her chest like a schoolbook. "How involved do you think Oliver was in all this?"

"I honestly don't know," Levi sighed.

Sneakers squeaked against the linoleum floor and pulled their attention. Jocelyn did her best to not smile too wide when she looked back to see AJ standing there.

"Needed more fuel," he sheepishly said. Jocelyn had never seen him make a face like that before. He was usually so assertive that she wanted to smack him. "I'm not interrupting, am I?"

"Not at all." Levi got the words out before Jocelyn could calm the butterflies invading her stomach. "What's your opinion on Oliver Hughes?"

"In what capacity?" AJ asked, pouring the bold elixir into his cup.

Jocelyn cleared her throat and the butterflies. This whole thing was ridiculous. He was just a guy. A really cute guy who wore annoying T-shirts and has luscious brown eyes and pouty lips.

Knock it off. AJ sucks. That's final.

"I asked Levi how involved he thought Oliver was in this mess. Do you think his voicemail was sincere or another lie?"

She swallowed harder than intended as AJ intensely looked at her. Levi faded into the background, no longer there as far as she was concerned.

"I told her I wasn't sure. I mean I don't care for the guy, but I think what he said might've been legit," Levi interjected, ruining the moment.

AJ broke eye contact with Jocelyn and took a quick sip from his steaming cup.

"It's possible he knew what they were doing but wasn't directly involved. I listened to his voicemail a handful of times. Now I didn't run a formal test on it or anything, but I'm considered an expert in voice analysis." He smiled that cocky smile and popped his eyebrows up one time in celebration of his accomplishment.

"Of course you are," Jocelyn huffed under her breath.

"I'd say he either deserves an Oscar or he's telling the truth."

AJ might be arrogant, but he was good at his job. Discounting his opinion would be reckless on her part.

"I would question the authenticity of his death," AJ continued. "I was able to triangulate his phone and get a location not too long ago. Have they found an actual body? And is it really Oliver?"

AJ ripped open the questions secretly tumbling in her mind and pushed them through the air like a pop-up sprinkler. Jocelyn sharply looked at Levi, his reaction less shocked than she expected.

"I've been wondering that too," she offered. "So far, no word on if they've found him. But to be honest, I won't believe it until I see it with my own eyes and science proves it."

"Science for the win," AJ smiled, sending a new wave of warmth through Jocelyn.

"Agreed," Levi chimed in.

The fact of the matter was, they were searching for Oliver and a possible third suspect. If they were one in the same, they would know soon. Until then, she had two suspects who weren't talking and it was up to her to crack them, but she was going to need information to help with that.

"Do either of you think Mia's involved?" she bluntly asked.

Levi's frustration was evident. Jocelyn had seen far too many nice and good-hearted girls do awful things because their boyfriend or husband convinced them it would be okay. After pouring over the financials and statements, nothing pointed to Mia. She wanted to let her go as a suspect, but she'd feel better if they both agreed with her.

AJ broke the silence. "Based on her behavior, she seems broken and in shock rather than a mastermind of some sort."

Levi hesitated another moment before speaking. "No." He put his hand up, palm toward her. "I know because of my history with Mia you think my opinion is skewed, but I know her." He lowered his hand into his lap and swiftly shrugged his shoulders. "Sure, she's a lot more broken now, but underneath all of that, she's still the same Mia I've known since we were kids. She's compassionate and loving. Flawed? Absolutely, but there isn't an evil bone in her body." He looked up at Jocelyn with big sad eyes. "She'd never be capable of something like this."

Jocelyn nodded her head with a warm smile. "I agree." Levi couldn't hide the joy on his face. "I have a question," she continued. "What do you know about this vet murder? Do you still think it's connected, or did you drool on the reports rather than read them?" Jocelyn joked.

"I'm certain it's connected. The antibiotic we found on the scene is the same one missing from the vet's office. The bucket of cold water we found matches the make and model of buckets carried by the clinic. In the initial sweep, they found a partial print, but nothing had popped in the system so far. They swabbed her mouth and found a second unknown DNA. So it was possible her killer kissed her corpse before leaving or she had a date that went really well before someone else came and killed her."

"I'll see if I can get some more information from the sample." AJ pumped a quick smile.

"Thanks, man. That would be super helpful." Levi thumbed through the papers. "The ME ruled the cause of death as blunt force trauma to the back of the head. He believes she was hit with the base of a high-powered surgical tool that is also missing from the clinic. They attached a picture of what it possibly looks like..." He thumbed forward in the papers. "Here." He handed the picture to Jocelyn.

AJ moved in closer to see the tool, and she ignored the giddiness that exploded.

"It kind of looks like a tattoo gun, just bigger," Jocelyn offered.

"Right? And if you look at the top, it looks like it has attachments for various uses. The report said they found all the attachments except the saw."

Jocelyn's eyes flickered up from the picture. "Would something like this be operational on its own?"

"This model has a built-in battery, so yes."

Jocelyn went to respond, but AJ cut her off. "I think I found something to connect these two cases." They both looked at him with lasting intensity. "In the back of the car we recovered from the scene, there was a black carrying case with tools. I wasn't sure what it was until I saw the name on the handle in this picture. It matches the name on the case. OrthoPro." After a brief pause, he added, "These two cases are connected, and your third suspect has a car and a new set of tools to kill again."

⚬⟶✕⟵⚬

Mia walked into the room where Charlotte lay peacefully, despite the trauma, pneumonia, and sure dehydration. She couldn't stop the tears from returning. If she had spoken up about Oliver's behavior sooner, if she hadn't been so scared to ask questions, if she had just sold that property... maybe they wouldn't be here right now.

Mia grabbed Charlotte's hand and rested her forehead on it. "I'm so sorry. I'm so, so sorry," she sobbed over and over again.

Forty-Five

LEVI DRUG HIS HANDS down his tired face as the rough stubble rasped against them. Jocelyn pinched the bridge of her nose with a grumble in her chest. The answers they desperately searched for seemed so close, and yet, the dots refused to connect.

"I need you to see if the lab has anything yet," Jocelyn huffed.

"Joce, it hasn't been that long since AJ called up to let us know the results of the rape kit for Charlotte." Levi's stomach churned at the thought of what that girl endured.

Jocelyn shot him her signature annoyed look, one he got far too often. "I can't interview these two suspects without information to help break them. I need you to go. *Now.*"

Levi put his hands up in surrender and headed for the lab. No use in arguing with someone who carried the weight of the world on their shoulders.

The elevator doors rang out at the arrival in the basement. Levi stepped out of the box and into the dimly lit hallway. He never enjoyed coming down here. There was something weird about knowing this was where they held prisoners back in the late eighteen hundreds when the station was originally built. Countless prisoners died here from disease or other inmates.

Some officers claim it was haunted. Although it gave him the creeps, Levi didn't believe in ghosts. He did, however, know without a shadow of a doubt, demons were real, which might explain his uneasiness.

Lord, protect me.

The door to the lab swung open and slammed into the wall behind it.

"Oh geez," Levi barked out. "My bad. Sorry." He looked over to each person with a whispered apology.

"Reed," AJ blurted out. "What can I do for ya, my man?"

"Joce sent me down here to see if you have anything new?"

AJ huffed with amusement. "That girl." He shook his head. "She's so impatient."

Levi smiled, noticing something more to AJ's reaction than just amusement. He'd watched Jocelyn dance around this guy several times now. It was clear she had some sort of crush on him, but this relentless grin on AJ's face at the mention of her name made it clear. He was crushing on her too.

At first, Levi wasn't sure how he felt about AJ. But, after seeing him at the crime scene, he'd concluded that AJ was more than human when it came to forensics.

His mind lingered on the thought of the land turned crime scene. He had said goodbye to that future long before now, but there was something about Mia holding onto it that brought heartache. This plot of land would always be different after this. Even if he wanted their dream life, it would never happen there.

Before all was lost, hope bubbled up within. Regardless of what took place out there, she kept the property. Not to mention, she didn't push him away the last time his hand lingered on her skin.

He wanted to call her, to rush to the hospital and be by her side, but this case had to come first. Since his mom died, Levi carried the weight of everyone's happiness and safety on his shoulders, and when it came to Mia, that job took over his whole world. It was hard to fight the internal demand to fix this for her, to ease her pain, but the only thing he could do was solve this so she could move on. He couldn't save her. Not from the hurt or from the emotions that threatened to swallow her whole, no matter how much he wanted to.

"So, like I said earlier," AJ interrupted his thoughts. "We know Charlotte was definitely raped, and according to the physical findings, it was pretty bad."

Heartbreak rippled through him again.

"As awful as that is, there's good news," AJ continued.

Levi was unsure how that could be true.

"She was assaulted without protection, which means DNA was left behind."

Levi swallowed hard. "Did they run a pregnancy test on her?" The thought of Charlotte pregnant with this guy's baby was a burden he'd never wish on anyone.

"They tested her blood, but it'll take a few more days to confirm." Levi leaned in with eyes wide. "So far, it's negative." Relief hit with a prayer for the Lord to protect her from such a horrific thing. "But this means we have the guy's DNA. We're running it specifically against the male DNA found on the vet to see if it's a match, and against all samples collected from this case." AJ gestured toward the empty chair across from him. "Have a seat, it should be done any minute."

The longest minute later, the computer alerted it was done. Levi saw it plain as day on the screen. It read: DNA MATCH 100%.

Levi went to text Jocelyn and let her know, but AJ interjected. "Hold on a second. There are more matches here."

He scanned the computer screen over AJ's shoulder, unsure what to look for. He waited patiently for an explanation while trying to look like he didn't need one.

"Looks like the second match came from one of the hair samples initially collected at Charlotte's apartment." AJ turned to face Levi. "The third suspect was in her apartment at some point."

Levi thought about the last words Charlotte said to him. *He's so familiar.* She knew him. She let him into her home. It was someone she saw regularly.

AJ picked up the phone.

"Who are you calling?" Levi pressed.

Before he could answer, a muffled voice picked up on the other end. "This is forensic specialist AJ Spalding. I need to speak with Captain Woods immediately."

⸺✕⸺

Back in her room, Mia prayed for healing and peace to surround Charlotte. Tears steadily streamed down her face. Too many emotions orbited to pinpoint anything, but what currently rang the loudest crippled her.

She'd killed a man and found out Oliver had a hand in the torture of several women and committed suicide—all within one night.

She was disgusted with herself for crying over monsters. The man she killed was in self-defense, but it didn't alleviate the heaviness attached to taking a life.

Oliver did unspeakable things, but part of her still loved him. She loved the man he used to be and relished in the moments he surfaced, no matter how brief, in the last year. He had been the man who brought her back to life, the man who loved her even when she was unlovable, and the man she leaned on for support when life got too much. The awful things he did didn't cancel out the depth of love built over the years.

Just this once, she let the guilt of it all fall to the wayside to grieve the loss of her husband, her friend, and the father of the child she lost. Even if he didn't deserve her love and tears, she deserved the time to grieve and heal.

She couldn't understand how Oliver connected with such darkness. The Lord would have to lead her to forgiveness so she could leave the unanswered questions at His feet—a task easier said than done.

A ping of her phone snapped her focus to the screen that blurred through the tears. She wiped away her sorrow. A text from Levi.

LEVI:
We got the names of the suspects we brought in. Todd and Vivian Banister.

Mia couldn't breathe. She stared, suspended in time, at their names. It was an answer she wasn't prepared for.

Mia was the architect of her own demise. She pushed Oliver to invite them to lunch so they could get to know the new couple at church. A friendship easily blossomed as she welcomed them with open arms into her home and life.

It wasn't until a month or two later, an uneasiness flourished. Mia backed off, but Oliver and Todd were already best buds by then. It was too late to stop it.

She sent Oliver into the lion's den, and they devoured him whole.

An awful thought crossed her mind. What if Oliver was the lion in the den? What if he was the spark that started it all? How many women met their Maker by his hands? How many lives were ruined because of him?

The full weight of the eight murders, Charlotte's torture, her husband's involvement, and her killing someone, gathered on her chest, suffocating her. Shrieks of agony wailed in her mind as if she were in the room when they were killed. She tightly closed her eyes. When they opened, blood momentarily saturated her hands.

She cried out for the Lord's mercy as the room filled with her brokenness.

—✕—

A woman falling apart over a man would forever be the most pathetic thing Jezebel watched. These idiots didn't even need men anymore. They could have those dreadful babies alone and could take care of their own intimate needs. They could take whatever they wanted without apologizing for it. They were women. They ruled the world while so many unknowingly allowed Jezebel to tear them apart, piece by piece.

The nuclear family was finally dead, thanks to her efforts. She orchestrated the entire thing with the help of some particularly wicked friends. The corners of her mouth turned up at the memories.

Her primary goal was to cut men down and eviscerate them into useless shells of what a man used to be. The femininely charged men who'd become gender fluid and unpicky about who they slept with made her happy. The alpha men of the world were now demonized, which lay the perfect foundation for Lucifer's plans. If they pulled this off, it would be the biggest destruction of the world, including that Idiot who thought he was in control.

She knelt and came face to face with this pathetic excuse for a woman, crying because her husband was dead. Jezebel thought about vulnerable little Charlotte, unconscious in a bed three doors down, like easy prey.

Both women threatened to wake up to the truth of who they were created to be. It was too dangerous to let it continue. This had to end here and now.

A knock at the door interrupted her plans. "Mrs. Hughes?"

Mia sat up in bed and wiped her pathetic tears. "Yes?"

"I wanted you to know that Charlotte has been stirring. You asked to be with her when she woke. We believe it could be any moment now."

Jezebel growled with delight and stalked after Mia as she headed to Charlotte's room. As the saying goes, two birds with one agonizing stone. The corners of her mouth pulled upward with a snicker.

Forty~Six

AFTER LOOKING OVER THE files for the millionth time, Jocelyn couldn't stall any longer. The interrogations had to start, whether she had anything to help her or not.

Never go in unprepared, Abby's advice rang through, leaving her stomach in knots.

It'll be okay, she lied to herself.

She was hoping to do this with Levi. Even though he wasn't a detective, he was quick on his feet and understood how to stand against whatever evil lurked within these two. Since he wasn't back from the lab yet, she had no other choice but to go in alone.

"What'cha thinkin', Maddox? Want us to take the husband?" Detective Diego Maltez smiled that crooked smile that could melt just about anyone.

She held back a laugh at the leather jacket and aviators that hung from his shirt, despite the fact the sun went to sleep hours ago. His whole persona was that of a tough guy, like it was him against the whole world, alone. Jocelyn could relate.

Detective Jerry Walsh rounded the corner, looking dapper in a well-tailored suit. Jocelyn didn't know many detectives who dressed so nice for the job, or that any of them had the fashion sense to do so. Despite all that, Walsh looked well-polished next to his—too cool for words—partner. What an odd pair.

"Yeah, I think the wife will respond better to me than the two of you," Jocelyn finally spit out. "Here's the file on Todd Banister. Take a few minutes to look it over." She sighed. "We honestly don't have much to go on at the moment, but we need the name of the third suspect before they lawyer up, so don't push too hard, too fast." She looked straight at Maltez when she said that. It was clear who the risk taker was.

"This isn't our first rodeo, detective," Maltez scoffed before walking off into the interrogation room alone.

"We got this. I know Diego seems like a loose cannon, but he's a good detective. We've been partners for years, and we work well together. He's a good man to have at your six."

With a quick nod, Jocelyn gave her blessing.

Being in control wasn't something she typically cared about, but this case opened up something new. She found it hard to trust those around her. The stakes were too high to leave in the hands of just anyone. Bottom line, she didn't want to be the one who let this guy get away, not again.

Walsh joined Maltez in the room. Jocelyn decided to watch for a minute before starting on Mrs. Banister. This was her not-so-clever way of stalling the inevitable, praying Levi would show up. The last time she faced demons, it wasn't pretty. Her hand reached up and instinctively rubbed her head, remembering the searing pain and temporary blindness.

"Mr. Banister, I'm Detective Jerry Walsh, this is Detective Diego Maltez, and we'll be conducting this interview."

"Don't you mean interrogation?" Todd hissed.

"We just want to get to the bottom of things, Mr. Banister," Jerry continued. "Have you been read your rights?"

Silence filled the room as the detectives waited for an answer, but none came.

"You have the right to remain silent," Maltez broke the lull. "Anything you say can and will be used against you in the court of law. You have the right to an attorney…"

At the word attorney, Todd's head rose and deadpanned at the mirror, as if looking straight at her. The rest of the Miranda Rights faded away as her stomach twisted. Her hand went back up to her head as a sharp pain sparked through.

She closed her eyes, *Lord, help me.* The pain faded and a calm rested on her shoulders. *Protect me. Please. I don't know how to do this like Levi. I need him.*

A small still voice responded within her. *You don't need Levi, you only need Me.*

Jocelyn nodded her head in agreement. *I need You. Come with me in that room. Protect me.*

A boldness trickled down her spine. She stood taller and gripped the file tight. She could do this.

The door to the interview room swung open and hit the wall behind it. She wanted to apologize but refused. If she had, it would either open Vivian up or be perceived as a weakness to prey on. It was safer to make no apologies or show weakness of any kind.

"Mrs. Vivian Banister, my name is Detective Jocelyn Maddox." She sat down across from the sullen suspect and opened the file. It stated she was Mirandized on scene by Bex. "Do you know why you were arrested today?"

Vivian sniffled several times and wiped the tears from her red and swollen eyes. "They said I killed someone?" Her voice strained. "I would never. I couldn't. That's not me."

"Mrs. Banister—"

"Vivian. Please call me Vivian." She softly smiled as a few tears escaped down her cheeks.

"Vivian. Why were you at eight-seven-seven Heartly Drive tonight?"

"That's my friend's property. She called me on my cell phone earlier and told me to meet her out there."

"What friend would that be?" Jocelyn pressed, already knowing the answer.

"Mia Hughes."

"How do you know Mia?"

"She's our pastor's wife. That's how we met."

"Why would Mia ask you to come out to a property she didn't tell people she had?"

"I don't know. Maybe she lured us out there to frame us." Vivian cried out, "I'm telling you, we didn't do this! We're innocent!"

Jocelyn examined Vivian's face as she continued the outcry of her innocence. Her lack of eye contact, the overzealous performance, it was all too much.

"How did Mrs. Hughes call you?"

Vivian's eyes sharply darted around the room as if the question had thrown her off guard. Her hands fidgeted with the chain securing her cuffs to the table. The panic didn't last long and would've been easy to miss if Jocelyn hadn't been paying attention. Vivian conjured up a few sobs and finally answered.

"First, she called our house and spoke with my husband, looking for Oliver. She asked us to meet her out there. And then, she called my cell from some number I didn't recognize."

Jocelyn opened the file in front of her. "According to your cellphone records, there's only one unfamiliar number here."

"That must've been the number," she cried.

"But it shows *you* called this number three times in a row about six hours ago." Despair fell from Vivian's face. "So how could this be Mia calling, when you initiated contact here and multiple times over the last few days?" Jocelyn pointed to the number of an untraceable burner phone. "Who'd you call, Vivian?"

Every ounce of grief and innocence vanished, as if she stepped into another person altogether. Her eyes dried instantly with a sharp look at Jocelyn. The atmosphere in the room shifted, leaving the air thick as fear clawed at her chest.

A menacing smile contorted Vivian's pale face. One eyebrow quickly lifted with such arrogance.

"I don't know what you're talking about, detective. I didn't call anyone." She sat straight up and calmly folded her hands on the table in front of her.

"Then who did?"

A faint chuckle held in her throat. "You have my husband next door. Why don't you ask him these ridiculous questions?"

Jocelyn's pulse raced as droplets of sweat formed on her upper lip.

Lord, help me. I don't know what to do.

"Do you really think that's going to help you?" Vivian's words cut like glass.

"What are you talking about?" Jocelyn's eyes widened.

"Praying. Do you really think *praying* will help you now?"

Jocelyn wanted to run, to hide, but she had to pull it together. Her head spun out of control along with her pulse. Without thinking, she calmly leaned forward.

"Pretty sure even *your* knee must bow to the Almighty. Now *silence.* Let *her* speak."

They held in a standoff, neither one willing to budge. Jocelyn couldn't believe the words that came from her mouth. Her mind focused on the verse her grandmother used to tell her about how every knee in existence bows before Jesus. She now believed it to be true with all her heart and stood firmly on it.

Sobs burst out of Vivian like a waterfall breaking through a dam. "Please. Help me. Please," she pleaded.

Jocelyn didn't move. Instead, she studied Vivian as she gave the performance of a lifetime. It would be easy to fall for this act. She was even surprised as a few of her heartstrings were pulled with every plea of remorse. Alas, a performance was all this was, and Jocelyn was done listening to it.

"Enough!" Jocelyn slammed her hand on the table. "You're not fooling anyone."

A sinister laugh vibrated through the air. "Oh, you're good."

—⦿—✕—⦿—

"We're the chosen ones. You'll see." Todd smiled, giving Jerry the full-on creeps.

This guy went around in circles for an eternity. Jerry casually checked his watch. It had only been seven minutes. He drew in a deep breath and slowly exhaled.

"Todd, we found you at the scene, running from the cops. That already doesn't look good for you." Diego pointed at the file Jerry had in front of him. "Wanna know what I think?"

"Please, enlighten me, detective," Todd sneered.

"I think you saw Miss Scott and decided you needed to have her. I don't know if it's some twisted fantasy with you and your wife, but you chose to kidnap and rape her together."

Todd abruptly stood up. "I would never defile myself with that wicked being!" he loudly declared.

"Sit down, Mr. Banister," Jerry demanded. Todd softly returned to his seat and folded his hands on the table. He straightened himself with arrogance. It was obvious to Jerry why Ken Grant didn't care for this guy. "What did you mean when you called her a 'wicked being'?"

"She's a sinner. My wife and I are kept pure, like snow, by God Himself."

"How does kidnapping a girl and holding her hostage keep you pure?" Diego interjected.

"We operate outside your laws here on this wicked earth. We answer only to God."

"So let me get this straight," Jerry wearily said. "*God* told you to do this?"

Todd Banister scoffed, seemingly offended by the question. Jerry wasn't quite sure what to make of this guy. His body language indicated he fully believed this twisted reality to be true.

Jerry internally searched for the details of this case. They believed it was connected with a string of occult killings. The stones and red paint found in the trunk of the car on scene matched the style, type, and color of the previous murders. He remembered seeing the coroner's report that stated he believed the victims were cut into pieces while still alive.

Jerry wasn't much for religion, but he did know the sacrifices made in the Bible were humane. The animals didn't suffer like these women did. This ritual was unnecessarily brutal.

"How many are part of the chosen ones?" Jerry calmly asked.

"We're not privy to the information God holds."

"Are there other teams out there right now?" Diego pushed.

"I suppose so." Todd shifted in his seat, appearing uncomfortable.

"So, I guess you're not quite as special as you were led to believe," Jerry huffed.

Todd restlessly fidgeted with his fingers. "No. No. That's not right." His breath increased. "No. We're the chosen. We're special. We answer to God."

"Who's we?" Diego asked.

"We are the chosen. We are the chosen. We are the chosen." Todd repeated the phrase over and over, rocking himself back and forth.

Jerry sighed. Maddox was going to be ticked.

"We'll get you some water, Mr. Banister. Sit tight. We'll be right back." Jerry looked at Diego and nodded his head toward the door. This guy needed a break, and they needed a new strategy.

———————— ⚹ ————————

Mogrin, a loyal soldier of Occult, attached himself to the woman. He was a glorious soldier who embodied everything this mission was—pride, arrogance, and a holier-than-thou standpoint. He snickered at the relentless chanting of the simpleton next door. His brother-in-arms, Shabak, had done quite a number on him over the years. The man needed to surrender prior to meeting the woman for the plan to work.

Occult told Mogrin the mate was a woman handpicked by Jezebel herself. It happened long ago, when Vivian's father abandoned her and her mother to suffer alone. Her childhood was agonizing, by the queen's design. She conjured up giant hurdles for them to endure, making their mere existence a harrowing feat of torture.

Jezebel sunk her talons deep within the woman, shaping her to be the head of the home and the mission. Soon after, a delightfully wicked plan formed—create a team to take out those with the brightest anointing and make them think it was all for God.

Genius really, to remove the biggest threats before they came to the Lord. And if by chance their stupid parents taught them early, do their best to insert rebellion and peel them away from the light or break them down trying. The mission was of the utmost priority, and Jezebel obliterated anyone who stood in her way. The anointed must be killed—whether it was physically or spiritually was of no concern to the queen as long as it was carried out properly.

The man was never meant for anything of value. He cowered to any fight that found him throughout his adolescence. His only job was to follow the direction of the woman, and he did it with more excitement than they expected. He was the perfect puppet, a big, dumb puppet, and it was enjoyable to hear him unravel.

"No more games, Vivian," the detective demanded.

This awful little tyrant was on his last nerve. She needed to be put in her place.

"You'll never win. You're a pathetic excuse for a detective. You traipse around here like you own the place when it's probably your first big case." The noted fear in her eyes told Mogrin all he needed to know. "Oh wait," he cackled through Vivian. "This is your first big case, isn't it?"

"Who did you call six hours ago, Vivian?"

The detective's breathing increased. She was right where he wanted her.

"Gabby." The name fell from the woman's lips with a twisted thrill. He was glad to know what to use against her, thanks to Occult's knowledge of the woman. He somehow knew a guy that knew a guy who orchestrated the whole beautiful thing. It was delightful to watch these puny creations suffer a treacherous death like Gabby. The detective's eyes were as wide as saucers, as indiscernible words swirled on her trembling lips. "No matter how many cases you solve, nothing will ever be able to bring Gabby back." The woman smiled, a twinkle in her eye. "You failed her. She died because you left her alone. You thought you were better than her, and she died knowing she was nothing more than street trash."

His words, designed to cut like a hot knife and filet open the old wounds that hid behind her badge. The detective abruptly got up, grabbed the file off the table, and stormed out of the room.

Mogrin looked at himself through her eyes in the two-way mirror. He longed to see his own reflection and not the blonde ringlet curls that fell past her shoulders or her large light blue eyes and thin lips. He missed his real face. The slender fangs that protruded past his lips. His black eyes that struck fear into the hearts of those around him. He missed the relenting terror he caused everywhere he went.

Playing God hadn't been as fun as he was promised. Vivian didn't tremble before him, but being worshiped was a delightful twist. And then there was the first cut of the anointed ones. The metallic odor that poured out with every drop as they wailed in pain was something to hold dear. Yes, he would miss that very much.

— ✕ —

Jocelyn leaned against the closed door, breathless. How on earth did that woman know about Gabby? It was pretty clear that something sinister entangled itself within Vivian Banister.

She wondered if it would leave now that Vivian was arrested, or if she would continue in prison to murder people for the sheer thrill. There would be plenty of sinners around to choose from. Solitary confinement would need to be considered.

The door to the other interview room opened, causing her to jump.

"We are the chosen. We are the chosen," Todd Banister muttered over and over.

As the door shut, Walsh and Maltez held similar expressions to hers, shocked with a hint of fear.

"Did you get anything?" Jocelyn shook off her rapid heartbeat and sweaty palms.

"This dude is out of his mind," Maltez blurted out. "We might need a psych eval for this one."

"It's almost like he's…" Jerry's thought trailed off.

"Possessed," Jocelyn finished for him. The two men looked at her with horror. "I know that makes me sound crazy, but seriously it's the only explanation I can think of. Mrs. Banister literally changed personalities right in front of me and then mentioned…" She paused, fighting her emotions. "Something she shouldn't have known."

"Our guy thinks they're the chosen ones of God to carry out His punishment on the sinners of the world." Maltez scoffed. He pointed his finger at his head and swirled it around his ear. "I told you. He's crazy."

To Jocelyn, it confirmed what she already knew. All nine victims had religious backgrounds and all lived lives contrary to God's desire, from homosexuality to drugs to simple denial of His existence. To this team, each victim slapped the face of God with their choices, so they believed it was their job to fix it. It seemed wild that someone who attended church could get things so twisted.

"Do you have a psych person on call?" Jocelyn asked. They both looked at each other, a blank look on their faces. "Never mind, I'll ask the captain."

Jocelyn headed for the captain's office, fighting the grief threatening to take over. Reality cut deep when it came to Gabby. A part of her had always thought her friend was ridiculous for wanting to join the gang. It was something below both of them, but Gabby had been just desperate enough to do it. It cost her life.

Jocelyn took a deep breath. Forward was the only way worth going. She couldn't change what happened then, but she could focus on the now. Another suspect was likely out there, and countless lives could be saved by catching him.

Two steps down the hall, her phone rang.

"Detective Maddox," she answered.

"Joce!" Levi sounded out of breath. "Joce, oh my gosh."

"Levi, slow down." She turned back to look at Walsh and Maltez on her heels and put it on speaker as they stepped closer. "What's going on?"

"Joce, it's AJ." He was either on speaker or, more likely, AJ took the phone from Levi. "I have news." She heard the clacking of the keyboard. "First things first. We also have both Banister's DNA all over the inside of the vehicle and the trunk, which places them in the car on multiple occasions. Plus, it came back as a match to the two unknown DNA at your previous crime scene. The machine is still processing the national data base, that can take a while, but I suspect they'll connect with other unsolved crimes. Hair and blood samples were found in the trunk of the car they abandoned and they're a match for at least four of your victims, including Charlotte Scott. I expect more to pop because it's not done running yet."

"Are you serious?" A smile spread wide.

"Yes. Also, there was a third sample pulled from inside the car, and that sample matches the DNA from the rape kit, the sample from the vet, and samples collected at Charlotte's house." There was a moment of silence as Jocelyn, Walsh, and Maltez looked at each other, holding their breath for what came next. "We know who the third suspect is."

Forty~Seven

She fluttered awake and took in the hospital room. Despite the anchor of weakness that weighed her down, she forced herself up in bed. Countless machines encircled her and wires spread from them to her. Two IVs painfully invaded Charlotte's arms. The tubes in her nose tickled as air pumped through. She yanked the oxygen from her face, sniffling several times as she did.

Next to her, an unfamiliar woman sat in a chair, and a gasp hung on her lips. There was no time for pleasantries or pain. The familiar twist in her gut and the fear pricking her throat alerted—Big Mama was here.

Charlotte scanned the room, quietly hunting the invisible threat. Her dry, parched throat caught on itself. Hurled forward she whooped in protest. The unknown woman sprang into action with a bucket. Within seconds, bile burned as it forced its way out.

The woman rubbed Charlotte's back like her mother used to.

"Who are you?" Charlotte grunted.

Right then, she saw it. A monstrous dark intruder behind the caring stranger.

"Big Mama," Charlotte whispered.

The woman clutched a brown leather Bible in her hand. Without thinking, Charlotte snatched it from her grasp and held it out in front of her with both hands. Her heart raced and her breath quickened as an ache reverberated in her chest. Her back rounded at the pain.

"Leave! Now!" Charlotte's voice strained.

A low rumble of laughter followed in her ears.

"There's nothing you or that Bible can do to make me leave my new friend here," the beast hissed.

Charlotte flipped her attention to the woman. "You have to tell her to leave. You have to do it right now before she kills us both!"

The woman looked around. "What are you talking about? There's no one else here."

"Jezebel. You have to make her leave. She's here to kill us," Charlotte pleaded.

—◦—✕—◦—

On a backcountry road, as the sun threatened its arrival with shades of purple and orange bouncing off the pillowy clouds, the trap was set. For about fifteen years now, all cars came equipped with GPS. They easily tracked the black Chevy Impala, thanks to a court order and a genius hacker in the lab. The pieces almost effortlessly fell into place once they learned his name.

Jocelyn parked in the middle of the road as two black and white patrols flanked each side. Guarded by her open door, she mounted the HK and pointed it down the stretch of road. A hundred and fifty yards out was a bend that provided the element of surprise she hoped for.

The cool air pushed shivers up her spine. Levi and all the officers around held the same stance with various firepower in their steady hands.

She checked the red dot on the tracker. "Hold your positions," she boomed. Each word brought a puff of white mist into the air. Levi repeated her orders on the radio like an echo. "We should have a visual in one minute."

"Suspect's vehicle just past us, should round the corner in thirty seconds," Walsh's distinct voice stated over the radio.

"Remember, don't fire unless necessary. A reporter from WKT was reported missing less than an hour ago. It's possible he has her in the vehicle."

Nods came from all around while the word "copy" echoed off the radio speaker. This was it. They found him. Now for the hard part, justice.

Jocelyn kicked herself for not seeing it sooner. She looked into this guy but found no link between him and the other victims, only Charlotte. Maybe the kid knew how to get away with murder—his father sure did.

Lord, let us take him alive, please.

The thought of killing anyone, even someone evil, made her stomach coil in knots. She would prefer a peaceful end, but that wasn't up to her. Whatever happened next rested fully on his shoulders.

The Impala flew around the corner. Tires screeched against the pavement, sliding to a halt. Exhaust billowed a cloud of smoke into the air. She took it all in as her body tensed. The windows were too dark for a visual confirmation.

"Hold your positions," she reminded. The tracker confirmed they had the right vehicle.

Her fingers gripped the megaphone. Another deep breath burned in her lungs. No one moved a muscle.

She placed it in front of her mouth. "Bradley Wright. There's nowhere to go." Patrol units from down the road pulled in behind him, blocking a possible escape. "Put the vehicle in park, turn it off, roll down your window, and toss out your keys."

—⚹—

Knowledge of Jezebel fought its way past the hate that had suddenly encapsulated her heart while waiting for Charlotte to wake up. Mia lived with so many demons for so long that she worried somehow her authority in Christ had faded. She actively ignored them, entertained them, and let them flourish in her home.

The rush of hostility toward Oliver made her feel empowered. And although Oliver didn't deserve her tears, she deserved to grieve. So much had been lost, not just today, but throughout her life.

Hell hoped to rob her of healing and growth to keep her in turmoil, and she almost let it happen.

A fire ignited within her. Enough was enough.

"Jezebel," Mia called out. "I stand in the authority given to me by the blood of the Lamb. And I command you to leave this hospital, in the name of Jesus!"

Mia saw things so clearly now—a black shadow filled the room. Dawn rapidly approached and yet the room remained muted in wretched hate. The sooty fog swirled Mia's legs.

"In the name of Jesus leave," Charlotte echoed.

The creature pulled back but remained close enough to touch Mia. Calling on the name of Jesus worked countless times in the past, but there was something here she didn't understand.

"Jezebel, get out in the name of Jesus!" Mia demanded with aggression. Her heart raced with fear. It wasn't working. The demon remained firmly in place with a huff of amusement in its chest. "You *will* listen. You *will* heed the name of Jesus. You have been defeated!"

Tears pricked at the back of her eyes. Mia tried with all her might, but darkness remained, feeding off her failure.

Mia, the Lord spoke to her heart. *Do not entangle yourself with darkness.*

"Father God, my soul cries out in a desperate plea. Help me resist the temptation to entangle myself with this demon. Your Word says You'll fight for us, we only need to be still. So, I'm asking for You to come now, please." The threat pulled away. Mia grabbed Charlotte's hand. "We stand together on Your foundation, Lord. We know one can put a thousand demons to flight and two ten-thousand." She dropped her focus from above and put it back on the shadow. "In Jesus' name, I command you to leave."

Hidden from sight in the hospital room, Viveka crouched in the corner. Her orders were clear. Mia had to do this with the Lord alone. She must learn to walk in victory and how to truly be a warrior for Christ.

An excitement curled on her flawless face when He walked in as a Majestic Lion. Golden light shimmered from his perfectly governed mane. His head held high with confidence—the King above all other kings, the Son of God, the Lamb who was slain for all mankind.

In reverence, Viveka placed her right fist across her chest and bowed low before her King.

The demon now hid in the dark closet out of sight, but Mia remained watchful with discernment.

Unsure Mia understood the power and authority of Christ, Viveka stayed ready in case the King ordered her to step in. A lack of trust was evident in Mia's life, but all it took was one moment of clarity to turn it around.

It was known amongst the warriors Mia would one day be the rock in which Jesus rescued many from the claws of the enemy. She made Hell nervous. Viveka loved that about her.

"Jesus, I look to You. Come fight for us and remove the threat of darkness. Bring Your strength and Glory, for I know Hell cannot stand in the midst of it," Mia boldly prayed. "Fill us with Your presence, Holy

Spirit. May Your fire ignite and flourish within our hearts. We are but Your vessel. Fill us with Your Authority and Might."

The once dingy, ratted armor Mia wore in the spiritual realm now glistened with the Light of the Lord Jesus, beaming through the room. A muffled hiss and several bangs came from the closet. The devil knew its time was short.

Viveka watched as Mia caught sight of the Lord next to her. Still clutched to Charlotte, she strategically moved in front of the wounded girl. A shield from the fight. Mia put Charlotte's safety and needs above her own as a leader and warrior—the first step was complete.

The Lord locked eyes with Mia. No words were audibly spoken, but Viveka was given the privilege to hear what he said to her heart—a rare gift.

You've forgotten who you are in Me, but today you've returned, and I'm so proud of you. In the coming months, you'll learn and grow as I show you exactly who you are. Be still, as I bring victory to you in this moment. You are My daughter, My prized possession. My victory is yours. Learn to walk in this and see what I do.

A lone tear trickled down Viveka's face as the fire of the Holy Spirit exploded across Mia's chest. The Lord's words were planted deep within the woman's heart.

She was finally ready.

Mia gripped her spiritual sword tight and turned fully from the threat tucked away in the forgotten corners of the closet to face the Lord. With a simple nod of her head, she slowly knelt and bowed low before the Lord God Almighty.

Rays of gold burst forth from the King, basking the room in Pure Glory.

The lion lunged into the closet. Mia and Viveka stood and intently watched the door. The ground beneath their feet rumbled, erupting in a violent quake. Mia braced herself on the bed behind her. Confusion and panic contorted her face.

"Be still," Viveka assured.

A legion of wicked beings violently surged from their obscure hiding place. Shrieks came from deep within their chests as they scrambled to get away. The rot of darkness crinkled Viveka's nose.

The last to run out was Jezebel with an awful hiss and howl. The face of the lion emerged through the closet door, stepping forth. Viveka gripped her sword as the room filled with evil beings, all facing Jesus.

What happened next was shielded from their ears, for none of them could withstand the magnitude of His roar. The world fell silent as it forcibly built, shaking everything within the room, including the bed. In a snap, every devil left all at once.

Viveka bowed at the waist in reverence for the mighty King. Mia released Charlotte's hand as she dropped to her knees. Her sobs hiccupped in her throat.

"I had no idea how many there were. Forgive me, Jesus." She bowed before the Lord as her elbows rested on the floor. "I'm sorry."

Jesus nudged at her with His nose and rubbed His ample body against her like a cat. "You're forgiven, my child," He audibly spoke.

The room filled with the Victory of the Most High.

⬥

A few grunts escaped as she pulled herself from the bed. Charlotte placed a hand on the woman's back. The power that rippled through the room was like nothing she ever knew before. Clueless as to what happened, she offered comfort the best way she knew how.

"Are you okay?" she asked.

Tears stained the stranger's face and neck. "Oh my gosh. You need to get back into bed."

The woman quickly helped her back to the safety of the bed. Every fiber of Charlotte's being rejoiced as she sunk back on the lumpy mattress. The woman gently adjusted the pillows behind her head and tenderly tucked the blankets around her.

"You never got a chance to answer me," Charlotte lightly chuckled. "Who are you?"

The woman briefly smiled before it fell from her face. "My name is Mia."

"It's nice to meet you, Mia." Charlotte smiled. "Are you the one who found me?"

"Not exactly." Mia cleared her throat and bit her lip. "I need to start by saying, I'm not here to hurt you." Everything within Charlotte tensed. A plan formed to push the nurses' button at the first opportunity. "I guess

I kind of helped them find you, but I was only there because of what my husband did."

The thought of being brutally assaulted flashed in her mind. A surge of emotions welled up and broke free down her sore cheeks.

"I had no idea what was happening there to you, to the others." Mia's voice strained. "I'm so sorry, Charlotte. I'm so, so sorry." Several sobs unleashed.

Charlotte relaxed, unsure why she trusted this woman. There was something disarming about her and her brokenness that allowed Charlotte to say three powerful words.

"I forgive you."

"You're surrounded, Bradley." The screech of that woman's voice made Occult cringe. "Roll down your window and throw the keys out," she demanded.

Occult remained silent, ignoring the throbbing wounds on his once magnificent body.

"Gun it," Ketaton cut in.

"No!" Occult shouted. "This is *my* puppet. The queen gave this job to *me*, so back off you half-wit!" he growled at Ketaton. "Stay put," he demanded his puppet.

Ketaton thought he was so tough, but he was also cut to shreds by a little girl, so any and all respect was officially lost. Occult refused to conceal his amusement at how pathetic this sissy looked tore open, hemorrhaging black tar.

Dozens of cops filed in on both sides of them. The forest must be lined with backup from SWAT teams and snipers. Occult missed the days when none of this existed.

Unprompted, Bradley rolled down the window, turned off the car, and got out with his hands raised in surrender. Occult was furious his puppet would defy orders like that. Coloring outside the lines would not be tolerated.

He needed to salvage this nightmare.

"We need to go," Ketaton barked. "Leave that idiot!" He removed himself from the puppet. "Heavenly Hosts are everywhere. I know you feel them. They're probably in the trees with weapons drawn, ready to banish us!"

As the words slurred from his mouth, out stepped that ridiculous leprechaun, Finn. He towered above the swarm of police and their vehicles. In one hand, he held a mighty sword and in the other, a shield. This wasn't the first time Occult battled this Irish prick. He'd been a part of the crew that saved Levi's hide in the desert.

"I'm not running from one measly moron," Occult snapped.

More warriors poured in from the trees and took position between the cars. Occult looked back at those still latched onto the puppet.

"Sorry, old chap. I'm not going back there for you." Hexiathan pulled out and zipped off through the sky.

"Coward," Occult barked.

With a grunt, Ticano jammed out right on Hexiathan's tail. Occult and Fear were the only two left, with uncertainty brewing fast.

"Sir, I do believe this one is a lost cause," Fear offered. "Maybe we need to go to plan B."

This made Occult sick. He planted Todd Banister at that white water rafting camp for at-risk youth, waiting for a puppet just like this for so many years. It wasn't every day you stumbled onto a rich entitled young man with so much anger that allowed their wicked ways to flourish to great lengths.

So much damage would be left undone in his absence.

"What a waste," Occult huffed. He turned and whispered in Bradley's ear, "You cannot let this play out. You're of no use to me in a cell. Come home, my son. Come home to Heaven with me. We can go there together." His sultry voice sunk deep within the puppet.

—⊶✕⊷—

Finn noticed a shift within Bradley as hopelessness radiated from his heart.

"You have another choice here, Bradley," Finn shouted out. "It doesn't have to end this way."

"Turn around, place your hands on your head, and walk backward toward me," Jocelyn commanded.

"They're lyin' to you, Bradley. They're not your friends, lad," Finn pushed.

"Hush," Occult spat in Finn's direction. "Come home with me, son. Come home."

Bradley reached toward his back underneath the light jacket he wore.

"Keep your hands where I can see them, Bradley," Jocelyn urged.

Unable to wait any longer, Finn lunged into action. Other angels followed behind. Everything slowed. Bradley reached toward the waistband of his jeans and pulled out the matte black pistol he stole from his father's safe three days ago.

"No!" Finn shouted.

"Do it! Now!" Occult demanded.

Time stood still for Jocelyn, Levi, and the officers surrounding the vehicle. Finn sprinted with everything he had to get the weapon away from the head of someone God loved.

The crack of the gun echoed off the trees and mountains surrounding them, replaying the devastating moment of death for all to hear. Bradley's lifeless body plummeted to the ground, stopping the warriors in their tracks.

Pain contorted Finn's face, making new patterns in the freckles tossed over his nose and cheeks. Useless to stop it, he watched in horror as Bradley's spirit separated from his body. The fight for his soul was over. What was done couldn't ever be undone.

Finn clutched his chest as dark shadows seeped through the ground. They grabbed Bradley's spirit, clawing and biting him with razor-sharp teeth. They pulled him down and attempted to rip him apart. Horrific shrills of a man destined for an eternity of torment filled the air.

Finn would carry that sound with him, another scar for another soul lost to darkness. The God Head would grieve this loss in incomprehensible ways, but that didn't lessen the sting of defeat. Bradley Wright was lost forever.

Finn looked back toward Levi and Jocelyn. Time on Earth continued in slow motion. Occult swirled around Levi's head as the soldier lunged out from behind the car after Bradley.

"Until we meet again, solider boy," Occult chuckled before fading out of sight.

Forty-Eight

Jocelyn locked eyes with Vivian Banister as she and Todd were escorted out of the building for transport to the county jail. A twisted, poisonous smile flashed on Vivian's supple face. It sent the hairs on the back of Jocelyn's neck straight up. The depth of evil cinched onto them was vile. She wondered if their children would carry on the legacy. Just the thought of it made her skin crawl.

"We are the chosen ones. We are the chosen ones. We are the chosen ones," Todd continued to recite the five words that echoed through the open room.

Vivian let out a vicious laugh like a hyena. "Fools," she yipped. "You can't stop God. He *always* gets His way."

Her threat of Divine retribution was muffled as they exited the door toward the white van with bars on the windows. They would go before the judge within the next forty-eight hours to enter their plea and set bail.

Pride for her team, here and in Durham, welled up within Jocelyn. Their tenacity and persistence brought this ruthless group to justice. Although this wouldn't bring back the victims or fix the lives they ruined, it would bring peace to know the women of Durham were safe tonight.

Before gathering her things, she was finally able to put to rest the idea that Oliver Hughes faked his death when she saw him in the morgue with her own eyes. Plus, DNA and dental records were a match to the body found. There was no denying it, Oliver Hughes killed himself in the parking lot where he and Mia got married.

Joni Jacobs was found drugged and bound in the trunk of the Impala. She was transported to the same hospital where Mia and Charlotte were, to be monitored and treated for minor injuries. Jocelyn hadn't interviewed her yet, but the officers assigned to question the news staff discovered Bradley posed as an intern named Landon Barnes to gain access to the building.

Several workers said he asked a bunch of questions about Joni which they found odd, but they assumed he had a harmless crush.

No matter how hard Jocelyn tried to stop it, her heart ached for Bradley Wright. The choice to take his own life didn't make much sense. He was the son of the best defense attorney in North Carolina who, by far, won more than he lost. It was no secret James Wright kept hardened criminals as clients, so his son would have been protected.

"Great work, detective." Captain Hendrix held out his hand with a grin.

"Thank you, sir." She smiled, firmly shaking his hand. She released her grip and pushed both hands into her pockets, nibbling at her inner cheek.

"Whatever's eating at you, just ask," he huffed in amusement.

"I do have one question I can't shake."

"What's that?"

"How did the Banister's and Bradley Wright become a trio?"

"I thought you'd seen that part of the file," he retorted. "Looks like the three of them started meeting a handful of months before Charlotte was taken. We'll probably never know if the Banisters sought him out or if it was a meeting of chance, but the barista your team back in Durham spoke to confirmed the three of them got together regularly at the Roasted Bean on Lex."

"So essentially they groomed him," Jocelyn thought out loud.

"It's possible, but again, we don't know." He cleared his throat. "We do believe it was Bradley's idea to take Charlotte. We have him on video leaving shortly after Charlotte the night she was taken. They assumed he left in his car, but cameras outside the shop show the two-thousand-fifteen Cabrera Porsche registered to him was still there two hours after he supposedly left." Hendrix walked over to grab the file off his desk. "Plus, there's this." He handed her an array of photos taken of a wall covered with candid pictures of Charlotte.

"Whoa."

"Yeah, I'd say he was more than obsessed with her. Your team in Durham found these when they looked deeper into his life."

"How did he get his hands on the Impala?" She handed him back the photos.

"The VIN matches one reported stolen six days ago. Crime of opportunity, perhaps?"

Jocelyn stood, frozen. These women never stood a chance. Each kidnapping was meticulously planned. Three monsters circled Charlotte and struck hard when the time was right. The broken glass, the deserted street, the coffee shop, the rape—a well-choreographed routine of tribulation.

Hendrix softly placed his hand on her shoulder. "Closin' cases like this can be hard. We desperately want to find a reason, any reason that'll help us understand, but we don't always get that. Sometimes, it comes down to the mere fact that evil exists in this world, detective.

"I know that's not a reason, but it's true," he continued. "Evil doesn't make sense, but it does make us feel insignificant in making a difference. Just remember, if you hadn't caught them, more lives would have been lost.

"Sure, we can't predict the next evil and awful thing, but we can always be ready to bring justice for their victims and their families." He gave her a brief hug.

"Thank you," she whispered.

Pulling away, he left her with one more piece of advice. "Celebrate the wins, learn from the losses, and keep putting one foot in front of the other."

Jocelyn smiled and hoisted her bag over her shoulder, glad she took the time to thank the team here in Knoxville. She headed for the door. Captain Hendrix was right. The wins are worth celebrating, even if she couldn't understand why someone would believe God sent them on a mission to eradicate people.

Not everyone who claims to know Me does and not every eye is open to see clearly, a voice whispered to her heart. She wondered if it was God talking.

Levi annoyed her with his puppy dog eyes and terrible decisions when it came to Mia, but somewhere along the way, he became less of a nuisance and more like a little brother. She now felt protective over him and wanted him to grow as a cop and a man.

Jocelyn had no clue if he and Mia would ever find their way to each other through the catastrophic damage done. They could be great together if they allowed the storm to settle before moving forward. She mildly shared that with Levi before she left him to collect evidence on that back country road, unsure he listened.

It was hard to say goodbye standing in the middle of the road, locked in an embrace neither wanted to relinquish.

"I'll be back soon." Jocelyn sniffled, doing her best to hide her tears. "There's still loose ends to tie up, not to mention the trial," she added.

They reluctantly let go of each other. "You know, you're welcome to stay in my guest room, plus the rent is better than cheap. It's free." He beamed.

"I'll certainly take you up on that." She giggled, and every part of her meant it.

"Be sure to bring AJ too."

Levi nudged her with his elbow, just like a little brother would. She didn't conceal the sparkle in her eye at the mention of his name.

Such a brat, she huffed to herself, thinking about it.

The station door pushed open with ease. A new pep settled in her step. After feeling like a failure for almost a year, this whole thing was finally put to rest. Rays of sunshine burst up through the sky as the sun held to the mountain peaks. The purple clouds faded to a warm golden glow with the blue sky making its presence known.

Exhaustion lost its hold as she caught sight of AJ leaning up against her car like James Dean. She leapt with attraction and excitement. When their eyes met, a smile spread wide as his face danced with joy.

"There you are, Superstar," he called out. "Wanna get some breakfast to celebrate?" Butterflies swarmed within her. Her feet picked up speed. "Are you a waffle or an eggs and bacon girl?"

She ignored the breakfast babble from his pouty lips. No part of her cared. All she needed was him. Her teeth scraped against her bottom lip. Her stomach coiled. She refused to let her nerves talk her out of what she'd wanted to do since the gas station, ten miles out of town.

Mid-sentence, she abruptly stopped right in front of him, close enough to smell the lingering scent of mouthwash. The sweet heat from his breath danced on her lips. Without further hesitation, she lifted to the balls of her feet and pressed her lips onto his.

He stood frozen, like a statue. It mimicked the time in fifth grade when she and Gabby practiced kissing on the back of their hands. Regret boiled over. This had been a mistake. He wasn't kissing her back.

And then, as if he'd finally woke up, his lips firmly pressed into hers. His hand swept into her short hair. A burst of excitement exploded within her as a breath caught in her throat. AJ spun her around and pushed her into the car before parting their lips.

"What was that for?" He smiled like a kid on Christmas.

Jocelyn sheepishly grinned. "You know you're cute. Don't even right now."

"True." AJ batted his long lashes. "But honestly, I've never felt this way about anyone before."

"Me either."

He pulled her closer. "I'm not a perfect man, but I'll strive to be the man you deserve, Jocelyn Maddox."

Her heart exploded with irrevocable joy. "You already are."

He pushed into her lips and held her face in his soft hands. She never wanted this moment or this feeling to end.

—❊—

She sat in a chair, looking out the window at the beautiful morning sky. Despite the bruises and bandages that dressed her face and torso, he loved her. His gaze lingered, losing the fight to keep a single tear from spilling over and down his cheek. She was alive and finally free.

Mia turned to meet Levi's gaze. "When did you get here?" she softly asked.

"Just a second ago." In a few elongated steps, he knelt by her side. "What are you doing in here?"

"I've been sitting with Charlotte. They took her out for an MRI."

More tears spilled over. "I thought you were dead." His voice cracked. "And all I could think about were the last words I said to you." He dropped his head, heartache gathered in his chest. "I shouldn't have spoken to you that way. I'm so sorry, M."

Mia placed her hand on the side of his cheek and gently lifted his head. She was blurry behind the pool of tears in his eyes. Neither of them moved, locked in a loving gaze.

"You said what needed to be said. I forgive you," she whispered.

He leaned in. Being this close to her made his heart race. "I wouldn't know how to live in a world without you in it."

Her eyes flickered to his lips. Uncertainty caught in his throat. She'd been through too much. This was too fast, and it wasn't fair to her for him to be this close. He should pull back, give her the space she needed, but his loudest desires took over.

No part of her seemed uncomfortable with him nearby. Levi went against his instincts and her best interest and leaned in. His heart coiled as their lips brushed against each other.

With a shudder, Mia dropped her head and pulled back ever so slightly. Still nose to nose, their breath swirled together in a cloud of limerence. Levi fought the urge to close the gap and take her in his arms.

"I can't do this," she whispered with tears building in her eyes. His heart shattered and fell in his chest. "I'm a mess, Levi. I have to work on myself. I deserve time to heal." Their lips threatened to touch when she leaned closer. "Wait for me?" Mia cocked an eyebrow with a smile, amused to ask the same question he did all those years ago.

A chuckle held in his chest as he rested his forehead on hers. "You know I will."

It didn't matter how long it took. A life without Mia wasn't a life he cared to live because there was no one he'd rather spend forever with than her.

In the meantime, Levi decided to work on himself too, so he could be a man worthy of her love, affection, and grace. Plus, he desired to be free of the deeper things harbored in his heart. They were too heavy, too bulky, and it was time to let them go.

———✕———

In the filthy barn where Occult hid his plans, she waited for the incompetent fools to return. The floor groaned beneath her as she paced back and forth.

"Where are they?" Jezebel hissed to her messenger.

"I don't know, Your Highness," he explained. "They should be on their way."

The barn door flew open. Ketaton limped in looking as pathetic as ever. Dragging his left leg behind him, black tar continuously oozed from several places. That girl worked him over well. She chuckled in amusement at his pathetic state.

"Ketaton." She bit her lip to stop her laughter. Seeing men and beasts cut down to size made her relish with delight. "Where have you been?" she snapped.

"We were with the successor, but he's gone now." Ketaton's deep voice slurred. "But before you lash out, Your Highness, you should know this is Occult's fault, not mine."

Occult slammed into the door jam, pouring his battered body into the barn. He slithered across the weathered floorboards, falling to his knees before her. He may be a big, dumb oaf, but at least he knew how to greet royalty.

"Your Highness. The boy is dead," he cried out. "We're left with no successor. I've failed you. I've failed my prince."

That idiot, Ketaton, finally got the hint and dropped to one knee before her. A sea of darkness filled the barn. That was more like it. Empowerment collected on her shoulders with delight.

"Although I would love nothing more than to turn all of you into ash." She whipped her gaze to Hexiathan who now knelt near Ketaton. "And I mean *all* of you." He lowered himself further until his face was on the ground. "It's not up to me."

Jezebel unleashed her talons in an unexpected fit of rage. The inferior demons closest to her shrieked in pain. The air filled with ash as black tar cascaded across the floor.

Someone had to pay for the transgression of morons.

A slew of sad, miserable, and incompetent fools remained on their knees, begging to be spared from torment.

"Get up, you half-wits!" she screamed. "On your feet!" They scramble off the floor. "Your prince spared you, not me. He said something about you being valuable to the cause." She scoffed with disgust. "We must start over someplace new, right away. Our Enemy has gained too much ground, and it's time we remind Him the world is ours to rule."

Shrieks of celebration tore through the still morning air. There would be more empty and pathetic vessels out there. A slew of humans ready and willing to let darkness disguised as light in.

Forty-Nine

Two years later

With the car in park, Mia took in the sight before her. The Butterfly Exhibit at the Museum of Life and Science in Durham, North Carolina was incredible. Gorgeous shiplap dressed the side of the glass habitat as metal butterflies of various sizes floated up the wall. Abundant foliage permeated the space through every window. Beautiful, vibrant butterflies seen from afar fluttered around inside. Pristine flowers lined the path toward the lawn outside the exhibit.

"I wasn't sure what to think about a wedding being here, but wow," Levi breathed.

"I certainly never imagined this." A smile lifted her face. "It's kind of the perfect place for a bug guy and a detective to get married though."

"This place definitely screams AJ and Jocelyn." Levi smiled at her. "Can you believe it's been two years since…" His voice trailed off.

"I can't."

Time had been an elusive thought through Mia's healing journey. Often old wounds seemed closed, only for the scabs to fall off and bleed again. In the last seven months, massive progress had been made. Occasionally, phantom pain cried for attention, but in those moments, she remembered forgiveness was the key to freedom.

Forgiveness seemed impossible a year ago. When she walked into Callie's office, it was too much to bear. When she saw her therapist's youth and pocket-sized frame, Mia internally scoffed, unsure this sweet girl could help carry the burden of such hurt.

There was only one thing left to do—spill the whole ugly story and see if Callie broke by the end. When Mia was done, she composed her tears and waited to hear her story was too much, she was too damaged, and there was nothing she could do.

Callie leaned forward with tender admiration. "I feel like the first thing I want to mention is this is a lot for you to carry around."

Mia braced for disappointment.

"But I want you to know," Callie continued. "None of this is too heavy for me to help you hold and work through."

Unable to stop the release of emotions, Mia realized how alone she felt in all of it. Sure, Levi was there as a friend, but he couldn't be her rock, not anymore. She had to learn to make Jesus her foundation, her refuge, her everything.

Callie helped her to forgive Oliver and Levi for the pain they caused. She also realized the role she played in her shattered marriage and accepted she had to forgive herself.

Six months ago, when the trial started, Mia felt strong and ready. After testifying, she sat there day after day listening to every detail that threatened to send her back to the bottom of the hill she worked so hard to climb.

Turns out, Todd Banister volunteered at a camp in the Rocky Mountains where they took in at-risk youth from all over the country. They spent the summer hiking and whitewater rafting. That was where they first met Bradley Wright.

His father sent him to the camp the summer before he turned eighteen, after he got high and wrecked his dad's boat.

The Banister's kept in touch with Bradley through a secret email account and when the time was right, they packed up their life and moved their family across the country to be near their prodigy.

Mia's stomach curdled when it came out that the Banister's children were being groomed to take over the family calling, all four now placed in extensive psychiatric care.

Through matching their DNA, they were able to link them to seventeen other unsolved murders in the Mountain West area by Utah and Arizona. It appeared this was the place the killings started and the rituals were perfected.

She felt relieved to know Oliver never participated in the heinous crimes, not for lack of trying on Todd's part. He did, however, know what they were doing and turned a blind eye, which brought its own wave of disgust within. Thankfully, Callie helped her sort through each emotion and hardship as it surfaced.

—✕—

He held her gaze as the rest of the world faded away. Mia had been clear about her needs and the role he played in that. Setting boundaries wasn't easy, and he applauded her for doing it. As he healed the broken parts of himself, maintaining those lines became easier.

Before the trial started, he opened up about why he left all those years ago, sharing all the shameful details of his descent into madness. He hid for so long behind a shield of protection when it came to her. He desperately wanted to control the world around her, to protect her. What was perceived as love, he now saw as a govern of fear.

Over the last two years, they built a strong friendship. He learned to cherish her as she discovered who she was and not who everyone around her decided she needed to be. Together, they discovered a healthy place for individual growth as well as strength in friendship. The last year, they'd become inseparable.

It was suggested they find new hobbies and interests, so they tried a few things together. Pottery was interesting. Well, Mia was a natural, but Levi's bowl looked like the ceramic equivalent of a Picasso painting.

He enjoyed camping. Mia, on the other hand, loathed sleeping on the ground, the massive mosquitoes, and using a bucket as a bathroom. So, Levi kept his camping adventures to guy trips, and they compromised by hiking together.

Cooking was a pleasant surprise for both of them when they took a class. That grew into weekly cook-a-thons where they made a plan, divided up the work, and created an elaborate dinner. This usually took place at Mia's new house since she went all out with a grand kitchen remodel before moving in.

"Are we going inside or what?" A voice crashed their heartfelt moment.

"Charlotte." Mia smiled. "I thought you would've beaten us here." Mia reached out and hugged her.

Levi shook her boyfriend Paul's hand. "Hey, it's good to see you again."

Paul evidently was Charlotte's ex from several years ago. Levi didn't know the details as well as Mia, but he was a nice dude who treated

Charlotte right and after a long struggle with trust, he applauded his patience with her.

Mia and Charlotte reconnected a month or so after everything died down in the media and life resembled normalcy. Mia initially reached out to her, but Levi was against it. He worried it wouldn't be good for either of them, but he was happily wrong. Charlotte and Mia leaned on each other during their healing and were there for each other as much as they could be throughout the trial.

Walking up the pathway, Levi thought of how far they all had come. Mia was stronger than ever and so confident in her own skin. She also returned to her maiden name, Foster, as the last severance to her old life.

Charlotte changed majors to psychology. She and Paul got back together a few months ago and were going strong. As for Jocelyn, she received the Medal of Valor by the Governor of North Carolina for her leadership that brought these heinous killers to justice. After that, she fielded offers from neighboring departments and even one from the FBI last month.

She and Levi kept in touch regularly and during the Banister's trial, as promised, she stayed with him. During the day, they sat outside of the courtroom awaiting their turn to testify and at night, they played card games. They were joined by Mia and AJ, when he was able to come. Needless to say, the four of them become rather close throughout the trial.

The Banisters were both found guilty and received the same sentence, life with no chance of parole. District Attorney Harmon for Durham requested the court consider Capital Punishment for the crimes committed, but the request was denied. Rumors were, the DA would try again in Tennessee, but Levi didn't think they'd say yes to it either.

The death penalty wouldn't heal what had been broken, but Jesus would. What demons intended for destruction, the Lord would use for good. He prayed one day those affected by these tragic crimes would know that fully.

—◦✕◦—

Her slippers easily slid across the hardwood, making it difficult to pace with anxiety. It wasn't that she thought marrying AJ was a mistake but doing it in front of a hundred and eighty people might be.

The door let out a quick screech, causing her to jump. Her grandmother popped her head through with a smile.

"I didn't mean to scare ya. I just wanted to see how you were holdin' up, and by the looks of it, I'm right on time." Her southern drawl comforted Jocelyn. It was the voice of reason in her head when she needed it. Loretta stepped in and closed the door. She shuffled to one of the chairs in the bridal suite, provided on-site. "Talk to me, sugar. What's wrong?"

Jocelyn fought the urge to bite her bottom lip, which would ruin her makeup. The only thing left was to put on her dress and shoes, but she hadn't built up enough courage to do so yet. Thanks to her slippers, Jocelyn looked like a baby trying to walk when she made her way to the open chair. Kicking them off, she vowed to never buy the knock-off brand again.

Finally in the chair, she sighed. "It has nothing to do with AJ, Mam-aw. I honestly can't wait to marry him and call him my husband." Jocelyn grinned, ignoring the schoolgirl squeal begging to come out. "It's the crowd of people." Loretta huffed a chuckle and nodded her head. "Why did we invite so many people?"

"Oh, child, I know exactly what you mean. When I married your pop-pop, I was a nervous wreck. Now I knew he was the man for me, I just hated that Mama and Daddy invited the whole neighborhood to watch." A faint smile dressed her lips at the memory. "You know we were quite poor back then, so my weddin' looked nothing like this one, but we had about a hundred people show up, which was just an awful lot." Loretta gently grabbed Jocelyn's hand. "I know this feels like too much but let me tell ya this. One of the most special parts of our weddin' was seein' all the faces we'd grown up with surroundin' us with love and encouragement—plus the massive amount of gifts helped too," Loretta chuckled.

"Mam-aw," Jocelyn laughed.

"I know the thought of being up there in front of everybody scares you. Just remember, seein' all their faces beamin' with joy'll be somethin' you cherish as time goes on." Loretta leaned toward Jocelyn as far as she could. "If it ever becomes too much, just look at the man you love and let the rest melt away." She winked. "Thinking about the weddin' night helps too."

Laughter erupted between them both.

"Mam-aw, you're terrible. But thank you." Jocelyn wrapped Loretta up in her arms. "I love you."

"I love you too." They pulled away but stayed loosely entangled. "Time to get that dress on, sugar," Loretta chimed in. "You've got a wonderful man ready to marry you. Let's not keep him waitin' longer than he has to."

—※—

Charlotte took her seat between Levi and Paul, admiring the beauty around them. The big beautiful trees and lush green grass reminded her of her time with Jesus. In an instant her whole life changed, and she couldn't be more grateful for it.

Celebrating the worst moment of your life seemed odd, but in that dungeon, she encountered Love. She thought taking her own life was the only way out, but Jesus met her there, in the dirt and grime, to remind her that she was worth fighting for.

Leaving the hospital, a drastic life change loomed on the horizon. As soon as she was able, she went straight to Duke and transferred from law to psychology with a focus on helping rape victims.

Charlotte's therapist was instrumental in her healing, and she wanted to be the same for others like her. No one deserved to endure that level of pain and trauma, but sadly it happened far too often and most didn't get justice like she did. Victims deserve a safe place to expose their wounds and heal, and Charlotte wanted to provide that for anyone who may need it.

Soft music queued guests, and the wedding started. A hush fell over the enchanted garden and as if on cue, the sun descended as the sky morphed into an array of colors. Charlotte was ecstatic to partake in such a beautiful ceremony for an amazing couple.

She looked over at Paul and the countless possibilities their young love held. She owed Mia for convincing her to track him down a few months ago. A few exchanged messages on social media grew into coffee and now into a committed relationship. He happily gave her a second chance, and Charlotte asked the Lord to help her navigate it in a healthy and fulfilling way.

Being friends with the detective who saved her life just made sense to Charlotte. For so long, Jocelyn had a wall up, but Charlotte didn't take offense. She assumed it was to protect both of them. Alas, fate or whatever you want to call that, had other plans as they ran into each other in the most random places—the grocery store, the park, and they even had the same dentist. There came a point it just seemed unavoidable and that's when Charlotte invited Jocelyn to lunch. With juicy burgers and over-salted fries, a friendship was born.

AJ looked dapper in his three-piece suit as he walked in from the side with Pastor Wilkinson—the church was another place where they ran into each other frequently. Both mothers were escorted to their seats by unfamiliar men in tuxes. AJ's father passed away about four years ago, so there was a reserved seat for him next to his mom and a lit candle at a table off to the side.

Everyone was shocked when AJ and Jocelyn didn't want a wedding party, but Charlotte loved the idea of them being up there alone before God. AJ and Jocelyn had the kind of relationship Charlotte wanted with Paul—honest, real, loving. They weren't perfect, but at the end of the day, they were in it together.

Out of the corner of her eye, she watched Mia reach over and inner-lace her fingers with Levi's. She wondered if those two finally crossed over from friendship to relationship. Mia was finally whole, and Charlotte admired her strength and boldness. Most people didn't recover from damage like that and get a second chance at love. She hoped Mia would take it.

Through all of this, Charlotte thought there was more the church could do to help people heal and disciple them into freedom with Christ. When Mia presented the idea of building a ministry to help other women, just like them, Charlotte practically jumped out of her skin to say yes. In the Lord's timing, things really did fall neatly into place. She smiled up at Paul as he pulled her close.

—✕—

Her chest fluttered as she held her father's arm tight. The speakers played a soft piano intro of the song "I Get to Love You" by Ruelle. Jocelyn slowly exhaled with a quiver in her full lips.

She thought about how AJ's hand felt in hers when they prayed together before the ceremony. A wall stood between them, blocking their ability to see, but they kept God first in all things they did, especially today.

"Lord, we invite you here today, for this is not two hearts becoming one, but three. Without you, we wouldn't have the solid foundation needed to stand boldly together in this world. We pray for a lifetime of memories and for Your hand to be upon our union." AJ earnestly prayed with such humility, and she couldn't wait to be his wife.

Jocelyn's mother stood and faced the entrance of the aisle as the lyrics sang out. Everyone followed suit. Excitement twisted in the pit of her stomach.

"You ready, peanut?" Her father smiled with a tear in his eye.

Jocelyn looked up at him, too nervous to speak. With a nod, they stepped out in unison.

Rounding the corner, she saw AJ and couldn't stop the tears from trickling down her face.

⊶ ✕ ⊷

Jocelyn's dress was exquisite and hugged her frame well in a mermaid cut. Mia especially loved the detail of sheer butterflies in a whimsical line down the front. Jocelyn really did make the most beautiful bride.

Mia couldn't help but think about her own wedding day and how she felt so full of hope for the future with Oliver, even though she held a secret deep in her heart. A third person walked down the aisle with them that day—Levi. After five years of marriage, she never let him go. She tried, she really did, but every time she came close, a new wave of heartache and love flooded her.

The last year was perfect with Levi. They focused on friendship, and he never pushed for more, which made her nervous that maybe he didn't want it anymore. But when he looked at her with such love, all those fears melted.

He squeezed her hand in his as they took their seats once again.

⊶ ✕ ⊷

The ceremony was short and sweet. They had standard vows since neither of them was fond of baring their hearts to a lawn full of people. Instead, they wrote letters to each other for a more private declaration. Levi only knew that because AJ called him in a panic, two weeks ago, begging for his help.

Levi couldn't stop thinking about how Mia would look as a bride, walking down the aisle toward him. He wanted that more than anything but was content to wait as long as she needed. For now, he basked in the moments she grabbed his hand and leaned into him.

"I now pronounce you husband and wife," Pastor Wilkinson announced.

AJ took Jocelyn in his arms, dipped her low, and laid a passionate kiss on her lips. Everyone whooped and hollered at the display. AJ, the perpetual goofball and genius.

They were officially husband and wife, and Levi was so happy for them. Mia and Charlotte casually wiped the joy from their eyes, and Levi was ready with a few tissues from his pocket.

Over one hundred monarch butterflies were released into the air as Mr. and Mrs. Spalding walked down the aisle and into Forever.

Fifty

THOUSANDS OF TWINKLING LIGHTS dressed the trees and the darkened space above their heads. Everything was so perfect. The meal was incredible, and the evening was filled with such joy.

"Hey." Mia leaned over toward Levi. "Wanna take a walk?"

His face lit up with that smile that melted her heart. "Absolutely."

Several trees around the area let off a golden twinkle of light as they slowly walked through the outlying landscape. Mia immediately regretted the heels she wore and took them off to avoid a losing battle of sinking into the grass. Carrying the black pumps in her hand, a shiver vibrated through her body. It was much colder than expected away from the lights and people.

Unprompted, Levi removed his jacket and wrapped it around her shoulders. His warmth lingered in the fabric, making her shivers instantly cease. It smelled like him, a nice bonus.

"It really is beautiful here," Mia finally spoke.

"It is, isn't it? Who would've thought?" He smiled.

A knot of nerves coiled in her stomach. She abruptly stopped and turned to face him, less graceful than she hoped. She bit at her inner cheek, trying to calm the anxiety percolating.

He really did look handsome in his suit and tie. His freshly shaven face was a change from the scruff she'd grown to love. His pocket square matched her forest green calf-length chiffon skirt. The black top she wore matched the black of his suit. He was so adorable sometimes.

Her heart twisted with nerves, but she ignored it.

"When you left for Afghanistan, my whole world stopped. I didn't know how to just carry on with life when my heart was out there in serious danger." She took a shaky breath, exhaling it through pursed lips. "And when you ended things"—her voice cracked—"my world shattered."

Levi took her hands in his. "I'm so sor—"

Mia put a hand up to stop him. "I didn't think I would ever recover from you. And I know you explained everything that happened, and I understand why you thought it was the best thing to do. You were protecting me. You lost your mind over there and didn't want to drag me into the mess.

"But I want to be in the mess. I want to be in the battle *with* you. I don't want to sit on the sidelines of your life. I want to be right there in the middle of it all, holding your hand.

"I know I went off and got married, but you never left my heart. I've carried you with me everywhere since the day we met as kids, and I'll never stop." She wiped a tear from her cheek. "I don't want to feel that way ever again, okay?"

"Is it my turn now?" Levi asked and Mia nodded. "M, I've loved you from the moment I laid eyes on you, and letting you go was the biggest mistake of my life. If you give me a second chance, I'll never let you go again."

"And we fight our battles together from now on, okay?"

Levi stepped forward. His warm minty breath swirled with hers. "Are you sure that's what you want?" A mischievous smile curled on his soft lips.

"Shut up and kiss me, you brat."

His lips pressed into hers. With strong hands, he pulled her against him. A warmth burst within her chest and radiated out to every part of her body. She was back in his arms, once again hoping it would never end.

Levi pulled back ever so slightly, his lips still brushing hers. "I love you."

Mia smiled. "I love you too."

Her hands cradled his face, pulling him back in for another kiss.

<hr>

Finn awkwardly averted his eyes from the tender make-out session these two were having. It was intrusive to be this close to such a private moment. With a look of regret on his face, he turned on his heel and took a few steps back.

"It's about time for those two crazy kids." Andrew smiled, looking over Finn's shoulder at them.

"We should give them some privacy," Finn added.

A few steps later, they were with the small group of angels here to make sure things went smoothly for Jocelyn and AJ. They were there to witness this budding romance, therefore, it was theirs to help protect.

"Did we hear you right? Mia and Levi are kissing?" Kano said with a cheesy grin.

"Looks like those two are finally together," Finn announced with a smile.

"Good for them," Viveka softy acknowledged.

Footsteps quickly approached, forcing the warriors to unholster their weapons and be ready to fight whatever lurked in the shadows. Finn's eyes narrowed, taking in each frame at a time.

Viveka crept forward with stealth. No sound came from her feet as she stepped out with her sword drawn, ready to fight.

"Whoa, V! Careful with that thing," Kafziel objected with a mouth full of cake.

"Kaf, you shouldn't be eating cake," Finn scoffed, placing his sword back in its sheath.

Kafziel raised his shoulders. "It's really good cake though." They all chuckled at the young warrior's reasoning. "Where we headed next?"

Amusement fell from Finn's face. "Reports have been made of a demonic movement gaining traction in the East." He paced before his humble team like a drill sergeant making eye contact with everyone, including Dante, Leon, and Ashanti. "The task won't be easy. China is crawling with darkness, so we'll have to tread under the radar." He turned to face them. "You up for the challenge?"

Metal scraped against metal as Viveka once again unsheathed her sword. "Sounds fun."

Letter to the Reader

Dear Reader,

I truly hope you enjoyed this incredible story of triumph and hope. Maybe your story looks similar to Mia's or the fear of failure holds you back, like Jocelyn. Or maybe Charlotte's doubt hit you hard, or you feel the need to rescue those you love no matter the cost, like Levi. Or maybe, you're a little bit of every character… yeah, me too.

If we're being honest with ourselves, doubt and fear can play a huge role in our lives, and the enemy of our soul loves to exploit them any chance he gets. One thing I've learn in the last seven-ish years is our feelings are big, fat liars. Fear tells us not to trust the Lord because things don't *feel* good. I'm not quite sure at what point I began to believe that a life with God would be easy, but when it became too heavy to handle, it about crushed every ounce of my faith. I would imagine on some level you can relate because we all endure things that overwhelm and terrify us.

But, there's good news… Jesus gets it. He really does. And He loved you and me so much he left His throne in Heaven to endure the suffering of a broken world to offer salvation. Remembering this helps me to come boldly to the Father with brutal honesty and reverence. I mean, He knows exactly what we're feeling so why dress it up like we're fine? Personally, that's gotten me nowhere in the past, what about you?

My goal for this novel was simple—expose darkness. Peel back the curtain between our world and the spirit realm. A spiritual war plagues us all. It overwhelms and suffocates each of us. We're living in a time where that battlefield is evident in the music we listen to, the movies and shows we watch, and even on the political stage.

The idea of this book came to me about seven years ago. I held onto it in my heart, unsure what to do. I had experienced the enemy first hand on multiple occasions in my life, but I wasn't sure how people would respond to something like this. I had recently come back to the Lord after about two decades of self-involved living so I had yet to hear of authors like, Frank Peretti. It's funny how God works because about a month later, in a conversation with my mom, this book idea came up. That's when she introduced me to Peretti's work, and I was hooked.

I've gotta be honest here, I had no idea what I was really getting myself into. When I started, I wrote thirteen chapters and the Lord said, *No. That's not the book I told you to write. Start over.* YIKES. I obediently did as he asked, despite how painful it was to watch weeks of work disappear in one fell swoop. What I didn't know then was how amazing the story He did want me to write would become.

This book was written one step at a time as I walked in-sync with the Lord. He told me what to write, what to delete, and the direction in which to take these characters, whom I love dearly. All of that makes it sound like writing this story was some romantic notion where I hooked arms with God and we rode off into the sunset together, but that couldn't be further from the truth. Let me be very clear here, writing this book was a war. The enemy has been relentless in its attacks on me and my family from the moment God dropped this idea in my heart. And I never thought I'd say this, but I'm so thankful for the battles I endured.

Growth doesn't take place in soft, comfy places. It takes place in hardship, battles, grief, uncertainty, and a million other places that make us want to scream, "Why are you doing this to me?!" I don't know what difficulty you might be walking through at this moment, but I do want to encourage you with this. There is goodness, even in the midst of this unimaginable pain, task, or difficulty. I can say this with the utmost confidence because I've lived it too. Goodness exists there because God exists there with you. You're not alone. Ever. He never drops us in the middle of nowhere and says, See ya! Hope you survive! Instead, He says, I know how much this hurts. I've got you. Lean on Me, and we'll get through this together.

Maybe you're reading this and you don't have Jesus in your heart. Please read this next part carefully… He is standing before you, waiting for you to simply reach out and grab ahold of Him. He loves you more than you can possibly fathom right now. If you're on the fence. If you think, I don't want anything to do with God's dictatorship or rules, I hear you. I used to feel the same way. It took me almost two decades and a whole lot of hurt to see how wrong I really was about God and who He is. So maybe you can do what I did, and give Him a real chance. Put both feet in the boat with Him, and let Him show you how much He loves you.

Every demonic attack in this book is based on attacks I personally walked through as I learned how to walk in Victory. The battle truly belongs to the Lord. It's not ours to agonize over and worry how to win because, spoiler alert, with Jesus in our heart, we've already won. Victory is yours. On the cross, Jesus spoke His last words, "It is finished." The actual word He said was "Tetelesti" which is a Greek word meaning a debt has been paid. We were in debt to death. Death owned us. And Jesus paid the ultimate price to set us free. Death no longer has a hold on you or me. The devil cannot overthrow us or stop the Lord's work from happening. Victory is ours! So, let's walk boldly in it together.

♡ *Bethany Sustaric*

PS: Please don't forget to leave an honest review of Hush where you purchased it. If you bought it directly from me, please leave it on Amazon. Every review helps more than you know! Love you all!

Acknowledgements

I think that first and foremost, I want to thank the Lord for entrusting such an incredible story to me. Thank you for the journey to surrender. Thank you for breaking me so that I may truly heal. May you be glorified not only in these pages, but in my everyday walk with You. You are my breath. You are the words I speak. You are the details of this story. Keep me upright with You, always.

To my girls, Alyse and Isabella, it has been quite a wild ride, hasn't it? Thank you for putting up with all my crazy, and for your grace when I've needed it the most. Thank you for being there to remind me to never give up, and for putting up with the never-ending tears being poured out from a broken person who loves you more than life itself. I'm so thankful for the last seven years with you and the healing that took place in each of us, and in our family. We not only love each other, but we like being together, and I love that so much.

Mom and Dad, thank you for everything you've done for me and the girls. Thank you for reading every draft and for your advice, even when I don't take it. Thank you for sticking by my side and cheering me along. These last few months have been difficult to say the least. Know that I love you both so much and I truly believe the Lord is in control, come what may. And FYI, cancer can suck it. It can't have you, Dad, because you belong to the Lord. You're victorious for eternity. Thank you for stepping into the father role for my children, and for fixing the mountains of things that break around here. Now it's our turn to take care of you because you've taken such great care of us. Mom, you're one of the strongest people I've known. Thank you for being there to hold me in my darkest moments and for boldly saying what the Lord asks of you. You both helped make me into who I am, and I love you for it.

Theresa, Meegan, and Nicole, you ladies have been three of the best friends a girl could ever ask for. Theresa, what started as a mentorship, radically grew into friendship because the Lord knew how much we would need each other as we both learn to navigate new terrain. You're an inspiration more than you know and I admire your wisdom and sassiness. Meeg, my sister from another mister! Thank you for always being in tune to the Lord and for your boldness. I love your advice and laughter. Never lose that infectious smile. Thank you for being willing to read the first draft of Hush and give me your honest feedback. Nicole, you and I are like twins. Every rough patch we've endured has made each of us stronger. I find it rather amusing that if I'm struggling, I can almost guarantee you are too, and I love how that has helped prompt us to check in on each other. The Lord has done some impressive things in our lives, and I can't wait to see where he takes each of us next.

Holly Compton, I love you dearly and adore our friendship as it's grown over the last year and a half. Thank you for reading my first draft and for the feedback you've given. Thank you for being a sounding board and one of my biggest cheerleaders. The Lord has great plans for you, my dear, and I'm blessed to have a front row seat.

Penny Childers, thank you for taking the time to encourage me and bestow upon me some fantastic advice. Also, I appreciated your feedback and for introducing me to the next incredible person.

Joan Alley, thank you for being the most amazing person and editor ever! Thank you for pushing me, even when it was uncomfortable. You have helped build me into a better writer and that is utterly priceless. I appreciate your patience with me and my million questions, uncertainties, and mistakes. Thank you for making me look as if I'm great at grammar although I'm not… that'll be our little secret, LOL. I look forward to the next book!

And lastly, I want to thank Google for always being there, day or night to answer the weirdest questions imaginable… Most of the facts would've been wrong without ya, bud!

HUSH PLAYLIST

In no particular order are the following songs that encompass warrior vibes to help fully immerse us into the world of *Hush*. You can find this playlist available on Spotify. Enjoy!

WARRIOR – LEDGER (FEAT. JOHN COOPER)

UNSTOPPABLE – THE SCORE

BEFORE YOU GO – LEWIS CAPALDI

BORN FOR GREATNESS – PAPA ROACH

YOU CAN'T STOP ME – ANDY MINEO

STANDING IN THE STORM – SKILLET

COUNT 'EM – BRANDON LAKE

EVEN IN EXILE – CROWDER

HOPE – NF

DEVIL IS A LIAR – COLTON DIXON

LEDGEND – THE SCORE

HIGH LOW (REMIX) – ALIVE CITY, TRYHARD SOCIETY

FINISH LINE – SKILLET

CAN'T TOUCH THIS – MC HAMMER

HARD FOUGHT HALLELUJIAH – BRANDON LAKE

GOD ONLY KNOWS – FOR KING AND COUNTRY

THE BREAKUP SONG – FRANCESCA BATTISTELLI

BREATHE INTO ME – RED

HOLDING ME UP – STEPHEN STANLEY

GOOD GOD ALMIGHTY – CROWDER

TAKE IT ALL BACK – TAUREN WELLS

Bethany Sustaric

Christian author, Bethany Sustaric is a self-proclaimed recovering hot mess and has lived the testimony of a prodigal who's returned home. As a former paramedic of almost twenty years, she developed a foundation of leadership with compassion and has transferred those same qualities into ministry.

Almost seven years ago, an injury ended her career, and when she feared all hope was lost, the Lord mightily showed up. During that time, the Lord taught Bethany how to trust Him and how to battle against the schemes of our very real enemy. She lovingly refers to this season of life as her tailor-made wilderness journey. In that desolate place—the Lord restored a broken woman and tempered her into a warrior.

Today, Bethany uses her gifts of writing and speaking to share the Lord's truth. Her passion is to help the church boldly stand on God's Word and teach what it means to be a warrior in His army. Be sure to check out her podcast, Confessions of a Recovering Hot Mess, to learn more.

She resides in a small mountain community in Central California with her two daughters, their lovable Pitbull, and two sassy chickens. Sustaric is just warming up as she continues to work on future books sure to captivate audiences everywhere.